Praise for Mariah Stewart

THE LAST CHANCE MATINEE

"The combination of a quirky small-town setting, a family mystery, a gentle romance, and three estranged sisters is catnip for women's-fiction fans."

—*Booklist*

"A good read, with a nice blend of mystery, family drama, and romance. Readers will look forward to the next installment."

—*Library Journal*

THE CHESAPEAKE DIARIES SERIES

"The town and townspeople of St. Dennis, Maryland, come vividly to life under Stewart's skillful hands. The pace is gentle, but the emotions are complex."

—*RT Book Reviews*

"If a book is by Mariah Stewart, it has a subliminal message of 'wonderful' stamped on every page."

—*Reader to Reader Reviews*

"The characters seem like they could be a neighbor or friend or even co-worker, and it is because of that and Mariah Stewart's writing that I keep returning again and again to this series."

—*Heroes and Heartbreakers*

"Every book in this series is a gem."

—*The Best Reviews*

"Captivating and heartwarming."

—*Fresh Fiction*

A DIFFERENT LIGHT

"Warm, compassionate, and fulfilling. Great reading."

—*RT Book Reviews*

"This is an absolutely delicious book to curl up with . . . scrumptious . . . delightful."

—*Philadelphia Inquirer*

MOON DANCE

"Enchanting . . . a story filled with surprises!"

—*Philadelphia Inquirer*

"An enjoyable tale . . . packed with emotion."

—*Literary Times*

"Stewart hits a home run out of the ballpark . . . a delightful contemporary romance."

—*The Romance Reader*

WONDERFUL YOU

"*Wonderful You* is delightful—romance, laughter, suspense! Totally charming and enchanting."

—*Philadelphia Inquirer*

"Vastly entertaining . . . you can't help but be caught up in all the sorrows, joys, and passion of this unforgettable family."

—*RT Book Reviews*

DEVLIN'S LIGHT

"A magnificent story of mystery, love, and an enchanting town. Splendid!"

—*Bell, Book and Candle*

"With her special brand of rich emotional content and compelling drama, Mariah Stewart is certain to delight readers everywhere."

—*RT Book Reviews*

MARIAH STEWART

dune drive

POCKET BOOKS

New York   London   Toronto   Sydney   New Delhi

Pocket Books
An Imprint of Simon & Schuster, Inc.
1230 Avenue of the Americas
New York, NY 10020

This book is a work of fiction. Any references to historical events, real people, or real places are used fictitiously. Other names, characters, places, and events are products of the author's imagination, and any resemblance to actual events or places or persons, living or dead, is entirely coincidental.

First Pocket Books paperback edition August 2018

POCKET and colophon are registered trademarks of Simon & Schuster, Inc.

For information about special discounts for bulk purchases, please contact Simon & Schuster Special Sales at 1-866-506-1949 or business@simonandschuster.com.

The Simon & Schuster Speakers Bureau can bring authors to your live event. For more information or to book an event, contact the Simon & Schuster Speakers Bureau at 1-866-248-3049 or visit our website at www.simonspeakers.com.

Manufactured in the United States of America

10 9 8 7 6 5 4 3 2 1

ISBN 978-1-5011-5441-6
ISBN 978-1-5011-5442-3 (ebook)

*With grateful thanks to my readers who have
stayed with me from the beginning.
You know who you are.*

Acknowledgments

Every author needs a great editor, and I do believe I've been blessed with the best. Lauren McKenna makes my books oh, so much more, and I'm so lucky to be working with her. I'm lucky as well that the wonderful team at Pocket Books is my village—and it takes one to bring a book from the writer's mind to the hands of the reader. I'm thankful for everyone at Simon and Schuster who works so hard on my behalf.

Thanks, Chery Griffin, for being my first reader and for picking up all those little things I miss. I'm always happy to return the favor.

The Writers Who Lunch gives me an excuse to get up from my desk at least once every month. I am so thankful for these ladies who know when to laugh and when to commiserate, and I'm always happy to have spent a few hours in their company.

My family is my reason for everything: Bill, Kate and Mike and the boys—Cole, Jack, and Robb—and Becca and David. Love you all more than you will ever know.

Diary ~

It's been such a busy spring! Even though I've cut back my time at the inn and passed on much to Dan—who, let's face it, is a better innkeeper than either his father or I had ever been—it still seems as if there aren't enough hours in a day. I've also given Ford more responsibility at the newspaper, though not my weekly features column. I do so enjoy talking to people and writing about them. I think in another life I must have been the village storyteller.

Some might say in this life as well, but I digress.

I've decided it was time for my children to understand what it means to inherit a business. Dan's done an amazing job turning the inn into a resort, and Lucy's contribution as event planner par excellence has made us the destination wedding venue on the Eastern Shore. The paper has been increasing circulation, which in itself is a bit of a miracle since so many others have lost subscribers. But Ford was quite right when he thought some of our summer regulars might like to see what's going on in St. Dennis during the rest of the year, and he was absolutely on target. I've raised such clever, industrious children.

I'm taking a long moment to pat myself on the back.

One night soon I'll be having dinner with my dear friend Ruby Carter. Her great-granddaughter, Chrissie Jenkins, has been staying on Cannonball Island with her since the fall. Ruby tells me she's quite the cook, so I'm looking forward to a wonderful meal. I might even skip my afternoon tea. Well, probably not.

Years ago, I was friendly with Chrissie's grandmother, June Singer Blake, who'd grown up on the island but had always favored the town. I can't fault her for that—St. Dennis has been much more progressive than our neighbors on Cannonball Island. Yes, of course I know that Ruby had her issues with June, but one tries to stay neutral in these things. Come to think of it, Ruby had issues with several members of Chrissie's family, starting with her mother, Dorothy, and that idiot man she married. No wonder the girl's been lost for so long, with the parents she had. Well, we all must play the hand we're dealt. I will say that it appears Chrissie's getting her cards in order these days. She's come back to the island, and she'll be better for the choices she'll make. Who knows where the road ahead will take her?

Oh, who am I kidding? We both know the girl's worst days are behind her now, and if she follows her heart, she'll be just fine.

It just may take Chrissie a while to figure that out.

~Grace

Chapter One

Chrissie Jenkins sat at the end of the pier on the spit of land known as the point at the end of Cannonball Island and watched the sun begin its drop over the Chesapeake Bay. It had been a fine April day, and the water was calm and smooth as glass and just as peaceful as Chrissie remembered from her childhood. After the past five unsettled years, the pink and lavender sky seemed like an old friend, and for the first time in at least that long, she felt like she just might be home.

She tried to remember the last time she'd spent more than a day or two on the island, and figured it had been almost three years, when they'd laid her grandma June to rest. Of course, June Singer Blake had insisted on being buried in the Presbyterian cemetery in St. Dennis, right over the bridge from the island—no burial in some forgotten family plot on Cannonball Island for her. Chrissie smiled, recalling the flap June Blake's viewing had stirred up. Before she died, she'd given Chrissie an envelope containing eight thousand dollars, and told her to make sure she bought the best coffin she could find. Most important, it had to have a pink satin lining. Grandma June figured if she had to meet her maker, she wanted to arrive in style. Chrissie'd thought it was a bit much, but it wasn't her money, and she wasn't the one about to leave this world. If her grandmother wanted a coffin with pink satin lining, that's what she'd have. The extravagance had set tongues wagging in the small bayside town where her grandmother had spent her entire life.

Of course, Doug'd had a fit when he found out what Chrissie'd done.

"Are you crazy?" He'd grabbed her arm, twisting it as he held her against the wall. "You paid eight thousand dollars for a coffin for a dead old lady?"

"It was her money, and it was her last wish." Chrissie'd tried to wrest away from him, but as always, the struggle had been fruitless. He was too much bigger, and way too much stronger. Chrissie'd never had a chance against Doug when he was angry. And it seemed the longer they'd stayed together, the more often he was angry.

"Do you know what we could have done with eight thousand dollars?"

"It wasn't my money, and it certainly wasn't yours, so there's no 'we' to talk about. And let go. You're hurting me," she'd pleaded. But he hadn't let go, and he hadn't stopped hurting her.

Well, all that was behind her now. It had taken a while, but she'd finally found enough strength to leave. The best thing she could say about the five years she'd spent with Doug was that she never married him.

On a Tuesday in late September, she'd left for work, and for the last time, locked the apartment they'd shared in West Orange, New Jersey. She'd left behind everything she owned except what she'd been able to move out over the preceding month, secretly, piece by piece, in her bag, and stashed in her locker at work. That last day, she'd gone into the restaurant as usual, but at the end of her shift, she'd asked the owner if she could speak with him in his office.

"I hate to do this to you, Rob, but tonight's my last night. I swear, if there was another way, I'd do it," she'd said with tears running down her face. "But if you knew I was planning on leaving, you'd deny it when Doug asks and he'd know you were lying. And he will ask."

"Where are you going, Chris?"

She'd shaken her head. "He'll ask you that, too. If you don't know, you won't have to lie. Just know it's someplace where I know I'll be safe."

He'd put an arm around her and hugged her. "I hate to lose you—you're a good cook, Chrissie, and could be even better with a little more training and experience. You have such natural talent, so much potential. I had high hopes for you."

"Thank you. For everything. For giving me a chance to learn in your kitchen. For teaching me so much. It's meant everything to me. I'm so sorry to be leaving you like this, but—"

"I'm sorry you're leaving, too. But at the same time, I'm glad. You don't know how many times we've been tempted to either call the cops or take matters into our own hands," he'd said. "And by 'we,' I mean me and Jim, the entire kitchen staff, and half the waiters."

He'd pulled up the right sleeve of the white T-shirt

she'd been wearing and exposed an ugly circle of purple and yellow bruising on her upper arm.

"Don't tell me the neighbor's dog did that when he jumped up on you."

Chrissie'd looked away, unable to meet the eyes that knew her story without her having said a word.

"You go, and you don't look back, hear? We all love you, honey, but the most important thing is that you're safe." Rob'd gotten up and gone to the filing cabinet that stood inside the door. He pushed it aside to reveal a wall safe, which he opened with his back to Chrissie. She heard it click when he closed it again.

"Here's what I owe you for this past week, some severance pay, and your Christmas bonus." He pressed a stack of bills into her hand.

"You don't pay severance to someone who's quit, especially when that someone hasn't even given you the courtesy of a week's notice." She smiled. "And Christmas won't be here for another couple of months."

"Details!" He fluttered a hand in her direction. "Look, if you need help, or a reference, anything, you get in touch with me. But don't call here, in case Doug comes in and starts asking if anyone's heard from you. Call Jim's cell, and leave me a message. He'll let me know as soon as he hears from you, or if someone calls on your behalf." His laugh was harsh, and just a little forced. "Listen to me, I'm starting to sound paranoid, like you."

"I don't know how to thank you, Rob." Her eyes filled and she reached out to hug the man who'd done so much for her during the year she'd worked for him. He pulled her into a tight embrace and let her hang on for a moment. "Please give Jim my love.

The two of you have been such good friends to me, it's making this even harder."

"Aw, we both love you, honey. Don't forget, you need anything, your first call is to me," he told her. "Promise?"

Chrissie nodded. One more hug, and she'd tucked the envelope into her bag and opened the office door.

"Did you say good-bye to anyone on the floor?" he'd asked as they'd stepped into the short hall from the office to the kitchen.

"No. Like I said, if—when—Doug comes in and asks, if no one knows anything, no one has to lie." Besides, it wasn't as if she'd made any real friends other than Rob and his partner, Jim. Friends asked questions, friends expected to spend time with you, wanted to share confidences. Doug would never permit her to share her time—or her thoughts—with anyone but him. Rob had recognized her situation immediately, and though they'd never spoken about it, Chrissie had known he'd help her if it came to her needing to quietly escape—and he had.

"Then slip out the back, here." He'd touched her arm and pointed to the door at the end of the hall. "My private in and out."

"Thank you again, Rob, I don't know how—"

"Stop. Just go. Be safe. Be happy. Find another restaurant and cook amazing food." He took her face in his hands and added, "Find someone who loves you the way you deserve to be loved. And never doubt for one minute that you deserve to be loved, Chris." He opened the door for her and she walked out.

"Let me know when your feet hit the ground," he'd called to her.

"I will."

There were exactly thirty-two steps between the door and her car, and she'd counted every one. When she got into her old Nissan sedan on that early autumn night and locked the door, she felt ten pounds lighter. In another few hours, she'd be lighter still. Once she crossed over the bridge from New Jersey into Delaware, and on into Maryland, she'd head for the Eastern Shore of the Chesapeake, and the only place she'd ever really felt safe.

It had been fate, she'd decided, that her cousin—second cousin, really—Lis had called with an invitation to her wedding just as Chrissie had faced the inevitable conclusion that it was time—past time—for her to move on. Her relationship with Doug had been steadily declining as his drinking and drug usage had accelerated, and she'd realized several important truths: Doug was an alcoholic and a drug addict; he was never going to change; their relationship had long been over. And the biggest realization was his abuse of her was escalating and would end in either her serious injury or her death. The when to leave, the how, the where to go, kept her wide awake every night as she examined every possible option, but it all became clear with that one call from Lis.

"Chrissie, I'm sorry for calling so late, but I'd mailed your invitation to my wedding to the only address I had for you, and it came back," Lis had said. "I tried your mom as well, but couldn't track her down, either. Finally, it occurred to me that maybe Ruby might know how to contact you, which of course she did. If you give me your new address, I'd be happy to mail the invitation."

The call had caught Chrissie off guard, but it only took a moment for her to respond. After expressing her joy for her cousin, Chrissie'd said, "No need to mail the invitation. Just give me the date and the time, and I'll be there."

She'd been surprised by the call—she and Lis hadn't seen each other in years, but they'd been friends when they were younger. Not particularly close friends, but friends, the way you are with cousins who are the same age with whom you spend the summers. The more she thought about it, the more she believed it had been fate that had prompted Lis to pick up the phone. She suspected perhaps Ruby may have been behind it, but it hardly mattered who or what was responsible for opening an escape hatch for her.

She'd never told Doug that her family's roots went deep on the Eastern Shore, and with no paper trail regarding Lis's wedding, he'd have no way of finding out where she'd gone. He knew she and her mother had lived outside of Pittsburgh, but he had no idea that her mother had been born elsewhere. While he'd been furious about her having carried out her grandmother's last wishes, as always, he'd shown no interest in where Chrissie was going, since it didn't involve him and there was nothing personal to be gained.

When the call from Lis had ended, Chrissie had made a call of her own.

"Gigi," she'd said when her great-grandmother answered the phone. "It's Chrissie."

"I know who it be." Ruby had sounded as if she'd been expecting the call, and perhaps she had.

It was generally accepted by pretty much everyone in the family—everyone on Cannonball Island and in St. Dennis, the town across the bridge on the mainland—that Ruby Carter, great-grandmother— Gigi—to Chrissie, her brother, Luke, Lis, and Lis's brother, Owen, along with several other cousins who were scattered here and there, had been blessed, or cursed, with "the eye."

"I'd like to come for Lis's wedding, Gigi. Could I stay with you for the weekend?" Chrissie had asked.

"You be staying more than the weekend, girl. You bring what you need. It's time for you to come home." She'd paused. "Past time."

"Yes, ma'am."

Chrissie'd broken down and sobbed after the call ended. While she and her mother's family had never been particularly close, she'd always looked up to Ruby with a combination of awe and trepidation. Besides her rumored prescience, Ruby was one hundred hearty years old, still in good physical health, and sharp as the proverbial tack. Her piercing green eyes with their steady gaze never seemed to miss a thing, and her regal bearing alone was intimidating to an awkward child like Chrissie had been. She'd not been a faithful visitor to the island, yet when she arrived, Ruby had welcomed her with open arms. She hadn't realized how much she'd missed the island's sights and sounds, the smell of the bay, the distinctive dialect spoken by the old ones, the sense of peace she'd always found there. Most of all, she'd missed Ruby.

Chrissie stretched one leg as close to the water as she could and with her big toe traced her name onto the surface, the way she had when she was a child. The water was cold, true spring being just around the corner, and the chill ran up her leg, but it made her feel alive. Her brother, Luke, once told her that writing your name on the Chesapeake meant you were part of it, would always be part of it. She wondered where Luke was now, and if writing his name on the bay had brought him back from time to time.

When their parents, Stephen and Dorothy, divorced, Luke went with their father, and one-year-old Chrissie stayed with their mother. As far as Chrissie knew, neither father nor brother had ever looked back. It was as if the earth had opened up and swallowed Stephen and Luke Jenkins body and soul, as far as she was concerned. Chrissie wouldn't recognize either of them if they stood in front of her. Her father had been from the mainland and had no ties to the island except her mother. Once that bond had been broken and her mother remarried and moved to Pennsylvania, Chrissie figured her father had no reason to return. If her mother had heard from either of them, she'd never told Chrissie, and the few times Chrissie'd asked, her questions were ignored.

The last time Chrissie had asked, her mother had snapped, "That's the agreement we made, no contact, and I'm sticking by it. So far, he has, too. What difference could it make now? He's never been part of your life. He never wanted to be. Leave it alone, Chrissie. Don't ask me again."

To Chrissie, it was unforgivable on the part of both her parents—her mother for not telling her why her father left, and her father for never coming back. Once she'd started examining her life in earnest a year ago, it hadn't been difficult for her to figure out that being abandoned by her father had contributed to the fact that her self-esteem had been so low she'd permitted herself to be abused. That her mother would never tell her why had only added to her poor self-image: as a child, she'd assumed he'd left because she was a bad girl. What other reason could there have been? Now, as an adult, she realized there'd had to be something other than that, that while children see everything that happens through their eyes as it relates to them, the constant arguing between her parents had probably been about something else. Try as she might, though, her mother would never tell her what that something had been.

She still thought of her father with a mixture of anger and longing. Had he ever remarried? Was he still alive? And Luke . . . ? She had no idea if he was dead or alive, either.

It would have been nice to have had a big brother growing up, though. Chrissie had no memory of him, and that made her sad. She'd been barely a year old when Stephen had picked up the then-four-year-old Luke and left their home in Salisbury, Maryland. Over the years, Chrissie had searched for Luke on social media, but she'd never found a trace of him. No Facebook, Instagram, or Twitter accounts that she could find, and nothing for Stephen, either. It was bizarre, she thought, that neither father nor son had left a footprint anywhere. She hadn't been aware that anyone could fly so far under the radar these days.

She stood and brushed off the back of her jeans, pulled down the sleeves of her sweatshirt, and picked up her sneakers. She retied the ribbon that held back her dark blond hair, and with one look over her shoulder at the setting sun, she walked the length of the pier and hopped onto the cool grass. Less than seven months ago, the point had been lit up like a thousand Christmas trees, a tent set up down near the road, and chairs had lined the lawn area for Lis's wedding. There'd been fairy lights in the trees and happy chatter, a string quartet, and later, in the tent, a band. Now there was only a light breeze shushing through the pines and the occasional caw of a gull to break the silence.

She passed the old cottage that Lis and her new husband, Alec Jansen, had renovated, the house where Ruby and her husband—known to all as Ruby's Harold—had raised their family. Chrissie's grandmother, Mary Elizabeth, had been one of their daughters, as had Lis and Owen's grandmother, Sarah. Chrissie remembered playing there with Lis when they were little girls. The cottage had been uninhabited then, Ruby and Harold having moved to the general store when they took it over after Ruby's mother passed away.

Sometimes Lis and Chrissie had pretended to be Mary Elizabeth and Sarah, though they'd never ventured upstairs to the second-floor loft, where the Carter girls had had their dormitory-style bedroom. There were rumors among older folks on the island that the ghosts of the Carter children who'd died young—Gloria, at age eight, and the stillborn son they'd named John—had never left the only home they'd known and came out at dark to reclaim their space. Chrissie wondered if Lis and Alec had made their acquaintance yet.

Chrissie skirted around the marsh where red-winged blackbirds guarded their territory on swaying dried fronds of last summer's cattails. She wrinkled her nose at the first faint whiff of decaying organic matter—crabs, seagrass, a fish dropped by a gull and forgotten—and turned her face to the bay for a deep inhalation of salt air. As the days grew warmer, she knew the scent would intensify.

Across the sound, the pleasure boats had been put to bed in the marina, the stragglers easing into their berths before the sun set and darkness settled over the bay, but up and down the uneven coastline, fishing boats had been moored at private docks for hours. Chrissie knew they'd be leaving before dawn to get a jump on another workday.

She'd watched that same scene for as long as she could remember, and it had never varied—unlike Cannonball Island, which showed signs of change, something Chrissie thought she'd never see, but it was obvious that a new day was coming. Houses that had been boarded up during her last visit were showing signs of life. Owen's new wife, Cass, was an architect whose father had bought up most of those abandoned places, and Cass was redesigning them for modern living. Chrissie and Cass had discussed it several times, and Chrissie'd been fascinated by the fact that almost all the locals had been on board with the idea.

Ruby'd been 100 percent behind the project, Cass had confided, so pretty much everyone else on the island had followed suit.

Chrissie climbed the worn wooden steps leading to the wide front porch of the Cannonball Island General Store and pushed open the decrepit door. Inside, an ancient Coca-Cola sign hung over the door, and an old metal bait cooler stood off to one side. There were rows of wooden shelves that supplied the islanders with paper and cleaning products, canned soups and meats, cellophane bags of noodles, bottles of soda and juices, jars of condiments—everything the locals needed on a daily basis, it seemed, except meats and fresh produce. One small freezer held ice cream and some frozen vegetables, and just yesterday, she and Ruby had talked about maybe bringing in some seasonal local produce.

The wide-planked wood floor showed the wear of more than two hundred years where countless feet had left their mark, and on the far side of the room stood a round oak table with claw-and-ball feet that dated from the 1870s. Placed next to a window on the sunny side of the building, it was Ruby's favorite place to sit and read, drink a cup of tea, or pass time with a friend. It was there that Chrissie found her, the day's newspaper open in front of her and an empty mug at her elbow, her stark white hair pulled back into a tight, neat bun that sat low at the nape of her neck. As usual, Ruby had dressed in one of her favorite outfits, a skirt the color of cotton candy that reached her midcalf and a white blouse with a round collar, a look that never failed to remind Chrissie of her mother's high school yearbook photo. On her feet she wore white tennis sneakers. Chrissie couldn't remember her ever wearing any other footwear.

Ruby looked up when the door opened, and asked, "You have a good walk?"

"I did." Chrissie stepped back onto the porch, wiped sand from the soles of her feet, and slipped into a pair of flip-flops she'd taken to leaving by the door. She came back inside and asked, "Are you hungry? Want me to start dinner?"

She walked to the table and checked the contents of Ruby's mug. Finding it empty, she asked, "Want another cup of tea?"

"Tea might be nice." Ruby handed her the empty mug. "Dinner be a little late, maybe. Might be we have company."

"Oh? Who's coming?" Curious, Chrissie thought. Except for Lis and Alec, or Owen and Cass, Ruby hadn't had dinner guests since Chrissie had come to stay.

"Might be my friend Grace stop by 'fore long." Ruby turned the page of the newspaper. "Might'a told her there could be oysters for dinner tonight."

"You know I picked some up in town this morning." Chrissie smiled. She liked Grace Sinclair, a kind and thoughtful woman whose family owned the famous Inn at Sinclair's Point in St. Dennis, just a mile over the bridge. "How would you like them done up?"

"Whatever moves you be fine with me. You be clever that way." Ruby's attention had turned to an article in the paper, thereby effectively dismissing her great-granddaughter.

Chrissie picked up the cup and took it into the kitchen, where she prepared another cup of hot water for Ruby. She carried it into the store along with a fresh tea bag. God forbid anyone but Ruby should dunk her tea bag in her mug—Chrissie'd made that mistake many years ago and hadn't repeated the infraction since.

"Here you go, Gigi." Chrissie set the mug in the middle of the table and handed the tea bag to Ruby. "What time would you like dinner to be ready?"

"By and by," Ruby replied.

Chrissie looked at the clock that hung over the counter where the old cash register stood on the other side of the store. It was almost seven.

"What time might Grace be stopping over?"

Ruby glanced at the door as if waiting seconds before it opened. A spry, tiny, birdlike woman with white hair caught up in a bun atop her head and wearing a light green polo shirt and a short skirt patterned with tropical leaves entered, waving and smiling as if she were Ruby's best friend. Which, in fact, she was.

"Am I late?" Grace Sinclair closed the door behind her.

"Right on time," Ruby told her. "Chrissie be just about to start dinner. Come in and set for a few."

"Chrissie, dear, you're starting to get some color in your face. Before long, you'll be sporting a tan." Grace hustled across the store and joined Ruby at the table.

"I've been spending some time outside," Chrissie said. "Mostly helping Gigi get the garden ready for planting in another month or so."

"I meant to say how nice it looks out there," Grace said as she pulled up a chair and sat. "Your beds along the front porch look good, and the garden out back looks so nice and tidy."

"That be Chrissie's doing. I be too old for all that bending and weeding and tilling. Chrissie got a nice feel for the earth. She'll do fine." Ruby nodded. "We been planning a nice herb garden."

"I should have the grounds crew at the inn do the same. The chef and his staff use a ton of herbs in the kitchen, and it would be nice to have freshly picked.

Oh, we do buy from the Madison farm—my daughter does most of the kitchen gardening over there, Clay's so busy with the brewery—but there's nothing like picking your own. I'll have to look into that." Grace patted Ruby on the hands. "Now, let's catch up since the last time I saw you . . ."

"I'm going to go on and get dinner started." Chrissie headed for Ruby's private living quarters in the back half of the store's first floor.

The kitchen, sitting room, bedroom, and bath were all new since Chrissie's last visit. Alec had reclaimed unused storage areas and fashioned the space into new rooms for Ruby, who, everyone agreed, should not have been hiking up to the second floor every night to her bedroom. Her new apartment was perfectly suited to her needs, and she'd been more than happy to move into it.

Chrissie loved working in the kitchen, and she'd come to look forward to preparing meals for herself and Ruby, and occasionally Lis and Owen and their spouses. Within a few miles, there were organic farms where vegetables were field-grown in the summer and grown in greenhouses in the winter. There were farms where chicken and organic eggs could be purchased inexpensively, and of course there was the bounty from the bay—rockfish and oysters and blue claw crabs in their season. Chrissie enjoyed shopping for herself and Ruby in the mornings, then using her purchases to re-create dishes she'd learned from Rob or dream up new ones of her own.

When she first arrived on the island, she'd started out baking on Sundays and Wednesdays, so Ruby could sell fresh baked goods to the store's customers. It

was her way of paying back Ruby's kind offer of an in-
definite home and making a contribution. Early mornings, when the watermen crowded in for their coffee
and snacks and lunch provisions, she'd set out a tray
of whatever she'd baked, and most days by 7 a.m., the
tray would be empty. At the request of their customers,
she was now baking almost every night of the week:
brownies—chocolate and blondies—muffins, scones,
cupcakes, cookies, and various kinds of cakes that she
sliced into large wedges and wrapped in cellophane.
They all sold out by the time the watermen left for
their boats. Ruby'd seemed more pleased by Chrissie's
initiative than by the unexpected income.

During the days, Chrissie worked in the store
with Ruby, checking invoices when deliveries were
made, stocking the shelves, helping customers carry
their purchases to their cars—whatever needed to be
done. She was infinitely grateful to Ruby for giving
her time to heal from her five-year ordeal with Doug,
and though Ruby had never asked, it was as if she'd
known what Chrissie'd gone through.

Of course Ruby had known. Chrissie heard it in
her voice when she'd called to say she was coming
back for Lis's wedding, and she'd seen it in her eyes
when she'd stepped out of her car when she arrived
on the island in the wee hours of the morning after
having driven since ten the night before. Chrissie'd
eased into the parking lot at the store very slowly,
her headlights off, intending to stay in her car until
the morning rather than awaken and very possibly
frighten Ruby at such an hour.

Chrissie should have known better.

The light over the porch was lit, and a figure sat

in one of the rocking chairs. Chrissie hadn't had to think twice about who it was.

"You be done with him and all his nonsense" were the first words Ruby'd said when Chrissie came up the steps.

"I *am* done, Gigi." She'd wanted to ask Ruby how much she knew, but she didn't have the strength. That would be a conversation for another time. Growing up, she'd heard the stories about Ruby's "eye." For years she hadn't wanted to ask, fearing it might be considered bad manners to ask someone if they had psychic abilities, where they'd come from, and how did one manage such a thing, if in fact it could be managed. And since family legend held that Mary Louise, Ruby's mother, had possessed such a gift, was it hereditary?

Ruby'd opened her arms and, in an uncommon show of affection, held Chrissie while she cried and soothed her with whispers. "You be home now, Chrissie. No harm be coming to you again. Not while there be life in me."

These days, Chrissie woke early so Ruby didn't have to, put the coffee on in the store, and took care of business until Ruby made her way from her apartment to the counter, and did whatever she could think of to make Ruby's life easier. In return, Ruby gave her a home and enough time off during the day for Chrissie to wander the island and reacquaint herself with the place her ancestors had helped settle. The homes of her Blake and Singer relatives were among those that had been sold to Cass's father's construction company for renovating, and the small private family graveyards commonly found next to the old homes still held the remains of many of Chrissie's kin. She walked among the gravestones, reading the names of those who were long gone, and even helped Cass tend the plots that had been overgrown and forgotten. Her life on the island was simple, and in its own way, productive, but most of all, it was healing. The bruises on her body had disappeared months ago, but the bruises to her psyche had taken longer to heal.

She had motivational tapes and books about finding oneself and one's best life. She listened and she read, and over the period of months since she arrived on the island the previous fall, she'd grown stronger. Why it had taken her a full five years to find herself she still wasn't certain. She was pretty sure she'd loved Doug back when they first started out, but she was hard-pressed to remember what it felt like.

For Chrissie, part of the healing process involved cooking. That she could cook every day in a beautiful new kitchen made her happy. She had time to experiment and time to re-create dishes she'd watched Rob make at the restaurant, and to create dishes of her own with all the wonderful ingredients that were available to her. Sometimes when she'd made something especially delicious, she'd send a photo to Rob, no text, just the photo. Though she'd tossed her old phone the day she left so Doug couldn't trace her whereabouts, she knew that even without recognizing her new phone number, Rob would know instinctively whom the texts were from. His return message would always be something simple, like *Wow!* or *So proud!* or *Go, you!* Always with the exclamation, never a name.

Oysters were on the menu for Ruby and Grace, and Chrissie was happy that something had moved her to buy a few extra that morning.

Maybe I inherited the eye from Gigi, she mused as she took the bowl of shellfish from the refrigerator.

Since arriving on the island, she'd experimented with any number of ways to prepare the oysters and crabs that were so bountiful. Tonight, she'd sauté the oysters in butter, some herbs, and white wine. She'd serve them over buttered toast next to fresh bright green asparagus spears she'd bought that morning, and some roasted cherry tomatoes with garlic and onion. She'd stopped at a nearby farm that grew greens all winter long in a greenhouse, and she'd picked up avocados and grapefruits at the market, and from those ingredients she'd make a salad. There were red onions in the pantry and leftover vinaigrette in the fridge.

She worked steadily, humming and occasionally singing along with a song playing on Ruby's radio on the counter. It was set to a station that played only tunes from the 1940s, and over the past several months, Chrissie'd learned the words to many of them. For her, the songs, the meal preparation, the vibe in this old building were both comforting and energizing. She'd slept well in the room on the second floor that had once been reserved for Lis, and she ate well because she was a firm believer in the healing properties of food. Being with people you loved, people who loved you, was healing as well.

"Dinner's almost ready. Gigi, would you like to eat out here or in the den?" Chrissie stood in the doorway between the store and Ruby's sitting room. "I can set up a table for you in the den if you like."

"That be fine, Chrissie. Thank you." Ruby nodded from across the room. "There be a card table in the storage room. Some folding chairs as well."

"I'll find them, thanks." Chrissie went through the den where shelves for Ruby's books lined one entire wall and her large-screen TV hung on another. A closed door led into an area that still served as storage. It took a few minutes, but Chrissie located the folding card table and three chairs. She brought them all into the den and set them up in front of the window that faced the bay. The chairs were a snap, but the table proved more challenging.

"You need a hand with that?" Ruby asked as she and Grace came into the room.

Chrissie had the table facedown on the floor.

"I can't seem to find . . ." She blew out an exasperated breath. "How do these legs work? Just tell me and I'll do it."

"Nothing to it." Ruby pointed to one of the table legs. "You pull that straight up . . . yes, like that. Now, see that little hinge? You straighten that as well. Mind you watch your fingers. There you go."

Chrissie managed to get all four legs secured, then, with Grace's help, turned the table right-side up.

"Thanks, Grace." Chrissie moved the chairs into place, then proceeded to set the table with Ruby's favorite pale yellow dishes. "Now, can one of you tell me why this is called a card table?"

"Used to play cards on it, why do you think?" Ruby frowned and took a seat next to the window.

"Did you used to play cards?" Chrissie asked

"Still do, time to time."

"What do you play? Canasta? Pinochle?"

"Sometimes one, sometimes the other. Why so many questions?" Ruby asked.

"I haven't seen you play since I got here, and that was seven months ago."

"Cards be a summer thing" was all the explanation Ruby offered. "Maybe you been around more, you might have more to remember."

"I guess you told me." Chrissie suppressed a grin.

"I guess I did."

Chrissie disappeared into the kitchen, then returned with a platter of oysters already on their buttered toast points in one hand and a bowl of asparagus in the other. She placed them on the table, then brought out the roasted tomatoes and the salad. After Ruby and Grace had been served, Chrissie served herself.

Ruby cut into an oyster. "These be quite nice, Chrissie."

"Thank you." Chrissie smiled at the compliment.

"Delicious," Grace exclaimed. "I've lived in St. Dennis all my life and have been eating oysters since I had teeth to chew with, and I've never had oysters that taste like this. They're absolutely perfect."

"Thanks, Grace. The owner of a restaurant I worked for back in New Jersey always had seafood on the menu, and he liked to experiment. He taught me a lot."

"And he taught you well, I daresay." Grace took another bite and rolled her eyes. "Delicious," she repeated.

"I'm glad you like them." Chrissie could feel herself beginning to blush.

"And the little roasted tomatoes with the garlic

and . . . what herb is that you've added?" Grace popped a cherry tomato open with her fork and the juice ran across her plate. "Never mind. Don't tell me. I'll be tempted to go back to the inn and give your recipe to our chef."

"Your chef is welcome to it," Chrissie told her. "Though since he's been recognized as one of the premier chefs on the Eastern Shore, I doubt he'd be interested."

"We're always interested in finding new ways to cook old favorites." Grace ate the last bit of oyster on her plate. "And these . . . to die for."

Grace continued to comment on each of Chrissie's dishes, ending with the dessert—scones that had been left over from the morning and had been heated and topped with whipped cream and a warm compote she'd made with some cranberries, chopped apples, and oranges.

"Now, that was one of the tastiest scones I've had in a very long time," Grace said after she'd taken several bites.

"Grace, you're being too kind."

"I'm not being kind. I'm being truthful. I'm tempted to ask you to show our pastry chef how to make these the way you do. I have a tea every afternoon at the inn, as you know, and I'd love to be able to serve these."

"I recall having had tea at the inn with you one day, and everything was delicious. I'm sure your pastry chef does a fine job, whatever she makes. I'm sure she doesn't need any help from me."

"She does some things exceptionally well, dear. Scones, alas, aren't one of them."

"Chrissie does a lot of things better than most," Ruby said.

"You're certainly right about that." Grace nodded. "Now, tell me where you studied. Where you went to school."

"I didn't go to culinary school, if that's what you're asking."

"You're self-taught?"

"Mostly. I've always liked to cook. My first jobs out of high school were in diners. My last was with a wonderful café called La Luna in northern New Jersey. The owner was an incredible chef, inventive and so enthusiastic about food." Chrissie rested her chin in her palm, her elbow propping up her arm on the table. Thinking about Rob and his kindness brought a lump to her throat. "He taught me so much. I wish I'd had more than a year with him."

"He taught you well, dear." Grace exchanged a look with Ruby.

"Might be I'd have another one of those scones if there be some tea to go with it," Ruby said pointedly.

"Yes, ma'am. On my way." Chrissie paused on her way into the kitchen. "Gigi, don't think you're fooling me. I know you set up this dinner to show off my cooking to Grace because Grace owns a restaurant and you wanted to see what she thought of my skills."

"Nothing wrong with sharing with a friend," Grace said.

"I guess not." Still, Chrissie felt slightly embarrassed that Ruby had tried to show her off.

"That all you have to say?" Ruby asked, one perfectly white eyebrow raised.

"Thank you." Chrissie stepped back to the table

and hugged her. "It makes me happy to know that you think so much of my cooking that you wanted to share it with your best friend." She kissed the top of Ruby's head, and before the woman could react, Chrissie ducked into the kitchen. Ruby's displays of affection were few and far between, and it always seemed to embarrass her when others were overt in showing their love for her.

Chrissie cleared the table and went back into the kitchen, where she filled the tea kettle with water and placed it on a burner, all the while listening to the soft chatter from the other room. It pleased her to see Ruby happy and relaxed with her friend, and it occurred to her that almost every day since she'd arrived on the island had been pretty much like this one. Right from the start, she'd taken over the cooking for Ruby, and had enjoyed the easy smiles and gentle laughter of the islanders. It had been years since she'd lived in such a place, a place where there was no angry shouting or the fear of saying the wrong thing, a place where people listened when you spoke and cared what you thought. Right now, Chrissie thought that might be enough, regardless of what else may be missing in her life.

Chapter Two

Chrissie's first thoughts upon rising were of gratitude that she had awakened in this place where she felt no fear and where she was loved and appreciated. It had been the same every morning since she'd arrived on Cannonball Island. Each new day, she rose cheerfully before the sun and dressed with a smile on her lips. She happily greeted everyone who came into the store, laughing at the same jokes the old watermen had made the week before, looking into the eyes of everyone with the growing sense of being one of them, of belonging, of being accepted for who she was. And for the first time in a long time, Chrissie knew for certain who she was and where she belonged. She had Carter, Singer, and Blake blood commingling in her veins: she was a child of the island.

Living with Doug had taken so much from her, starting with what Ruby had dubbed her *Chrissieness* when she'd first arrived for the wedding. While she was still searching for her self-confidence—always fragile—and her self-image had suffered immeasurably, she was over blaming herself for the way Doug had treated her and accepting of the fact that she deserved better. Every day now she felt a little stronger, and every day she gave thanks for the fact that she'd somehow found the strength to leave and not look back.

Every morning she looked forward to those first few moments alone in the store, when she'd walk through the quiet dark, turning on the lights as she crossed the scuffed floor to unlock the door. She'd step onto the porch and pause to watch the sun begin to rise over the river. Then she'd go back inside and make coffee in one of the oversized pots that Ruby kept on a counter. Then she'd make hot water for those early folks who preferred tea or hot chocolate. She'd go back into the kitchen and bring out the trays of whatever she'd baked and wrapped the night before and set them on the counter near the cash register.

Alfred Dooley, a wizened man of indeterminable age, was almost always first through the door, and he always greeted her the same way.

"Good morning, sweet cheeks. It's gonna be a cold one." Or a warm one, or a windy one, depending. His greeting changed only with the weather. He'd go directly to the pots of water and ask, "Got that tea water ready yet?"

"Almost, Mr. Dooley," she'd tell him.

He'd lean over the trays, as if checking out every piece of whatever she'd baked before making his selection. He'd eat standing up there at the counter, and when he was finished, he'd announce, "If I were fifty years younger, I'd marry you, girl."

And inevitably, someone else who'd come into the store would call to him, "Al, if you were fifty years younger, you'd still be an old coot!"

The banter would continue until every one of the island's watermen had come and gone. Ruby'd join her at the cash register before the last of the early crew had left for their boats, and she'd contribute to the chatter.

"Hmmm. Looks like those baked doughnuts you stayed up to make last night are gone," Ruby noted the morning after their dinner with Grace.

"They sold out really fast. I left a couple in the kitchen for you."

"I had me one with my first spot of tea," Ruby said. "Savin' the other for later, maybe for my afternoon break."

The early rush of watermen being over, Chrissie poured herself a cup of coffee and had time for two sips before a truck drove up and parked in front of the store. Grace craned her neck to see out the window.

"Hmmph. Tom be early today," she said.

"I'll take care of him." Chrissie went to the door and opened it. "Morning, Tom."

"Morning, Chris. Got a big delivery today."

"Can I help?" she asked.

"Nope, but thanks. I got it." He opened the back of the truck and began to unload some large cartons that he stacked on the ground next to the truck. When he finished, he brought them inside, one by one.

"Got that extra carton of soup you asked for, Miz Carter," he told Ruby, and she nodded in acknowledgment.

"Where do you want these?" he asked Chrissie. "Usual place?"

"That would be fine, yes. Thank you. Right there near the first set of shelves would be fine."

Tom stacked the boxes neatly for her, then held out a clipboard onto which he snapped an invoice. He went over each box and its contents before Chrissie signed for it.

"See you next week." He smiled at Chrissie and blew a kiss to Ruby, who rolled her eyes.

"What man think it be cute to pretend to kiss an old woman?" Ruby said when Tom had closed the door behind him. "He means well, and he has a good heart, but he still be a bit of a fool."

"I think he's just showing affection for you, Gigi." Chrissie left her coffee on the counter and grabbed a box cutter from a drawer in the counter. She lifted the top box from the stack closest to her and sliced it open. "Paper towels," she told Ruby.

"You know where they go."

"I do indeed."

"Newspaper here yet?" Ruby asked.

"It's already on your table." Chrissie nodded in the direction of the round table on the opposite side of the store.

"Thank you. I think I be setting for a bit."

Chrissie proceeded to open each box, unpacking the contents and placing them on the shelves where they belonged. The first week she'd been there, she'd thought she'd rearrange some items, but she'd inadvertently caused a panic.

"Folks know where things supposed to be," Ruby'd told her. "Don't be messin' with the natural order of things."

It had been on the tip of Chrissie's tongue to ask what was natural about the order of toilet paper stacked on a shelf next to bags of potato chips, but apparently that was what worked on Cannonball Island. Who was she, Chrissie wondered tongue in cheek, to question it?

When she finished with the shelves, she broke down the boxes and piled them next to the bait cooler near the front door for Tom to pick up next time. She picked up her coffee where she'd left it, but before she could raise the mug to her lips, Ruby said, "That be cold by now. Pour yourself some new and come over here and set for a minute."

Chrissie did as she was told and took the chair opposite Ruby. The coffee was delicious, and she wondered as she took a sip why it seemed better than any coffee she'd had before. *Must be some of Ruby's magic*, Chrissie mused, though she dared not voice that thought.

"What be your plan for today?" Ruby asked.

"I thought I'd clean up around the store, then go into town and see what the market has that I can make for dinner."

Ruby held her tea with both hands, her fingers tapping impatiently on the side of the cup. Chrissie'd come to recognize the gesture to mean Ruby was gearing up to make a pronouncement, but she knew it wouldn't move the conversation along to ask. She'd just have to wait Ruby out till she was good and ready.

Finally, Ruby said, "How long you plan on hiding out here in the store?"

"What?" Chrissie was taken aback. "I'm not hiding."

"Course you are."

"Gigi, I'm out and about on the island every day. I go into St. Dennis every morning to shop."

"And then you hightail back here fast as you can." Ruby's eyes narrowed. "Don't think I don't see."

"I don't know what you think I'm hiding from. I'm not even hiding from Doug, because he has no idea I'm here. He doesn't even know this place exists. He never cared enough to ask me about my family and he never listened when I tried to tell him."

"I'm not talking about that fool boy you took up with. Not even worth my breath, him." Clearly annoyed by the very thought of Doug, Ruby dismissed him with a wave of her hand. "You be hiding from yourself, Christiana, and that be a fact. Time to take a few steps out of that box you got yourself in. Time to start to shine, way you supposed to."

Chrissie took a deep breath. No one ever called her by her given name, and most people, when seeing it written out, thought it was misspelled, assuming her name was Christina. Somewhere in her father's memory the name Christiana had left a mark, and when she was born, it had resurfaced; at least that was what her mother had always told her.

"I don't know what you want me to do." Chrissie rested her arms on the table.

"I want you to be yourself. I want you to do what you be meant to do."

Chrissie shrugged. "I don't even know what that is."

Ruby smacked the table with the newspaper, not enough to make Chrissie jump, but enough that it got her attention.

"Why you being so dense, girl? You been in that kitchen three, four times every day since you got here, and you worked your own kinda magic. You need to get out of my kitchen and into someone else's." Ruby stared at Chrissie as if waiting for her to catch on. Finally, when Chrissie hadn't responded, she said, "I spell it out for you, since you don't be as quick as I be giving you credit for: you need to get a job."

"Gigi, I can pay you rent, if that's what this is about. I should have thought of that sooner, all these months I've lived here and—"

"Oh, you hush. I don't need your money. What'd I do with more money? Got all I need. What I need is to see you moving on. Not moving away—just getting on with your life. Got me thinking you're afraid, like you were before you got here."

"I was afraid for a long time," Chrissie admitted.

"You think I didn't know that? Girl, remember who you're talking to here."

Chrissie's mouth stretched into a smile. "You know everything, don't you?"

"Not everything. Can't always see what was, sometimes just see what is. It's just a knowing. Don't need to be putting a name on it. No rhyme or reason, far as I can tell. Some things I just know or see. Not everything, and not all the time, and just mostly things about them who be one of mine."

"And I'm one of yours."

Ruby nodded. "Always have been. Your mama, she be on her own. I can't be helping her. She burned her bridges, sure as life. She tried taking you away from the island, but you found your way back, just like you had to. Lisbeth did the same. You and Lis, you're my girls."

Chrissie came up behind her and put her arms around Ruby, and for a moment, Ruby let her hold on.

"You understand why I think you need to get out in the world again, make your own way?" Ruby asked softly.

"I do. But my only work experience is in restaurants, Gigi."

"Seems then you answered your own question." And just that quickly, the moment was gone, and Chrissie released the hold she'd had on her. Ruby took a sip from her cup, then frowned. "Cold."

"I'll get you another cup." When Chrissie reached for the cup, Ruby grabbed her hand.

"You be good at what you do. Too good to be spending all your days cooking for just yourself and an old woman."

"I enjoy cooking for you, Gigi. And I thank you for . . ." Chrissie paused, trying to find the words to tell her great-grandmother how much it meant to her that she'd opened her home and taken her in when she had no place else to go where she'd be safe.

As if Ruby knew, she released Chrissie's hand and said, "This be your place, Chrissie. Always been, always will be. No need to thank me for what's already yours. No harm ever going to come to you here. But you got to do what you be meant to do. More in store for you than cooking in my kitchen. Grace said you do as good as the cooks at the inn, maybe you should be there with them."

"The inn has the reputation for having the best kitchen on the Eastern Shore. The chef is the best. I'm not sure I'm ready for the inn. But if you think I should, maybe I'll stop and talk to Grace when I go into town this week."

"Not about what I think you should do. What you think you should do. What's in your head, girl?"

"I've never cooked for that many people, in that big a venue. I'm used to a smaller kitchen, and I don't think I'd like the hustle of one that big, one that has so much going on, and such a lofty reputation to uphold. I don't think I'd be comfortable there."

"You be afraid of it?"

Chrissie shook her head. "I just know what makes me happy. I've never been comfortable in a crowd. I've been to the inn. I've seen their kitchen. They have a big staff there. It's not fear, Gigi. I'm just more of a small-pond kinda girl."

"I understand that. Some of us be all right in any pond. There be other places in St. Dennis. Seems to me soon enough some be hiring, tourists be on the rise in another month or so, might be a new baby on the way be slowing someone down. You need to get out and look around on your own."

"I've seen most of the other restaurants in town. They're all so much more upscale than the places I've worked for. Lola's is so gourmet; they do so many French entrées, I can hardly read the menu in the window. I've only worked in one place that wasn't a diner."

"Don't need to be gourmet—whatever that means. And don't need to be selling yourself short."

"I'm really not. I'm a good cook, I know that. It's just been easier to stay here and do for you while I— well, got over things."

"You not be over everything. I know what I see. Right now, I be knowing it's time for you to get out and do what you do."

"You're right, but some things take longer than others to get over."

"You can leave that load right where you left that man. Not worthy of you, him."

"I know that now." Chrissie nodded. "And you know that I know that."

Ruby nodded, her green eyes twinkling. "Don't never be thinking you be fooling me."

"I wouldn't dream of it. I'll definitely check around, see what's available." Chrissie stood, then leaned over and kissed Ruby on the cheek. "Thanks, Gigi. It's been so long since someone was in my corner, since someone believed in me. Well, other than Rob at the café. Before that, I didn't think I was good enough to move on to something better. It seemed I was always moving backward. It's taken me a while, but I feel like myself again."

"You keep that little man's voice outta your head," Ruby said sharply. "He had his say long enough. Time to listen to yourself." She smiled. "And to me, of course."

"I'm listening, Gigi." Chrissie smoothed back a wisp of thin white hair from Ruby's forehead. "I still want to take care of you, though."

As soon as the words left her mouth, she regretted them. She felt Ruby tense, then grab hold of her wrist.

"Now, who do you think be taking care of me before you?"

"Ah . . . I didn't mean . . . I thought Owen . . ."

"Owen had his hands full, missy. I been taking care of myself since my Harold died, and that be before you were born. I don't need no one to take care of me." She loosened her grip. "But if sometime you be wanting to cook me some oysters like you did last night, or some crab like you did the night before, I be here to eat them."

"Got it." Chrissie nodded. "I think I'll just go on into St. Dennis now, see what the market has today."

Chrissie backed up a step or two, then headed toward the second floor to get her bag. She was half-way to the stairwell when Ruby called to her. "Won't hold it against you if you come back with some rock-fish and a couple'a lemons. Course, would be nice if you got me that tea before you took off . . ."

CHOOSING TO WALK into St. Dennis had been the right choice. She'd changed from her early morning work clothes into a pair of black yoga pants and a pale pink top. She'd tied up her hair in a ponytail, slipped on her dark shades, and put on her running shoes, since the walk would be her workout for today. The sky was blue, the air temperate, and there was just enough balance of sun and shade to make it a perfect morning. Chrissie crossed the bridge between Cannonball Island and the mainland and strolled along the sandy shoulder of Charles Street, St. Dennis's main street, which stretched from the island through the center of town, and clear out to the highway. She passed a pond where a heron feasted on its morning catch and several Victorian-era houses that were set back from the road. The trees were just beginning to leaf out and the birds had started their migration north. The bare branches were filled with the transients that stopped at the bay to refuel before resuming their flights.

With every step, her mind replayed her conver-sation with Ruby, who of course was right about everything she'd said. It *was* time for Chrissie to step out and join the world again. She'd gotten too com-fortable at the store, the routine easy and gentle on

one who'd been kicked around—mentally and physically—for far too long. Another life, Chrissie told
herself. Not this one. Not anymore.

She hadn't been kidding when she told Ruby that
she always seemed to be sliding backward, because
she had been. Whenever she'd been moved up in
whatever kitchen she was working, Doug had been
relentless in convincing her she'd fail if she tried to
move to the next level, and he'd talk her into quitting
and going elsewhere, where she'd start at the same
low level she'd been at. The cycle had been broken
when Rob, who'd been the head chef at the last diner
she'd worked at, left to open La Luna and begged
Chrissie to come with him.

"You're too good—way too good—to work in
diners like this one the rest of your life. Come with
me," he'd told her, "and I'll make a head chef out of
you one day."

Of course, Doug had done his best to undermine
her confidence, telling her Rob would end up firing
her once her true lack of skill was exposed, that roadside diners, not fancy cafés, were where she belonged.
But Rob had been as tenacious in helping her believe
she deserved better, she deserved more. In the end,
Doug had given in, though Chrissie knew it wasn't
because he believed in her but because Rob offered
to pay her more than she'd been making at the diner.
That she had thrived at La Luna had been her little
secret. She'd never once shared Rob's words of en-
couragement or praise with Doug, because she knew
he'd somehow turn those words around. For reasons
she'd never understood, Doug took every one of her
accomplishments as a slap in his face, which he'd

then take out on her. Over the past year she'd read enough—on her breaks, of course, never at home—to begin to recognize that only a badly damaged person would react to another's success the way Doug had, and in a way, she'd felt sorry for him. She'd tried to get him to open up about his past to help her understand him a little better, but all he'd say when she asked about his childhood was, "It wasn't good."

There were days when she could barely believe she'd walked away from him and left behind all the baggage he'd refused to share. Maybe someday he'd get help to overcome his anger and his bitterness, both of which had fueled his drug and alcohol addictions, but she doubted it.

Why had she stayed so long? She'd loved him, or thought she had. Over time she began to understand that what had drawn her to him was the mere fact that such a beautiful man had desired her. She'd always considered herself the ugly duckling of the family. So when a man like Doug paid attention, she was beyond flattered. From the first time she met him, she'd been drawn to his good looks, his easy charm, and the fact that he'd made her feel like the most beautiful woman in the world. Because she had self-esteem issues, he'd struck all the right notes. He was four years older, had already graduated from college, and seemed to have a brilliant future as an accountant. He'd talked her into quitting college in her junior year and moving in with him. If things went well, he'd said, they could get married after they'd had time to build up savings for a house. She couldn't believe that such a man wanted to share his life with her.

But by the time she realized his beauty was only superficial, they'd moved in together and she knew moving out would not be that simple. Over time the girl she'd been—the one who'd loved to dance, loved eighties rock and who'd sing "Come On, Eileen" at the top of her lungs in the shower, who loved to read and would spend hours in the library, picking up random books to learn something she hadn't known before—was lost, and she didn't know if she'd ever be able to bring her back.

And over time, Doug'd stopped talking about marriage, and for that, she'd been grateful.

She'd learned a lot since then. She still had some self-esteem and self-image issues, but she'd been working on that.

Chrissie pushed aside any thoughts of Doug and the life she'd left behind. She was a new person now, a person who was finding her own happiness in her own way and in her own place. She wasn't about to let anything or anyone take her joy or spoil this morning for her.

In one hand she carried a hardcover book Ruby had asked her to drop off to Grace, so she turned at the entrance to the Inn at Sinclair's Point. The driveway was fairly long and curved in several places, so the inn didn't come into view until you were halfway there and the ancient pines gave way to gardens and hedges. The venerable building was three full stories of white clapboard with a front porch that went clear across the inn. Tall white pillars reached to the second floor to support the balcony. On one side, a wing stretched into a lawn that even now, at the end of April, was thick and green. The wing on the opposite side overlooked tennis courts, and a well-equipped playground stood between the inn and the bay.

Several guests, some wearing tennis whites, sat in rocking chairs on the front porch as Chrissie took the steps two at a time. She went inside the wide front door and followed the hall past a large ballroom where a young woman with long blond hair appeared to be setting up for an event.

"Hey, Lucy," Chrissie called in through the open double doors.

"Hi, Chrissie." Lucy Sinclair Montgomery, Grace's daughter and the inn's event planner, waved back.

Chrissie glanced around the room, which appeared to be in the process of being dressed up.

"Looks great." Chrissie nodded in the direction of the large round tables where lush, colorful floral decorations were being placed.

"Thanks. Fashion show tomorrow night. You should come. Lis and Cass will be here, and I know you've met most of their friends from town." Lucy reached into her pocket and took out an envelope. Handing it to Chrissie, she said, "Two tickets. It'll be fun. Besides, I need to fill chairs."

"Thanks, but I don't really know anyone to give the extra ticket to. I doubt that you'll have a problem packing the place, but I'll try to make it." She tucked the envelope into her bag. "Any idea where I'd find your mom this morning?"

"Try her office," Lucy said. "Third door on the left. If she's not in there, check out the lobby."

"Will do. Thanks. I'll let you get back to work."

"See you tomorrow night."

Chrissie knocked on Grace's closed office door

when she reached it, but there was no answer. She turned the door handle and gave it a slight push, and when it opened, she peered inside. The lights were on and there were papers scattered upon a desk, but no Grace.

Chrissie closed the door and walked toward the lobby, which was straight ahead. There she saw Grace at the registration desk in conversation with a family that appeared to be checking in or checking out. Chrissie walked the perimeter of the room, glancing at the artwork, while she waited. Finally, Grace was free, and seeing Chrissie, she broke into a wide smile.

"Thank you so much for dropping off the book," Grace said as she drew closer. "I meant to bring it home with me the other night but it slipped my mind." Her smile widened. "Must have been those delicious oysters that made me forget everything else."

"Thanks, Grace." Chrissie handed her the book. "Anytime you'd like to come by for dinner with Ruby and me, you just let us know. You're always welcome."

"Thank you, dear. I'll certainly be back," Grace assured her. "Now, where are you off to?"

"The market, but I really want to stop at Scoop. I've had this craving for ice cream for the past few days."

"There's no ice cream like Scoop's. Have a cone for me." Grace paused. "On second thought, I might have to make my way down there later this afternoon."

"I could bring you something if you like," Chrissie offered.

"Thank you, but as you know, part of the fun is walking into that sweet little shop and reading the day's flavors for oneself." The phone in Grace's pocket began to ring.

"You take that," Chrissie said. "I should be moving along anyway."

"Thank you again." Grace took the phone from her pocket and headed back toward her office.

A group of seven women who appeared to be in their midtwenties came in through the automatic double doors at the side of the lobby. They stopped at the registration desk and one by one dropped their luggage to the floor. A minute later, a tall man wearing worn jeans, a checkered shirt with the sleeves rolled to the elbows, and a Philadelphia Eagles ball cap approached them and struck up a conversation with the last woman in the line, a short pretty blonde. Her eyes appeared to shine approvingly as she turned to look into his face. As Chrissie passed by, she heard the woman say, "Just till Sunday. Girls' weekend."

Chrissie went through the automatic doors and onto the small back porch, where she stood for a moment to look around. She'd been to the inn before, but she'd never taken the time to discover all the resort offered. On a whim, she walked down to the bay, past a large shed where bicycles stood waiting to be rented. Ten feet away, kayaks and canoes stood up against the wall of the boathouse. Chrissie passed by it all and went right to the bay. The grass grew almost to the water's edge, and off to the right the wetland was teeming with life. She sheltered her eyes from the sun with one hand to look across the bay, but the Chesapeake was too wide to see clear to the other side. A clang of the metal gate at the opening to the playground drew her attention, and she heard several very young children shrieking to be first on a slide. She knew that in the summer months, the inn employed its own babysitters so parents could enjoy a game of tennis while their offspring played in the sand or on the swings, but today, the parents were on their own. As she looked around the inn's grounds, it was pretty clear that Dan, Grace's son who'd taken over running the inn, had thought of everything.

Thinking of Dan Sinclair brought to mind his wife, Jamie Valentine, the writer whose books about relationships had been bestsellers the year before. One of the waitresses at the café had left one of the titles in the small break room in the back of the restaurant, and it was there that Chrissie had first picked up the book that helped her to change her life. In the pages of *The Honest Relationship*, Chrissie had recognized exactly what her relationship with Doug had become. She'd gone on to read *The Honest Life*, and by the time she'd gotten to the last page, she realized that every day she stayed with Doug was one more day she'd spend lying to herself. It had taken her close to a year to leave, but in that year, she managed to quietly do what was necessary for her to step out of her dishonest life and leave her toxic relationship behind. When she'd met Jamie at Owen's wedding, it was all she could do not to gush.

"Your books have changed my life," Chrissie'd told Jamie.

"Tell me." Jamie'd sat next to Chrissie and listened.

And Chrissie had told her everything.

When she was finished, Jamie's eyes were filled

with tears, and she'd hugged Chrissie tightly. "Thank you," she'd said. "You have no idea how much it means to me to know that my books helped you in some small way to help yourself."

"No small way. It's no exaggeration to say you probably saved my life," Chrissie'd told her, and from that conversation, a friendship was born.

As she walked toward the driveway, Chrissie looked back at the building, wondering if Jamie had returned from her latest book tour. Not that she had time to visit, Chrissie reminded herself. She had an errand to run and she really wanted to stop at Scoop.

She'd just reached the driveway when she heard someone calling her name.

"Hey, Chrissie?"

She turned, not certain she was the Chrissie who was being paged. The tall guy with the green Eagles cap she'd seen in the lobby chatting up the pretty blonde was jogging toward her.

"It's Chris, right? Chrissie?" He stopped ten feet away, and she realized who he was. Jared Chandler. Owen's friend who'd made Chrissie feel like a stammering idiot at both of her cousins' weddings when he'd tried to make conversation with her, but she hadn't been up to the challenge of talking to him for any length of time. She'd still believed that guys like Jared were way out of her league, and she'd acted like it. She'd danced with him when he asked, but there'd been little conversation. When the song ended, he'd walked her back to her table like a gentleman, then disappeared. She noticed him dancing later with a friend of Cass's from college, with whom he'd left at the end of the evening.

That Chrissie—the one who couldn't carry on a conversation with a hot-looking guy—was the old Chrissie. The new Chrissie was determined to do better.

"Right. Hi, Jared." She could almost feel a blush beginning to rise from her chest to her face, but she mentally beat it down. Hopefully his shades were dark enough that he couldn't tell.

"I thought that was you. Owen's cousin, right? From the weddings?"

She nodded.

"So how've you been?"

"Good. You?" Apparently the new Chrissie was still working on her conversational skills.

"Work's a little slow right now." He gestured toward the general direction of the island. "The state is trying to decide which is more important, the Native American settlement at the bottom of the river, or the merchant ship from the early 1800s that's sitting on top of it, so things are a little quiet."

"That's right. You're a diver, like Owen." She tried to recall what her cousin had told her about the boat they were salvaging, but Jared had removed his sunglasses, and at the moment, all she could think of were his dark blue eyes, which were looking directly into hers. "He mentioned something about an old camp but didn't go into detail."

"We're naturally more interested in getting to the ship—that's what we're here for—but no one's made a decision yet, so everything's on hold."

She nodded again. She wasn't sure what the laws were regarding salvaging archaeological sites, and didn't know if Jared would be inclined to explain them.

"So where are you off to?" he asked.

"I have a few errands in town, then my weekly stop at Scoop."

"You're going to Scoop? I keep hearing about that place. Supposed to be the best ice cream on the Eastern Shore."

"It totally is. I'm surprised you haven't checked it out yet. It's a definite must when you're in St. Dennis."

"Hey, do you mind if I tag along? I'll even drive."

"I don't mind, but I'm walking. If you want to ride, I'll meet you there." Pat on the back for not taking the ride with the hot guy when she really did want to walk.

"Well, it's a beautiful morning. I guess I'll walk with you."

Chrissie smiled. "Try to keep up."

Jared laughed and easily kept pace. His long stride soon bested hers, and she had to ask him to slow down.

"Your legs are longer than mine," she said. "Not a fair contest."

"Hey, you were the one who told me to keep up with you."

"A mistake on my part."

"So tell me again, what you do? I know we talked at the weddings, but I don't remember what you said about that."

"Probably because I didn't say anything about working. Because I'm not. Well, I do work in Ruby's store, but it's not like a job."

"Ruby's store? You mean the general store on the island?"

Chrissie nodded.

"I've been there a couple of times. I don't recall seeing you there."

"When were you in last?"

Jared appeared to think about that for a moment before saying, "I guess the end of the summer or so. I left this job to work on another job my dad had lined up. When we finished up that dive at the end of February, I came back here to work with Owen, but then we got put off." He shoved his hands into his pockets as they walked. "Which is okay, I guess, since it's been a while that I've taken any real time off."

"I didn't get here until the end of September for the wedding, so I wouldn't have been around when you stopped in."

"So Ruby's your, what, grandmother? Great-grandmother?"

"Great-grandmother, yes."

"She ever spook you?"

"What?" The question was totally unexpected.

His grin was that of a seven-year-old who knew he'd said something provocative. "Ruby. She ever say anything that made the hair on the back of your neck stand up?"

Chrissie laughed. "Many times. But you—?"

Jared nodded. "Oh yeah. One time I dropped in at the store to see Owen but he wasn't there. Ruby was just getting ready to have dinner and she asked me to join her. So I said sure, since it was nice of her to invite me, plus I was starving. I'd just gotten into town and didn't know anywhere else to go, so it seemed like a good idea at the time."

"What did she do? She read your palm? Tarot cards?" Chrissie asked, knowing full well Ruby did neither of those things.

"No. We're sitting there talking, and all of a sudden she says, 'You're heading south.' And yeah, I was. My dad opened up new headquarters in South Carolina and that was going to be my next stop, so I figured that was what she was referring to.

"But then she tells me there was going to be stormy weather soon and I needed to mind my instincts. Which I thought was strange, but, okay. Then my dad calls out of the blue and tells me he needs me to fly down to the Keys and look at a job he'd been asked to take over from another salvor who'd botched it. So I go down there and right from the start, everything's off. The crew, the equipment, the salvage boat itself—nothing's up to our standards, so I called my dad and told him I didn't want us to take the job. Fortunately, my dad trusts me, and he turned the job down. Someone else came in, took it over, and four days into it a hurricane hit and the ship went down with everyone on it." He shook his head. "Trusted my instincts, all right. Funny thing is, I'd forgotten about what she'd said about a storm until after I'd heard what happened. Then I got goose bumps, head to toe. Seriously freaked me out."

"Did you ever tell Owen that story?"

"Yeah, but he didn't seem to think it was anything out of the ordinary. I guess he's used to it. Her coming out with stuff like that." Their arms touched as they walked. "Don't you think it's odd? Or are you immune to that sort of thing, too?"

"Not immune so much as not surprised. I guess the only thing that surprises me at all is that she said something to someone out of the family. So she must like you."

"Better to be liked by the woman who knows all than not," he said.

Chrissie laughed again. "She can be disconcerting, that's for sure, but she has the kindest, truest heart of anyone I've ever known."

"Owen said the same thing."

She found him easy to talk to, and she relaxed enough to enjoy their chatter as they walked along the shoulder of the road.

"So you grew up around here?" he asked.

"No. Born in Salisbury, south of here, raised outside of Pittsburgh, but my mom was from Cannonball Island. She's Ruby's granddaughter. I spent most of my summers on the island growing up."

"It must have been pretty cool. There's so much for a kid to do there. Ponds, the marsh, the point, the bay."

"Crabbing from the dock, digging for oysters in the bay, swimming. Catching frogs and other fun critters in the marsh."

"You're the first girl I ever heard say she liked catching frogs. I'm impressed."

"When you're a kid, and you've read every book you own, and there's no TV, you learn to play with what you've got. In our case, it was the island."

"Back then, it must have seemed like one big playground," Jared said.

"That's exactly what it was. One big playground, and for the most part, it was just ours."

"No other kids on the island?"

"There were some friends that Lis and Owen went to school with in St. Dennis, but odd as it seems now, back then, a lot of island families sent their kids to relatives off island for the summer. In retrospect, I think maybe they didn't have anyone to watch the kids while they worked, so sending them off to Grandma's might have been easier than finding a babysitter."

She stumbled a little on a stone and he caught her elbow. "Thanks," she said. "So how 'bout you? Where are you from?"

"I grew up in Boston."

"Siblings?"

"I have a sister, Rachel. She's a diver, runs salvaging jobs for our dad, and is married to a marine archaeologist who also works for the company. They have two little demons—I mean, little boys. When my nephews get a little bigger, we're going to teach them to dive, too. We're thinking we'll be able to pass the business on to the third generation."

"So I'll go out on a limb and guess that your mother is a diver as well?" she asked.

"My mother hated anything to do with the business," he said briskly. "She was a concert pianist and died when I was twelve."

"I'm so sorry, Jared. I had no way of knowing."

"You wouldn't. And it's okay. It was a long time ago. I don't remember her much."

She thought he was about to elaborate a little, but he left it at that. She sensed there was so much more to the story that he'd left unspoken, and that he remembered more than he wanted to admit.

"So what's so cool about diving? Obviously you like it, and I know Owen loves it, but I don't get it. No offense, but the thought of going underwater freaks me out."

"You're kidding?" When she shook her head no, she wasn't, Jared asked, "What is it that bothers you?"

"The whole thing. Looking up and seeing the surface of the water above you just seems weird to me. And all the things that live under there! Sharks, rays, barracuda." She shivered. "If God meant for people to go down there, we'd have been born with gills."

"If you'd ever gone, you'd look at it entirely differently. You'd see the beauty in the silence, in the way the sunlight shimmers below the surface, the gracefulness of all those things you just named that you're afraid of."

"If you say so."

"You should try it sometime. I could take you, or Owen . . ."

"Not gonna happen in this lifetime."

"Your loss. Really. It is," he said to emphasize his point. "But if you ever change your mind—"

"I know who to call. Thanks."

They reached the light at the center of town and walked left down Kelly's Point Road, past the municipal building that housed the police department as well as the town's administration offices. Once past the free parking lots that stretched along each side of the road, Kelly's Point ended at a boardwalk. To the right was the marina, Captain Walt's ("Best Seafood on the Bay"), and the boat shop owned by

Lis's husband, Alec. To the left was One Scoop or Two—Scoop to the locals—the ice cream parlor that had once been an old crabbers shack.

Jared reached around Chrissie to open the door, and the bell that hung over it rang weakly. She smiled a thank-you as they stepped inside and started toward the counter. The interior of the shop was much like the exterior, with a rough-hewn floor and walls. There were three people ahead of them in line.

Chrissie whispered to Jared as she pointed to the wood-covered walls. "So much in vogue right now."

"What, wood walls?" He stared at the wall for a moment. "Says who?"

"Says HGTV."

"I don't know what that is."

"Where have you been for the past couple of years?"

"On a boat in the middle of the Gulf of Mexico. Before that, I was in Bermuda, then Costa Rica."

"I guess we could give you a pass. It's a television channel about home renovating and decorating."

Jared made a face. "Sounds like must-see TV."

Chrissie pointed to a blackboard where a list of flavors was written in different-colored chalk. "Those are the specials," she told Jared. "But there are other flavors in the cooler."

He walked closer to the board.

"Hey, Chrissie," the woman behind the counter called as she filled a cone and handed it to a customer. "What can I get you today?"

"Hi, Stef. Give me a moment to check out the selections." Chrissie turned to Jared. "Have you met Steffie MacGregor? Owner and creator of the finest ice cream on the Eastern Shore."

"No, I don't think so." Jared took his eyes from the board. "Jared Chandler."

"Stef, Jared's with the salvage company—" Chrissie began.

"That's searching for the merchant ship that went down in 1812 or thereabouts. Yeah, I heard about it." Tall and leggy with honey blond hair and a quick smile, Steffie nodded as she went to the cash register to ring up the sale. "We've had some of your crew in here. Not to mention Owen and Cass."

"What's the newest flavor?" Chrissie asked.

Steffie pointed to the board. "The strawberry festival is new this week. Tons of berries and pieces of pecans. The rhubarb pie is also good—not quite as sweet but really tasty. Oh, and the spring fling is amazing if you like chocolate and raspberries."

"Sold." Jared moved ahead a few steps as the line moved. Chrissie was still staring at the board.

"I love anything with mint," Chrissie said.

"Then the mint julep is for you. Best mint flavor I've ever been able to make."

Chrissie nodded. "I definitely need to try that."

"This is a very cool place," Jared told Steffie when he and Chrissie had moved to the head of the line.

"Thanks." She beamed, clearly proud of her business. "It's all mine. It was a mess when I got it and it seemed like it took forever to fix it up, but it's my little corner of the world." She paused, ice cream scoop in her hand. "What can I get you?"

"Chrissie?" Jared deferred to her.

"One scoop of the mint julep," she said.

"Cone or dish?" Steffie asked.

"Cone, please."

"And you?" Steffie turned to Jared.

"I'll have that chocolate thing with the raspberries. Two scoops. You can top them off with some of that strawberry pecan. Cone."

"A triple-decker cone?" She raised an eyebrow. "I hope you're a fast eater."

"Good point. Make it a dish."

"Coming up."

The bell over the door rang and several other people filed in as Steffie worked behind the cooler. In no time, she had Chrissie and Jared's orders ready and met them at the cash register. Jared dug in with the spoon before taking his wallet from his back pocket.

"You know, Chrissie, you can come in more than once a week," Steffie said.

"Right." Chrissie shook her head. "I think the ice cream looks better in the case than it would on my hips."

Jared reached behind her and handed several bills to Steffie.

"This is for both," he told Steffie.

"Jared, you don't have to pay for my cone," Chrissie protested.

"A small price for letting me tag along with you." He took another spoonful of the strawberry. "And for introducing me to the best ice cream I ever had."

"Thanks." She grabbed a handful of napkins from the counter. "Stef, I'll see you next week."

"Right. Wednesday right before noon. I swear I could set my watch by you," Steffie said as Jared and Chrissie turned away. "Oh, wait. Chris, you going to the fashion show at the inn tomorrow night?"

"I'm thinking about it. Need a ticket? I have two."

"I have mine, but thanks. I'll see you there," Steffie said. "A whole bunch of us are going. Maybe we could have our own table. I haven't had a girls' night since I had the twins, so I'm beyond due. Vanessa's doing the show, all new stuff from her shop, and somehow she talked my sister-in-law into modeling."

"Sounds like fun."

"You know who my brother's married to, right? My husband's sister?"

Chrissie nodded. "Dallas MacGregor, the movie star. I heard."

"May I interrupt your conversation by saying that I have been in love with Dallas MacGregor for my entire adult life?" Jared leaned an arm against the cooler.

"You and every other guy who ever gazed upon her gorgeousness," Steffie said, then added with a smile, "Don't think it makes you special.

"Anyway, she usually keeps a low profile and only agreed to do it because it's a charity thing. The money's to go to the new women's shelter that's being set up over on Pearl Street."

"I heard about that."

"Yeah, so that's tomorrow night." The doorbell rang again and Steffie glanced at the growing line in front of the cooler. "I'll look for you then. Jared, nice meeting you. Come back again."

"Count on it."

They had to cut through the line of customers to get to the door. Jared reached for the handle, then stopped. "Want to get a table in here or go outside?" he asked.

"Outside, for sure," Chrissie said.

Outside on a small patio were several small tables with umbrellas to block the sun, and along the board-walk there were backless wooden benches. Chrissie headed for the benches and sat facing the marina and the bay beyond the pier.

"Good choice." Jared sat next to Chrissie and gazed out at the water. "I noticed these benches earlier."

"I like watching the water. The sailboats especially. Oh, and those speedy little boats. They look like so much fun." She licked the side of the cone where the ice cream was starting to drip. "And those big yachts. They look so majestic going by."

"Sounds like you spend a lot of time watching the bay."

"Sometimes I like to go out onto the point and just sit at the end of the pier." She turned to him and asked, "You know the pier, right? Where Lis and Alec's wed-ding was?"

Jared nodded. "I remember. That was some party. So was Owen's. It's still hard to believe he's married, though. Owen was always such a rolling stone. Had some of the best times of my life with your cousin."

"I always remembered him as sort of a good-time kind of guy."

"Understated, but we won't quibble. Doesn't mat-ter now, though. Cass put an end to his wild times." Jared nudged Chrissie with his shoulder. "I gotta admit, I miss the old Owen sometimes."

"I guess everyone settles down at some point."

Jared shook his head. "Not this guy. I can't see my-self ever doing the whole domestic scene."

"Born to run, eh?"

"Something like that." He'd finished the top scoop and had started on the middle. "How 'bout you?"

"Tried it once. Didn't work for me." She could have said more, but figured the short version was all he really wanted to hear anyway. "So did you get her name?" she asked to change the subject and lighten the mood.

"Whose name?" He frowned as if not understanding the question.

"The blonde in the lobby, the one checking in."

A grin spread across his face. "Oh, you caught that?"

"I did."

He didn't answer one way or the other, but she figured he'd scored the name and probably her phone number. If he'd waited till she'd checked in, chances were he had her room number as well.

He'd finished his ice cream and was wiping his hands off on one of the napkins she'd given him.

"Thanks." He rolled the napkin into a ball and tossed it with a flourish in the direction of the trash can on the opposite side of the path from where they sat. The napkin went in and he snapped his fingers.

She took the last bite of her cone and looked out at the bay. About two hundred yards from the pier, a trio of sailboats skipped along on the breeze. She wondered what it would feel like to be flying across the water in one of those narrow crafts.

"So I guess you want to get on your way, get your errands done." Jared stood.

"I really should. Gigi will start to wonder where I am."

"Nah, the woman who knows everything knows where you are."

"It wouldn't surprise me," she said as she stood.

They strolled to the end of the walk, then Jared stopped. "Alec's boat shop is right down there, right?" He pointed to the left.

"It is."

"I think I'll stop down and say hi. I heard he has an old skipjack he's restoring, and I'd like to see it."

"My great-uncle Eb's skip," she said. "It was outside Ruby's store on cinder blocks forever. It's a long story how it got to Alec. You might ask him about it."

"I might do that. Hey, thanks again for letting me tag along this morning."

"Anytime. And thanks for the cone. My treat next time."

He took a few backward steps. "Right. Next Wednesday. Same time. Same place."

Chrissie smiled, then with a wave of her hand started the walk back toward Charles Street. She looked back once, when she got to the parking lot, but by then he was gone.

"*Next Wednesday,*" he'd said. "*Same time. Same place.*"

She wondered if he'd remember, and if so, if he'd show—and if he'd even been serious. If she were a betting woman, she'd bet against it.

Chapter Three

Jared stood on the deck of the *Cordelia Elizabeth*, one of several salvage boats owned by his family's company, Chandler and Associates, and watched the sun go down. He'd stayed at the inn for the past week, leaving a crew member on board in his absence, but he didn't think it was fair that the poor guy was stuck on the ship while Jared got to enjoy the comforts of the town. After dinner, he borrowed an outboard from Owen and headed out to the *Cordy E*, as he referred to the boat, and traded places with the crewman with instructions on where to return the outboard.

That act of altruism might have caused another man to rethink his generosity, but Jared didn't mind being alone on an anchored boat. Being stationary in the Chesapeake was nothing like being anchored in the ocean. Here the waves were much smaller and the evening more peaceful. He'd sit in his cabin and read for a while, then he'd let the natural rhythm of the boat rock him to sleep. It would be a win-win sort of night for him.

He could have talked the blonde he'd met at Captain Walt's the night before into sharing the bunk with him, but she'd fawned over him to the point where he couldn't take any more, and the thought of spending more time in her company gave him a headache, regardless of the fact that she'd made it apparent she'd be happy to share his bed, on land or at sea. He'd admit he'd considered it for the briefest moment, but in the end, he realized he just didn't want to be bothered with a woman who just couldn't stop telling him how cool she thought he was, and who constantly called him cutie or handsome or hot stuff, as if he didn't have a real name.

Where had his head been when he'd even considered it?

He was pretty sure he knew.

While he liked to be appreciated—who didn't?— he hated to have anyone hang on him. He didn't understand why certain women thought that was the way to get a man's attention. Maybe that worked for some guys, but he was thirty-six, way beyond the age where he needed that kind of ego boost.

Why couldn't all women be like Chrissie Jenkins? He'd spent the better part of an hour with her and she'd not even so much as batted her eyelashes at him. She hadn't acted flirtatious or silly or laughed too much at things he said.

Not that he was interested in Chrissie *that* way, but still. That's how women should act, in his opinion. Just natural and carry on an adult conversation without showing off what you knew about anything. That's what made him think twice about a woman. Like he was thinking about Chrissie.

Not that he was attracted to her in *that* way, but he liked to be with her. He liked her no-nonsense personality.

Which wasn't really a surprise, since he'd been raised by a no-nonsense kind of guy. His father, Gordon, was one of the best-known and most highly respected salvagers in the country, maybe even the world. He'd been called upon by governments, corporations, and private citizens to retrieve the lost—artifacts, ships, remains of crew members—from the bottom of the sea. He was scrupulously honest and was recognized as a man who respected the past. Such a man had no time for silliness or frivolity—especially having found himself a single parent when his children were twelve and eight.

Jared had few memories of his mother, who, as a concert pianist, had been away from home almost as much as his father had been. He and Rachel had been raised by their mother's aunt Bess in her Boston home. Most of what he remembered of his early childhood was someone coming home and someone leaving. Both parents had rarely been home at the same time, and Jared had been an adult when he discovered the reason their mother had made fewer and fewer visits home.

After their aunt died, Jared had been designated executor of her will, which meant, among other things, he'd be responsible for cleaning out the Boston house in which he'd grown up. Rachel was on an important dive at the time, or he'd have talked her into joining him. But as it was, he'd been alone in the old brownstone for the weeks it took him to go through the contents of the house and decide what to sell, what to put in storage. The furniture was easy enough to dispose of—he'd called in an antiques dealer, and having determined that neither he nor Rachel wanted any of the large pieces, sold almost the entire lot on the spot. It was the small things he'd gone through that had been the most difficult to part with.

The jewelry had been set aside for Rachel, everything in the old wooden chest where Bess had kept her good things. Some pieces called up memories, like the gold brooch in the shape of a rose that she wore most frequently on the collar of her favorite coat, and the sapphire ring that had belonged to *her* mother that Aunt Bess had always worn on the middle finger of her right hand. Then there was the envelope he'd found marked with his mother's name—Amelia.

He'd held on to the envelope—unopened—for most of that day, opening it only later when he took a break. He'd poured a cold beer and taken it into the living room, where he sat on the sofa, opened the envelope, and spilled its contents onto the table. Inside had been a plain gold wedding band and a gold ring with a diamond flanked by two sapphires—these, he assumed, had been her wedding and engagement rings. But there were other pieces as well, pieces that were obviously expensive, beyond what he would have expected his father to have bought. Then again, he'd thought at the time, who knows what gifts a man might choose to dazzle the woman he loves?

Jared had packed up the envelope and sent it to his father, thinking Gordon might reminisce about the moments he and Amelia shared when he'd gifted her with each piece before passing it all along to Rachel.

Then Jared found the cache of letters his mother had written to his aunt.

Amelia had poured her heart out about the man she'd fallen in love with, the man she couldn't have because he, like she, was married. Reading the story of his mother's love affair had felt like a sucker punch to the jaw. Jared'd never questioned that his mother's artistry as a pianist had been in such demand that she'd traveled through Europe pursuing her career. Finding out so many years later that she'd chosen to stay away for the sake of a man she couldn't have—a man she'd chosen over her son and her daughter—had shaken him to his core. He hadn't planned to tell his father, but by the time he'd made his discovery, the package had already been delivered. It had been Gordon who'd later called to say he'd sold every piece and wanted the proceeds to be shared equally between his children. Without thinking, Jared had declined.

"I don't want any part of it," he'd snapped. "Nothing that she'd—" He stopped midsentence, remembering whom he was speaking with.

"Nothing she'd been given by her lover." Gordon had seemed matter-of-fact about the situation. Jared thought his father had probably known the truth for years. "I understand. What shall we do with the money?"

"Burn it." Jared had shrugged. "I don't care."

"What if we do something a little more constructive with it? Delia told me about a proposed women's shelter outside of West Chester, where she lives. The money would go a long way toward purchasing the building they want to buy," Gordon said.

"Fine. Let's do it," Jared had readily agreed. "Dad, I haven't said anything to Rachel. About Mom, I mean."

"I see no reason to do that at this time. However, if at some point it becomes relevant, by all means, share what you know," Gordon had said stiffly before immediately changing the subject to an upcoming dive he wanted Jared to make in his father's stead.

He and Gordon had never really addressed his mother's infidelity. Jared could understand his father not wanting to discuss it, but there were times when Jared wished he'd bring it up. He had so many questions, and he was pretty sure his father had the answers. It wasn't an easy subject to approach. How did you ask your father to tell you about your mother's affair with another man?

It bothered Jared sometimes, mostly when he'd been dating someone he liked. He'd start thinking about how maybe things could work out, then he'd think about his mother, and he'd remember how she'd abandoned him and his sister, how she'd betrayed his father. Then he'd break off any relationship that looked like it might go somewhere beyond the superficial, because all things considered, superficial was good enough for him. Superficial didn't burn when either of you moved on.

He knew how cynical he was. He just didn't care. Even his sister had called him out on it, but he'd merely agreed with her.

"You don't give anyone a real chance," she'd said after he broke off with a woman Rachel had liked.

"Maybe I just haven't found someone I thought was worth taking a chance on," he'd told her.

"Yeah, well, I think you're going to die a lonely old man."

"Maybe so. But at least I won't be a lonely old man with a broken heart."

"As far as I know, all the broken hearts have been on the other side of your relationships," Rachel had said. "So why would you even say something like that?"

Rachel wouldn't understand. She didn't know about their mother's betrayal, so it had been easy for her to fall in love and marry a guy who she could believe loved her enough to stay true to her and to be a loving father to their boys.

Sometimes Jared wished he didn't know, either.

For some reason, he thought about Chrissie, about how she'd alluded to having had a relationship that hadn't worked out, and he wondered who had been responsible for the breakup, her or the guy.

Jared guessed it was the guy's fault. She didn't seem like the type to mess around. Of course, he didn't know her all that well. He could be wrong.

He sat on the deck, leaning back against the cabin wall, and raised his eyes upward to where a thousand stars were beginning to shine through the dark of the night sky. It was a sight that always comforted him as a young boy when he'd accompany his father on one of his ventures. He'd been nine the first time. They'd gone searching for a lost Spanish galleon off the coast of Florida. At night he'd sit out on the deck, just like this, and look up and wonder if his mom was looking at the same sky, the same stars. He hadn't known then about time zones or love affairs. All he'd known was that he missed his mother, and that maybe right at that moment, she was thinking about him, and they were sharing the stars.

Jared didn't have anyone to share the stars with, and he was okay with that. He was here to do a job, but he was growing impatient and bored. He just wished he could get on with it. There was only so much one could do in a town like St. Dennis.

He went downstairs to his cabin, turned on the lights, and picked up the book he'd started reading the week before. Propping pillows behind his head, he found the place where he'd left off, and fell back into the story.

IF LUCY HADN'T given her tickets and a personal invitation, Chrissie most likely would have skipped the fashion show. She'd never had much interest in clothes, mainly because for most of her life she hadn't been able to afford much beyond the basics. Over the past few years, she'd almost completely given up on the way she looked. Doug didn't appear to notice, though she knew he'd beat the crap out of anyone who did. Best to not stand out, she'd learned.

She showed the tickets to Ruby and said, "Lucy gave me these for a fashion show they're having at the inn tomorrow night."

"Be nice for you to get out with others your age."

"Come with me?"

"What I be wanting to do that for? I got no interest in clothes other than what I got to wear. No." Ruby shook her head. "You be going without me."

"Nope. If you don't go, I'm not going."

"Oh, yes you are. Lucy be nice enough to give you those tickets, you be using one."

"Ruby—"

"Don't want to hear another word 'bout that. You be going and you be having a good time."

Chrissie'd never been to such an event, so she had no idea what to expect, but she'd gone, and was surprised that she'd had a great time. For one thing, the food prepared by the inn's kitchen had been incredible. She couldn't remember the last time she'd been served such a meal. The appetizers had been as delicious as the entrée and the dessert, though she had to stop herself from mentally critiquing the sauce for the chicken, which she thought was a little heavy on the blood orange juice, and the chocolate caramel crème brûlée, which would have benefited from just a smidge of coarse sea salt sprinkled on just before serving. Still delicious, but she'd have tweaked the recipes.

It seemed that in St. Dennis, casual dress ruled, so most of the items on display were easy, seasonal, pretty, and too often expensive. The models were all local women, including Dallas MacGregor, who'd married the town vet, and Mia Shields Beck, the wife of the police chief, who both modeled casual attire. Shirley Wyler, Steffie's mother, modeled vacation wear, and Carly Summit Sinclair, the wife of Grace's son Ford, modeled the more formal dresses in the show. Savvy businesswoman that she was, Vanessa offered a 20 percent discount on the purchase of any of the items shown that night and had made certain to include clothing appropriate for women of every age. To this end, she'd asked Dallas's grandmother, the film actress Beryl Townsend—known to all in town as Berry—to close the show wearing a cocktail dress that proved that even at eighty-something, a woman could shine. Berry definitely brought down the house.

To Chrissie, the best aspect of the evening hadn't been the remarkable food or the beautiful clothes. It had been so long since she'd had friends that she'd forgotten how good it felt to spend time with other women who laughed and chatted and freely shared bits of themselves. That she could make friends of her choosing, enjoy an evening out without worry of how to explain where she'd been and whom she'd been with, felt like the greatest gift she'd ever been given. Stepping out on her own meant she was free of her past. All friends of Lis's, the women had been fun and lively and accepting of Chrissie into their group, which consisted of Lis, Cass, Steffie, and Sophie.

"Do you love that yellow sundress?" Steffie had whispered to the group. "I do."

"I'd wear that," Cass agreed.

"What about that red and white one?" Sophie asked.

They all agreed the red and white sundress was perfect.

"How 'bout that pale pink shirt and the white pants?" Lis nodded in the direction of the model who was just hitting the runway.

"My dear, this year it's *blush*, not pale pink." Steffie adopted an affected accent. "Please. Keep up with the trends."

Lis laughed. "I stand corrected. I do love that *blush*-colored silk top. It would look great on you, Stef."

Steffie shook her head. "My boobs are too big to wear something that low cut. Those ankle pants, though. I might stop at Bling this weekend and try those on. They're perfect."

Everyone agreed.

"Stef, there's your mom," Lis pointed out. "She looks stunning. Actually, she's looked fabulous in every outfit she's modeled. I want to look like her when I'm in my sixties."

"I love that fuchsia dress on her." Stef beamed as her mother turned and posed. "Maybe I'll buy it for her birthday. She'd never spend that much money on one outfit for herself and it's so her. And Vanessa's giving us a twenty percent discount, so I'm in."

Chrissie sat silently for the most part. When she said she really had never been into clothes, she hadn't been kidding. She'd never been in Vanessa's shop, but it had the reputation of being pricy. Still, she was surprised to see a few items she liked in spite of herself and might actually wear. A pretty sundress, a few tops, and those ankle pants—she might stop into Bling one day soon and try on a few things.

Then again, where would she wear such pretty clothes? She really didn't go anywhere other than the store, the inn, and a few shops in St. Dennis when she ran errands for Ruby or to food shop. Those were the boundaries of her life, and she was okay with that. Small though her world might seem, it was infinitely wider than the one she'd left behind.

Vanessa had pulled out all the stops at the end of the show, and the dressy outfits on the runway took everyone's breath away. Dallas modeled a stunning blue silk dress that hugged her beautiful figure and set off the platinum of her hair and the lavender of her eyes.

"She'd look that good in anything. An old grain

sack, muddy boots, and ripped jeans—it doesn't matter," Steffie'd said with a sigh. "It was my luck to marry the guy whose sister was one of *People* magazine's most beautiful women in the world." She sighed. "I could hate her if she wasn't also the nicest person I ever knew."

After the show ended, Lucy proposed they move to the inn's bar for a glass of wine to top off the night. She'd asked the server to push together several tables so they could sit together, and several bottles of wine appeared—on the house, at Grace's direction before she called it a night. Vanessa joined them after she had the clothes from the show packed up and ready to return to her shop. Her arrival was met with applause and a toast.

"To Ness, who keeps us well dressed and stylish. May she never forget that friends-and-family discount," Lucy said.

Steffie entertained them with the latest antics of her two-year-old twins, Daisy and Ned, who just that morning had decided to make cookies. On the kitchen floor. With an entire bag of flour, a canister full of sugar, an entire carton of eggs, and half a stick of butter. All of which they mixed together with their bare feet.

"I just stepped out onto the deck to take a call from one of my suppliers. I thought the kids were in the TV room watching cartoons. Came back inside to find two cherubs covered with mooshed-up eggs and butter and flour and sugar sticking to them everywhere." She took a drink from her wineglass. "'Yook, Mama! Neddie make 'ookies!'" She took another sip and with a wide grin added, "Wade said it took him all morning to clean up the mess."

"Wait, you left your husband to clean it up himself?" Chrissie asked.

"He offered. Besides, he wasn't going anywhere, and I had to open the shop. He's great about stuff like that, and frankly, I wouldn't have married him if he wasn't. This girl has a business to run."

That tale was followed by Vanessa's lamenting that her husband, Grady, a former FBI agent, was thinking about going back to the bureau.

"I thought that wilderness guide thing he had going for him was doing well," Lucy said.

"It's doing really well. He's just getting bored. He talks to his brothers and his cousins, all of whom are agents, and he starts thinking he's missing something." Vanessa held her glass up to Lucy for a refill. "Once a G-man, always a G-man."

"Maybe he'll get over it," Lucy said.

"Maybe." Vanessa sighed, then brightened. "But someone here has good news." She looked directly at Sophie.

Sophie Enright Bowers, who owned Blossoms, the only eatery on River Road, laughed. "Okay, yes, fine. I'll spill." She took a deep breath. "Jason and I are having a baby."

"Which explains the glass of club soda," Lis noted. "I was going to ask you about that. Congratulations to you both."

"Do you know what you're having?" Lucy asked.

"I do, but Jason doesn't want to know, so I haven't told him. I just have to be careful not to let it slip."

"You can tell us," Vanessa whispered. "We won't tell anyone."

Sophie laughed. "Uh-uh. Not sharing. It wouldn't be fair to Jason. But I appreciate the offer of confidentiality."

Lucy made a toast to the parents-to-be, and everyone raised their glasses, then took a drink.

"So I guess you're going to be cutting back your hours at Blossoms," Cass said.

"Eventually. I've been having leg pain, which isn't helped by standing in the kitchen, cooking from before dawn till two in the afternoon." Sophie rubbed her temples with her fingers. "I love my restaurant, but this is our *baby*."

"What did the doctor say?" Steffie asked.

"I'm going to see her on Monday."

"You have employees, though," Cass pointed out. "They can take over, right? You still live upstairs from the restaurant, and Jason's business is right next door."

"Joan, our other cook, is leaving in two weeks for Hawaii with her boyfriend. His father owns a pineapple grove and they're going to work for him so the dad can retire." It was obvious she was forcing her smile. "I'm not going to worry about it now. I'm going to assume all is going to work out and I'll have lots of time to find someone to replace Joan."

Chrissie felt as if her heart stopped in her chest. She looked up to find both Cass and Lis staring at her, slight smiles on their lips, as if they knew what questions were going through Chrissie's mind.

How big was the restaurant? What sort of food

did they serve? How many employees? How extensive was their menu?

It was neither the time nor the place to ask. She'd check out Blossoms for herself, see what it was like, then maybe she'd approach Sophie about applying for a job when Sophie was ready to hire someone. She'd already checked out Captain Walt's, but she thought it was too heavy on seafood. As much as she liked cooking fish, crabs, and oysters, she did prefer a little more variety in the menu. The same held true at the Blue Claw, a seafood restaurant on the highway. It was to be expected, she knew, since St. Dennis was on the Chesapeake, but still. Variety was important to her.

The party began to break up, and after saying their good nights, Chrissie, Lis, and Cass walked out together.

"Chrissie, do you need a ride home?" Cass asked. "Owen's picking me up. We can drop you off."

"I drove, but thanks for the offer," Chrissie replied as they crossed the lobby.

"We should have coordinated this better," Lis said. "I drove, too. And there's Owen, right on time."

"Is that Jared he's talking to? Damn, it is. I hope they're not going to start diving again this week. I was hoping to put Owen to work painting the new kitchen."

Owen looked up and smiled broadly when he saw his wife, and it was obvious to everyone but Jared that Owen had tuned him out.

"You ladies done for the night?" he asked, his eyes still on Cass.

"We are," Lis replied.

"Hey, Chrissie." Owen appeared to have just noticed her. "How's Gigi this week?"

"She's great." Chrissie hung back a bit, the feeling of belonging she'd sensed just a few minutes ago ebbing. Owen had had that effect on her even when they were kids. She wasn't sure why, but she always had the feeling that he barely tolerated her, and then only because he had to.

She turned to Lis. "Are you free for lunch tomorrow around noon?"

"Sorry. I have an appointment at ten that will probably stretch right on into the afternoon. Thinking about a trip to Blossoms?" Lis asked.

Chrissie nodded. "It's okay. I can go by myself. I just thought it would be more fun if someone else was along."

"I'd go with you but I'm meeting my dad at one in Baltimore," Cass told her. "Another day, though—"

"I'm curious. I've heard about it but I've never been. I guess I just don't think to go out River Road," Chrissie said.

"It's a darling café with tons of charm and excellent food. Sophie's really into the whole locavore thing. I think you'll love it. Make sure you check out the St. Dennis wall."

"The St. Dennis wall?"

"You'll know it when you see it." Lis leaned over and kissed Chrissie on the cheek. "I'm so happy you came with us tonight. I love to see you out and about. As much as we all love Gigi, you need to get a life, girl."

"I'm working on that, thanks."

The entire group headed outside, except Jared, who'd been quiet until he'd said his good nights and walked across the lobby.

"Hey, Chrissie, I'm free for lunch tomorrow," he called to her.

At the sound of her name, she'd paused and turned as the others passed through the double doors just as Jared stepped into the bar area. Judging by the look on the pretty hostess's face, he'd focused that megawatt smile on her, and whatever Chrissie'd thought to call back to him died in her throat.

CHRISSIE PULLED INTO the parking lot at Blossoms just before noon. There were already a dozen cars in the lot, and she had to park around the side of the building. She got out of her car and took a long look around. She'd already learned from Ruby that the building had been boarded up and pretty much abandoned when Sophie Enright—she'd been single then—had moved to St. Dennis to work with her brother Jesse in the law firm that had long been a staple in St. Dennis. Their great-great-grandfather had founded the firm in 1890, and there'd been an Enright practicing law in St. Dennis every year since. Though she'd passed the Maryland bar, Sophie's heart wasn't in law. Her dream was to own a small restaurant of her own. When this old building out on River Road came up for sale, she'd grabbed it, spent her time and money to renovate it, and molded it into the image she'd carried in her head. She met and fell in love with Jason Bowers, who owned the plant nursery and landscaping operation next door to the restaurant. They married, moved into the apartment on the second floor, and took care of their thriving businesses. Soon, apparently, there'd be something else for them to take care of.

Chrissie stood for a long moment and took it all in. There were woods that led from the back of the restaurant down to the river. Behind the restaurant was a patio with several tables and a tall fence that overflowed with vines that were still a month or two from flowering. Chrissie didn't know what kind of vine they were, but she was sure they'd flower, and in her mind's eye she could see colorful blooms spilling over the fence. The scene was so vivid to her she had to blink, but then it was gone. She walked around to the front of the building, where a bouquet of three flowers, tied with blue ribbon, had been painted on the large square window that faced the road.

Inside, the restaurant was alive with happy chatter. She was met by a waitress who apparently served as hostess as well.

"Table for . . . ?" she asked.

"One," Chrissie told her.

"This way." The waitress wore a name tag on which the name *Dana* had been written in red ink over a sketch of the same bouquet appearing on the front window.

Chrissie followed her to a small table with two chairs that sat next to the side window, through which she could see the nursery operation next door.

"I'm Dana. What can I get you to drink?" The waitress handed her a menu.

"Unsweetened iced tea, thanks." Chrissie tried to remain calm even as she wanted to take it all in at one time. She forced a deep breath, then picked up the menu and studied it. It took her mere minutes to know that Sophie was a woman after her own heart.

If Chrissie were to design her own restaurant and plan her own menu, it would look so very much like this. There were the staples—crab cakes, burgers, quiche, mac and cheese, crab bisque—then a special soup, salad, entrée, and dessert of the day, and everything sounded delicious.

Dana returned to the table with Chrissie's iced tea and a bowl that she placed in the middle of the table.

"Roasted chickpeas," she told Chrissie. "It's one of our signatures."

"Nice." Chrissie nodded and popped a few into her mouth. She tasted garlic and sea salt. "Perfect," she told Dana.

"Everyone says that." Dana smiled. "Did you see our specials when you came in? On the board near the door?"

"No, I missed that."

"Our soup today is a creamy fresh green pea with mint, and the salad is watercress with avocado and grapefruit with almonds in a citrus vinaigrette. The quiche of the day is asparagus, spring onions, and goat cheese, and our entrée is a Yukon Gold potato and sausage hash."

"Hmmm. Tough choice." Chrissie frowned.

"Oh, and you could have a small watercress side salad with any of the entrées, if you like."

"I would like, thank you, with the quiche." Chrissie handed back the menu.

"And I'd like the Jason burger and an order of potato wedges. Oh, and a cup of oyster stew, if you have any left." Jared slid smoothly into the chair opposite Chrissie, whose jaw had started to drop. He smiled at her. "I told you I was free for lunch today."

"So in other words, your regular. Hi, Jared," Dana said. "What would you like to drink with that?"

"Hi, Dana. I'd like a beer, but since I know you don't serve it, I'll have a Pepsi."

"I'll get your orders in right away." Dana went off to the kitchen.

"Why are you looking at me like that?" he asked. He was still smiling.

"You surprised me."

"Why? I said I was free today. I thought you heard me."

"You must eat here often," Chrissie said, "if you have a regular order."

"At least once a week. It's one of my favorite places."

"The food must be really good then. I can't wait to try it."

"You know why Sophie named it Blossoms?" he said.

"No idea."

"Years ago, there were three girls in St. Dennis who were the best of friends. Rose, Lily, and Violet. Sophie's grandmother was Rose. Violet was Rose's best friend and the secretary at the Enright law firm for about a million years. I hear she still goes in part-time just to make sure the 'new girl' isn't messing up her filing system. The 'new girl' is in her fifties and has been there for two years now, they tell me."

"So who was Lily?"

"Lily was . . . I forget the exact relationship, but I

do remember that she was related to Ellie O'Connor somehow. Ellie's married to Cameron O'Connor, the contractor, if you ever need any carpentry work done."

"Thanks, but I think Alec has that covered."

"Right. Anyway, it's a really long story, but Ellie inherited the house, and she says Lily's still there, if you get my drift." He wiggled his eyebrows.

"You mean her ghost?"

"So I've heard. Except Cameron called it her spirit. He plays poker with Owen, and whenever they need an extra guy, they call me. So I heard it straight from the source."

"I don't believe in ghosts."

"I'm just telling you what the locals say about the place." Dana brought his Pepsi and Chrissie's iced tea along with a glass dish holding several kinds of sweeteners. "Just sharing a little local color with you. Now, me, I keep an open mind. I've seen too many things I can't explain to never say never."

"So name one thing that you've personally seen that you can't explain."

"UFOs," he said without hesitating.

"You saw a UFO." She rolled her eyes.

"Not UFO. *UFOs*. Plural." He picked up a few chickpeas and rolled them around in his hand like dice.

"Come on."

"Hey, you asked. I answered." He shrugged. "Believe it or not."

"Not."

"Why not?"

"Because . . . because there's no proof. You'd think if they were real, there'd be some sign. Like, how come none of these supposed vehicles from out of space have ever landed somewhere?"

"What makes you think they haven't?"

"Because we'd know."

Now he laughed. "You know, you're quick to scoff, but you haven't even asked me what I saw with my own eyes."

"Okay. What did you see? Or what do you think you saw, I guess, is the better question."

"The first time, I was on board one of our salvage ships off the coast of Yucatán. It was just around midnight, and I was doing my last check around the boat when I saw lights directly overhead. Seven lights. I counted them. They hovered over my ship for about five minutes. Then they took off across the sky and vanished."

Chrissie stared at him.

"Anyone else witness this?"

"Three of my crew saw them."

"These lights just sort of hung over your ship."

"Well, from time to time, one would drop down closer, then go back up again. Then a minute later, another would do the same thing."

"I don't suppose you have photos."

"Of course I do. I sent copies to the Federal Aviation Administration and the Pentagon, but I never received an acknowledgment from either." He tossed the chickpeas into his mouth. "And that wasn't the only time."

"Where else?"

"Once when I was hiking in the Rockies, and another time when I was camping in Maine."

"You're just a regular magnet for these things,

aren't you?" She leaned forward and whispered, "Maybe you're actually an extraterrestrial."

"Maybe I am." He smiled.

"You're a good storyteller, I'll give you that."

Dana brought their food, and after she'd served them, asked, "Can I get you anything else?"

"I'm good," Chrissie told her.

"You could do a little karaoke while we eat," Jared suggested.

"Oh, you." Dana laughed. "You'll never let me live that down."

"Nope." To Chrissie, he said, "Dana does a mean 'Proud Mary.'"

"That's the problem with small towns," Dana said as she turned away from the table. "You have one night you'd like to forget, but no one will ever let you."

"Hey, you were entertaining," Jared told her.

"Glad you thought so. Enjoy your lunch."

"Where do they have karaoke around here?" Chrissie asked.

"The Blue Claw, out on the highway." He grinned. "You interested?"

"Oh, dear God, no. That would be the last . . ." She shuddered at the thought of getting up in front of a roomful of strangers and singing. "Nope. You?"

"Well, I guess you'd have to come out to the Claw some night and find out." He winked, then turned his attention to his lunch.

They ate in silence for a few minutes, Chrissie watching as he attacked the oyster stew like a starving man.

"How is it?" she finally asked.

"Amazing. The best. If I don't have Sophie's oyster stew once a week, I go into withdrawal."

"Really?" He had her attention. "What's in it? What makes it so great?"

Jared shrugged. "I don't know. Oysters."

"Well, is it herby? A lot of butter? Chopped celery, carrots, potatoes? What's in it?"

He reached across the small table for the spoon at her place and scooped some stew onto it, then handed it to her. "Here."

She tasted the stew. It really was delicious.

"Tarragon." She licked the spoon. "Very buttery, and the oysters weren't overcooked. Very nice."

She looked up to find him staring at her, his eyes narrowed.

"Thanks," she said.

"So . . . you're a chef?"

"I wouldn't call myself a chef, but yes, I've been a restaurant cook."

"How come you're not now?"

"Well, for one thing, since I came back to the island, I've been helping out Gigi in the store."

"Who helped her before you?"

"To hear her tell it, no one. But I know Owen and Lis both looked in on her and helped her out."

"So why does she need full-time help now?"

She put her fork down. "She's one hundred years old, Jared."

"She looked pretty lively when I saw her at the inn a few weeks ago having lunch with Grace."

"Gigi aside, I needed to work through some things. Being around the store helped me to put things into perspective."

"You okay now?"

"Yeah, I'm good."

"So why aren't you"—he waved his fork around—"cooking in a restaurant?"

"You're really nosy, you know that?" She dug into her quiche, which was getting cold.

"I have been accused of that many, many times in the past. I'm just a curious guy." He took a bite of his burger, and when he'd finished chewing, he said, "You know, just because someone asks you a question doesn't mean you have to answer."

"I know. It just seems rude not to."

"Not if the question was rude. Which I guess mine was." He put down the burger. "I didn't mean to be."

"Just curious?"

He nodded.

She turned her attention back to her lunch.

"So what's in the quiche?" he asked, and she laughed.

"The obvious: goat cheese, green onions, asparagus, chives. As advertised."

"No hidden ingredients to discover?"

She laughed again. "No. It's pretty straightforward. Really good, but no surprises."

"By the way, did you get to see the St. Dennis wall before I came in?"

"Cass mentioned that. What is it?"

He pointed across the room to a wall covered with photos and what appeared to be newspaper articles.

"Old photos of the town and some of the people who live here. Stuff going back seventy-five years from the local newspaper, which maybe you know Grace owns. Birth announcements. Weddings. Obituaries. It's a real who's who in St. Dennis. Take a look when you're finished. It's like a history lesson on the wall."

Jared's phone rang, and he took it from his pocket to look at the number.

"Excuse me," he said. "I should answer this."

He got up and walked outside. She watched through the front window as he paced, stopped, paced, stopped. She liked watching him move. He was graceful for a man his size, his movements fluid and smooth as a dancer's, but masculine at the same time. There was something in his gait that reminded her of Owen's, and she wondered if somehow divers all moved in a similar fashion. Because of the way they moved underwater, maybe?

He was sliding the phone back into his pocket as he came back in.

"Well, this has been fun, but I gotta scoot." He picked up the burger and took a last bite.

"Everything okay?"

He nodded. "Peachy. See you around, okay?"

"Sure."

"Don't forget the wall." He turned and flagged down Dana, who met him at the cash register. He paid for his lunch, then walked out without looking back.

She couldn't help but wonder what the emergency was.

"So, if I could ask—not that it's any of my business—but are you and Jared . . . ?" Dana began to clear away Jared's place.

"Oh no. We're just friends. Really. My cousin works with him," she felt compelled to add, as if that would explain the casual relationship. "Why, you interested?"

"If you're not, you're probably the only woman in town who isn't." Dana laughed. "It's hard not to like him even if he is a huge flirt. Not that you'd want to get involved with him in any serious way. He's not a serious person. At least, not when it comes to, you know, dating. Women. He's sort of a playboy, actually."

"He does look the type."

"I know, right? Not that I'd ever fall for him, but still, he's adorable in his own way." She finished picking up his plate and the soup bowl. "I bet he's more fun to have as a friend."

Before Chrissie could respond, Dana had turned away and gone into the kitchen.

She finished her lunch, making notes of the flavors in the salad dressing—honey, orange juice, balsamic—and imagining what changes she might make, should she have the chance. Skip the balsamic and use apple cider vinegar? Toast the almonds before adding them to the salad? And the quiche—maybe use a mild jack cheese instead of goat?

Dana returned and asked if she'd like dessert, and Chrissie hesitated.

"We have bourbon brownies with roasted pecan ice cream today."

Chrissie groaned. "I want to, but I can't. There just isn't an inch of space left."

"I understand. We have the combo on the menu maybe once every other week since it's a favorite of our customers, so maybe next time." She glanced out the window. "Actually, we always have it when Dallas MacGregor is having a meeting at her place down the road. You know those old warehouses? You can always tell when all the staff is there because you'll see more than half a dozen cars. So if the lot is full, chances are there's bourbon brownies and roasted pecan ice cream."

"I will keep that in mind."

Dana handed her the check, and Chrissie rose, but instead of going to the cash register, she went to the wall Jared had previously pointed out to her. The tables closest were unoccupied, so she could take her time looking at the photos. Except for a photo of Ruby standing in front of the store that might have been taken within the past ten or fifteen years, she had no idea who the others were, but Jared'd been right. It looked like a history of the town in photos.

"See anyone you know?"

Chrissie turned to find Sophie standing behind her.

"No. I was just thinking that other than my great-grandmother Ruby Carter, I don't recognize anyone in any of these pictures."

"I'm sure you know this family." Sophie pointed to a photo where a tall man stood behind a much shorter woman and three young children, two boys and a towheaded girl. "I'll give you a hint. She's still really blond."

"Is that Lucy?" Chrissie guessed.

Sophie nodded and pointed out the others. "Grace and her late husband, Daniel, then Dan, Lucy, and Ford."

She went on to point out several other photos, ending with one of her own family. "My grandmother Rose Enright and my grandfather Curtis on their wedding day."

"Jared told me she was one of the women you named the restaurant for. She was beautiful."

Sophie nodded. "I never got to meet her when she was alive. Though I've been in her presence from time to time." She smiled. "Everyone in town knows she never left the old mansion, even after my grandad gave it to the town for the arts center.

"My grandmother was very fond of gardenias. Grew them in the greenhouse there, and it was the only scent she ever wore. She's been gone for more than twenty years now, but sometimes you can still smell gardenias in the house."

"Because they're still in the greenhouse?"

"No. Because she comes back to be with my grandfather. Ah, I can see you're a skeptic. I was, too, for a while, but I've experienced it myself so many times it hardly makes me blink anymore. The first time, I was freaked out. I was visiting my grandfather, and all of a sudden there was this really heavy fragrance. I went into every room in the house looking for a gardenia, or a plant, or even a diffuser, but there was nothing. When I came back into the room, my grandfather was in the rocking chair and he looked me straight in the eye and said, 'She said you're lovely and she's proud of you.'"

"I'd have freaked out, too."

"Yeah, it was a moment."

Sophie lowered herself into the nearest chair. "Thank God it's a slow day. I'm exhausted and it isn't even one thirty yet."

"I noticed on the menu it says you close at two."

"These days I'm hard-pressed to make it till two. Then it's close up, clean up, prepare for tomorrow.

And the worst part?" Sophie beckoned Chrissie closer. "I'm still having morning sickness. Try whipping up a big fat batch of eggs when you feel like . . . you know. My cook's only here for the lunch shift, but she's not going to be here much longer."

"You need someone to take over for you."

"It'll take me months to find someone good enough."

Chrissie took a deep breath. "I could probably help you with that."

"You know someone?"

"I've worked in restaurants for years. My last position was with a trendy café in northern New Jersey."

Sophie looked stunned. "Why didn't I know this?"

"It never came up in conversation. Not that we've had that many conversations since I got to town. But I'm good, and I think I'd be a really good fit for Blossoms."

Sophie looked away and seemed to stare into space for a long time. Finally, she looked up at Chrissie and said, "Come in around seven tomorrow morning and work with me. Let's see what you can do." Sophie pushed herself out of the chair and walked to the kitchen. "I hope it works out. For both of us."

"All right. Tomorrow, then."

Sophie disappeared through the kitchen door, her voice trailing after her. "See you at seven . . ."

Chapter Four

Gigi, think you could handle the coffee crowd tomorrow morning? I'll be here to set up, but I have a chance to work with Sophie at Blossoms. She really needs someone to help her out, and—" Chrissie turned and was pinned by what she and Lis used to secretly call Ruby's death stare.

"Who you think be making the coffee before you?"

"I know you did, but . . ."

"There be no buts. You be at Blossoms when you supposed to be, and don't be worrying about the store." Ruby shuffled to her table, a book in her hand. "Wouldn't hurt none if you baked up a little something for the early customers, though. Spoiled 'em. Seems they look for whatever treat you make."

"I'd planned on it. There's no reason why I can't bake at night like always." *And set up the coffee to brew and the water for tea and take care of the earliest of the early before I leave for River Road.*

You'll always come first, Gigi. I promise. Whatever else I do, you come first.

* * *

WHEN CHRISSIE LEFT the store at 6:50 the next morning, the coffee was on its third pot, there were fresh tea bags in a basket, the pitchers had been refilled with milk, half-and-half, and 1 percent milk, respectively, and two trays of apple crumb muffins were displayed near the cash register. Her trip to Blossoms was held up several times because of the school bus she had the misfortune to be following, which made her three minutes late. She hoped Sophie wasn't a stickler about such things, and she was grateful to find she was not.

"What would you like me to do first?" Chrissie asked after she arrived in Blossoms's kitchen.

"You could start by making blueberry muffins." Sophie looked relieved to see her. "The recipe is on the counter."

"I have one in my head," Chrissie told her. "All right?"

Sophie considered for a moment, then said, "Sure. Show me what you've got."

Chrissie had the muffins mixed and in the pans in under twelve minutes. She turned to Sophie and asked, "What else?"

"You can mix up the pancake batter. But I'd like you to use my recipe for these. My customers are mostly repeat this time of the year, and they expect their pancakes to taste the same way."

"Got it." Chrissie followed Sophie's pointed finger to the counter where the recipe awaited, and proceeded to mix the batter.

"You can leave it there," Sophie told her. "We'll pour onto the griddle from the mixing bowl."

"Okay. Next?"

And on it went through the morning's prep time, Sophie directing and Chrissie following orders.

At seven thirty, Dana arrived to admit the early risers, who came in for breakfast.

"Hey, you're . . . I don't know your name but you were here yesterday," Dana said when she saw Chrissie taking the last batch of muffins from the oven. "Why didn't you tell me you were going to be working here?"

"At the time I was eating lunch, I didn't know I'd be here today," Chrissie said. "And I haven't been hired. Yet."

When breakfast hours had ended, Chrissie could see the fatigue in Sophie's face.

"Look, I hope this isn't out of line, and I know you don't know me very well, and if I were you, I'd be hesitant to leave my business in the hands of someone I'd only known a few months, but I think you should go sit for a while. Put your feet up, have something cold to drink, and just relax. I can get things prepped for the lunch rush."

Sophie appeared to think it over. She'd spent the morning chopping vegetables for omelets, turning ground beef and herbs into burgers, making turkey chili, and rolling out dough for the quiches.

"You could keep an eye on the soups and maybe start prepping the salads until Joan comes in. She should be here in about"—Sophie checked her watch—"twenty minutes. Plenty of time for me to get my second wind."

Chrissie warmed up the carrot soup that Sophie'd made the night before and added the cheese and veggies of the day to the pie crusts to bake the quiches.

Joan came in right on time, and when she entered the kitchen, she was clearly startled to see Chrissie at the stove stirring the pot of soup. She stopped and stared at the newcomer.

"Sophie didn't tell me she'd hired someone." Joan was tall and apple shaped with short brown hair that feathered around her face. When she moved from the doorway it was to tie on a Blossoms apron over her jeans and white T-shirt.

"She hasn't. Not yet anyway. I'm sort of on trial." Chrissie turned to face her. "I'm Chrissie Jenkins, by the way."

"Joan Allen. Nice to meet you." Joan brushed past her. "Now, let's see what else we'll need for lunch."

They were going over the menu together when Sophie returned to the kitchen.

"Thanks. I feel almost like a new person." She directed the comment to Chrissie. "Not quite new, but it'll do. The first of the lunch crew is in the house, guys. Let's get this done." She went to the cooler and removed the large container of beef she'd earlier mixed for burgers. "Oh, and Chrissie? The blueberry muffins were delish. Thanks."

"You're welcome. And thank you. Glad you liked them."

"There was just a touch of cinnamon in the batter. I liked that."

"Good. I'm happy to make them whenever you like." Chrissie took the pan of beef and began to make patties.

For the next three hours, the women worked tirelessly as Dana and a second waitress named Margarite brought in orders. Chrissie hadn't moved that fast for that long since she'd left La Luna, and by closing time, her legs let her know how out of shape she was.

When Sophie said they closed at two o'clock, she meant two o'clock. Dana locked the door and turned the sign to the CLOSED side. The last customer left at 2:17. Dana swept the floor and tidied the dining area while Sophie, Chrissie, and Joan cleaned the kitchen.

"Let's grab a cup of coffee while we look over tomorrow's menu," Joan said after they'd finished emptying the dishwasher for the third time.

"Water for me, please," Sophie said. "On second thought, make it iced. I'm dying. My body thermostat is out of whack today."

"Why don't you go back out there and sit down while you have your water," Chrissie suggested.

"I want to get the menu worked out for tomorrow and make sure we have all the ingredients on hand."

Chrissie went out into the dining room and returned with a chair.

"Sit, please. You look like you're about to fall over." Chrissie pointed to Sophie, who sighed. Then sat. Then smiled.

"Thank you. My thighs ache." She rubbed them with both hands. "You'd think I'd be used to all the standing and walking. All of a sudden, it's as if my legs forgot I've been doing this every day for two years." She paused. "Except for Sundays and Mondays."

"You close two days every week?" Chrissie leaned on the counter.

"If I didn't, I'd never see my husband, even though his business is right next door. I decided after six months of working every day that enough was enough. I wanted my business to be a success, but it had to be on my terms. I wanted to have a life. I wanted time with Jason before we started a family. And now I'm so glad I took that time for just us. I have a feeling it's going to be a long time before it's just the two of us again."

Dana poked her head into the kitchen.

"Margarite left at three, and I've finished cleaning up," she told Sophie. "We need new flowers for the tables, though. The old ones are pretty beat. Want me to stop in at Petals and Posies and see what they have this week?"

"That would be great, thanks, Dana." Sophie rested her head back and closed her eyes. "Remind them they give us a nice discount in case whoever's working the counter forgets again."

Joan set a glass of ice water in front of Sophie and handed a mug of coffee to Chrissie.

"Okay, so for tomorrow . . ." Her eyes still closed, Sophie rattled off the next day's menu. "Check the fridge and just make sure we have enough greens for salad."

Joan opened the cooler door and brought out the large bin of greens. "Getting low, Sophie." She held it up so Sophie could see.

Sophie took her phone from her pocket, punched in a number, and while it rang, took several sips of ice water.

"Clay, it's Sophie. How're you fixed for greens this week? And is there enough asparagus for me? It's on tomorrow's menu . . ."

She finished working out the details of her purchase, then disconnected the call. One by one, she went over the list for the next day, and they checked the ingredients.

When they'd finally finished, Sophie said, "Chrissie, could you stay for just another few minutes?"

"Sure." Chrissie took her time removing her apron, which was in need of a wash after she'd spilled a little carrot soup.

"I guess I'll see you tomorrow, Sophie." With a glance and a quick wave toward Chrissie, Joan left.

Chrissie heard the front door open, then close, and the restaurant fell silent for a few minutes. Sophie sat with her eyes closed again, her dark hair falling out of the neat bun she'd had when she'd arrived that morning. Finally, she opened her eyes and said, "Want to do it all again tomorrow?"

"I'd love to," Chrissie told her.

"I'd like to try you out for two weeks. I'll pay you by the hour. I don't mind saying I'm impressed with what you did here today. In a strange kitchen, working with recipes that you hadn't tried before, not knowing where anything was—you held your own. I just don't want to make a decision based on one day, if that's all right with you."

"It's fine with me. I enjoyed it. It felt good to be back in a working kitchen again. I didn't realize how much I missed it."

"Even without being familiar with the way I do things?"

Chrissie shrugged. "Not so different from the way I cook, actually. In the last place I worked, I had shelves arranged in pretty much the same manner as you have here. I used the same spices. The recipes are different, but not so much so that I stumbled. A few things I do differently, yes, but you're the boss."

Sophie smiled weakly. "A tired boss."

"How far along are you, if you don't mind my asking?"

"Almost five months. We hadn't wanted to spread the word too soon because we lost our first one in the third month." An unmistakable sadness crossed Sophie's face like a shadow. "Jason thinks I pushed myself too hard last time, and maybe I did. This time, I'd planned on working my regular schedule through the end of my sixth month, then I thought I'd taper off a bit, let Joan take over a lot here in the kitchen." Sophie smiled. "Joan had other plans. So—"

"So you need a plan B. I'd like to apply for that spot. I'm good at what I do, I'm organized, I can think on my feet, I—"

Sophie held up a hand to stop the flow of words. "I think you're probably all those things. I'll check your references, and if they turn out the way I'm sure they will, and you do well over the two weeks, we'll talk about a more permanent position. Are you all right with that?"

"Yes, of course."

"Did you bring your résumé with you?"

"I did." Chrissie opened her bag and removed the envelope she'd prepared the night before. She hesitated for a moment before handing it over. She knew she'd have a lot of explaining to do.

"Is there a problem?" Sophie asked.

Chrissie bit her bottom lip. If she'd listed all her previous employers and Doug contacted one of them, even at this late date, there was the possibility he could discover where she'd gone. There was always the chance someone clueless about her situation would answer the call, and he'd learn that a restaurant in St. Dennis, Maryland, had called for a reference.

So she'd written down the information for La Luna only along with the cell number of Rob's partner, Jim.

She handed the envelope to Sophie, who took out the single sheet of paper, looked it over, then eyed it suspiciously. "I thought you said you'd worked in several places."

"I did. But I only trust this one." Chrissie sighed, and said simply, "Bad ex-boyfriend. Rob—he owns La Luna—is the only person who knows where I am. The other places—I don't trust them to not tell my ex whatever he wants to know."

"You think he's still looking for you?"

"I don't know if he'll stop until he finds me. Not that he loves me," she hastened to add, "but I think he sees me leaving as some sort of challenge. He might want to 'win' by finding me. Just to prove he can."

"Rob can corroborate your story?"

Chrissie nodded. "You can call him right now while I'm sitting here. But you have to call his partner, and he'll call Rob, and Rob will call you back."

"Seems a little convoluted for a simple phone call."

"Not if someone overhears the conversation and passes on whatever they might hear. I don't want Doug to ever find out that Rob knows where I am."

"This man is dangerous?"

Chrissie sighed, and told Sophie the entire story.

"So yes, he could be dangerous, but only to me." Chrissie watched Sophie's expression change, and knew immediately what she was thinking. "He's only interested in finding me, Sophie, and since only Rob knows where I am, that's not going to happen. He'd hurt me, yes, but he's not interested in hurting anyone else. Rob, maybe, for covering for me and giving me the means to leave." Without going into too much explanation, she added, "A little financial boost."

"He can't trace your phone?"

"Tossed into a trash can at a rest stop on the New Jersey Turnpike." Chrissie smiled. It had felt so good, so liberating, to have dumped that phone. She wondered how many times it had rung since then, and if anyone had picked it out of the trash to answer it.

"You could understand why I might be concerned about someone coming into my restaurant—which is also my home—looking to do harm."

"I do. Of course I do. But I don't know how he'd find me. I covered my trail, and he has no reason to look for me here. But I can see you're distressed, and with the baby coming . . ." Chrissie sighed. "Maybe this wasn't such a good idea after all."

Sophie nodded slowly, apparently as conflicted as Chrissie. "I don't think I can hire you under the circumstances. I don't think I'd feel comfortable. I'm so sorry."

"It shouldn't take you long to find someone permanent. If today was any indication, this would be a great place to work."

"Today was actually pretty slow."

"Well, good luck. And thanks."

"Did you really just thank me after I said I wouldn't hire you?" Sophie pushed herself out of the chair.

Chrissie could have told her how much it had meant to her to be amid the hustle and noise of a working kitchen again, to be with people who enjoyed cooking and were good at it. She'd felt alive in a way she hadn't felt since she'd left La Luna. But she couldn't get the words to come.

"Yes," she replied. "Thank you."

She picked up her bag and was at the door, her hand on the knob and just about to unlock it to leave, when she heard the kitchen door open with its soft squeak.

"Chrissie, I'm sorry. I really like you and I like the way you work. I wanted this to happen, for both our sakes. I'm so torn over this. You probably know I'm a former lawyer. I was a prosecutor when I first got out of law school. I've seen things . . . cases where an ex has used unbelievable means to find someone. I took cases like yours to trial, I put guys like him in prison, and I—"

"You don't have to explain. It's all right. I understand. I do." Chrissie forced a smile for Sophie's benefit. "I guess I'll see you around St. Dennis."

She could tell Sophie wasn't happy about having to let her go. But she had her family and her customers to think of. Even though Chrissie believed it could never happen, there was no way Doug could ever find her here, she could understand Sophie being uneasy.

She drove back to the island, comforting herself with the knowledge that she had the store and its early morning crowd of watermen to take care of. She knew that Emily Hart, one of the old women on the island, ran a sort of under-the-radar restaurant. Maybe she could use some help.

Tom's truck was in front of the porch when Chrissie pulled into the driveway. She drove around it and parked behind the store and went in through the back door.

"Tom, did you find the stack of boxes I left near the cooler?" She dropped her bag onto the counter next to the cash register.

"I did. All loaded up. I got your invoice for today right here." He held up the clipboard.

"Show me what we've got here." Chrissie noticed Ruby at her table reading the newspaper as if she'd known her great-granddaughter would be there to deal with the delivery. She'd barely raised her eyes from the page she was reading.

Chrissie got Tom squared away, then grabbed a bottle of water from the cooler and walked over to the table.

"Busy here today?" she asked as she sat next to Ruby.

"Pretty much. Same as always early, quieted down till about eleven, then picked up some. Busy for a time this afternoon, now be the lull." Ruby folded the newspaper. "How be you, Chrissie?"

She wanted to say that she was fine, but she wasn't fine, so she said nothing. Her hands were folded in her lap, and she stared at them. Before Chrissie could tell Ruby about Sophie letting her go, she reached out to pat Chrissie's hand and said, "She be coming around, no need to fret, girl."

"What do you mean?"

"You go on upstairs now, take a good long shower, rest just a bit," Ruby said, ignoring Chrissie's question. "Then come back down here and cook up that piece of rockfish Alec dropped off. Go on with you now."

A hot shower had been just what Chrissie needed, Ruby had been right about that, and a quick nap had been restorative, but she woke feeling just as down as she'd been when she left Blossoms. She'd really liked the restaurant—liked the pace, liked the food, liked the ambience of the place. Still disappointed, she made her way downstairs to start dinner.

By six thirty, they'd finished eating. Throughout the meal, Chrissie'd tried to be upbeat, but her heart wasn't in it, and she knew Ruby saw through her. She finally broke down and told Ruby everything.

"Should I have not told Sophie about Doug, Gigi?" Chrissie asked.

"That be your truth, Christiana, and that's what you need be telling. Can't change what be."

"I know, but maybe a little less of my truth will land me a job. Then again, with Sophie being pregnant, and her having prosecuted guys like Doug for doing just what he did to me, I guess I can't blame her for being afraid to have me around." She got up and began to clear the table. "Maybe I should go to Grace and tell her everything and see if she thinks it would be problem at the inn. Not my first choice, but beggars can't be choosers."

"No need to beg, girl. Things be righting themselves."

Chrissie finished clearing the table without further comment. She'd just started to load the dishwasher when she heard the bell in the store buzz.

Ruby had always locked up the store at seven, but she'd had a loud doorbell installed in case one of the islanders really needed something.

"I have it," Ruby called to her.

Chrissie could hear Ruby's sneakers shuffling across the floor, then the opening of the front door. It was still early enough that it wasn't unusual for one of the locals to stop by. She heard voices—Ruby's and several others—so after she turned on the dishwasher, she went into the store to see what all the chatter was about.

Ruby sat in her chair at the table, and Sophie sat across from her. There were two men with their backs to Chrissie. Besides Owen, she recognized Gabriel Beck, St. Dennis's chief of police.

"What's going on?" she asked as she approached the group. She walked up behind Owen and placed her hand on his back.

"When were you going to tell me about this crazy man who might be coming after you?" Owen turned to face her. "You think you could have mentioned it?"

"It's not a problem, Owen. No one's going to come after me. He can't find me."

"Sophie's not so sure." He nodded in Sophie's direction.

"Really, this wasn't necessary, Sophie. I told you I'm okay with your decision—"

"But I wasn't okay with it. It bothered me on so many levels. It bothered me that you'd been treated like that, and it bothered me that I hesitated to hire you because of him. I discussed it with Jason and he agreed it isn't fair. Not fair that this guy got away with his abuse of you, and not fair that you're being punished because of his actions. So we talked to Beck, and he had some thoughts on the subject."

The chief of police nodded. "I need to know about any potential threats to anyone living in my town."

"Beck, I don't think there's a threat." Chrissie outlined the steps she'd taken to hide her whereabouts.

"Good for you," Beck said. "You did a great job of covering your tracks. But the fact that you took such pains tells me you're not one hundred percent certain he won't keep looking." He crossed his arms over his chest. "Can you tell me honestly that you think he's forgotten? 'Cause my experience with this type of personality tells me he hasn't."

"No, he hasn't forgotten, but like you said, I covered my tracks. He isn't going to find me."

"What I want you to do is give me his name, a physical description—a photo would be better—what kind of car he drives, license plate number. I'd like to have it on record. If he's still looking for you, and if he should somehow stumble onto the Cannonball Island connection, I want to have a file on him." He smiled reassuringly at Chrissie. "And I never forget a face."

"I thought about a protection-from-abuse order," Sophie said, "but then he'd know where you are, so that's obviously out of the question."

"Look, I appreciate the concern, I really do. I still don't expect this to be a problem, but I'll give you any information that you need, Beck. You're right. Better to be safe than sorry." She turned to Sophie. "I'm embarrassed that you were the one who thought to bring it to Beck's attention. I guess I should probably have told him."

"Or me. You should have told me." Owen poked her in the side.

"Can you understand why I didn't want everyone knowing what an idiot I was? That I was so weak it took me years to stand up for myself?" She willed the tears not to spill down her cheeks.

"You're not weak, Chrissie. As a matter of fact, I have a whole new respect for you, that you were able to walk away as cleverly as you did. That took strength and smarts." Owen put his arm around her and hugged her. "We just want to make sure that if this guy ever figures things out, we are ready for him." He tilted her face to his and stared into her eyes with steely resolve. "We'll take him down, Chris."

"Thanks," she whispered, a lump forming in her throat. "And thank you, Sophie."

"You can thank me in the morning by making some of these for my customers." Sophie held up one of the apple crumb muffins Chrissie'd made that morning. "They're delicious."

"Wait, you want me to come in tomorrow to work?" Chrissie wasn't sure if Sophie was asking for her to work, or merely to bake.

"Tomorrow, and for the next two weeks as the rest of your trial period, then after Joan leaves, if all goes well, and I'm sure it will, you'll be hired full time. " Sophie stood. "I'm sorry I didn't think this through as thoroughly earlier today. I was just sort of blindsided. I had no idea . . . anyway, I want you to work with me."

"I'll be there. Thanks for giving me a chance to prove myself." Chrissie could have hugged her.

"Don't forget the muffins." Sophie walked around the table to give Ruby a hug. "Thanks for the snack."

Ruby smiled and patted Sophie on the arm. "You come back and see me in the spring. We be planting lots of herbs for your kitchen and flowers for your tables."

"I'll take you up on that. See you, Chrissie. Owen. Beck." Sophie headed for the door.

"I'll walk you out," Beck told her. He turned to Chrissie. "You get me the information, I'll take it from there. And don't forget the photo."

"I think they all were lost when I ditched the phone I took them on, but I'll see if I can find something," Chrissie told him. "And thanks."

"Of course." Beck looked at Ruby. "You really should have your own police force on the island, Miz Carter."

Ruby smiled. "Now, why would we be needing our own when we have you, Gabriel Beck?"

He laughed, and caught up with Sophie, who was waiting for him at the door.

"Maybe we should have our own police," Owen said after Beck and Sophie left.

"Never did before, son. Don't see no reason to change things."

"Gigi, we don't even have a town government," he reminded her.

"Don't have a town, neither, boy. It's just the island, same as it's always been." She hoisted herself from her seat. "See you take a few of those muffins home to Cass. I know she favors them."

"Why were any left over from this morning?" Chrissie asked.

"Figured we'd be having company, by and by. Always hospitable to have something to offer." She walked toward her apartment. "Night, Owen. Thanks for stopping by."

"Thanks for calling me, Gigi." He kissed her on the cheek as she passed by.

"Wait, she called you . . ." Chrissie frowned and turned to Ruby, who hadn't missed a step. "How did you know to call him?" she asked.

"I told you she'd be coming 'round, didn't I?" Ruby kept walking. "I told you not to fret. Should be payin' better attention when I be talking to you . . ."

Chrissie rubbed the back of her neck. "I'm never going to get used to her. Honestly, Owen, I've been here for months and she still surprises me. What does she know and when does she know it?" She shrugged.

"No rhyme or reason that I can tell." He stood in the doorway. "And this from someone who sometimes knows things himself."

"I hope you're kidding. The last thing I want to be thinking about is whether or not that eye is in our DNA."

"Not kidding. I do try to ignore it, though. I don't want to know things. I just want to live my life and love my family." He gave Chrissie one last quick hug. "That includes you, kiddo. You know I'd do whatever I had to do if this guy shows up."

"I know. Thanks."

Owen stepped outside, then, before she closed the door, said, "Don't forget to give Beck the info he asked for."

"Got it. Thanks again." She watched him walk to his car, then shut the door and locked it.

Chrissie heard another door open, then close. She went through Ruby's apartment and to the screen door that led to the back porch.

"I thought you were going to read for a while." Chrissie went out and sat in the rocking chair next to the one Ruby occupied.

"Why you be thinking that?"

"Well, you have that new thriller to read."

"It's a good one, yes." Ruby's chair began to rock slowly. "I be going back to it soon enough."

Chrissie rocked along at the same pace as Ruby.

"It's a really pretty night," she said. "Lots of stars, and it's quiet enough to hear the waves hitting the shore."

Ruby merely nodded and continued to rock.

"I guess it's going to be time to plant up that garden of yours soon," Chrissie said. "I guess you're thinking about what you want to plant this year."

"No, I be thinking about those perennial flowers that already be pushed out of the ground. I'm pleased to see my old friends come back around again this year."

"Where are your flowers?"

"The Shasta daisies be here." Ruby pointed to a bed that ran along the fence. "Pinks be there, too, and peonies. They be in bud already. Hollyhocks over there close to the house. Roses along the fence. Be real pretty here come summer."

"When do we plant new stuff? And what do you want to plant, Gigi?"

"I be about to ask you the same thing." Ruby rested her head, her eyes fixed on the stars. "What do you want to grow?"

"Whatever you like. It's your garden."

"That garden be ours, not mine. I just asked you

what you wanted. What do you like to cook? What do you like to eat?"

Chrissie took a few minutes to think it over. "I like to cook with herbs. Thyme, tarragon, chives, sage, rosemary. Oh, and curry, and parsley, and I love different kinds of mint. And tomatoes—I love the varieties. So versatile. Lettuces. Eggplant. Summer squash. Melons. Cucumbers. Green beans, definitely. Golden and white beets, maybe. Carrots for sure."

"Might have to make the garden bigger, but that be fine. You want to plant all that, best get busy. Seeds on sale at the hardware store in town right about now. Heard Clay Montgomery has seedlings left over, might be he'll sell you a few. Hoes and rakes and trowels in the shed out back. Best get busy."

Ruby stood suddenly. "Lettuces be cool crops. You want them in now. Plan for the weekend. Monday be the day to plant. The weather be just right, spring being late this year, even if it be May already."

She went inside, leaving Chrissie alone on the porch to contemplate her garden. Tomorrow after work she'd stop at the Montgomery farm and see if Clay had any plants to sell, then see what she'd need to pick up at the hardware store. She'd had a garden when she was young, and she'd loved it, so she welcomed the chance to grow some of her favorites.

Tomorrow she'd begin by choosing her plants, and then she'd figure out how much bigger the garden would have to be to hold it all. It made her happy to know she'd have this bit of ground to work on her own. Growing things had always seemed both empowering and soothing to her. Empowering because you were tapping into what she thought of as the life force, watching seeds become plants that would eventually bear fruit or flowers, and soothing because the time you spent in the garden was quiet time to enjoy nature.

The very thought of it energized her. She went inside, singing "Girls Just Want to Have Fun," and after saying good night to Ruby, went upstairs to make her list of herbs and vegetables to buy and to sketch out where in the garden she'd plant them.

Chapter Five

Chrissie fit so comfortably into the routine at Blossoms it almost frightened her. Sophie ran a tight ship, but she was a pleasure to work with, and Chrissie could not have been happier. She easily made it through the first week of her trial period, and after they'd closed up on Wednesday, on her way home she'd detoured at Kelly's Point Road and parked behind Scoop.

Grace's daughter, Lucy, who was married to Clay Montgomery, had set aside some vegetable seedlings for her, and by the time Chrissie had picked them up and chatted for a while with Clay, she was later than usual, so much so that the schools had already been let out and the small shop was crowded with kids who all appeared to be in their early teens. There was so much chatter and laughter it reminded her of a diner she'd once worked in that had been a block away from a high school. The students would descend in droves, and for an hour every day, she and the others would run themselves ragged because the owner refused to bring in the late shift an hour early to help deal with the barrage of kids. Chrissie had hated the job, the tips were terrible, the owner not only an insufferable bore but a grouchy one at that, and she'd quit after six months.

She got in line behind a pair of giggling girls and tried hard not to listen to their whispered conversation, but it was hard not to overhear. Chrissie remembered a time when she'd been the object of such groundless gossip and how it had hurt when untrue stories made their way back to her and there'd been no way to defend herself. In high school, it had sometimes seemed that backstabbing was an intramural sport, and no one had been immune for the entire four years.

"Yeah, and she wore black jeans. Who wears black jeans? So uncool."

"Connor said when she and James got out of the car, her clothes were all jumbled."

"Figures. Slut."

When she couldn't listen to another snarky word, Chrissie cleared her throat. Loudly, making eye contact with the girl who was facing her.

"You know, girls, you're in a public place," Chrissie said, her voice barely above a whisper. "You never know who might overhear what you're saying."

The girl who'd been doing most of the talking turned away, her face red. The one whose back was to Chrissie muttered, "Mind your own business."

"I'm trying to," Chrissie whispered.

The line moved slowly and the girls fell silent until it was their turn to place their orders. They got their ice cream and eyed Chrissie suspiciously as they passed on their way to the door.

She turned her attention to the chalkboard list-ing that day's specials. The chocolate raspberry that Jared had tried was on the board again but with a twist: marshmallows. Chrissie was a sucker for marshmallows. She'd even learned to make her own, which tasted nothing like the commercial ones. She was pretty sure Steffie used the packaged kind, but she was intrigued, and when she got to the counter to give her order, a frazzled Steffie grinned and said, "An adult! My kingdom for an adult."

Chrissie laughed.

"They're all good kids for the most part, but today it seems like there's an unending line of them. And the girl who works for me in the afternoons had to stay late at school for a makeup test."

"Want me to pinch hit? I can scoop—ha-ha-ha, see how I slipped that in there?—with the best of them."

"Ha-ha. Yes. I caught it." Steffie rolled her eyes but laughed all the same. "The worst is over, but thanks. Besides, I heard you have a new gig. Working with Sophie at Blossoms."

"Still on my trial period but I'm crossing my fin-gers. Of course, it means I have to wait till later in the day for my Wednesday fix at Scoop, but it's worth it."

"Oh, that reminds me. Your friend was in around noon."

"What friend?"

"The diver. The guy who owns the boat out in the bay over near the island? I can't think of his name."

"You mean Jared Chandler?"

"If he's the guy you were here with last week, yeah." Steffie looked behind Chrissie and noticed the line was starting to grow again. "What can I get for you?"

"I'll have a cone with the chocolate raspberry marshmallow. One scoop in a sugar cone, please."

"You got it. Anyway, he came in around noon and sat at the table near the door. Finally, I told him we were counter service only, because I didn't know if he was waiting for someone to take his order. So he looked at his watch—it was around twelve thirty or so by then—and came up to the counter. Funny, but he ordered the same thing you just ordered. Only three scoops, like last week. Guess he was feeling brave, 'cause he ordered a cone, had to be close to a foot high. Sat back down near the door while he ate the top scoop, then grabbed a bunch of napkins and walked out."

Steffie handed the cone to Chrissie and moved to the cash register, continuing to chatter as she rang up the sale.

"Yeah, he's a cutie. Were you supposed to meet him here?" Steffie asked.

"I don't think so. Why?" Chrissie handed over several bills.

"He looked like he was waiting for someone. I just thought—" She shrugged. "Maybe he was simply passing time."

"Probably." Chrissie dropped her change into her bag and grabbed a few napkins out of the container on the counter. She said good-bye to Steffie and walked out onto the boardwalk, trying not to think about the possibility that Jared had been waiting for her.

It *was* Wednesday, and Steffie had commented on the fact that Chrissie stopped in every Wednesday right before noon. What were the chances he'd have remembered such an offhand remark? And even more unlikely, that he'd be there today, on Wednesday, around noon?

It sure sounded as if that's what had happened.

She'd been trying not to think about Jared at all. Working from early morning to late in the after- noon was exhausting and gave her little time for idle thoughts about great-looking guys with smiling eyes. The truth was she really wasn't ready to think about any guy. The last one had damn near killed her, and she wasn't about to go down that road again. Besides, it felt good to be just Chrissie for a while. She needed to get reacquainted with all those parts of herself she'd lost, those parts Doug had forced out of her with his bullying and his fists.

That was never going to happen again. New Chrissie knew there were pieces of the old Chris- sie she'd liked, and she was going to find every one of them and put herself back together. She'd made inroads to that end since she came to the island, read- ing all those books she'd passed on because Doug liked her attention at night. She hadn't baked for pleasure in forever, since Doug had told her she was getting fat. To a girl who'd grown up overweight, with image issues that had followed her into adult- hood even though she'd lost the weight years ago, his words had made her go cold inside.

She'd stopped running in the mornings because he didn't want other men watching her. She'd given up her long walks because he didn't like to go, and if she went alone, he'd interrogate her for an hour when she got home. Where had she been? Whom did she talk to? Did she meet up with another guy? Who was he? And depending on his mood, she was likely to get smacked around a little before he was finished.

She sang in the shower whenever she pleased now without fear of giving anyone a headache, since Ruby was the only other person in there, and she was downstairs on the other side of the building. This morning, Chrissie'd belted out an entire Bangles medley: "Manic Monday," "Eternal Flame," and "Walk Like an Egyptian." It had felt great.

New Chrissie would never allow anyone to smack her around again. That knowledge was empowering. It made her stand a little straighter and walk with a greater sense of confidence.

Still, the thought that Jared Chandler *might* have been looking for her was intriguing.

A woman with a baby in a stroller sat on the first bench drinking coffee from a paper cup, and an older couple sat talking quietly on the second one, so Chrissie strolled toward the pier. Many of the boat slips were empty, though from the end of the pier she could see a bow rider heading toward the dock. The engine had been cut and the driver was backing the boat into the slip on the rise and fall of the wake he'd churned up. A cruiser moored at the dock swayed with the tide. A catamaran sailed by and a kayaker with uneven strokes kept close to the shore, paddling around the pier and the outcrop of land where Captain Walt's restaurant sat overlooking the bay. On the boardwalk two gulls fought over a piece of a discarded bagel.

The fishing day had ended and most of the watermen in town tied up their boats overnight at the marina past Alec's boat shop, where the water was deeper. She walked in that direction, thinking she'd poke into his shop and say hello. When she reached the long, low, and wide building that housed the business Alec had taken over from his uncle, she saw that, although he'd been running the shop for several years, the original sign—ELLISON'S: BOATS FOR THE BAY SINCE 1896—still hung over the door. Right now, the sign Chrissie was most interested in was the one in the window: CLOSED.

She'd finished her cone, and after dabbing the napkin at the sides of her mouth, she balled up the paper and dropped it into the trash can that stood next to the walk that led down to the marina. From there she could see the point where the New River entered the bay. At a higher elevation, she could probably have seen the warehouses Dallas had turned into a film production studio, and farther up River Road, Blossoms.

She'd promised herself that with the warm weather, she'd spend more time exploring St. Dennis. She knew the area was rich in history, and while she'd read about how the town was founded and how they'd duped the British during the War of 1812, she wanted to find the one house in town that had taken a cannonball, and the tiny church that the earliest settlers had built. She knew, too, there were stories she'd yet to hear about the island as well as the town, and Ruby knew them all. She intended to hear every one. Whenever she'd asked her mother what she knew about their family, Dorothy would brush her off, saying, "Old news. Who cares?" Well, Chrissie cared, and she wanted to learn. Ruby knew all of Cannonball Island's secrets, and before long, Chrissie would, too.

From now on, she promised herself as she walked back to her car, she'd take two hours every Sunday and walk around St. Dennis. That would be her primer, and after her walk, she'd tell Ruby what she'd seen and ask her what she knew.

TRUE TO HER promise, on Sunday morning, Chrissie dressed in shorts and a cotton tee and tied on her walking shoes. She grabbed her sunglasses from her bag, then went into the sitting room to let Ruby know she'd be gone for a few hours. To her surprise, Ruby stood in the doorway wearing a blue skirt and a white blouse topped with a red sweater, her feet in her favorite white sneakers, her handbag over her arm.

"Gigi, you look so patriotic."

"And I guess you be going on a picnic."

"Just going on a walk. I thought I'd walk around St. Dennis a bit, do a little sightseeing. Maybe learn more about the town."

"You want to be knowing St. Dennis, you be asking Grace. Her family ran the only paper in town for over one hundred years."

"I saw some of the clippings on the wall at Blossoms. Weddings, funerals, births."

Ruby nodded. "If it happened in St. Dennis, the Ellisons wrote about it."

"Ellison." Chrissie's brows knit together, trying to remember where she'd just seen that name.

"That be Grace's maiden name."

"I saw the name on the sign by Alec's boat shop," Chrissie said. "I walked down there the other day after work."

"That be Grace's brother, Clifford. He took in Alec and raised the boy after Carole—his mother—died. Carole be Grace and Clifford's sister."

"I'd heard Alec was Grace's nephew, but I didn't

know about his mother, or that he'd been raised by his uncle. Well, I learned something today, and I didn't even have to leave the house to do it." She slipped her sunglasses onto her face. "I'm taking that walk anyway. After being inside for most of every day, I need to move my legs."

"Been walking plenty around the island at night," Ruby reminded her.

"That's different. That's just a stroll after dinner. Today, I'm walking with a purpose."

"I be heading to the inn to have lunch with Grace. Might as well walk with you." Ruby headed to the door.

"It's a pretty long walk, Gigi."

"One I've made many a time before." She opened the door and stepped through it.

"For crying out loud, the woman's gonna freaking kill herself," Chrissie muttered. She followed Ruby outside, then turned and locked the door behind her. "Wait up, Gigi. I'll drive you. I can walk from the inn."

"All right." Ruby smiled.

"Oh, you." Chrissie laughed as she went to the car, her keys jangling in her hand. "You knew I wasn't going to let you walk a mile in this heat."

Ruby was still smiling as she got into the car.

"Might be we'll sit out on that covered porch at the inn for lunch," Ruby was saying as they drove over the bridge.

"You two have been friends for a long time, haven't you?"

"Can't even tell how many years. Course, I be older, but age just be a number."

"True enough." Chrissie grinned. "Well, you know

they say that sixty is the new forty, and seventy is the new fifty."

Ruby gave her a side-eye. "And one hundred is still one hundred."

"You'll be one hundred and one soon," Chrissie reminded her as she turned at the sign for the inn. "We should have a party."

"Best be making it a good one."

Chrissie found a parking spot near the inn's back door. She helped Ruby from the car and walked her inside. Grace greeted them in the lobby as if she'd been waiting for them.

"How nice," Grace said. "You brought Chrissie with you today."

"Oh, I'm not staying. I'm taking a walk," Chrissie explained. "I want to become better acquainted with St. Dennis. I've heard so much about the history, I'd like to see more of it myself."

"Do you know what you'd like to see?"

"I thought today I'd check out the art center. I heard Sophie's family used to own the place."

"Folks 'round here always called it the mansion. First true mansion ever built in St. Dennis. Generous of Curtis—he's Sophie's grandfather—to give it to the town for the center."

Chrissie recalled that ridiculous story Sophie'd told her about how Rose never really left. "Sophie seems to think her grandmother still stops by there from time to time."

"Oh yes, Rose." Grace nodded vigorously.

"Yes what?"

"Yes, Rose still stops by the old place. Mostly when Curtis is there, or one of her grandchildren." Grace's voice dropped to a confidential level. "You probably know that their son, Craig—he was Sophie and Jesse's father—was the black sheep of the family. Left home under a dark cloud, stayed away for years while he sowed his wild oats. Married—oh, I don't know how many times now, three or four at least. Sophie's mother was his second wife, I believe. Maybe the third. Anyway, Sophie and Jesse never got to meet their grandparents when they were younger. Never did get to meet Rose. They just met Curtis a few years back when Jesse came into town and told his grandfather he wanted to know him and wanted to work for him at the law firm."

"That took a lot of courage," Chrissie said.

"Indeed it did. Curtis Enright is one formidable man. But it all worked out, and Jesse took over the firm from Curtis so he could finally retire." Grace sighed what sounded like a happy sigh. "Rose was a lovely woman, and she and Curtis adored each other. They were one of the happiest couples I ever knew, wouldn't you say, Ruby?"

Ruby nodded. "Rose do still be around. She showed up the night Lis showed off her paintings down at the mansion."

"Gigi, you really believe that?"

"Sure as I'm standing here. And standing is not what I be here for."

"Goodness, you're right. We're having lunch." Grace took Ruby's arm. "Now, veranda today?"

"That be fine."

Grace turned Ruby in the direction of the dining room through which they'd pass to the veranda. Grace glanced over her shoulder. "Chrissie, are you sure you don't want to join us?"

"Positive, but thank you. Gigi, I'll be back for you later." Chrissie watched the two women walk past the hostess and head for the French doors that would lead them outside.

It must be nice to have a friend who's known you for much of your life. Someone you don't have to explain yourself to, who knows what's important to you and knows your heart, what makes you laugh and what makes you cry. She'd never had a friend like that, though there was a time when she thought Lis might be that person, but they'd lost touch for so long.

She was so deep in thought she almost walked right into the double doors, and the man who was coming through them.

"Hey, you know that walking while zoned out is considered an offense around here, right? Like jaywalking except you don't have to be crossing the street. I heard the fines are pretty steep if you get caught." Jared grabbed her by both arms to pull her out of the doorway and out of the path of a family of five who were coming in behind him. He was wearing tennis shorts and a white polo shirt and held his racket under one arm.

"Sorry. My mind was wandering."

"I figured that out. Where are you off to?"

"Just going for a walk."

"No destination?"

"I'd like to check out the art center. Lis has some paintings on display in the gallery. I'm embarrassed that I haven't made time to go before this."

"Okay if I tag along with you?"

"Sure. You're done playing?"

"Got stood up, so I never made it onto the court."

He grinned, then shrugged. "Sometimes you score, sometimes you don't. If you could wait till I ditch the racket, I'll be right back."

"Okay."

He crossed the lobby and took the steps two at a time. In less than five minutes, he was back, still dressed the same except he'd added the green Eagles ball cap he'd worn the first time she saw him.

He opened the door and held it for her, and they walked side by side toward the main road.

"What brought you to the inn?" he asked.

"I dropped off Gigi—Ruby—to have lunch with Grace."

"No lunch for you?"

"I need to walk. To stretch my legs."

He glanced down at her legs as if about to comment, then apparently thought better of it.

She thought about asking him about Scoop, but was afraid she'd look foolish if it had only been a coincidence that he'd been there on Wednesday around noon. She was relieved when he said, "You still owe me ice cream. Don't think I'm going to let you off the hook just because you didn't bother to show on Wednesday."

"You were there?" she said, though she knew he had been. "It never occurred to me that you'd actually go."

"There was ice cream involved. Steffie's ice cream. Wasn't going to miss out on my payback. So you still owe me, and I expect you to ante up."

"I'd be happy to, if you could wait till late afternoon. I got a job. I'm working at Blossoms, of all places." She explained how she'd been hired, leaving out the hired-fired-hired part.

"I guess Sophie heard about your breakdown of her oyster stew and figured you knew your stuff, huh? Maybe she was afraid you'd take her secret recipe and use it as leverage to get hired somewhere else."

"It was more like her cook is leaving at the end of next week and she wanted to hire someone pronto. I applied and she's given me a two-week trial."

"When's the trial up?"

"The end of this week, and as far as I know, she hasn't interviewed anyone else, so I've got my fingers crossed."

"Is this what you want?"

"I was beyond ready to go back to work, and Blossoms is definitely my kind of place. I just wasn't sure about leaving Ruby to deal with the store by herself. Of course, she reminded me that she's been doing that for about the past million years. And I know she's capable of handling the customers—most of them are islanders and they know where everything is, so she just pretty much stays behind the cash register. I still take care of the earliest morning crowd and I still bake stuff for her, but I worry that she'll get overtired. And with new people coming onto the island to check out the new homes that are being built, I guess I'm afraid no one's checking up on her."

"Owen told me about Cass's father wanting to build on the island and buying up some abandoned houses and Cass designing the homes to replace them."

"Cass's houses are going to be built using as much of the old ones as possible. The old brick, the old floors, the old wavy glass in some of the windows. Very clever, I thought. Way to blend the old with the new."

"But they're really small, right?" he asked.

"The originals were small, but Cass is making them a little larger. I think she's trying to appeal to singles and couples, maybe a family of three but no more. She's marketing them as little getaways, weekends, vacations, in an unspoiled, natural setting."

"Where do I sign?"

"I think she only has something like fifteen to twenty places to sell, so you better move fast. She has a big advertising campaign set to start this weekend in all the big papers—D.C., Baltimore, Philly, New York. She's pretty sure she'll sell out before the end of the summer."

"Good for her. It does sound like a good idea."

"Ask her to show you her designs. They're beautiful. I'd be tempted to buy one myself if I could afford it, but she's going to be getting top dollar for those little places. Exclusivity is apparently a big draw."

"Yeah, Owen says the houses are going to be really cool, with views of the bay or the river. The right advertising will bring in buyers in droves. But I see your point about having a lot of strangers on the island with Ruby being alone in the store." His mouth upturned on one side in a sort of half smile. "Course, someone acts shady, she could always strike 'em down with some spell or something. I bet she's got some serious mojo."

"Watch what you say. She might decide to turn you into a toad."

"You think she could do that?"

"No."

"Yeah. Me neither."

They reached the center of town and waited at the crosswalk on Charles Street as the light turned red.

"Which way?" Jared asked.

"Let's cross here and go up Cherry Street to Hudson Street."

"I'll follow you, since I don't know one street from another and I have no idea where any of them lead."

"How long have you been in St. Dennis?" The light turned green and they crossed the street.

"Long enough to have made an effort to find my way around on my own. Which I haven't done, but I'm making up for it today," he said.

The houses on Cherry Street were an odd hodge-podge of architectural features. At first glance, they appeared to be bungalows, with all the charm and front porches and gables. But they were all built before bungalows came into fashion, and had elements of various styles, with Victorian trim here and a mansard roof there, and almost every one boasted flowering shrubs and masses of daffodils that spilled almost onto the sidewalk. Chrissie paused briefly in front of a white clapboard house with second-floor gables and a slate roof and a fenced-in front yard that was a riot of color.

"Vanessa lives here," she told Jared.

"Vanessa . . . ?"

"She owns Bling, the women's store right in the center of town. She's Beck's half sister."

"Right. Tall, long dark curly hair. Pretty. Married to that guy who does the guided adventure tours out in Montana. Used to be in the FBI."

"That's the one." She smiled slyly. "Now, if it's a witch you're looking for, people tell me the woman who used to live in this house was the real deal." She lowered her voice to a whisper. "They say she's still here."

"Who's 'they'?"

Chrissie started walking and Jared fell into step with her.

"Vanessa. Steffie. I'll bet Grace knows about it. You should ask her."

"Maybe I will. You believe it?"

"No. But I think *they* believe it."

When they reached the corner, Chrissie pointed to the left.

"I'm pretty sure the art center is down this way," she said.

"I guess we'll find out."

They walked in silence for a few minutes, then Chrissie asked, "So what else did you see that you can't explain?"

"Çatalhöyük," he said without hesitation.

"What's that?"

"Maybe the world's oldest city. The houses were built together like a giant beehive. You had to get inside by going through a hole in the roof because they had no doors."

"Why didn't they have doors?"

"Because the walls were all contiguous to the house next door. Like I said, a giant beehive."

"Where was this place?"

"Southern Turkey. The city was alive and thriving between—are you ready for this?—7500 B.C. and 5700 B.C."

"So the thing you can't explain is why they built their houses like that?"

"Nope. I can't explain what happened to the people who lived there. The entire civilization disappeared without a trace."

"Have you ever been there yourself?"

Jared nodded. "Rachel is married to a guy whose sister is a famous archaeologist—Daria McGowan. Sometimes she takes a group of friends and relatives to different sites she's worked on."

"So where does she think all these beehive people went?"

"She has no idea. So if she can't explain it . . ."

"Neither can you. Got it. No woo-woo factor there, like the ghosts we were discussing, but I get it."

They arrived at Hudson Street's dead end at Old St. Mary's Church Road. Across the street was the St. Dennis Art and Community Center.

"That's the old Enright mansion," Chrissie told Jared. "Sophie's grandfather owned it and he gave it to the town. And that"—she pointed to a stone building directly across from where they stood—"is the carriage house. They use it for special exhibits. Lis's work is hanging in there."

"Let's see if it's open."

The door to the building was unlocked, so Jared pushed it open and they stepped inside. An older gentleman stepped out from a side room.

"Hi, folks. Come on in," he said. "We're only open for another half hour, but the mansion's open till five. I'm the docent of the day, if you have any questions. Anything in particular you're looking for?"

"We heard there's an exhibit of Lis Parker's work."

"Ah, yes. Lisbeth Parker. Local artist, grew up on Cannonball Island right across that bridge at the end of Charles Street." He gestured for Chrissie and Jared to follow him.

It was a small room, and partitions set at ninety-degree angles to the walls created a sort of maze. They followed him around to look for the beginning.

"Here you go," the docent told them. "Parker's work starts here."

"Thanks." Chrissie waited for Jared to catch up. He'd paused to look at something on one of the walls near the door. She pointed to the large watercolor of the marsh on Cannonball Island.

"Wow. That's really lifelike." He stepped closer. "Beautiful use of color. I had no idea she was this good."

He went on to the next painting and had a similar reaction.

"Did you know how good she is?" Jared asked.

Chrissie shook her head. "I knew she always wanted to paint, and I remember when we were little that she always had one of those little art kits and she drew and painted all the time. So I wasn't surprised when she grew up to be an artist. I'm not surprised at how good she is. I'm only surprised that I hadn't realized it."

They went through the maze, commenting on the works displayed, one after another: the view from the point, foam-covered driftwood on the bay's wrack line, the abandoned chapel down the road from the store on Dune Drive, the rocky jetty that helped form the cove where the locals tied their boats up at night, a stack of crab traps on the sand. By the time they reached the end of the exhibit, Jared was ready to move on, but Chrissie wanted one more go-round of Lis's work. He followed along patiently and even commented several times about aspects of this painting or that he'd missed the first time through.

"Stop back again in a few weeks," the docent told

them when they'd finished. "She's supposed to be bringing a few new ones in to add to the collection."

"We'll definitely do that," Chrissie said.

On their way out, Jared grabbed her arm and whispered in her ear, "I call this one *Nightmare on Charles Street*."

Chrissie paused to look at the painting he was pointing to.

"Oh my God. That's hideous. What is it?"

"The little card here says it's a cat." Chrissie could tell he was struggling to keep a straight face. "*Tiger, Tiger, Burning Bright*, by Hazel Stevens."

The docent cleared his throat.

"That's one of the paintings that was entered in the local artists' competition. One of the perks of entering was having your work displayed here in the gallery. We'd promised to exhibit all the paintings submitted."

"It's—" Chrissie struggled for a nonjudgmental word. "Very different from . . . the others in the gallery."

"Yes, indeed. It is that." The docent held the door for them. "That's one of Mrs. Stevens's cats. She has several others. Cats, that is, and she painted each one of them." Without cracking a smile, he added, "This was judged the best of the bunch."

"Well . . ." Chrissie tried to think of something else to say about the painting, but couldn't come up with anything other than "Nice of them to be true to their word and hang the painting."

"Not sure about the decision to hang it next to the door, though. It might deter people from viewing the rest of the exhibit," Jared said as they followed the path from the carriage house to the mansion. "I bet they're sorry they ever made that promise. That thing was downright awful. I'm probably going to have nightmares tonight."

Chrissie laughed. "Maybe we'll see some pretty in here to chase the creepy out of your head."

The path led to the mansion's main door, and once inside the huge foyer, they were met by another docent, this one a woman who appeared to be in her late seventies.

"You're free to wander anywhere that's open. If a door is closed, however, we ask that you respect that," she said.

Chrissie and Jared acknowledged the request and set out to explore the huge old house, from the first floor to the attic. It had been set up to accommodate everything from children's crafts in two rooms on the first floor, to a conference room on the second floor that, according to the note on the door, was used primarily for social and civic meetings. Another room served to display works by a local sculptor, and yet another, miniature boats made by a retired waterman, which caught Jared's eye. It seemed every craft and hobby had its designated space in the old mansion, and when they made it back to the first floor, they went into the parlor that was open to the foyer by a large pocket door.

The walls were lined with bookshelves, and around the room, various chairs and sofas were arranged for group discussion or for solitary reading. Chrissie sat in a rocking chair and put her head back and rocked slowly, while Jared walked around the room, stopping occasionally to read the title of a book.

"I don't smell anything," she said.

Jared turned to her, a book in his hand. "What did you expect to smell?"

"Gardenias. Sophie said her deceased grandmother Rose comes back here. When she's here, you can smell gardenias."

He took a deep sniff. "Nope. No flowers of any kind."

"I knew it." She closed her eyes again and rocked peacefully.

"Are you all finished with your nap?" Jared said a while later.

"I wasn't napping. Just rocking." Chrissie got up and smiled. "Ready to resume the tour? I think you can walk around the grounds, too."

"I think I'd rather save that for another day. I'm getting hungry."

"We can walk back to town." She pulled her phone from her pocket and checked the time. "I should be picking Ruby up soon anyway."

Once outside, Jared started to cross the street to go back the way they'd come while Chrissie had taken five steps to the right.

"Where are you going?" he asked.

"I wanted to check out the old church." She pointed to the street sign. "Old St. Mary's Church Road. The church—Old St. Mary's—is up this way. But you know your way back to the inn."

"Yeah, but . . ." He appeared torn. "Where's Charles Street from here?"

"It's at the top of this one. That's where the church is. You've probably passed it fifty times without realizing it."

"Well, if it's Charles Street either way, I'll go with

you." He walked in her direction. "There are places to eat on this end of Charles, right?"

"We're not far out of the center of town. Like, two blocks from the light."

"Seemed like we walked farther than that."

"Time flies when you're having fun."

"It has been kind of fun. Not my usual kind, but still." He nodded as if to himself as they walked along. "The architecture on this side of town is interesting. I'll bet some of these old houses could tell some wonderful stories."

"And I'll bet Grace knows them all." Chrissie thought about that for a moment. "Gigi probably does, too."

Up ahead was the library and a series of brick buildings that served as professional offices. Chrissie saw signs for engineers, accountants, and law firms.

"That must be Sophie's brother," she told Jared as they walked past a building with a sign out front reading ENRIGHT AND ENRIGHT: ATTORNEYS AT LAW. "And a few doors down is Alec's office. You know he's an environmental consultant, right?"

"I did know that. We've talked on several occasions about efforts being made to clean up the bay and renew the fishing and crabbing industries. He says they've come a long way over the past ten years."

"Oh, there's the church, on the corner." She pointed up ahead.

"That little bitty building?"

"Hey, show some respect. That's the oldest building in St. Dennis, which just goes to show that they regarded their faith as more important than anything else."

When they reached the church, Jared read the sign posted out front. "The sign says it was built in 1718. That's really early," he noted. He tried to peek through the windows but it was pretty dark inside.

"It was open this morning but closed about a half hour ago." Chrissie pointed to the sign that told the church's story.

"Guess you'll have to take another walk next Sunday if you're going to get inside."

"Guess I will." She walked around the small building. Rosebushes had been planted on each of its four corners, and ivy trailed over the arched front door, which was barely tall enough for a man of Jared's height to enter without ducking. "It's pretty. I bet it's nice inside. So I will come back. You?" She looked back at Jared, who hadn't bothered to walk around the church when she did.

"Probably not."

Chrissie took a few pictures of the church on her phone, including one of Jared standing next to the sign.

"So I guess you're more interested in food right now." Chrissie put her phone back into her pocket.

"Way more."

"Help is just a few storefronts away." She pointed up the street. "I see two restaurants, a take-out place, and a bakery within steps of each other."

"On my way." He set off across the street. "Lag behind and you'll be left in the dust."

She laughed but took her time catching up with him.

"Here we are. The Checkered Cloth. I heard their takeout's pretty good." He stopped in front of the shop, his hand on the door handle. When she didn't move toward the door, he asked, "Aren't you coming in?"

"I think I should get back to pick up Gigi. She's probably waiting for me."

"You sure?"

"Yes, but thanks. Enjoy whatever you end up getting."

"One of everything on the menu." He grinned. "Thanks for letting me join you. It's a pretty cool little town. I enjoyed the company."

"Thanks. Me, too." She started walking toward town.

"Maybe we could do it again sometime," he called to her.

"Maybe we could." She kept walking, afraid if she turned around she'd change her mind and follow him into the shop. She thought he'd gone inside, but then he called, "You still owe me an ice cream cone."

She stopped and turned to him. "I owe you a dish."

"Huh?"

"You had a dish last week, not a cone. A cone would be an upgrade."

He laughed, and while she'd thought he'd go directly into the shop, she could swear she felt his eyes on her. She didn't have the nerve to turn around again to see if she was right.

The center of St. Dennis held a number of wonderful shops, some in storefronts, others in old houses that had been retrofitted for retail purposes. The gourmet spice shop, Curry Favor, and the children's clothing store, Giraffe, were both in Victorian houses with wide porches and bay windows. The bookstore, Book 'Em, was a storefront, and its big window facing Charles Street never failed to lure Chrissie inside.

Five minutes won't make a difference to Gigi, she assured herself as she stepped inside.

She spent well more than five minutes going through the stacks of sale books, then the new releases that were on a table near the front window.

"I thought you were in a hurry to get back to the inn," she heard a male voice say behind her.

"I am," she said without turning around. "But I had to make a quick stop. Gigi loves thrillers and mysteries—the gorier the thriller, the more convoluted the mystery, the happier she is. I see her favorite author has a brand-new book out this week, so I thought I'd surprise her."

Jared took the book from her hand and placed it back on the display. "She already has this one."

"No, it just came out." She picked it back up again.

"And she's probably holding an autographed copy in her hand right at this moment." He returned the book to the stack.

Chrissie stared at him blankly.

"You want to know how I know?" He leaned closer. "Maybe I'm psychic, too. Maybe I know things. Maybe I have, you know, that eye thing."

"If you 'know things,' what am I thinking?" she asked, even as she tried unsuccessfully not to smile.

"You're wondering how I know that Ruby has this book."

"Ha. Nope. I was wondering how you ate so quickly if you were soooo hungry you were going to order one of everything."

"How long does it take to eat a couple of burgers and an order of onion rings, and a handful of cookies?"

"You must have inhaled it all."

He shrugged. "I told you I was hungry."

"I guess so. Anyway, back to the subject at hand." She pointed to the book under discussion. "So how does Ruby already have the book?"

"Delia Enright, the author, sent a copy to Grace and one to Ruby, because she knows they are both fans."

Her eyes narrowed suspiciously.

"Delia's my dad's girlfriend. If you can refer to people in their seventies as boyfriend and girlfriend."

"You're kidding."

"Nope. They've been together for years. Delia loves to come to St. Dennis and stay at the inn. She's done a couple of signings here at this store. She said she always feels inspired here. She and Grace have become great friends."

"So she's related to Sophie and Jesse then? That's why she comes here?"

Jared shook his head. "No. Delia's husband was Curtis Enright's son. They divorced, and her ex remarried. Actually, he's remarried a couple of times. One of those wives—maybe the second or the third, I don't remember which—was Jesse and Sophie's mother."

"Got it. Well, you just saved me twenty-five bucks, so thank you." She left the book where he'd put it and walked to the cash register with the others she'd selected.

Barbara Noonan, the shop owner, asked Chrissie, "Find what you were looking for, Chrissie?"

"I did. Thanks."

Barbara glanced over Chrissie's shoulder to Jared. "Hi, Jared. I understand we're going to be seeing your dad this summer."

"Yeah, I heard Delia's having a signing here."

"She's such a good sport to come here every year. The customers love meeting her and we sell a ton of books, but it has to be exhausting for her. This place is always packed for hours when she's here, and she never turns anyone away."

"I remember from last year. It was pretty intense, but she likes to meet her readers."

"And we're so glad she does." Barbara bagged up Chrissie's books. "Tell Ruby we'll have another new Burke in two weeks. She can call me if she wants me to put one aside for her."

"I'll do that, thanks, Barb."

On the way back to the inn, Jared asked Chrissie, "Tell me the truth. Were you just ditching me back there, when you said you had to get back?"

"Of course not. Honestly, as hungry as you said you were, I figured it would take you about an hour to eat, and I knew I wanted to stop to pick up a couple of books, so I just thought I should keep moving."

"You swear?"

"I swear. Truth zone."

"Huh? Truth zone? What's that?"

"That's when you have to tell the truth, no matter what, and the other person has to promise not to hold it against you. You just have to accept that what you're hearing is the pure, unadulterated truth, no malice intended."

"So let's suppose I asked you out to dinner—just as a friend—and when I came to pick you up, you asked me if your dress made you look fat and I said yes, because it did, you wouldn't get mad?"

She laughed in spite of herself. "Frankly, I can't

see myself ever asking you or any other man for his opinion on how I dress." *Been there, done that. Not gonna happen again.* "But yes. If we're in the truth zone, I can't get mad. It's like you've made a pact to let the other person speak honestly."

"Got it."

They crossed at the light and continued the walk back to the inn on the sandy shoulder of Charles Street, the sidewalk having ended at Kelly's Point Road.

"So what you're saying is there's *nothing* that might be exempt from that whole, tell-the-honest-truth thing?" he asked.

"No exemptions, no exceptions."

"Interesting."

"What is?"

"I've found that a lot of the time, people don't really want to hear the truth. They want to hear what they want to hear."

"Agreed. But the whole idea behind the truth zone is that you care enough about the other person—as a friend, a lover, a relative, whatever—that you tell them the truth. If I was wearing something that looked terrible on me and I asked you about it, as a friend, I'd expect you to tell me the truth. What good would it do to tell me I look fine when I don't? Not that I'd ask, but you get the point."

"I do." He seemed to think about that for a minute or two. "Who came up with this truth zone idea?"

"I did. And before you ask, it was because I was lied to for so long about so many things, I never knew what to believe."

"Wow. I'm sorry. Can I ask . . ."

"No. You can't." She forced a smile. "But thanks anyway."

There were some things you didn't discuss. Like where your father went and why, and why did he take your brother and leave you behind? Surely your mother knows, so why has she been lying to you for all these years? The truth zone had never been part of that conversation, and probably never would be. Dorothy Jenkins had never met a lie she wouldn't tell. And then there was Doug, and the lies he'd told to keep her from leaving. Like how he'd stopped drinking and how sorry he was for what he'd done and said the night before.

"So about that ice cream you owe me," Jared said when they reached the inn's lobby.

"Wednesday. Five o'clock."

"I'll be there."

Chrissie went into the dining area and searched for Ruby and Grace. She could see them through the double doors, sitting on the shaded veranda and sipping cool drinks. When she reached the table, she pulled out a chair, asked the waiter to bring her an iced tea, and turned to Grace.

"So tell me how you know Delia Enright . . ."

Chapter Six

Jared sat on the balcony outside his room at the inn, his feet up on the railing, a cold beer in his hand via room service, and reached for his ringing phone. He checked the caller ID and smiled.

"Hey, Dad. How's it going?"

"Good. Very good. How's our sunken ship doing?"

"Same thing it was doing the last time you asked. Nothing."

"Still waiting for someone to make a decision?"

"We are. On the one hand, they want the ship removed because there's evidence of a Native American settlement beneath it. On the other, no one wants to be the person who gives the order to demolish the ship to get to the settlement. It's frustrating. I can't leave because we could get word any day now. But I can't work, either, so my hands are tied."

"But you've already given your report, right?"

"Two weeks ago. It was pretty straightforward. I explained how we could salvage the artifacts from the wreck, then we could bring up what's left of the ship piece by piece depending on its condition. Obviously there's a lot of rot. I also mentioned we'd bring in Sam as the marine archaeologist." As Jared spoke, he could almost see his father nodding in agreement.

"Exactly what I'd have done," Gordon assured him. "I know you're not a patient man, but try to hang in there. We've committed to this project, and right now, things are a little slow. Which is fine. We all need downtime." Gordon paused. "You in particular. You haven't taken time off since last year."

"Somewhere I heard someone say, 'When you're doing what you love, you never work a day in your life,'" Jared said, half in jest. "I had a great time diving in Costa Rica not too long ago, and before that, we were in Australia." Thinking of Australia made him remember something else he'd seen that he couldn't explain, which made him think of Chrissie. He tucked away the thought to save for Wednesday. "Anything going on I should know about?"

"Actually, there is." Jared heard his father take a deep breath. "Delia and I are getting married."

"This must be a bad connection. It sounded like you said you and Delia were getting married." His eyes were on the bay and the sailboats that flashed by in the early morning sun.

Gordon laughed. "I know, hard to believe, after how many years we've been together?"

"So why now?" Jared swung his legs down from the railing. This was the last thing he'd expected to hear from his father.

"It's time, that's all. I want to. And after she and I talked it over, she's agreed."

"Wow. That's some news, Dad. Have you told Rachel?"

"Right before I called you. She's obviously thrilled." Gordon paused. "How 'bout you? Aren't you going to wish us luck?"

"Of course I wish you both all the best, Dad. I'm just surprised. I had no idea you'd wanted to get married again."

"'Again' makes it sound like I've been married several times over, and recently, at that. I've been single for twenty-four years now."

Jared was not oblivious to the edge in his father's voice.

"I just meant I didn't know you were thinking about marriage. I guess I thought since you'd been together for so long, neither one of you wanted to make it permanent."

"We both feel the time is right for us."

"Then I'm happy for you. I really am. For both of you. Delia's . . ." Jared laughed. "Delia is Delia."

Gordon laughed, too. "I couldn't have said it better myself."

"So when's the big day? And where? And do I need to get a tux?"

"Three weeks from Saturday, at Delia's home in Pennsylvania."

"Three weeks? That's not a lot of time. Are you sure you can pull off a wedding in three weeks?"

"This is Delia we're talking about. She has everything under control, as you'd expect."

"So how do her kids feel about having a stepfather after all this time?"

"They're really happy. Nick is walking his mother

down the aisle and Delia's daughters and daughter-in-law will be bridesmaids. I'd like you to be my best man, son."

"I'd be honored, Dad," Jared said sincerely. "I truly would be honored."

"Great. That's settled, then. Hold on, Jared . . . here's Delia."

"You may call me Mom, or not," Delia Enright said in that always slightly dramatic tone of hers. "Or you may continue to call me Delia. You may not, however, refer to me as your stepmother. It sounds so Grimms' Fairy Tale–ish. In return, I promise not to be evil."

"You've got a deal." Jared was grinning. Whatever he felt about his father remarrying, he was glad it was Delia whom Gordon had fallen in love with.

"Did your father tell you the festivities are going to start on Thursday night?"

"No, he just said the wedding was three weeks from Saturday."

"Take all this down. Thursday night we're having a general get-together. Both families. All the kids and grandkids. Very casual. It'll be such fun. Then Friday during the day, we'll have activities for everyone. The Brandywine Valley is such a beautiful part of Pennsylvania, I want to share it with you all. Plan on sightseeing. It's a very historical area—the Battle of Brandywine, the Brandywine River Museum, the Wyeth paintings, Longwood Gardens. Look it up if you don't know it. Then Friday night, rehearsal dinner. Saturday, the wedding. Sunday, brunch and perhaps some more sightseeing if anyone is still on their feet from the night before. Questions?"

"No, ma'am."

"'Ma'am' is also off the table, Jared. It makes me sound ancient." Delia paused. "You haven't written down a word, have you?"

"No, ma'—Delia. But I have an excellent memory."

"That's what your father says, too. I've found it to be an exaggeration. Of course, he claims his age is responsible. You have no such excuse. I'm giving the phone back to your father now. Oh, and bring a date or you'll throw off the seating."

"Did you catch that last part?" Gordon was back on the phone. "Bring your latest girl."

"I caught it, but there is no latest girl. I'm not dating anyone right now."

"Well, sometime over the next few weeks you're going to have to find someone. Delia is deadly serious about the seating." Gordon chuckled. "Besides, knowing you, there'll be someone soon enough."

"Doubtful. But hey, I wish you both all the happiness in the world, Dad. Let me know what you want me to wear, and I'll take care of it."

"Thanks, Jared. I'll see you soon." Gordon paused. "I love you, son."

"I love you, too, Dad."

Jared remained on the balcony, staring at the water, wondering what had possessed his father to want to get married. You'd think after Amelia . . . But that wasn't fair, and Jared knew it. Delia wasn't his mother. She wouldn't be going off and disappearing into another life that didn't include him. Funny, though, that his father had fallen in love with two women who were independent and had careers that took them away from home. The difference between them, as he saw it, was that Delia had been going on book tours for many years, and she'd never failed to come back to her children.

For a time, when he was younger, he thought that's what mothers did. They traveled and did things that were so important they didn't come home. Then he got a little older and had friends whose mothers were home every night, and he started to wonder what his mother did that was so important she couldn't come home, too. When she died, he'd expected to feel more than he did, but she was a woman he'd never really known, a woman who had so little presence in his life that he honestly didn't miss her.

Why would his father want to get married now? Jared was at a loss to explain it.

That's what he could have told Chrissie, that an unexplainable thing was how a man who'd been abandoned by one wife would want to marry again.

And Delia was demanding that he bring a date for the wedding. A date for a four-day weekend? Delia obviously had no idea what she was asking of him. He couldn't think of one woman he'd tolerated for four days except his sister, and sometimes that had gotten touchy. Besides, chances were Rachel would be bringing her husband.

He speed-dialed Rachel's number and couldn't help but smile when he heard her voice. He really did love his little sister.

"So, you've heard Dad's happy news," she said when she picked up. "Isn't it wonderful? He and Delia are really getting married. They're so perfect for each other, don't you think?"

"Yeah. Perfect." He tried to sound upbeat.

"We're over the moon. The boys are so excited.

They've never been to a wedding. Of course, they're mostly interested in the cake, but it'll be a great time. They'll meet their . . . what would you call them, stepgrandkids? What would the relationship be between Delia's grandkids and Dad's?"

"I don't know. Listen, Rach . . ."

"Dad says you're bringing a date to the wedding. Who's the lucky girl?"

"There is no girl. Lucky or otherwise."

"What, you can't decide between the bevy of beauties that always seem to follow you around?"

"There's no bevy. No beauties. Nada."

"Jared, have you been sick? 'Cause the only time I remember you not having at least one girl in your life was when you were in South America and caught that fever and—"

"I'm not sick. I'm just not dating anyone. I'm just working."

"I was under the impression you weren't working. Dad said there was a lull."

"Right. But we expect to get called back at any minute."

"How's that cramping your style?"

"Look, I'm just having a nice, peaceful layover in a quaint little historic town, taking nice long walks, eating some great food . . ."

"Okay, who are you really, and what have you done with my brother? Because if you knew him at all, you'd know he doesn't take nice, peaceful long walks in little historic towns."

Jared laughed. "It's just a change of pace while I'm waiting to get back to the diving, that's all."

"So how's there no woman involved?"

"There just isn't."

"Wow. This is a whole new Jared." Rachel paused. "Are you honestly saying you haven't had female companionship since you got there?"

"Well, I've made a friend, but seriously, just a friend. We just hang out."

"You hang out and take long walks through a charming little town, something you never do, but she's just a friend."

"Yeah."

"I don't remember you ever 'just hanging out' when it comes to women."

"Maybe I'm an older, wiser Jared."

"That's a novel concept. I wonder what that would look like." Rachel paused. "But back to the problem at hand. Delia said you have to bring someone. How 'bout that woman you dated last summer? Jenna?"

"Jessica. And no, thank you."

"The one from New York, the one you had with you at the Halloween party, then."

"She really was a witch."

"Ha-ha. And here we thought it was just a costume. Okay, then, I guess I'm just going to have to set you up with someone. Oh, hey, I have this friend who—"

"No. God, no."

"She's really nice, Jared. And cute. Well, in her own way."

He groaned. "Is she anywhere near as annoying as you are?"

Rachel laughed. "Almost."

"Look, it's not that big a deal."

"Apparently it is to our future stepmother."

"If you value your life, you won't let her hear you call her that. I've been warned. I'm passing that warning on to you."

"Please. I'm not the one who's threatening to throw off her seating arrangement."

"I don't even know what that means."

"It means she wants an even number of people at every table. If you come alone, there will be an extra space at your table and she doesn't want that."

"It sounds silly to me," he muttered.

"Well, you're not the one who's getting married. Find yourself a date, bud, or I'll be forced to find someone for you."

"Don't bother. I'll think of something."

"I'm not bluffing, Jared. I will bring someone, and if you don't act like she's your real date, you will look like the biggest loser ever."

The sad truth was that he knew Rachel'd be good to her word. And the only thing he could think of worse than spending four days with someone he didn't know just might be starting off on the wrong foot with his stepmother.

He corrected himself. *Delia.*

"OH MY GOD, Chrissie, you're not going to believe what happened." Sophie was waiting for her when she arrived at Blossoms on Friday morning. "Dallas called last night. She's having a big meeting of her entire production staff to introduce them to the actors she's chosen to star in her new movie. They're all coming to St. Dennis. The stars, the staff, right down to the script people and the camerapeople. And she

wants to have a brunch. Or lunch. I can't remember
which she said. My mind sort of went blank when I
realized what she was asking me. And I said yes. And
now we have to do it."

"What did you say yes to?" Chrissie's head was
spinning, Sophie'd been talking so fast.

"Brunch. Or lunch. Here. At Blossoms."

"Take a deep breath." Chrissie waited. "Now,
when is this brunch? Lunch. Whatever."

"Sunday."

"Next Sunday?" Chrissie walked past her and
hung her bag on a hook near the back door. "That's
totally doable."

"Ah, no. This Sunday."

"Day after tomorrow? You're kidding."

Sophie shook her head. "She's a friend, but she's
also Dallas freaking MacGregor. I'm really grateful
she thought of me. This could be really good publicity for Blossoms."

"Do you really need publicity? It seems to me you
do okay."

"We do okay, yes, but we're coming into tourist
season and there are a lot of places to eat in St. Dennis. There's so much competition for those tourist
dollars. This is free publicity. People are nuts, you
know that. They're going to want to eat where Dallas ate. Dallas and the stars she's bringing with her.
And people are going to wonder, *If I eat there, will
she come in?*" Sophie tied on her apron. "You can see
where this could be really big for me, right? We don't
get the foot traffic that places like Lola's and Captain
Walt's and the other places that are right in the center
of town do. We're off the beaten track. I mean, you

have to have a reason to come out this way. River Road isn't exactly Charles Street. But if Dallas can put us on the map, more of those tourist dollars will flow our way because people will come looking for us."

"True. So what are you planning on making?"

"I don't know. I can't pin down the menu. I think brunch, then I think maybe more like lunch."

The front door opened and Dana called to announce she'd arrived. Chrissie looked at the clock. It was getting close to opening time.

"Look, let's get through today and after we close, we'll sit down and work something out," Sophie said. "I know I'm a little rattled. It's just huge for a place like ours to have an opportunity like this."

"Well, you do takeout for Dallas and her employees all the time. This isn't so different. They're just all coming here to eat."

"You're right. I know I'm overreacting." Sophie took a deep breath. "Okay, I'm over it now. Let's get on with it."

They were particularly busy, it being Friday, a day when more people seemed to go out for lunch, and the first of the early season's visitors began to trickle in. Not the droves Sophie counted on for the summer, but a few more tables than usual were filled. By two o'clock, Chrissie was as ready as Sophie to put the CLOSED sign on the door.

After they'd cleaned up from the day, they went into the restaurant and sat at a table, Sophie with a yellow legal pad and a glass of decaf iced tea in front of her, while Chrissie had fixed herself a cup of coffee.

"Okay. Dallas did mention eleven thirty or so for

the time. So I'm thinking brunch, though I will confirm that with her. We'll need a few appetizers to set the mood; we'll make those stationary because we're not going to have a lot of waitstaff. We have Dana and Margarite, and they both said they could work on Sunday, but we'll need a few more. Dallas agreed to keep the number of guests to match the tables and seats we have, which is forty."

"The weather's supposed to be gorgeous on Sunday. Maybe we could do the appetizers out back on the patio, then come in here for the main course and dessert."

"I like it. I don't have that many outside chairs, but people tend to stand around and mingle at cocktail parties, so it'll be fine. And we'll have to get the outside furniture out of storage and clean it up. I'll ask my husband to do that." She made a note on her pad. "It's May already. I should have it out now anyway."

"So we need some appetizers," Chrissie noted. "Since we're on the Chesapeake, we should have something with crab. Either a hot dip or mini crab cakes."

"I think the crab cakes. Dip can get messy." Sophie made another note.

By the time they'd finished, they'd decided on three appetizers, a strawberry salad, and three main dishes.

"We'll serve the salads, then we'll set up the entrées on the counter and serve those buffet style," Sophie said. "And we can serve dessert at the tables. One dessert. Something springy."

"I have a great recipe for a rhubarb upside-down

cake," Chrissie told her. "I used to make it at Luna and everyone loved it. We should have an ice cream to go with it." She thought for a moment, then snapped her fingers. "Steffie had the best mint ice cream. I wonder if we could get her to make enough for Sunday."

"Perfect. Rhubarb is definitely a spring thing. And mint ice cream would be exactly right. I'll give Stef a call tonight." Sophie made a face. "I don't have a liquor license, though. I can't sell alcohol."

"Why not ask Dallas to bring the wine or whatever she'd like to have served? If it's a private party, I don't know why there'd be a problem."

Sophie nodded. "I'll ask Dallas what she wants and how she'd like to handle it. I expect she'll want to have some beer, since her brother is half of Mad-Mac Brews."

"Ah yes, the St. Dennis brewmeisters. I had some of their beer at Owen's. It was great, but I don't know that beer goes with brunch. She'll probably suggest it, but you might want to shoot that down. Gently of course, since the customer is always right." Chrissie got up and stretched. "So we have our menu. Let's go into the kitchen and see what we're going to have to bring in tomorrow to make this thing happen."

ON SUNDAY MORNING, Chrissie and Sophie stood side by side in front of the glass portion of the back door at Blossoms and watched the stars walk not the red carpet, but the blue-stone walk to the patio behind the restaurant. They'd been preparing, cooking, baking since five that morning, and were ready to start serving. Dallas's husband had dropped off the wine and champagne earlier, and had lent a hand by taking the wineglasses onto the patio and icing the champagne.

"All set to play bartender today?" Sophie had asked when he arrived.

"One of my favorite gigs," he assured her. "So much easier than spaying dogs."

Sophie had turned to Chrissie and explained, "Grant is the town vet. He also has a rescue shelter for dogs, if you ever find yourself wanting furry companionship."

"We do have cats, too," Grant told Chrissie as he carried the cases of wine through the back door and set them on the ground in front of the table that would serve as the bar. "Not so many, because we've found out that my daughter Paige is allergic to them."

"Okay, let's just take a moment and get all our fangirling out of our systems at the same time," Chrissie suggested now. "Otherwise we won't be able to function for the rest of the day."

"Agreed. I could die just looking at Chase Winston." Sophie clutched Chrissie's arm. "He's actually standing on my patio. Looking at my restaurant."

"Ah, actually, he's looking at you, Sophie." Chrissie turned away from the window. "He apparently likes what he sees."

"Wow. We made eye contact."

"Might be a good time to step away from the glass." Chrissie gently pushed Sophie aside. "Wait till he gets a glimpse of that belly of yours."

"I'll convince him it's his." Sophie definitely looked starstruck. "We'll run away to Tuscany and have a dozen more babies."

"Jason might have something to say about that." Chrissie laughed as she removed several trays of roasted tomato tarts from the oven and placed them on racks to cool.

"You guys! You're never going to believe who just got out of a limo out front!" Dana burst into the kitchen, her eyes huge and round. "Laura Fielding!"

"Oh, she's been here before. She came in a few times last summer with Dallas. She's so nice." Sophie turned the mini crab cakes over in their pans on the stove.

"Damn. I wasn't working here last summer." Dana looked as if she was about to cry. "She's my favorite actress. I loved her in *Pretty Maids*."

"That was the first movie Dallas produced on her own. Everyone had written off Laura Fielding as a flake and told Dallas she was making a big mistake casting her. Dallas went ahead and did it anyway," Sophie recalled. "And of course Laura won an Oscar for her performance, with Berry winning best supporting actress. That was the hugest night ever for St. Dennis."

"Berry is . . . ?" Chrissie turned her attention to the previously baked fingerling potatoes wrapped with bacon and placed them into the oven to warm.

"Dallas's grandmother. Beryl Townsend, the actress? She's ancient, but she's still a feisty number," Dana told her.

"She's the older woman who modeled in the fashion show," Sophie told Chrissie. "Everyone in St. Dennis calls her Berry."

"I remember her. Very powerful-looking woman, and I don't mean physically. She just oozed self-confidence." Chrissie knew it when she saw it.

"So everyone always thought she was Dallas's great-aunt, but it turns out she was actually the mother of Dallas and Wade's father," Dana confided. "What a scandal the tabloids made of that when the story went public, but no one around here cared."

"Who was the father? A famous actor? A director?" Chrissie found herself getting caught up in the drama.

"A local judge. He and Berry are engaged now. Finally. After all these years. True love always wins out in the end, you know?" Dana nodded slowly, as if she'd invented the concept.

Margarite came into the kitchen, followed by two teenage girls.

"Do you know who just arrived?" Margarite placed a hand over her heart. "Sidney Warren. Sigh."

"Sigh a few more times, then get ready to take drink orders," Sophie said. "Dallas dropped off wine and champagne earlier." She smiled at one of the girls. "Hey, Paige." To Chrissie, Sophie said, "Paige is Grant's daughter, which makes her Dallas's step-daughter. And Gabi is Ellie O'Connor's sister. Nice to see you both again. You girls prepared to work your butts off today?"

"We are," Paige said, and Gabi nodded.

"I'm going to have you two staffing the appetizer buffet, and then you can help out with the entrées, also being served buffet style. You'll keep an eye on the dishes, let us know when something needs to be replenished, keep the table tidy."

Paige nodded. "Like, if someone puts down a used plate, we grab it and bring it in here."

"Right. I forgot how many times you've done this

before," Sophie said. "Start by taking those small plates outside and put them on the table by the warming trays. Your dad is already out there. And grab that stack of napkins, Gabi . . ."

The patio was beginning to fill up with members of Dallas's staff from River Road Productions, her film company, and others who would be involved in Dallas's next project. A glance out the window assured Chrissie that all was going well. Grant had the bar under control even as he was chatting with some of the partygoers. Paige and Gabi kept the appetizers moving, returning occasionally to refill platters or return used plates.

"How's it going out there?" Sophie asked.

"It's a good party. Everyone's saying how great the food is," Paige said. "I'm hoping there's some of that tomato thing left over. It looks so good and everyone's coming back for seconds." She grinned. "And my dad can't stop eating those potato-and-bacon things."

"Tell your dad to knock it off." Sophie laughed and stirred the pot of asparagus soup on her way to the oven to check the strata she'd prepared the night before to bake today, while Chrissie was busy arranging the salads on their plates. "Dana, how are you doing with the setup in the restaurant?"

"All ready to bring them in whenever you want," Dana replied.

"We should start soon," Chrissie said. "Everything is pretty much ready to serve. We don't want the strata or the soup getting cold."

"Chrissie, when you're finished with the salads, can you turn the chicken and get the waffles going?"

Sophie pulled a baking dish from the oven. "And the oyster fritters—"

"I'm on it."

Before long, the business of serving the group took over everyone's attention, from soup to entrées, and before long, everyone had finished eating. Dallas had decided to talk to the group about her plans for her upcoming film over dessert, so the rhubarb upside-down cake was served along with the spring mint ice cream Steffie had made the night before. "I wouldn't do this for anyone but my brother's wife," she'd told Chrissie. But before dessert was brought out, Dallas had insisted on Sophie and Chrissie coming into the front room to introduce them to her group, and her staff to them. There'd been applause and phones raised to take pictures. It had all been in fun, except for that one moment when, while listening to Sophie thanking them all for coming, an assistant producer had moved a little too close to Chrissie. Before she could blink, his hand had traveled to her waist, and then had gone lower. She'd stepped away, shaking inside, and gone back into the kitchen without saying a word.

By three thirty in the afternoon, Grant had packed up the leftover wine and champagne and helped his daughter clean the patio. Dallas had come into the kitchen to plant a kiss on both Sophie's and Chrissie's foreheads.

"You two are amazing! Honestly, I don't think anyone, anywhere, could have done better than the two of you did today. Everything was delicious. My crew loved it. I can't thank you enough for pulling through for me, especially on such short notice," Dallas'd said.

"Anytime," Sophie told her.

"Actually, it was kind of fun," Chrissie said after Dallas had left and Dana and Margarite were busy cleaning the front room. Except for the creepy guy with the roaming hands. She wondered if she should mention it to Sophie. On the one hand, yes, she should. It had happened in her establishment.

On the other hand, Chrissie couldn't get the words to come out. It had embarrassed her that someone had thought her to be so easy a target. She didn't want Sophie to think of her as weak, or a victim. She couldn't make up her mind.

"Definitely worth losing the day off for, though I don't want to do this every Sunday. I really do need those two days off now more than ever," Sophie was saying as she slumped against the counter, obviously tired.

"I like having Sundays off, too," Chrissie said as she again brought a chair in for Sophie to sit on and rest. "I've got this," she told her.

Sophie sat and kicked off her shoes and uttered a long, happy sigh. "I swear, I could fall asleep right here."

"This is ridiculous. Forget the chair. Go on upstairs and take a nap. I'll finish cleaning up and I'll lock the door. Just leave me a key."

"I know I should argue with you, but I just can't. I'm too tired." Sophie got up. "Just text me when you're leaving and I'll have Jason come down to lock up. Thanks, Chrissie." She gave Chrissie a hug as she walked past her. "You're worth your weight in gold."

"Does that mean I'm going to move from temp to full time?"

"You have to ask?" Sophie smiled as she went through the door. "Silly girl . . ."

Chrissie smiled and mentally patted herself on the back. She'd really fallen in love with this place, and while she'd been 99 percent certain she'd made the cut, she had to ask. She was still smiling when Dana came into the kitchen.

"Boy, what a day, huh? I bet when word gets out, we'll be crazy busy every day this summer, right into the fall. Great for tips." She wiggled her eyebrows. "I might be able to pay my own tuition next semester, give my parents a break. Made a nice start toward that today. Dallas is a great tipper."

"Good for you. You guys worked really hard today," Chrissie said.

"Yeah. It's just amazing to see what's going on in St. Dennis. I've lived here all my life, and I never thought I'd see the day when Hollywood legends would come into town with the same regularity like it's LA or something." Dana shook her head and poured herself a glass of cold water. "Before it was 'discovered,' St. Dennis was just this little bay town with a pretty inn and some great views of the water and a lot of old houses. Then the tourists found us and the next thing we knew, there were shops opening up that sold stuff besides bait and tackle."

Chrissie laughed. "There must have been more here than that."

"Yeah, I'm exaggerating. There were a few restaurants—Lola's and Captain Walt's have been here forever—and the market was there, and a few other places. I don't even know how word got out, but it seemed like overnight, things changed. And every year there are more tourists and more things to draw them to town. There are even festivals now—the Pirate Festival, the Strawberry Festival, Founders Day, you name it."

Chrissie finished up and decided to walk out with Dana rather than bother Jason to lock up.

"And then there are the tours," Dana was saying as they walked out of the kitchen and Chrissie turned off the lights. "Garden tours, historic house tours, ghost tours . . ."

"Ghost tours." Chrissie laughed. "Get out. People fall for that? Let me guess. They have it around Halloween?"

"That would be the Halloween weekend tour. No, the ghost tours are in late May. People come from all over for that one, 'cause you get to go inside some of the houses. My grandparents' house is on it this year. They have the ghost of a five-year-old child who lives in their attic."

Chrissie fought an urge to swipe a hand over her face.

"Please. You don't believe that, Dana."

"Uh-huh. I've heard her. She talks to herself. When I was little, I was afraid of her. When I had to stay over there, I'd get so scared I'd end up sleeping down in the living room instead of in the bed upstairs, 'cause I could hear her. But now that I'm older, I just feel sorry for her. She had a fever and she died up in the attic. That was where she and her mom lived, up there, about a hundred years ago."

Oh brother.

Chrissie didn't trust herself to comment, so she

left through the front door and waited while Dana locked it.

"I can tell you're skeptical, and I don't blame you. If I didn't grow up here and see some of this stuff myself, I'd be rolling my eyes, too. But there are all sorts of things in St. Dennis that can't be explained. Most of us don't even try." Dana walked to her car. "See you on Tuesday."

"Right. Enjoy your day off." Chrissie got into her car and slid behind the wheel, thinking about unexplainable things.

Jared said he'd seen a lot of things he couldn't explain. Sometime she'd have to ask him what else besides UFOs and an abandoned city in Turkey where the houses had no doors.

Chrissie's natural inclination to believe only in what she could see was too strong for her to buy into any of that. Maybe if she saw with her own eyes, she'd feel differently.

She stopped at the sign where River Road flowed into the upper end of Charles Street and thought back to last Sunday when she and Jared had gone sightseeing, and wondered how he'd spent his weekend, and if he'd gone on a walking tour of his own.

WEDNESDAY WAS OVERCAST, and Chrissie had debated whether or not to stop at Steffie's on her way home. For one thing, she was late, since they'd been really busy at Blossoms at lunch. For another, she was tired. In the end, the pull of Scoop was stronger than her fatigue, and she turned onto Kelly's Point Road and parked behind the old crabbers shack. She got out of the car, and as she walked toward the weathered building, she saw Jared on the bench straight ahead. She slowed her step, wondering what he was doing there.

"You're late," he called to her. "I was wondering if I'd been stood up."

He rose as she drew closer. "It's Wednesday, right? Everyone knows that Wednesday is Chrissie's day at Scoop."

Chrissie laughed.

"Come on. Let's see what she has today."

Chrissie still had yet to say a word. All she could think of was that Jared had been waiting for her.

He opened the door, and when they stepped inside, Steffie looked up and said, "What did I tell you, Jared?"

"Okay, so I owe you five dollars," he said good-naturedly.

"And I will collect. I know my customers, and I know my friends." Steffie held out her hand. "Pay up, big boy."

Jared took a five from his wallet and handed it over with a smile on his face. Steffie tucked it into her apron with a grin and told Chrissie, "He was beginning to think you might not come today. I told him you would."

"Obviously you know me better than he does," Chrissie said.

"Obviously. Now, what can I get for you today, Chris?"

Chrissie looked at the board. "Strawberry walnut sounds good. One scoop."

"You should know it was inspired by that salad you made for Dallas's thing last weekend. She told me all about it. Said the food was out of this world. You ever consider catering?" Before Chrissie could respond, Steffie had handed Chrissie her cone and turned to Jared. "And for the man who is five dollars poorer?"

"Three scoops of plain old chocolate in a dish." He nodded in Chrissie's direction. "And she's buying."

Steffie filled a bowl and met them at the cash register, where Chrissie paid up.

"Maybe sometime you'll shock the world and stop in more than once a week," Steffie said as Chrissie and Jared left.

"Let's take a walk." Jared headed toward the center of town and Chrissie followed along. "So I guess you figured you'd learned all there was to know about St. Dennis, you've seen all there is to see."

"What are you talking about?"

"You skip your Sunday walkabout? Or you just wanted to go on your own?"

"Had we talked about doing that again? 'Cause I don't remember having that conversation." The sidewalk was so narrow their hips were almost touching as they walked.

"We didn't. I was just thinking it would have been fun to see the other side of town."

"You could have gone. What stopped you?"

He shrugged. "It was more fun when I did it with you."

"I had to work on Sunday," Chrissie explained. "Dallas had asked Sophie to open the restaurant for a special brunch meeting she wanted to have for her staff. Of course Sophie said yes. How often do you get to cook for Hollywood royalty?"

"Lots of celebrities?"

Chrissie nodded. "Actors, directors, producers, and assistants to all of those."

"So impress me. Who all was there?"

Chrissie rattled off some names.

"You had me at Laura Fielding," he said, his right hand patting his heart. "Another of my crushes."

"She was so nice. Almost all of them were really nice."

"'Almost all' implies some were not." He leaned in her direction and lowered his voice conspiratorially. "Who was the bad egg?"

"It doesn't matter." She shrugged it off and turned her attention to her ice cream. "Strawberry walnut really is good. How's your chocolate?"

"It's fine, and don't change the subject. Seriously, was someone rude to you? Come on," he prodded. "Spill."

"Just some guy. Some assistant something or other. Assistant producer, maybe. He was just . . ." Chrissie thought it over. "Entitled."

"Entitled to do what?"

"To touch me where I wish he hadn't."

"Seriously?"

When she nodded, he said, "What did he do?"

"Oh, you know how some guys are."

"No, I don't."

"He grabbed my butt."

"Did you call him out?"

She shook her head.

"Why not? He had no business doing that."

"I just . . . froze. Besides, I didn't want to embarrass

Dallas." *Or me*, she could have added. *I didn't want to call attention to myself for something like that.*

She had the feeling at that moment that he knew what she'd gone through, that he'd read into her and *he knew.*

"I don't want to talk about it," she said. They passed a trash can and she pitched the remains of her cone into it. She'd lost her appetite.

"You don't have to," he said. "But if you ever wanted to . . . I'm your guy."

"Thanks, Jared. I appreciate that."

I'm your guy. Did he really just say that?

They walked for another half block in silence and stopped in front of the pet store, Bow Wows & Meows, across from the market. In the window were displays of dog clothing modeled by stuffed dogs.

"Do you have a dog?" Chrissie asked him.

"Not right now, but we used to. You?"

"Uh-uh. Never did." She stared at the window. "I'm not sure I get the point of all that. Would you have dressed your dog up like that?"

"I don't know. If you put a rottweiler in a sundress, is it still a rottweiler?"

"Only if she was wearing that pearl necklace."

"Spike might have drawn the line at wearing jewelry. *He* really wasn't the pearl type."

Chrissie laughed again.

They crossed the street in front of Book 'Em and paused for a moment to see the new releases in the window, then they walked on.

"This is Vanessa's shop," Chrissie said when they walked past Bling.

"I know. My future stepmother shops there every time she's in St. Dennis. Loads up on stuff for her two daughters and her daughter-in-law and my sister and whoever else is on her radar that week."

"Is your future stepmother the same person as your father's girlfriend? Has something changed since last week?"

Jared nodded. "Delia. Yeah. They just decided to get married. The wedding's in a couple of weeks."

"That's great. I hope they're really happy and that she keeps writing those fabulous books."

For a moment it appeared he was lost in thought.

"Jared?" She waved a hand in front of his face.

"Oh. Sorry. I just sort of zoned out for a moment."

"I said, I hope your dad and his bride are happy and that she doesn't stop writing."

"She'll never stop. It's what Delia does."

They started to walk back toward Kelly's Point Road.

"So what did you and Sophie cook for the star-studded private feast?" he asked.

Chrissie ran through the menu for him.

"Oh man. That all sounds so good. I wish I'd been there. I love fried chicken and waffles, and you could feed me oyster fritters every day of the week and I'd be a very happy man."

"I make them all the time for Gigi. Next time I'll let you know and you can join us. If you want to, that is."

"If I want to? Seriously? Date and time, all I need to know and I'll be there."

"Okay. I'll keep that in mind."

They reached her car and she stopped. He'd finished his ice cream and tossed the empty dish into a nearby trash can.

"Thanks for the ice cream."

"Never let it be said I don't pay my debts."

"So are you touring the town this Sunday?" he asked.

"I'm planning on it."

"How 'bout I meet up with you again?"

"Sure."

"Put my number into your phone and give me yours. I'll send you a text or you can text me if there's a change. Otherwise, I'll meet you in the lobby at the inn around noon."

They exchanged numbers, and when she was finished putting his information into her phone, she said, "I'll see you on Sunday." She started to walk to her car, then turned. "Can I drop you off at the inn?"

"No, I think I want to walk," he said.

"Okay. If you're sure."

"I'm sure."

Before she could get to her car, he called to her.

"Last time you got to pick where we went. How 'bout this time I choose the itinerary?"

"Sure." She opened the driver's-side door and got in, wondering what he had in mind.

In four days, she'd find out. She could hardly wait.

Chapter Seven

"You be heading down to the inn now." Ruby stood in the kitchen, a mug of tea in her hand and that look on her face that Chrissie's mother always called Ruby's know-it-all look. Her gaze lowered to Chrissie's sandaled feet. "Might want to put on some sneakers."

Chrissie looked down at her sandals. They were white leather and were thickly cushioned, a good choice for walking, she'd thought, since it was Sunday, and Sunday meant walkabout with Jared.

"Might want to put on a shirt with some sleeves and maybe a pair of shorts 'stead of that short skirt you got on."

"May I ask why I should change?" Chrissie said as respectfully as possible.

"Sun gonna be hot today. Don't want to catch a burn." Ruby drank some tea, then opened the cookie jar. "Looks like Owen cleaned us outta those chocolate cookies you made the other day."

"I'll make more when I get back." Chrissie kissed Ruby on the cheek and tried to ignore the fact that the woman had that same look on her face, the one that said *I know things you don't know.* The look Chrissie had been trying to learn to ignore since she arrived on the island and still hadn't figured out how. "Are you sure you don't want to visit with Grace today? I don't mind waiting if you've changed your mind and you want to take a few minutes to get ready."

"I be fine right here. Got that new book to finish. But you see her at the inn, you tell her I'll be calling on her this week."

"I'll see you in a while." Chrissie went out the back door, then stopped. Had she told Ruby she was going to the inn? She didn't think she had. "Gigi," she called back into the store, "how did you know I was going to the inn?"

"How do you think I knew?"

Chrissie shook her head and went toward the car, then changed her mind and decided to walk. She was early, so she wasn't afraid of missing Jared. She went around the back of the inn and over the dune to the road, then crossed the bridge into St. Dennis. Ruby had been right about one thing: it was going to get progressively warmer as the day went on, but the white tank top and the short khaki skirt would be just right if the temperature rose, so what was all that about longer sleeves and sneakers and shorts? Chrissie wondered if Ruby had gotten mixed messages somehow from where it was that her *knowing* came from.

She smiled at a group of bikers who passed her who apparently were heading toward the island, since there was nothing else at this farthest end of

Charles Street except for a few short side streets.
The bikes and the helmets all had ISP stickers for
the Inn at Sinclair's Point, and she wondered if they
were just early season tourists or if maybe they were
there to check out the houses Cass had for sale. The
last time they'd spoken, Cass had said she had three
spec houses completed and they were beginning
their ad campaign. Chrissie wondered how having all the new people on the island would change
things. Ruby didn't seem at all concerned, so she
shouldn't be, either. She wished she could afford to
buy the house that would be built on the lot where
the old Singer house had stood. She knew ancestors
of hers had built that place. She'd stopped at the
graveyard that still stood undisturbed next to the
foundation of the old house. She was pretty sure one
of her great-grandmothers was buried in that yard,
and she kept meaning to ask Ruby about it. Her
mother had told her so little, she was never really
sure who was who.

She tried to keep her mind focused on the island,
and the graveyard, and the lost relatives—even the
bikers—anything to keep her from thinking about
Jared and the fact that he'd wanted to spend the afternoon with her.

How crazy was that?

The fact that he found her interesting enough to
spend time with, even as a friend, was mind-blowing.
Jared was everything she thought a guy should be
now that she knew better. He was respectful, he
seemed interested in what she had to say and listened when she spoke, he wasn't pushy—he'd even
seemed somewhat indignant about that staff member

of Dallas's who'd grabbed her butt—and he treated her like a person who had feelings and opinions of her own. The fact that he was probably the hottest guy she'd ever been within five feet of, well, that was a bonus. She'd always liked dark-haired guys with blue eyes, guys who were buff but didn't try to show it off, guys who had a sense of humor, guys who were nice guys.

Guys like Jared, but they'd never seemed to notice her.

She felt that just getting to where she knew definitively what she liked in a man was a step forward for her. It had been so long since she'd noticed. Not that she was looking for someone. There was that whole trust issue to get past, but she'd cleared one hurdle, and that was enough for now. She'd know when she was ready for another relationship. She was pretty sure she wasn't now, but being friends with Jared was helping her to relax and be herself with a guy. Knowing he didn't expect anything from her helped a lot.

Still, he was one gorgeous friend.

He was waiting on the porch outside the back door of the inn when she arrived, and she wasn't surprised to see a pretty redheaded woman talking to him. Jared seemed to be a magnet for beautiful women. Chrissie slowed her step. Had he forgotten they'd agreed to meet for a tour date? How embarrassing would that be? She'd almost stopped walking when he looked over and saw her there, and he smiled.

"Hey, Chrissie." He looked at his watch. "Right on time."

She tried not to let it show that she'd been holding a big breath that she now had to let out. As she walked toward him, she heard him say, "Gotta go. My friend's here. Have a great afternoon."

He came down off the steps and said, "So are you ready for our adventure today?"

"I am. Was there anything in particular you wanted to see? Someplace you want to go?" Chrissie felt the heat from the redhead's glare as the woman walked away. She tried really hard not to feel good about that.

"Yes, and yes. Come on."

They were at the end of the driveway where it met the parking lot. Chrissie started off down the drive, but after she'd taken several steps, she realized Jared wasn't with her. She turned to find him where she'd left him, his hands on his hips, his dark glasses covering his eyes.

"Where are you going?" he asked.

"I thought we were going to explore St. Dennis." She pointed toward the center of town.

"We are." He took several steps in her direction. "But I thought we agreed it would be my choice this time around."

"We did."

"Okay, then, come on." He took her by the elbow and led her down toward the water's edge.

"Where are we going?"

"We're going to explore St. Dennis."

Jared smiled at the young man standing at the water's edge as they approached the dock. "Thanks for watching this one for me. I'm sure you could have rented it several times over."

"I couldn't do that with your gear in it already," said the guy, who appeared to Chrissie to be about fifteen.

Jared slipped him what must have been a tip. The boy pocketed the bill and said, "Thanks. Have fun," before walking away.

Jared turned to Chrissie. "You ready?"

"For what?" She looked at the boat, which she recognized. "Is that Owen's boat?"

Jared nodded. "He loaned it to me for the day. I picked it up at Alec's earlier this morning. You know what it is?"

She rolled her eyes and pretended to be insulted. "Please, you're talking to a woman who's been living on the bay for the past eight—almost nine—months now, and who spent a lot of summers here when I was a kid. Like I wouldn't know a deadrise when I saw one. Especially since the name is right there across the back: *Gigi*. Duh."

He laughed good-naturedly. "I have to admit I'd never seen one before I started hanging around with Owen. Interesting design, that sharp bow and the flat bottom. I guess it makes a great work boat for shallow areas if you're crabbing or digging oysters." He reached a hand to her. "Come on. Let's go see what we can see."

He grinned and helped her step onto the deck. The soles of her sandals were leather, and she barely avoided slipping, catching herself before she fell.

"Where are we going?" she asked for the second time.

"Just relax and enjoy the ride."

He untied the boat from the dock and started the

inboard motor. There were two chairs fixed to the deck, and he pointed to one.

"I assume you know how to drive one of these."

Jared laughed. "I've yet to find the craft I couldn't drive. Have a seat and we'll be on our way."

"Do you know where you're going?"

"So many questions." That grin again.

He backed the boat away from the dock and straightened her out, then headed north, driving slowly, taking his time.

"Interesting perspective of the town from here, don't you think?" he said as they went a little farther out into the bay.

"There's the park," she said, stretching her neck and looking toward the shore.

He pushed the throttle a little to increase the speed. "And around this next bend . . ."

"Scoop and the marina." She got up and went to the side of the open cabin to lean on the half wall. "There's Captain Walt's. And there's Alec's boatyard. I've never seen the town from the water. It looks so quaint and picturesque."

"Everything looks different from the water." Jared stood behind her, one arm still on the steering wheel, and watched as they passed the big stone jetty upon which Captain Walt's restaurant had been built.

"Now for some fun." He slowly let out the engine until they were speeding into the bay. Chrissie held on to her sunglasses and tried to hold back her hair, which was whipping around her face like a pale blond curtain.

"Goat Island," he said, pointing ahead, but she couldn't hear him over the engine.

"What?" she yelled.

He eased back the engine. "Goat Island."

"Oh, I remember Goat Island. In late August, they have a weekend they call Discover St. Dennis. It's when they show off the town for tourists. They have a big parade and boat races. The island is the turning point for the race. The boats go around the island, then head back to the finish line." Chrissie remembered the last time she'd been in St. Dennis for the big celebratory weekend. Ten years ago? Eight? She couldn't remember. "They have a cocktail party on Friday night to raise money for community things, like new playground equipment. It used to be a big boon for the town because it brought people into the restaurants and the B and Bs. I missed it last year by a month. I didn't get here until September."

"Sounds like a fun weekend. Maybe I'll come back for it this year if I'm not out of the country."

They were almost to the island, which was small, rocky, and uninhabited.

"It looks smaller than it used to." Chrissie stepped away from the cabin to lean on the railing near the back of the boat. "Of course, I've only seen it from the shore, so maybe it's just a matter of perspective."

"It could be smaller now." He slowed the boat even more as they drew closer to the narrow beach. "I've read about the bay waters rising and devouring low-lying areas. I wouldn't be surprised if this little island has lost some ground. Owen told me that a number of islands have disappeared altogether. It's high toward the middle, but the beach is low."

He drove the boat around the island, careful to

avoid the large rocks that seemed to grow out of the water.

"Yeah, look there." He stood so close behind Chrissie she could feel his breath on the back of her neck. She tried to ignore the goose bumps that rose on the skin there and the warmth that spread through her body. "See the rocks jutting out of the water, and the ones closer to shore? I bet they were part of the beach at one time. And I'd be real surprised if they still had boats racing around out here. It would be too easy to rip open your hull." He turned back toward the steering wheel. "Which is why we're heading out."

He swung toward the center of the back, and once he hit deeper water, made a wide turn.

"Where to now?" she asked, stepping into the shade of the canvas canopy that hung over the open cabin. The sun was getting hotter by the minute, or so it seemed. She could feel her shoulders starting to sizzle in the short time she'd been out of the cabin area.

"Up a lazy river."

She narrowed her eyes. "All the rivers around here are pretty lazy."

He pointed ahead. "Keep your eyes open and you'll see."

Again, he took his time, keeping the boat at a slow and easy speed.

"Hey, look. That's the Altman House." Chrissie pointed toward land. "That's the only house to be hit by a cannonball during the War of 1812. The people in town knew the British would be sailing at night and would fire on the houses closest to the water. So they kept their houses dark and set lanterns hanging in the trees. When the Brits came close to the harbor—which was too shallow to bring them close enough to shore to see much of anything except the lights from the lanterns—"

"They fired at the trees. Owen told me that story."

"Only one house was hit, and that's it." Chrissie pointed to the redbrick house that stood back off the bay at the end of a lush grassy lawn. Pilings had been built to shore up the dock where a long cabin cruiser was moored. "Gigi told me one time that the cannonball is still embedded in the back wall of the house."

"Imagine, we're probably right about where that British ship was when it fired that cannon," Jared said.

"The town was besieged by more than the British. You might have heard the stories about the pirates that used to come into the cove."

"Pirates," he said flatly. "Now who's talking about the improbable?"

"No, they really did. Gigi used to tell us the stories when we were little. They'd tie up in the cove and come ashore in the middle of the night, then they'd capture all the young women in the town and take them over to the square, where they'd keep them for three days, then ransom them back to the husbands or fathers or brothers."

"And you believe that?" He scoffed. "Any self-respecting pirate would have just taken the women and rowed back to the ship. After they pillaged the town."

"No, it's true." Chrissie laughed. "Gigi said so. There's even a weekend in St. Dennis to commemorate the event every year."

"Sounds more like another event intended to bring in tourists than a commemoration of a real event."

"Well, of course they're exploiting it. But it did happen."

"So they, what, call Rent-a-Pirate?"

"No. Guys from town dress up like pirates and carry off their wives or girlfriends or sisters, then they have a sort of auction and someone has to cough up the cash to get them released."

"Does St. Dennis have some kind of commemoration every month? It seems like there's always something."

"That's because something is always going on. It's a tourist town, and the local businesses do well as long as the tourists keep coming back. They have events right through the winter. November and December are really busy around here."

"I'll bet." He turned the wheel slightly to the left. "Owen told me the War of 1812 was when some people were driven out of St. Dennis and onto the island."

"By 'some people,' you mean our ancestors—Owen's, Lis's, and mine," she said. "Did he tell you why they were sent across the river? They had to ford it, right about where the bridge is now, with only whatever possessions they could carry."

"He said they were loyal to the crown, and that after the Brits conscripted several young men from St. Dennis to serve in their navy, the loyalists were blamed."

"They literally forced them onto the island, assuming they'd most likely die there. Cannonball Island was considered to be uninhabitable. There was nothing there but a bunch of scrub pines and sand and marsh."

"I guess folks didn't take kindly to their boys being abducted," Jared said.

"You think that's a good enough reason to send twenty-some families to their death?"

"They didn't die, though, did they?'

"No, but only because they were tougher and smarter than anyone had given them credit for," she snapped.

"So, yes, they'd have been tough." He slowed the engine even more to the point where they were almost drifting. "How'd they build their shelters if there was only scrub pine available?"

"Relatives who were not loyalists brought them supplies by boat so the others on the mainland wouldn't see they were helping," she told him.

"Well, then, they weren't exactly left to die, and all the folks in St. Dennis weren't evil." Before she could reply, he said, "Just looking for facts here."

"Sorry. Depending on who you talk to, the people in St. Dennis were either the devil's spawn or folks just seeking justice for their lost boys," she said. "Gigi was always sort of proud to have been descended from one of the early people on the island. Owen's dad was obsessed with what he perceived as the injustice of it all. He never got over it, never let Owen or Lis make friends with any of the kids from St. Dennis. He was a mean cuss anyway."

"Well, both Owen and Lis are great people, so apparently none of his meanness stuck."

"Lucky for the rest of us." Chrissie walked out onto the deck of the slow-moving boat. "Oh, that's the New River over on the left."

"I know. That's where we're headed."

"Why the river?"

"We're sightseeing, remember?" Jared flashed a smile. "Get ready to see some sights."

He turned into the river and took the sharp curve gently. The banks were heavily wooded until they'd gone about a quarter mile upstream.

"There on your right are the warehouses Dallas bought for her studio." He pointed up ahead.

"How do you know that?" Chrissie frowned. "I've been in St. Dennis longer than you and I just found that out last week."

"I made it my business to find out. Okay, I just found out over the weekend, and that was by accident. Grace told me."

"Ha. So much for trying to pass yourself off as an expert."

Jared laughed. "And right up there, behind those trees, if you look up the hill . . ."

"It's Blossoms!" Chrissie grinned. "I knew the woods were thick behind the building, but I had no idea they extended so far along the waterline."

"Wait till you see what comes next."

"You seem to know a lot about River Road from the back side. Did you already make this run?"

"Only from the road," he admitted. "And that was a week or so ago."

The boat scared a small flock of birds that rested on the low limbs of a tree that hung over the water. They scattered in a cluster. Moments later, the woods gave way to spacious lawns that surrounded stately homes and that ended in docks where boats were moored.

"Nice neighborhood," Chrissie said. "I drive on River Road every day and I never saw this section."

"It's because the houses are set so far back, and most of them have evergreens or wooded areas planted along the roadway."

A little farther up the river, Jared cut the engine again. "See that house?" He pointed to a Victorian mansion. A carriage house overlooked the water and what might have been a boathouse sat close to the dock.

"Who lives there?"

"Berry Townsend. Dallas's aunt. She was—"

"I know. A great film star. She was in the fashion show last week. But I heard she's actually Dallas's grandmother, not her aunt."

"Really? Are you sure that's not just gossip?"

"Nope. Reliable source and all that."

"Interesting. Anyway, that's some pad, right?"

"It really is." Chrissie was still standing. "There's a fence around the front. I guess to keep the riffraff out. I don't blame her. It's a beautiful property. If I lived in a house like that, I'd probably have the entire place fenced in, too."

"Somehow I don't see you in a place like that," he said.

"Oh?"

"I think it's too over the top for you. Doesn't suit your personality. As least, as I know it."

She turned to look at him. "What do you think suits me?"

"Someplace . . . I don't know, someplace not ostentatious. More comfortable, more casual, relaxed, maybe. I don't see myself walking into that mansion and kicking off my shoes, for example. I don't see you comfortable in a place where you can't kick off your shoes, either."

"That's because neither of us are Hollywood royalty," she told him.

Jared nodded slowly. "That could be it."

"So where to now?" Chrissie asked.

"Now we turn around down here where the river gets wider, and we start back in the opposite direction."

He kept the slow pace so as to not disturb the boats tied at the docks they passed, but once back out onto the bay, he opened the engine and sped toward town. Chrissie'd expected him to dock at the inn, but he kept going.

"I thought you said we were going back." She pointed to the inn.

"Nope. We still have sights to see."

"The inn looks so regal from here," she said. "When you come in through the front, you don't appreciate that there are different wings. The porch looks like it came right off a southern plantation." She thought for a moment. "Which probably isn't a surprise, since I think I read somewhere that the original structure—that center part—was built in the 1850s."

"It's impressive." He pointed to the tennis courts. "Look, that's where I gave up three tennis games in a row to one of my crewmembers last week."

"Sounds like someone needs to practice."

"Someone needs to find a different game. For some reason, tennis just isn't mine."

"More into team sports?"

"Not really that, either. I played soccer when I was in school, but I missed a lot of games because my dad liked to take me with him when he went on dives, so I wasn't a reliable teammate."

"He just took you out of school whenever he felt like it?"

"Pretty much." He glanced over his shoulder at her. "Don't judge, or think he wasn't a great dad, because he was. Besides, I learned more on those trips than I would have learned in a classroom. Geography, history, anthropology, archaeology, languages— and I was exposed to so many different cultures at a young age. I learned to see the whole world as one. One planet. One people. I'll never forget the lessons I learned from him." They passed the remnants of a lighthouse that once stood at the end of Bayview Drive, and passed the cove that harbored Sunset Beach. Jared fell silent until they crossed the sound and the island came into view.

"Oh, I never saw the island from the water," Chrissie said. "It looks almost deserted."

"From here it does, yeah." He pointed off to the left. "There's the store."

She crossed the deck and leaned on the railing. "I can see my room from here. Second floor, third window on the right."

"Now I know where to put the ladder," he said.

She turned and looked at him. "Planning a little B and E?"

"You never know when wanderlust might strike and I might need my travel companion."

"Tossing a few stones at the window would be just as effective."

"I have a hell of a pitch. Ruby might get annoyed if I break a window or two."

"Good point. In that case, the ladders are in the garden shed."

"I'll make a note."

She turned back to the island view and he guided the boat into one of the coves.

"Owen said one reason why he likes his deadrise is the flat bottom," Jared said. "You can take it into shallow water and not get stuck. Unless, of course, you beach it. Then all bets are off."

"I can see some of those little houses Cass is selling. I think she was having them open to the public today. She's hoping to sell a few on spec." Having ditched the sandals, Chrissie stood on her tiptoes. "Have you seen any of them yet?"

"No. I keep meaning to, though. I'm curious."

"If I could afford it, I'd buy one. There's something so incredibly cool about what she's doing. Building new houses using as much of the old material as she can—the wood that made up the floors, the bricks from the fireplaces, in some cases the glass from the windows." Chrissie sighed. "I'd love to live in a place so full of history."

"You live in a place full of history right now. Owen said the store was one of the first buildings to go up on the island, maybe *the* first."

"True, but it's not mine. I've never had a place that was just mine. I think I'd like it." She shrugged. "At least, I'd like the chance to find out."

"Well, then, I hope one day you do that. Find a

place that's just yours. I think everyone should live alone for a while. It's easier to sort things out when you're by yourself."

He drove the boat out of the cove and toward the point.

"Lis and I used to sit on that pier," she told him as they passed by. "We used to crab there. Sometimes I still go all the way out to the end by myself and watch the sun set on the bay. It's such a peaceful place."

He drove around to the other side of the island where the house Owen and Cass were renovating stood in a clearing.

"My great-grandad—Gigi's Harold, her husband—was born in that house," Chrissie told him. "His father was a waterman and he built the place for his wife before he'd even proposed to her."

"Now, there's a confident man."

"No doubt," she agreed. "He had to have known she'd say yes. They raised a family of seven children and she died right after the seventh was born. Six months later, he married a younger woman and had seven more kids with her."

"Not only confident but virile."

Chrissie laughed. "She died before he did, then he passed away a few months later." She stared at the island and the house for what seemed like a long time. "For years I wanted to know about my family. My mother always blew me off, didn't think any of it was interesting. But Ruby comes out with these gems every once in a while without me even asking. I love to think about them living here and working so hard to make a good life for themselves and each other and their children. There must have been something really strong inside those people. I want to think that some of their strength has come down through the generations. I want to be able to be that strong."

"You seem pretty strong—pretty together to me," he told her.

"Do I?" Her smile was slow in coming. "That might be the nicest thing anyone's ever said to me. Thank you."

Could she ever tell him who she used to be? How New Chrissie had fought so hard and come so far from Old Chrissie? Would she ever be able to tell anyone just how bad things had been for her?

"Anyway, that old place was vacant for years, since Harold's youngest brother died. We used to play in it when we were kids. Gigi gave it to Owen to fix up. It's going to be beautiful when he's finished with it."

"He reminds me every chance he gets," Jared said. "They're going to have one hell of a view, that's for sure."

"If you're nice to him, maybe he'll let you sit on his back patio and watch the sun set sometime."

Around one more curve of land, and there was Jared's ship, the *Cordelia E.*

"It's bigger than it looks from the island," Chrissie said.

"She's a good size. Probably a little bigger than what I need for this job, but she's a favorite of mine. Dad's, too. He named her after Delia, as you can see." He pointed to the name of the ship painted across the back.

He drove around the ship, waved to the crewman

on the deck who watched him go by, then drove the deadrise into the mouth of the river, where he pulled back on the throttle.

"The ship you're salvaging, the merchant ship. It's around here somewhere, right?"

Jared pointed down. "We're over it."

"It's right down there?"

He nodded, and she leaned over the side of the boat.

"I don't see anything," she said. "The water's so dark here."

"The water in the Chesapeake is dark, and the river's no better. It's a tough place to dive, but that's what makes it interesting."

"But how can you see if it's so dark?'

"We bring in lights." He grinned. "They cast a ghostly glow over everything, so it's just a little on the creepy side the first time you experience it, but you get used to it soon enough."

"Not me. I'd never get used to it. Being underwater and in the dark?" The thought of it made her wince. "I don't think so."

"Anytime you want to go down there with me, you just say the word. My sister always keeps a wet suit on board here, so you could—"

"No. No, I couldn't."

"I bet if you dove someplace where the water was clear and there were pretty little fishes swimming around you, you'd love it."

"I'm pretty sure I wouldn't. But we'll never know, because I'll never do it."

"Well, your loss. It's a whole new beautiful, ever-changing world, Chris."

"I'm happy for you that you found something you love. Now change the subject."

He groaned, apparently frustrated, but did as she asked. She moved to the stern and took a long, deep breath. "The air smells saltier here than it did closer to St. Dennis."

"That's because the bay's saltier here. We're closer to the ocean, which is salt water. St. Dennis is close to the New River, which is freshwater, and there's more freshwater in the upper portion of the bay. Remember, the Chesapeake's an estuary, and the ocean water flows up into it just as the Susquahanna River flows down. So some areas have salt water, some fresh. St. Dennis is in one of those areas where the two meet and mix."

"I never think about the river flowing down," she admitted. "I just always think it's salty because the water around the island is salt water."

"Anyway, the ship is down there and it's making me crazy not to be down there with it. I know Owen's getting antsy and my crew got impatient, so I had to let most of them go home until we get the thumbs-up to dive. I did keep a couple of my guys to stay with the boat when I'm not on it. We alternate nights on shore and nights on the boat."

"So you have sleeping quarters?"

"Enough for eight men. And a cabin for the captain." He nudged her with his elbow. "That would be me."

She stared over the railing into the dark water. "Gigi always refers to that ship down there as the tea ship."

"That's what it was carrying when it went down.

It apparently was running from a ship that would have confiscated its cargo, so the captain tried to hide it in the river. Like you can hide a ship that big. He didn't realize how shallow the river is here, and he went aground, and then the storm hit. I have some photos we took on the last dive before we were shut down. They're on the *Cordy E*, though. I'll show you sometime."

"Can you see the Native American village in the photos?"

"Not really."

"Then how do you know it was there?"

"Artifacts that were found there. A lot of pottery. Some fishing implements, tools, arrowheads. Local legend pointed us in that direction, and the vestiges of the people who lived there proved the legend right."

"Gigi said that at one time, that piece of land"— she pointed across the river opposite the island— "extended clear on out past the middle of the river, so close you could walk from one side to the other at low tide."

"She wouldn't have been alive that long ago," Jared pointed out.

"I don't know how she knows." Ruby's words when Chrissie was leaving the store rang in her ears— "*How do you think I know?*"—and Chrissie smiled.

"What?" he asked.

"Nothing." She shook her head. "Just . . . nothing."

He idled the engine and opened the cooler that had been on the boat when they picked it up.

"Water?" he asked, holding up a bottle.

"I'd love one." She took the bottle and opened it. She drank some and wished she could pour the rest of it over her arms and legs. Gigi had been right about the danger of sunburn, even this early in the season. Her bare arms and legs were soaking up the heat. And if she'd known she'd have to be climbing on—then later off—a boat, she wouldn't have worn a short skirt. Gigi'd been right about that, too.

Of course she had.

She could feel his gaze and sensed there was something he was about to say, but he wasn't saying it. His indecision was making her a little uncomfortable.

"So what else can't you explain?" she asked to break the silence.

"What?" He seemed to snap out of the fog he'd been in.

"You said there were many things you'd seen that you couldn't explain. UFOs being one of them. The abandoned city. What else?"

He thought for a moment. "There's a place where airplanes disappear without a trace. They go missing, but no sign is ever found of the plane or the passengers or the cargo."

"The Bermuda Triangle. Everyone's heard of that."

"Correction. The Alaskan Triangle." He smiled smugly.

"I never heard of the Alaskan Triangle. I think you just made it up."

He shook his head. "Nope. It's true. Over sixteen thousand people have disappeared in the Alaskan wilderness. Did you ever hear of Hale Boggs?"

"No."

"He was the majority leader of the US House of Representatives. In 1972, the plane he was on disappeared between Anchorage and Juneau. There was a massive search, as you'd expect for one of our highest-elected officials. Civilian planes as well as military—close to one hundred planes—and an untold number of people searched on land over an area that covered thirty-two thousand miles."

"And . . . ?" She gestured for him to continue.

"And nothing. They never found the plane nor any trace of it."

"I thought we were talking about things you'd seen that you couldn't explain."

He nodded.

"A couple of years ago, the brother of one of my regular crew flew his plane up there, just wanted to look around, see what the wilderness was all about. Long story short, the plane took off one morning from Juneau and disappeared. Our entire crew went up to join the search team but nothing was ever found. No plane, no distress signal, no trace."

"I thought all planes had black boxes."

"It was an old private plane, but it should have had a locator transmitter on board, yes. There's no explanation as to why there was no signal. We searched for ten days, and I can tell you those were the roughest ten days of my life. I'd never want to do that again."

"None of the other planes were ever recovered, either?"

"Not that I ever heard about."

"Huh." She thought it over. "What do you think happened?"

Jared shrugged. "I honestly don't know. Some have suggested some type of magnetic field, others have said there are holes in the glaciers that can swallow up a plane and disappear after an avalanche. I have no theory. Like I said before, there are many things we can't explain. Even some things we've observed ourselves."

"There has to be a logical explanation."

"When you figure it out, make sure to tell me, okay? I'll pass on the information to my crewman. Maybe you can help him find his brother."

"I used to have Alaska on my bucket list of places to visit. I think I'll take that one off."

"Don't be so quick to dismiss it. It's beautiful, wild, and in the warm season—which maybe is July—it's worth exploring. But it can be a dangerous place, no question about it."

"Like I said. Off the bucket list."

"So anything else you want to see while we're out here?" he asked.

"I'd say your tour was pretty comprehensive. The wreck in the river? Check. Cannonball Island? The inn? Charming historic bayside town? Check, check, and check." She finished the last bit of water in the bottle. "Oh, and all the fancy houses on River Road. Check those, too."

"Then I guess we can give Owen's boat back." Jared stepped under the canopy and started the engine. Within minutes they were skimming the coast of the island, then St. Dennis, until they reached the small dock where Alec kept boats he was working on. Jared lifted the cooler and set it on the dock, then showed Chrissie how to tie the boat securely and helped her from the boat onto the dock.

She was prepared to walk back to the inn, so she was surprised when Jared took his car keys from his pocket.

"I drove down here to get the boat this morning," he explained as he grabbed the cooler. "I'll drive you back to the island."

"Are you sure you don't mind?"

"Positive."

He'd left his rented sedan under a tree, where the shade had kept the leather seats from frying in the full sun. He unlocked the car and Chrissie got into the passenger seat while Jared placed the cooler in the trunk and got into the driver's seat.

"So what do you have planned this week?" he asked as he started the car and pulled out of the parking place.

"Work, mostly." She thought about it for a moment. "Actually, that's pretty much it. How 'bout you?"

"I think I'll drive over to Annapolis, spend a few days with an old friend while I have the time, and hope we get the all clear soon so we can go back to work. At least Owen has his house to work on."

"Well, if you get bored, I'm sure Cass would be happy to give you a tour of her houses. It's a development, sort of, just not all the houses together on the same street or in the same area. There are a few on Dune Drive, but they're scattered here and there among the dunes."

Jared was already driving over the bridge onto the island. He pulled into the store's lot and put the car into park but didn't turn off the engine.

"Chrissie, I want to ask you something."

"What's that?"

"I told you my dad's getting married in two weeks. The Saturday after next."

"To Delia Enright, yes, you did. It's exciting."

"Well, for them it is. Not to say I'm not excited and happy for my dad and for Delia, but . . ." Jared paused. "So here's the thing. Delia told me I have to bring a date for the weekend. The entire weekend, which begins on Thursday and ends on Sunday night, so we might as well say Monday. She said something about wanting an even number at the table. The problem is I'm not dating anyone, and there's no one I could stand to be around for four days straight. Except you. Please don't take this the wrong way, but you don't act like most women." He paused again. "That was a compliment, by the way, in case you're wondering."

"Okay." Her brain was beginning to fog up. Was he asking her to be his date for his father's wedding?

"Would you go with me, Chris? Would you be my date for the weekend? No pressure on you to . . . well, you know, we'll be together a lot that weekend, but I don't want you to think I'm going to take advantage of the situation, if you know what I mean. You're the only woman I know whose company I enjoy enough to even think I could spend that much time with and not wish I hadn't."

He was. He did.

"Let me get this straight. You're asking me to be your date for your father's wedding, no strings, just to have as the obligatory companion for the weekend."

"That's pretty much it, yeah."

She needed to think about this. Four days away with Jared as his friend-slash-date?

"I need to think about it."

"What's to think about? We're friends, right? I just want a friend for those four days. Someone I feel comfortable with. That I don't have to feel like I'm on all the time, or that I have to try to impress her. I never feel like I need to be someone else when I'm with you."

"Who do you feel like?"

"I feel like myself. And I always feel like that's enough for you."

"Well, thank you." Chrissie paused. "But I still have to think about it." When he looked like he was about to protest again, she said, "For one thing, I have to make sure Sophie is okay with me taking off what for her is half her week. And she's getting more pregnant all the time. Which means she's more tired—" Chrissie stopped. "Wait. Your dad's marrying Delia Enright. Sophie's probably invited to the wedding. I couldn't ask for the same time off. If she's not going to be there, she's going to depend on me to—"

Jared held up a hand as if to stop the flow of words.

"Sophie isn't related to Delia. Delia was Craig Enright's first wife, remember? Sophie's mom was the second or third wife. While they're a pretty friendly bunch, I'd be real surprised if Sophie and her brother were invited to Delia's wedding. I think it's just going to be family and maybe a few very close friends."

Still . . . four days with Jared . . .

"So okay, take a few days to think about it." He opened the driver's-side door and got out, then walked around the car to open her door. "You can let me know this week. How's Wednesday sound?"

Chapter Eight

Chrissie arrived at Blossoms early on Tuesday morning hoping to have a few minutes to talk to Sophie before Dana got there.

She'd been awake the previous two nights, thinking about Jared's invitation and vacillating between accepting and making an excuse as to why she couldn't go to his father's wedding. She really wanted to go, even though at first she'd had a hard time admitting why, but in the end it seemed flat-out stupid to lie to herself. She liked him. A lot. And she was attracted to him—who wouldn't be? She hadn't wanted to, hadn't wanted to like or be attracted to anyone— but there it was. He was everything she needed to stay away from, and yet she felt like she was under some kind of a spell.

If he'd been trying hard to make her like him, if he'd come on really strong, or if he'd tried to seduce her, she'd have felt entirely different. But he'd done none of those things. He'd simply been a nice, friendly guy who said he enjoyed her company. Chrissie couldn't deny that she liked his. The fact that

he was movie-star handsome and had a great sense
of humor and a phenomenal build should have been
in his favor. But she'd thought the same about Doug
when they first met, and those things that had caught
her eye in the beginning hadn't served her well after a
while. With Doug, it had all been only skin deep.

Jared isn't Doug.

She'd spent the past two nights telling herself that
fact. So while she reminded herself of the similarities,
she also reminded herself of their differences. Doug
had been a flatterer, a man who always told you what
he thought you wanted to hear. At least, in the beginning he had. After a while, he no longer bothered
to tell her she looked pretty, maybe because she'd
stopped caring how she looked.

Things had become so strained that shortly before
she left, she'd asked him why he stayed with her if he
was as bored by her as he'd professed to be.

He'd grabbed her ponytail and pulled her head
back as far as it would go, exposing her neck. For
one terrifying second, she'd envisioned a knife in his
hand, saw her own blood spatter across the room.

"Because you belong to me," he'd told her. Long
moments passed before he'd set her free.

That was when she knew the time for her to leave
was closer than it had ever been. The day she'd
planned for would come sooner rather than later.
Within a week, she was gone, but the memory of that
mind-numbing fear had never gone away.

But Jared was nothing like Doug. And the chance
to attend such a fun, happy event with Jared, even as
a friend, was almost too tempting to pass up.

She decided she'd leave it up to the fates. If she

asked for that weekend off and Sophie said no, then that would be her answer to Jared as well.

"He invited you to his father's wedding to Delia?" Sophie had looked more than a little surprised, though she did try to cover it. "That's fabulous! You're going to have such a good time. Those Enrights know how to party, believe me. Have you met Delia before?"

Chrissie shook her head, surprised by Sophie's easy acquiescence. On the one hand, she was relieved of making a decision. On the other, now she had to go.

". . . and he's just darling," Sophie was saying.

"Wait . . . who?"

"Nick Enright. Delia's son. He's a marine biologist, works along the Delaware Bay. His wife, India, is an attorney; she's from Devlin's Light. They have a son who must be twelve or so, a daughter who's maybe eight, and they adopted a young girl named Corri, who's in her teens." Sophie went into an explanation about Corri's roots—she was the adopted daughter of India's deceased brother—even as the thought swirled around in Chrissie's head that she was actually going to do this.

"Chrissie, you look shocked. You didn't really think I'd say no, did you?"

"I wasn't sure. I thought maybe since I've only been working here a few weeks, you're not obligated to give me time off."

"I'd never want to be responsible for anyone missing out on a weekend like that," Sophie assured her.

"A weekend like what?" Dana came into the kitchen.

Before Chrissie could respond, Sophie said, "Jared

Chandler asked Chrissie to be his date for his father's wedding to Delia Enright."

Dana frowned. "I thought you said you were just friends."

"We are just friends. He didn't want to take a *date* date, but he had to bring someone to keep the tables balanced or something." Chrissie felt compelled to repeat, "We really are just friends. He's in a pinch and asked me to bail him out. That's all."

"I'm his friend and he didn't ask me," Dana pouted.

"Take it up with him, because honestly, I don't know why he asked me except—" Chrissie began, then stopped. Dana had a point. He could have asked her or anyone else, but he'd chosen Chrissie. "Except that we really are good friends. I think he didn't want pressure from anyone who'd expect anything of him. End of story."

"End my butt. It won't be the end until after the wedding and we hear all about who wore what. That's a pretty fancy crew, you know." Sophie slipped her apron over her head and studied the blackboard where the night before she'd posted today's specials. "Delia's daughter Zoey is a host on one of the shopping channels and she's married to a guy who used to race Formula One. Her other daughter was a professional ballerina and she's married to a vet. These people *dress up*. I mean designer duds."

"Then I probably should tell Jared no. I have absolutely nothing to wear to something like that." Chrissie's heart sank. She'd just accepted the fact that she was going, gave herself permission to get excited at the prospect, and then, bam. Back to earth.

"Go see our friend Vanessa at Bling. Tell her what

you're going to be doing, and I promise she will fix you up. Maybe not with Versace and Dior, but she sources things for her shop from little-known designers who've yet to make their name."

"I don't know . . ." Chrissie had no idea what such a venture would cost.

"Go talk to Ness. Trust me. She'll move heaven and earth to help you. She has the biggest heart in the world and she's sharp as a tack. She'll know what to do."

VANESSA HAD KNOWN exactly what to do.

"Find out what you're going to be doing every day," Vanessa had told Chrissie after she'd explained her situation. "Then you bring that list back in here and we'll find you just what you need. You tell Jared you want to know what, where, and what time of day."

"I don't know if he even knows."

"Then tell him to find out."

Chrissie must have been staring at her blankly because Vanessa explained, "There's bound to be a rehearsal dinner and it'll probably be the night before the wedding, right? Ask where it's going to be and how dressy. If it's going to be a barbecue in the backyard, you wouldn't pack a cocktail dress. But if it's a fancy restaurant . . ."

"I got it." The fog that had been in Chrissie's head began to clear. It was simply a matter of logic. Jared would give her the info, she'd pass it on to Vanessa, and then she'd shop.

She was actually looking forward to it. She'd looked around Vanessa's store and been dazzled by the beautiful clothes and accessories, the shoes and the jewelry. The thought of buying some of those beautiful things, of wearing them while she was with Jared and his family, was at once intimidating and exhilarating. New Chrissie could hardly wait to shop.

When she met up with Jared on Wednesday outside Scoop, before he could even ask her what she'd decided, she suggested they go inside, order, then sit at one of the tables instead of walking or opting for a bench outside.

"I need to go over a few things with you," she told him.

"Okay." He looked puzzled but agreed.

There was a line when they got inside, which gave them plenty of time to read the specials for the day, and for Chrissie to run through exactly what she was going to say. She didn't want him to think she was as excited as she was—so not cool, she'd decided. But on the other hand, she didn't want to come off as if she thought she was doing him a favor by going, even if she was.

"If it's Chrissie, it must be Wednesday." Steffie stood behind the counter with an ice cream scoop in her raised hand.

"It is on both counts. One scoop of strawberry rhubarb cheesecake in a dish, please." Chrissie stepped aside so Jared could place his order.

"Mexican hot chocolate for me."

"The usual three in a dish?" Steffie asked.

Jared nodded. "Perfect."

"So I hear congratulations are in order, Jared." Steffie handed Chrissie's order over the top of the counter. "Your dad is marrying a famous lady." She piled his ice cream into a dish. "We love Delia here.

She brought in a couple of her grandkids last time she was in St. Dennis. Cute kids." She passed Jared his order, then took a few steps toward the cash register.

"Yup. Another week and a half and I'll have a stepmother," he said. "Wait, scratch that. I'm not allowed to use that word. Delia's made it clear there will be no 'steps' in the family."

"Aw, that's nice." Steffie glanced at the door as the bell rang for the fourth time in as many minutes. "Must be getting warmer outside. The place is filling up. I'd love to hear about the wedding, but I'm afraid the crowd would get rowdy."

Jared paid for the ice cream, and when Chrissie protested, he told her she could buy next time. Since it appeared there most likely would be a next time, she nodded and staked a claim to a table.

"So." Jared sat with his back to the wall and an uncertain expression on his face. "You're either going to break my heart or make my day. What's it going to be?"

"I asked Sophie if I could have the time off and she agreed. So yes, I'll go to your dad's wedding with you."

"Yes!" His smile went all the way to his eyes. "Thank you. You're going to make a lot of people very happy, not the least of whom would be me and my dad and my step—ah, Delia."

Chrissie was surprised by how happy he looked. Genuinely happy that she was going with him. If she said it wasn't an ego boost, she'd be lying.

"Thanks, Chris. I really appreciate you doing this. If you ever need a favor . . ."

"Actually, I do." She took a small pad of paper

and a pen from her bag. "I need you to tell me what we're going to be doing every day, and what the dress code is."

"Huh?" He looked confused.

"I need to know what to pack." She didn't want to admit she'd be shopping for just about everything she'd be bringing with her.

"Oh. Well, I know there's a rehearsal dinner on Friday night, and the wedding's on Saturday. Does that help?"

"I sort of figured those out for myself. No, I need to know about Thursday. What time are we going? Is there something planned during the day? That night? Casual? Formal? Somewhere in between?"

"You're starting to sound like every other girl I ever knew," he said.

"It's what any girl would ask when going away to spend four days with people she's never met, especially when one of those people happens to be an internationally acclaimed author. So can you find out those things and let me know?"

"Sure." He looked slightly peeved at the prospect.

Chrissie laughed in spite of the fact that she could see he was perplexed. "Look, you have a sister, right? Just ask her."

His face relaxed a little. "That's a good idea. Better yet, how 'bout I ask Rachel to call you and she can tell you what she's bringing?"

"That would be great, thanks." She picked up the pad and the pen and started to drop them into her bag. "Should I write you a memo?"

"No, I'll remember. I have to call Dad anyway so he can tell Delia I will be bringing a friend to their festivities." His ice cream had started to melt, so he began to work on it. "Chrissie, thanks, I really am happy that you're going with me. Not just to please my dad and Delia, but because I know we'll have a good time."

"I'm looking forward to it," she said. "I really am."

AND SHE WAS. She was glad the decision had been made, and happy when Rachel, Jared's sister, called the following night.

"I knew there was someone," she told Chrissie. "I knew he'd break down and ask you to go with him. As soon as he said, 'There was this friend . . .' Well, Jared doesn't have women friends, so of course we were all wondering what he was hiding."

"Oh no. He's not hiding anything. We really are just friends. He wasn't kidding," Chrissie protested.

"I'll believe that when I see it." Rachel paused. "We're all looking forward to meeting the woman Jared claims is 'just a friend.' "

"Oh, no pressure."

"Sorry. I didn't mean it that way. It's just that . . . I guess you'd have to know how Jared's always been about women."

"Someone did describe him as a bit of a playboy."

"Playboy works. Not in a bad 'love 'em and leave 'em' way, but he's always been sort of lighthearted about his relationships. I never saw him in a serious relationship, so I don't even know what that would look like. But I digress. I'm sure you're fabulous and we'll all love you. If you're a strong enough woman to take on a relationship of any sort with my brother, you must be quite a girl."

"Thanks. I think."

"Now, I did manage to get an itinerary out of Delia, so take this down . . ."

Rachel ran through the weekend's events and Chrissie made notes. By the time the weekend had been laid out for her, Chrissie felt slightly deflated. There were so many things planned, so many choices of activities for the afternoons, her head was spinning.

"I'm packing a nice outfit for Thursday night—something I can wear anyplace that I can change the look of with different shoes—but am going with a casual sundress for the day. Delia lives in Chester County, and there's so much to see there, lots of great sightseeing, depending on your interests. Dressy for Friday night, very dressy but not floor length for the wedding, though some others may choose to wear something long. Totally casual for Sunday. Does that help?" Rachel asked.

"Enormously. Thank you so much. I think I can work with this." Or at least, Vanessa will.

CHRISSIE CALLED BLING on Friday morning and gave Vanessa the outline for the weekend.

"Come in on Sunday morning," Vanessa told her. "I'll have a bunch of things for you to try on. And don't feel you have to buy everything, or anything, for that matter. I'll be the first to admit I love clothes—hence my choice of profession—and I love to find things for other people to love. But even if you don't find something you want to buy, you can get an idea of what's available, what's in style this season."

"Thank you. I appreciate your help so much. I'll see you on Sunday morning." Chrissie ended the call determined to find at least one thing to buy from Bling.

She'd gone through the clothes she owned, what she'd brought with her as well as the pieces she bought after she moved to the island. Aside from a few basics, there wasn't a whole lot she'd want to take with her for the wedding weekend.

A pair of shorts, a few casual tops, walking shoes in case they did some exploring, and a pair of sandals that weren't particularly great looking but that she had a fondness for and were comfortable to walk in. She'd set them on the chair in her bedroom and regarded the small pile of clothing. Definitely not enough to take her through a weekend where many of the other women would be wearing designer clothes.

She checked her bank account and found she had more in reserve than she'd remembered. Then again, she'd had few expenses since she moved to Maryland, and there'd been that generous severance from Rob plus what she'd been earning at Blossoms. Armed with her checkbook and an open mind, Chrissie drove into St. Dennis on Sunday morning. She found a parking place directly in front of the store since it was early and the church parking lots would be filled at this time of the day. Most of the shops on Charles Street didn't open until noon on Sunday, and the only business that seemed to be busy at that hour was Cuppachino, the coffee shop directly across the street from Bling. Chrissie locked her car, and after a brief pause to admire Bling's front window, which sported a few things from the fashion show, she knocked on the locked door.

"Sorry," Vanessa said as she unlocked it. "We normally don't open on Sunday until twelve, but I wanted you to have enough time to try on some things that I think will be lovely on you."

Vanessa ushered Chrissie to the main section of the store, where she had a rack of pretty things on display. Chrissie's head began to spin.

"I thought we might want to go event by event, starting with Thursday." Vanessa stepped aside so Chrissie could look through the rack. "Any idea what you might be doing in the afternoon?"

"I think we're not leaving till around four. Jared said we'll get there in time for dinner and hang out with his family afterward," Chrissie said.

"So that's good. You only need something for the trip there and something for dinner." Vanessa pulled out several dresses from the rack. "Any of these speak to you?"

Before Chrissie could take a look, the door of the store opened and closed.

"Hey, we're here." Lis came into view, followed by Cass.

"What are you doing here?" Chrissie tried to remember if she'd mentioned her shopping excursion to either of them.

"When Gigi told me you were going to shop for some new things to wear next weekend, well, we had to be here." Something in the glass jewelry case caught Lis's eye and she paused for a moment.

"We thought we'd do a sort of girls' day. Girls' morning. Whatever." Cass placed a bag on the counter. "Coffee, scones, a few Danish tossed in for good luck." She handed Chrissie a paper cup of coffee. "Drink up. Then let's see what you decided to try on."

"Nothing yet. I haven't had a chance to look."

Chrissie took a sip of coffee and put the cup down on the counter. It was delicious, but so were the four dresses Lis pulled out from the rack.

"Any one of these would be perfect on you." Lis held up a blue sheath.

"We're going day by day, so we're on Thursday dinner and probably hanging out at Delia's house," Chrissie said as she began to go through the dresses. After she'd rejected them all as too dressy, Vanessa brought out several more.

"I still like the blue one." Lis held the dress up in front of Chrissie. "It's so pretty."

"It is," Chrissie agreed as she searched the rack. "But it's just not me. Maybe it's that ruffle around the neckline. I can't see myself in it."

Chrissie lifted a light gray dress of slightly marled cotton knit from the rack. It was fitted, sleeveless, and had a high neckline. "I think I'd like to try this."

"It's kind of plain," Cass said, then hastened to add, "but you could dress it up with a belt or a scarf."

"I want to try it." Chrissie held it up to her body.

"The dressing room is to the right in the back room." Vanessa pointed the way.

Once in the dressing room, Chrissie took a deep breath. She'd wanted not to feel overwhelmed by this totally new experience of shopping in a high-end boutique, one that had opened just for her. She was determined to enjoy herself, especially now that Lis and Cass were there, both of whom she felt sure had shopped here more than once.

She took off the white T-shirt and navy shorts she wore, and slipped the dress over her head. When she turned to look in the mirror, she did a double take.

The dress was slightly fitted to her body but not tight, so unlike most of her things, which were somewhat baggy. She'd been browbeaten for so long by Doug not to show off her body, she'd forgotten what it was like to wear clothes that actually fit well.

She stepped out of the dressing room in her bare feet and went into the front room, where Lis, Vanessa, and Cass were dividing up a huge scone. The three looked up when Chrissie came in.

"Well, there's a perfect example of how a dress can look like practically nothing on the hanger and then be a wow on the right body." Vanessa licked remnants of the scone from her fingers.

"I never would have guessed that would look so good on." Cass nodded. "It really sets off your hair and your cute shape. You need something here, though." She patted around the neckline. "Might be too warm for a scarf, but maybe a necklace."

"Something fun and summery," Lis agreed.

"I have just the thing." Vanessa opened one of the glass cases and brought out a necklace made of five strands of coral-colored beads. "Try this." She handed the necklace to Chrissie.

"Oh, and these shoes, Chris." Cass lifted a pair of sandals made of multicolored strips of leather. "They have heels, but not too high, not too low. And they have that coral color in them." She handed the shoes to Chrissie.

"These are my size," Chrissie said. She looked to Vanessa and asked, "May I?"

"Of course."

Chrissie slipped on the sandals while Lis fastened the necklace at the nape of her neck.

"Gorgeous," Cass said.

"Perfect," Lis agreed.

"That outfit's a winner, Chrissie," Vanessa said. "Look in the big mirror behind you to get the full effect."

Chrissie stood there for a moment, then pulled the elastic from her hair and let the long blond strands fall over her shoulder. She hardly recognized herself.

"Done. I love everything—the dress, the shoes, the necklace. I'm taking these." Chrissie removed the necklace, then the shoes, and handed them all to Vanessa.

"Great choice." Vanessa placed them on the counter. "Now. Friday. Friday night."

"Rachel said there was a lot to see around Delia's place. I checked out the area on the internet and found some Revolutionary War battlefields and a place with lots of gardens," Chrissie recalled. "So I'm guessing some sightseeing during the day, something sort of dressy at night."

They went through the entire weekend, event by event, just as Vanessa had suggested, and by the time Chrissie was finished shopping, she'd picked out a pretty sundress for Friday during the day and a beautiful silk dress in a medium shade of pink for Friday night. For the Saturday wedding, she'd chosen a dress in a shimmery blue-green that seemed to change with the light. It had thin straps and came to a V in the front that was, in Lis's words, deep enough to be interesting but not so deep as to get her in serious trouble. As soon as Chrissie had seen it, she'd known it was the right one.

"These shoes." Lis handed her a pair from the display. "With that dress. Put 'em on, please."

Chrissie did.

"I should have had you modeling in my show a few weeks ago. I will remember this for next time." Vanessa straightened out one of Chrissie's straps. "You wear everything so well. And those just sell the whole picture."

"You need long, sparkly earrings, and nothing else." Lis scanned the glass cases for something she deemed suitable.

"I have a pair of long gold earrings that look like they've been woven from solid strands. They're just the thing. I'll loan them to you," Cass said.

"I'd be afraid of losing them, but thanks," Chrissie told her.

"No, that dress needs those earrings. Trust me. You have to wear them," Cass insisted.

"I'll try them on. Thanks."

They finished the scones and the coffee, and Cass cleaned up the counter while Vanessa added up Chrissie's purchases and Chrissie held her breath. She knew the total was going to be steep, but she didn't care as long as she could cover it with a check. She'd set a spending limit for the day, and she was determined not to exceed it.

"Of course, you get the friends-and-family discount," Vanessa told her before she handed over the bill. "And I took a little extra off because it was fun for me. I never get to shop with my girlfriends anymore."

"Maybe because you don't have to go anywhere to shop," Cass pointed out. "And because when we shop here, there are always a dozen other people shopping at the same time."

"Yeah, the rest of us don't get the royal treatment that Chrissie got. No fair." Lis pretended to be put out.

"Maybe we should do this more often," Vanessa said as she began to bag Chrissie's things. "Open early on Sundays for private shopping." She nodded. "I like it."

"I like it, too. It's more fun this way." Lis turned her attention to the short skirts that were hanging on a nearby rack, then began to search through a pile of colorful T-shirts. "As long as I'm here, I think I'll pick up a shirt or two."

"Let me see that light green one, please." Chrissie held out her hand.

It would be cute with her denim skirt, which she'd decided she'd take with her for the weekend. She asked Vanessa to add it and a pair of white cotton shorts to her total, since—surprise—she hadn't reached her self-imposed limit. She knew that happy fact was due to the generous discount Vanessa had given her.

"Vanessa, this was the most fun." Chrissie gathered the bags that held her shoes and the jewelry she'd bought and the garment bags containing the dresses. "I'd hug you, but I have no hands left for hugging."

"I'll hug you, then." Vanessa did just that. "If I don't see you before Thursday, have the best time of your life. Imagine how much fun you're going to have. Delia is a delightful woman—she shops here when she's in town—and her daughters are just as much fun."

"I want to hug you, too." Lis set down the shorts she was considering and put her arms around Chrissie. "Thanks for letting us crash your party this morning. It's been fun. We'll definitely do this again."

"Thanks for bringing the refreshments," Chrissie said as Lis squeezed her.

"I might as well, too." Cass hugged her when Lis stepped away. "You're going to wow everyone with that beautiful blue-green dress. It's a shame you and Jared are only friends. He's going to be knocked out and not know what to do about it."

"The idea isn't to knock him out," Chrissie said before she left. "I wanted to knock me out. I wanted to feel good about the way I look. For me. Not for Jared."

"You go, girl." Cass held up a thumb.

"Oh, wait. Your hair." Lis came to the door. "What are you going to do about your hair?"

"And makeup?" Cass asked. "Do you even own any makeup besides mascara? And how old is it, if you don't mind my asking?"

Before Chrissie actually got out the door, Lis had made an appointment for her to have her hair trimmed and highlighted on Wednesday after Chrissie was finished working, and Cass promised to bring her some makeup samples to try out later that day.

"I have tons of stuff," Cass told her. "As much as I hate to admit I have a weakness, I am a makeup junkie. I order tons of kits, then end up using two or three things, so I have stuff that's never been used."

"I've never worn a lot of makeup," Chrissie said.

"The trick to wearing makeup is to look as if you're not wearing any. You want to look like Chrissie, but better. I'll show you," Cass promised.

"Do you need help getting to your car?" Vanessa asked.

"No, I'm good," Chrissie told her, "but thanks. I'm right out front."

Chrissie said her good-byes and somehow made it to

the car with all her goodies without dropping anything. She probably could have used a hand, but after two hours of girl talk, as fun as it had been, she was ready to go back to the island. She'd just started the engine and snapped on her seat belt when her phone rang.

"Hey, Chrissie. It's Jared. I was just wondering if you were planning on another of your tours today."

"Ah, actually, no. I have some things I want to catch up on at the store since I'll be away for a few days. I want to make sure things are set up for Gigi, and I want to bake some stuff ahead of time." She thought about the hair appointment Lis had made for her with her hairdresser, a woman who worked out of her home and was available 24/7 according to Lis. "No ice cream on Wednesday, either, I'm afraid."

"Oh. Well, okay." To her genuine surprise, he sounded disappointed. "So I guess I'll see you on Thursday. I'll get back to you with a more exact time, but it looks like around four in the afternoon."

"I promised Gigi I'd make oyster fritters for her for tonight, and I'm on my way to the market now. Do you want to join us around seven?" Actually, she'd told Ruby she'd make oyster fritters the following night, but all of a sudden tonight sounded so much better, especially if Jared could join them.

"Yeah, I'd really like that. Thanks. Can I bring anything?"

"Beer, maybe?" She tried to remember if there'd been any left from the last time Lis and Alec had stopped over.

"You got it. I'll see you at seven."

He hung up right about the same time she did, and just as Cass was coming out of Bling.

She called to Cass, who walked over to the car.

"Since you're coming over to the store later anyway for a makeup tutorial, why not bring Owen and plan on staying for dinner? I'm going to pick up some oysters."

"We'd love to. Funny thing, but Owen just asked this morning if we could have oysters for dinner. Thanks. What's a good time?"

"Dinner's at seven, but you can come earlier if you want."

"Will do. Thanks again. You saved me a trip to the market. Want me to bring dessert?"

"I'm going to be baking all day for the store, so I've got that covered. You could bring a salad, though."

"Consider it done. We'll see you then."

Chrissie turned off the ignition, got out of the car and locked it, then walked three storefronts to the market, where she bought oysters and a big bag of green beans, some grape tomatoes, a bag of lemons, and a couple of green onions. She tucked the packages into the back of her car and returned to the island.

"Gonna have some company, looks like." Ruby walked into the kitchen just as Chrissie began to clean and shuck the oysters.

"Owen and Cass." Then as if it was an afterthought, she added, "And Jared said he loved oyster fritters, so I invited him, too."

"Good. I like that boy. He has him some good manners. Got a good aura, too."

Chrissie put down her shucking knife and turned around. "Gigi, I have never heard you use that word before."

"Manners? Manners be important. I been telling you that since you were knee high."

Chrissie laughed. "You know what I mean. Aura. I've never heard you say that someone had an aura."

"Well, now you have."

"Do I have an aura?"

Ruby seemed to be studying her. Finally, she said, "Yes, but be different from the one you had when you got here."

"Why? How's it different?"

"Don't be asking me to tell you things you already know." Ruby shuffled in her white-sneakered feet to the door that led out to the store. "You be smart enough to figure that out on your own."

THROUGHOUT THE DAY, Chrissie baked. She made two kinds of brownies, chocolate chip scones, and two kinds of cookies. She froze the brownies and the cookies and wrapped the scones tightly for the following morning. She'd still need something for Tuesday, Wednesday, and Thursday morning, but those were all night-before goodies. The brownies and the cookies were for Gigi to sell while she was gone. There was no way she could leave her great-grandmother to a potential mutiny. The watermen were a tough crew, and she'd readily admit she'd spoiled them. She couldn't in good conscience leave them without their morning snacks.

She finished the baking and cleaned up the kitchen and was preparing to cook the dinner when she heard footsteps on the back porch. She looked out the window and saw Owen and Cass at the door.

"It's open," she called to them.

"I heard there'd be oyster fritters," Owen said by way of a greeting.

"There will be. I was just going to start getting them ready," Chrissie told him. "And you're welcome."

"Thanks." He grinned and looked around. "Where's Chandler? Gigi said he was coming to dinner."

"I told him seven."

"Why? I'm hungry now. And what's going on with you two anyway? Cass says you're going away with him for four days. You know what you're doing, Chris?"

"One, I baked all day, so you can wait another hour just like everyone else. And two, there's nothing going on. Jared has to bring a date to his father's wedding and he just invited me as a friend. So it's not like a romantic four days, it's a friends-and-family-having-fun weekend."

"Chandler doesn't know how to be friends with a woman," Owen cautioned. "I've known him a long time, Chris."

"Well, he knows how to be friends with me. Now, go inside and talk to Gigi," Chrissie said.

"Yes, please. Chrissie and I are going to play with makeup." Cass nudged him in the direction of the store.

"Maybe I want to play with makeup," he told her.

"It's Chrissie's turn tonight. Go." Cass pointed to the door.

"Yes, dear." He went into the store.

"No one's buying that meek-little-man act," Chrissie called after him. "Just so you know."

"Okay, so what do we want to do first?" Cass

studied Chrissie's face. "Maybe some foundation just to smooth out your coloring a little. Go wash your face, then come back."

"I don't really have time to—"

"So dinner's three minutes late. Go. We can't experiment on a sweaty face."

"Sorry. I've been baking." Chrissie put the bowl of cleaned oysters into the refrigerator, then washed her hands.

"I'll be right back." She went into Gigi's bathroom and washed her face with the soap from the dish on the sink counter.

When she came back out, Cass said, "Perfect. Now, sit down."

"I can't. I have to make dinner," Chrissie protested.

Cass went to the sink and rinsed the green beans in a colander, then dumped them into a bowl. She placed the bowl on the table and got out a pot.

"Sit down and snap the ends off these." Cass put the pot on the table next to the bowl. "In the meantime, I'm going to play with your face."

"Okay, but be gentle." Chrissie picked up a couple of green beans from the bowl. "And don't get too crazy. I don't want to scare off Jared, now that I'm looking forward to this trip. I saw some photos of Delia's home online and it looks amazing. It's like a true estate, with grounds and outbuildings."

"Take pictures on your phone and send them back while you're away so I can live vicariously through you. Now, close your eyes. I want to try this color foundation."

Chrissie snapped while Cass applied the liquid to

her entire face and blended it with a small sponge, then stood back to assess the results.

"The color's good, so we'll put this aside for you to take. You definitely need some blush, though." She tried and rejected several shades before settling on a rose. "You can use just a touch of this during the day, then layer a little more on for evening." She set it next to the bottle of foundation.

"Cass, I really should be starting dinner." Chrissie started to get up.

Cass pushed her back down. "Stay where you are. I'm not finished. Eyes. Close them." As with the blush, Cass tried several different eye shadows, removing the ones she didn't like and applying another choice. When she found something that pleased her, she added it to the collection on the side of the table.

"Eyeliner, mascara, then we're done."

"Cass . . ."

"Don't want to hear it. Close your eyes and keep them closed." Cass vacillated between two shades of eyeliner, then made a choice. "Open your eyes. Yeah, that's the right one. Now keep them open."

"Are you almost finished?" Chrissie was getting antsy. The last thing she wanted was for Jared to come in and find Cass showing her how to apply makeup.

"Just need the mascara. Keep your eyes open."

Chrissie felt the brush on her lashes. When Cass finished, she took a step back to admire her handiwork.

"Terrific. You look beautiful," Cass announced. "Like Chrissie, but more so; we've enhanced your Chrissieness."

"Let me see." Chrissie went into the bathroom and stared at her face.

Cass was right. She did look like herself, only more so. There was nothing overt that screamed makeup, just soft colors on her cheeks, and her eyes looked bigger, prettier, the green more pronounced.

"So what do you think?" Cass stood with her arms folded over her chest, a knowing smirk on her face.

"You were right. About everything. I like what you did."

"Want me to show you how to do it all yourself?" Cass asked.

Chrissie shook her head. "No, I remember how. I just haven't done it in forever."

"Then I'll leave these things with you. Anything else I can do?" Cass snapped her fingers. "Oh, the earrings."

She took a small jeweler's box from her bag and handed it to Chrissie. "Try them on."

Chrissie pushed back her hair and slid the long, shimmery gold earrings into the holes in her lobes.

"They are going to be perfect with that shiny dress. I wouldn't wear another thing, honestly. Maybe a pretty ring, a thin bracelet or three, and you are set."

Chrissie didn't want to admit she didn't own a ring that would do justice to the dress, so she merely nodded.

"I love the earrings. Are you sure you want to loan them out?"

"Absolutely. I love them on you." Cass gave her a quick hug. "I will want to see pictures of you in that dress, though. Make sure you take some."

"I will. Thanks again. For everything."

"You're welcome." Cass started to return all the rejected blushes and eye shadows to the bag she'd brought them in. "Now, let's do something about getting dinner ready."

Chrissie had just finished preparing the oysters for frying when she heard the bell in the store ring. A moment later, she heard Jared and Owen talking, then Cass went in to say hello and take drink orders.

Minutes later, both men came into the kitchen.

"Gigi wants to eat outside on the back porch," Owen told her. "She wants us to take a table and some chairs out."

"In the storage room." Chrissie turned around and smiled. "Hi, Jared."

"Hey, Chris." He tilted his head, looking at her as if he hadn't seen her before.

"Looks like Gigi's going to make you work for your dinner." She gestured toward the storage room at the back of Ruby's apartment. "Owen, I think she probably wants the long walnut table, but she probably doesn't care which chairs."

"I know which one. We've used it before. Come on, Jared. It's going to take both of us. That table is solid and weighs a ton." Owen opened the storage room door, and Jared followed after one look back at Chrissie.

Cass giggled softly. "He's looking at you like, 'I know that's you but something is different.' See what just a little of the right makeup can do?"

"I didn't want it to *do* anything as far as Jared's concerned. I just want to be able to hold my own among all the other women who are going to be at the wedding."

"The lady doth protest too much, methinks," Cass whispered in her ear as Owen and Jared brought the table out of the back room.

"Man, you weren't kidding," Jared was saying. "This thing is heavy."

"Solid walnut, bro. Gigi's grandfather made this about a thousand years ago," Owen told him.

"More like about a hundred and fifty years, but a little exaggeration never hurt," Cass said.

They took the table out to the back porch and Cass followed to move rocking chairs out of the way. Soon they had the table set up and chairs in place, and Cass proceeded to set the table for dinner while Owen grabbed a few beers and poured a glass of iced tea for Ruby before he and Jared went back into the store.

"What can I do next?" Cass asked.

"Just put the green beans in a bowl and take those out, and I'll be along with the oysters. I just have a few more to fry, so get the salad out, tell the guys to bring Gigi, and get drinks onto the table. By the time you've done all that, the oysters will be ready." Chrissie looked over her shoulder at Cass. "Aren't you glad you asked?"

"I've got it under control. Always glad to help when the reward is a delicious dinner. And I know this dinner will be amazing." Cass left the room to alert the others that it was time.

Chrissie piled the platter with the oyster fritters and cut lemon wedges to serve with them. She scattered grape tomatoes and finely chopped green onions over the oysters, and when she was satisfied with the way it looked, she carried it out to the porch. She served Gigi first, and then the platter was passed around the table.

She sat next to Gigi and across from Jared.

"Wow, you really do make the best oyster fritters on the planet," Jared exclaimed once he'd tasted one. "You should do these for Blossoms." He met her eyes across the table. "Does Sophie know you can do this?"

Chrissie shrugged and tried not to show how the praise made her feel slightly embarrassed. "I may have mentioned it."

"I think you should do more than mention it. You're sitting on a gold mine here," he told her.

"Speaking of gold mines, did you hear about the Spanish ship that was just located down in the Keys?" Owen asked.

"I did. Not one of our jobs, unfortunately," Jared said.

From there the conversation turned to the job they were on, when they might resume, what the latest word was from the agency that was reviewing the situation. By the time dessert was served—a plate of brownies Chrissie'd reserved for the purpose—she was ready to pass out. It had been an eventful and very busy day, from shopping to baking to cooking.

"You look wiped out, girl," Cass said as they were clearing the table. "Why don't you head on upstairs and go to bed? You worked like a dog today, all that baking you did, then dinner."

"That would be rude," Chrissie replied.

"No, it wouldn't be." Jared put one hand on her shoulder, and with the other, took the plates from her hands. "Ruby told me all you'd been up to today. It would be ruder if you collapsed and we had to revive you."

"Are you sure you don't mind?" She addressed

the question to Cass. "I hate leaving you with this mess."

"Those oysters were worth it. Totally. I'll wash and these two clowns can dry," Cass said.

"Okay, if you're sure . . ."

"We're positive," Owen told her. "Go."

"And if all I have to do for a meal like this is to dry dishes," Jared said, "count me in."

"See you all later." Chrissie stopped to hug Ruby on her way out of the room. "Don't eat all the brownies, Gigi."

Ruby cut a brownie in half and took a bite. "You be minding your own business."

Chrissie laughed and left the room, all the while knowing Jared's gaze followed her. If she hadn't been so tired, she'd have probably given more thought to that. As it was, it was all she could do to climb the steps to the second floor, toss off her clothes, and fall into bed.

Chapter Nine

"Chrissie, you best be getting ready to leave," Ruby called up the steps. "Jared be along anytime soon."

"I just need one more minute," Chrissie called back before ducking into the bathroom and taking one last look.

The hairdresser Lis'd taken her to the night before had worked a color miracle. Chrissie had never imagined her hair, which she'd always worn pulled back in a ponytail, could look as good as it did. The highlights were subtle, blending and shading different tones of blond, and the cut, while not drastic, had evened out the length all the way around. She'd put on a minimal amount of makeup, but even that had been enough to change her look.

"Pretty. I look—pretty," she'd whispered to herself, as if afraid to say it too loudly, in case she was wrong.

Chrissie heard the car pull into the parking lot out front and went back into her room. She grabbed the garment bag holding the dresses and the suitcase holding everything else. The one she'd brought with her when she'd fled to the island had been a beaten-up affair, and when Cass saw it, she said, "No-no-no," so quickly it sounded like one word. She'd brought Chrissie one of hers, an expandable Pullman with enough room for shoes and all the clothes that weren't on hangers. Chrissie'd filled it, debating unsurely over this shirt or that, these shorts or that skirt. Finally, she'd made her decisions and packed what she thought she'd wear. Only after she'd finished that chore did she get dressed.

The day was sunny and very warm, so the sundress she'd picked out at Bling was perfect. It had wide yellow and white horizontal stripes and wide straps, and the short white cardigan she'd bought was just right to toss over it. The dress was cotton, though, so she hoped she wouldn't be a wrinkled mess, but it was so cute she almost didn't care.

"Chrissie." Ruby called her name.

"I'm on my way, Gigi," Chrissie called back.

She grabbed the garment bag and the suitcase, which she had to roll down the stairs instead of carry. For one thing, her arms weren't long enough to lift it over the steps. For another, it was heavier than she'd thought.

"I'll get that." Jared came halfway up the steps and held out his hand for the suitcase, then he stopped. "You look . . . great. Great." He took the suitcase and carried it down the rest of the way.

"You behave yourselves, hear?" Ruby stood at the door. "You tell Delia I send her my best and that I be happy for her and her mister."

"I will. Promise." Chrissie kissed her on the cheek.

"Don't forget. Take the scones out of the freezer the night before and unwrap them but keep them covered. The brownies, same thing. The cookies—"

"Girl, I be pretty sure I know how to defrost. You just go on about your weekend and have a good time." Ruby appeared to be debating whether to say something else, then did. "I be fine here. No harm be coming my way. Owen and Cass, Lis, Alec, all be checking in."

Chrissie paused at the doorway, wondering if Ruby had sensed some threat that she'd since dismissed. A chill ran up her spine. She was never completely certain how to interpret some of Ruby's pronouncements.

"You sure everything's okay?" she asked.

"I just said so, didn't I?" To Jared, Ruby said, "You drive right careful now, hear?" before closing the door.

"Guess I got my orders." Jared lifted Chrissie's suitcase with one hand and carried it to the car. He put hers into the trunk next to his, and both fit easily. "You can put your dress bag in the back," he told Chrissie.

"This is one fancy ride." She opened the rear passenger door and laid her bag across the backseat over his. "Is this yours?"

"No. I left my car in South Carolina. I rented this one." He flashed a happy smile. "I thought we should travel in something a little more upscale than my beat-up old Jeep."

"It's beautiful." She was tempted to run her hand over the metallic silver paint of the Jaguar sedan.

"Yeah, she's a pretty thing. If I didn't live like a

vagabond, I'd want to own something like this." He stepped up behind her, then reached around and opened the front passenger door. "Ready?"

She nodded and slid into the light gray leather seat. *Here we go. God, I hope this isn't a mistake.*

Jared got behind the wheel and started the engine, which to Chrissie sounded more like a purr. He eased out of the parking lot and onto the road leading to the bridge. Chrissie turned in her seat and watched the store and the island disappear behind them.

"You worried about her?" Jared asked.

"Not really. I know Owen and Lis are going to keep an eye on her."

"But . . ."

"But she is going on one hundred and one. Her birthday's in another month."

"Planning a party?" he asked.

"I was thinking about talking to the others about that. Lis and Alec and Owen and Cass. I'm not sure who to invite."

"Other than everyone on the island and half the residents of St. Dennis, who else is there?"

Laughing, because he was right, everyone who knew Ruby would expect to be invited, Chrissie said, "We do have other relatives. I just don't know where most of them are."

"Well, you know where your mom is, right? And your dad?"

"I know my mother's still outside of Pittsburgh. My dad?" She blew out a long breath. "I've never known where he is. Actually, I've never known him. He left my mom and me before I was one, so . . ." She shrugged.

"Only child?"

"I have a brother. At least, I'm assuming I still have a brother." She told him the entire story—no reason not to, and there was no way to pretty it up. Her father had abandoned them, and she'd never known why.

"I'm trying to think of something to say," he told her, "but I'm at a loss. Except that I'm sorry. I know what it's like to have a parent leave. I don't know what I'd have done if I hadn't had my sister."

"You were lucky. This isn't something I normally talk about because I've never understood why he left and why he stayed away, and why he took Luke but not me, and if I do tell someone, they have the same reaction you just did. No words." She looked out the window. "Lots of questions, no explanations."

"What does your mother say?"

"Pretty much that it's none of my business."

"Of course it's your business. We're talking about your father."

"I agree. But tell my mother that."

"I think I would, if I ever had the chance."

Chrissie was pretty sure he'd do just that.

"Didn't you ever 'truth zone' your mom?"

"What would be the point? She isn't bound by rules of any kind."

"I'm sorry. That really stinks for you."

"Thank you." She didn't mean it to sound as formal as she said it. She really was thankful that he seemed to understand.

They drove in silence for a few minutes, then Jared pointed to the radio.

"Want to find some music? I think we have satellite but I'm not sure."

"Okay." She turned on the radio and searched for a station. Hearing Patsy Cline's voice, she said, "Oh, the forties! I love forties music!" She turned it up. "Ruby has an old radio on the counter in the kitchen, one of those plastic-case ones. Lis said when Alec built the downstairs apartment for her, he offered to buy Ruby a new radio, but she threw a hissy fit." Chrissie grinned. "I can just imagine. She loves that old thing."

"The thought of Ruby throwing a hissy fit is sobering. Almost frightening."

"It is. Her radio's set to a station that only plays music from the forties. I've heard all the songs so many times, I know almost every one from that era by heart."

"How 'bout this one?" He pointed to the radio to indicate the song that was playing.

She began to sing along with Patsy. "'I go out walking after midnight . . .'" and sang right through to the end.

"Impressive. And you have a good voice. We'll get you out on karaoke night yet."

"Not on your life. I don't sing for crowds." Actually, she was surprised she'd sung for him. It had happened before she'd had time to think about it.

"How 'bout this song? Title and artist?"

She listened for a moment. "Please. Bing Crosby. 'I'll Be Seeing You.' It's one of Gigi's favorites. I always thought it reminded her of her Harold somehow."

"Her Harold?"

"Her husband. My great-grandfather. I don't remember him—he might have been gone by the time

I was born, I don't know. But I've never heard him referred to as anything but Ruby's Harold. Even my mom called him that."

They picked up Route 301 at Wye Mills and continued north.

"This song?" he asked.

"That, sir, is 'Marie Elena.' Jimmy Dorsey. I remember this one especially because when I was little, one of my first friends was named Marie Elena. Her father used to sing this song."

"You really are good," he conceded.

"Not so familiar with popular singers these days, but damn, I do know my forties crooners." She settled back into the seat, much more relaxed than she had been when they'd started out. The music had taken her mind off herself and gave her something else to focus on. "How 'bout you? What's your favorite style?"

Jared smiled and turned the dial on the radio, obviously searching for something.

"Ha. Here we go." He turned up the volume. "Now, that's music."

He started singing along to "I Walk the Line."

Chrissie rolled her eyes. "That's Johnny Cash. Everyone knows that."

"Oh really? How 'bout this one?"

Jared began to sing something she'd never heard before. His voice wasn't all that good, but he seemed to give it his all.

"I can tell by that blank stare of yours that you don't recognize the great country classic 'Walking the Floor over You.'"

"And you're correct. I don't know that song."

"The late, great Earnest Tubbs sang that." He turned the dial again. "Maybe you'd recognize some more contemporary country songs. Ah, this one." He settled on a station and turned the volume up a little. He glanced over at her and sang a few lines, then asked, "Anything?"

She shook her head. "Nope."

"Girl, that is Blake Shelton. Don't you even watch *The Voice*?"

Another shake of her head.

"Do you live in a cultural vacuum?"

"Apparently."

"Now, this is a great song. 'I Lived It.' Listen up."

She listened. "I hadn't heard it before, but I admit I like that one." She turned it back to the forties. "Another golden oldie. There you go. Perry Como. 'Some Enchanted Evening.'"

"I admit that's a romantic sentiment, seeing a stranger across a crowded room and falling in love that fast. Never happens like that, not that I ever heard of. That's not real life." With a flick of his wrist, the country station was back on. "Now, this is Keith Urban. You ever heard of him?"

She nodded. "He's married to Nicole Kidman."

"Right. What I like best about country music is the stories the songs tell. This song that's playing now, 'Blue Ain't Your Color'? It's about a guy who walks into a bar and sees a woman sitting there alone, and he can tell that someone's hurt her, maybe abused her. He tells her that the guy who didn't treat her right wasn't worthy of her, that she should never look that sad, that blue. There's a line that says 'It's so black and white, he's stealing your thunder.' That's just the way you feel when you're in a relationship that sucks all the energy out of you, right? Know what I mean?"

She bit her bottom lip and tried to hold in the tears and find her voice. She knew Jared kept looking at her, knew she was expected to say something, but she couldn't.

"You okay?" he asked.

Chrissie nodded, but she still couldn't speak.

Jared put on his right-turn signal and pulled into a parking lot outside of Centerville. He put the car in park and turned to her.

"Chrissie?"

"I'm okay. Really, I am. You didn't have to stop."

"You were crying." He reached over and wiped a tear away with his thumb. "You're not okay. And I did have to stop. It's okay if you don't want to tell me why. We can just sit here until you feel better."

"It was that song . . ." She pointed to the radio, where Keith was still singing away. "It just made me think . . ." She couldn't put it into words. She'd come so far since then that talking about it would make it real again.

"Made you think about someone who wasn't particularly nice to you?"

She nodded.

"Want to tell me?"

She shook her head. "I don't want to think about that time in my life at all. I want to have a great weekend and just forget that any of that ever really happened to me. That I ever let anyone treat me like that . . ."

"Okay. I get it." He rubbed her shoulder. "You don't have to talk about it. Ever. But you're absolutely going to have a great time this weekend. I promise you."

He was so sincere she could have cried all over again. But she forced a smile. She found a tissue in her bag, blew her nose, and nodded. "I'm good. Really. It was just an unexpected flashback. Sorry. It won't happen again. We can go now."

"Don't apologize to me. And you can cry on my shoulder anytime, Chris."

"Thanks." She gestured with her hand for him to start driving again.

He put the car into drive and headed back onto the highway.

He reset the radio for classic rock and left it there until they reached Delia's house outside West Chester, Pennsylvania.

CHRISSIE THOUGHT SHE was dreaming when Jared stopped across the road from a matching pair of open tall black iron gates attached to even taller red-brick pillars covered in ivy. They'd passed several large homes set way back from the winding country roads, but they hadn't seen anything like those fancy gates with their lion emblems.

"Is this . . ." She pointed across the road.

"Yeah. Delia's place. It's really something. Wait till you see." He drove through the open gates and a moment later, the large house came into view.

"Holy crap," Chrissie heard herself say.

"Like I said. It's really something. Delia told me that's all native fieldstone. You see a lot of old places in Chester County made from that stone." Jared drove past the house and parked between a late-model SUV and a BMW sedan.

"I see Zoey is here." He pointed to the sedan on their right. "Ben, her husband, likes fast cars."

"Is he the one that raced?"

Jared nodded. "Till he had an accident and had to stop. It just wasn't safe for him anymore, but he never stopped loving it. He still goes to Europe for the races in Monte Carlo and France. His grandfather owns the shopping channel Zoey used to work for. Ben runs it now."

"Zoey works for her husband? That could be awkward."

"She quit when she had her third baby last year. Said one full-time job was all she could handle." He turned off the car and asked, "Ready?"

"As I'll ever be." She got out of the car at the same time as he did, not bothering to wait for him to open the door for her. She took a deep breath, pushed all her insecurities into a corner of her mind, and straightened her back.

"Here, hold on." Jared reached a hand to her and she took it. She didn't feel she needed to hold on, but felt somehow he did. Why, she couldn't begin to wonder, but she held on all the same.

Chrissie tugged on Jared's hand to get his attention. "Wait. Let me just take it all in for a moment."

The property on which Delia's house stood was as breathtaking as the house itself. A stone and clapboard carriage house was set off to one side, a well-cared-for barn on another.

"For Delia's horses," Jared told her. "She rides,

though not so much anymore. But she runs a camp for special-needs kids where they can come and ride. There's an indoor ring in the barn."

Chrissie looked out into the vast pasture behind the barn where several horses grazed. "How many horses does she have?"

"I don't know. A few years ago she started rescuing horses, but I have no idea how many. Dad said she's always bringing new ones home, the way some people do lost or unwanted dogs or cats."

"I've heard of rescue dogs and rescue cats, but I never heard of anyone who rescued horses."

"And now you have. It's the same idea. Someone has a horse they can't keep or don't want for whatever reason—change in circumstances, they think the horse is too old, they bought it for a kid who's no longer interested—whatever. If Delia hears about it, nine times out of ten she'll have it brought here. Dad said she's planning another addition to the barn."

"Surely she doesn't take care of them all."

"She has a hired crew."

He began to walk toward the house, so she fell in step with him.

There were gardens in front of, next to, and behind the house.

"She must like flowers," Chrissie said.

"She said all that digging in the dirt helps her to think. She claims her best plots come after she's weeded for a few hours."

The front door opened and laughter spilled out across the gracious porch and the early evening.

"Jared, is that you?" A dark-haired woman stood

on the porch watching them approach, a squirming toddler in her arms.

"It is. Is that my soon-to-be stepsister?"

"Bite your tongue. You know Mom said there were to be no 'steps.'"

The woman put the toddler—a girl with a very high ponytail, her hair dark like her mother's—down and the little girl ran into the driveway. Jared dropped Chrissie's hand and went after her, catching up in three long strides. He lifted her off the ground and returned her, laughing, to her mother.

"Thank you." The woman kissed Jared on the cheek. "Introduce me to your friend, Jared."

"Chrissie Jenkins, meet Zoey Enright." In a stage whisper he told her, "Zoey is the tall one. Her mini-me's name is Daphne."

"Hello to both of you." Chrissie smiled. She recognized Zoey from the days she'd spent watching shopping on TV those nights when Doug was out and she wanted the company of a human voice, though she doubted she'd ever admit that.

"I was watching for Georgia. She's not here yet and I was getting worried," Zoey told them. "But you guys go on in and see the folks. Rachel got here about an hour ago. Sam's coming later. He had some paper or another to finish. Apparently he's teaching the summer semester."

"It was nice meeting you," Chrissie said to Zoey as Jared took her by the elbow and steered her to the oversized front door.

"We'll have lots of time to get acquainted over the next few days," Zoey told her. "I'm looking forward to it."

"Me, too."

Jared ushered Chrissie into the front hall. There were voices coming from the right side of the house.

"My guess is the sunroom," Jared told her. "Delia's favorite room. Her kids call it the hanging gardens. Besides horses and people, Delia collects plants. She had a bar installed for my dad, who enjoys a cocktail while watching the sun set. Which it does right out behind those low trees. We'll go out and take a look later."

Chrissie'd never seen such a house, had certainly never been inside anything close to it. It had its fancy touches—she could see into the dining room, where a table was set for what looked like twenty people, a huge ornate crystal chandelier hanging over it—and there was lots of dark, highly polished wood—the floors, the wainscot. But there was also a feeling of hominess from the family photos on the walls and the child's tricycle in the hall. A peek into the huge living room as they walked by revealed upholstered furniture all covered in pretty colors, florals and stripes, solids and plaids, all happy-looking pieces that gave the grand house a much lighter, more informal feel than it might have otherwise had.

"This house is amazing," she said as they moved through the hallway.

"Delia's done a lot with it. She put an addition on the back with an indoor pool—she swims every morning she's here—and there's an exercise room downstairs, just in case you're wondering how she stays in such remarkable shape for a woman her age. She also had a second family room and a playroom built on to the other side of the house, off the kitchen, so her grandkids have a place to play and hang out."

They stepped from the foyer into the room where greenery ruled. Jared hadn't exaggerated. There were plants everywhere. It stopped short of appearing junglelike.

"There's my boy." A white-haired man in a linen jacket and pants put his drink down on the nearest table and held his arms open to Jared, who dropped Chrissie's hand. "Glad you made it early, son."

Father and son embraced, Gordon patting Jared on the back. "I missed you," Gordon told him.

"Missed you too, Dad." Jared returned the back pats, then broke away. "Dad, this is Chrissie Jenkins. She's Owen Parker's cousin."

"Ah, Owen. What a character he was. I heard he got married. Must have been from you," he said to Jared before turning to Chrissie. "We're so glad you joined us for the weekend." He lowered his voice. "Particularly Delia, who for some reason has a thing about having an uneven number of people seated at a table. I don't get it myself, but there it is."

Chrissie smiled. "We're all entitled to our little quirks."

"You picked the right one to bring with you, Jared. You'll fit right in, Chrissie. I'm delighted to meet you."

"Thank you, Mr. Chandler. Same here," Chrissie said.

"It's Gordon. We're pretty easy here, Now, come meet my bride." Gordon took her arm and led her away from Jared.

Chrissie'd spotted Delia the moment they came into the room. She looked exactly like the photos on the back of her books, of which Ruby had a ton.

"Delia, this is Chrissie Jenkins. She's a friend of Jared's," Gordon told the elegant, dark-haired woman in the emerald-green silk shirt and matching pants.

"Oh, the woman who's evening out my tables. I'm indebted to you. Thanks so much for agreeing to come out to the wilds of Pennsylvania with that rascal soon-to-be son of mine." Delia greeted Chrissie with a hug.

"I'm so happy to meet you. My great-grandmother is a huge fan of yours. I think you've met her a few times in St. Dennis."

Delia tilted her head, perhaps trying to place someone named Jenkins in St. Dennis.

"Ruby Carter," Chrissie told her.

"Oh my, yes." Delia smiled. "I adore that woman. So wise. Always has the most interesting stories. She and my dear friend Grace Sinclair are very close. When I think of St. Dennis, I think of the two of them. Of course, Ruby doesn't actually live in St. Dennis. She's on that island . . ."

"Cannonball Island, yes."

"I keep meaning to go there. I've heard so much. Now, did I read an article recently about a developer buying up old historic homes and building new ones with some of the original details?"

"Yes. My cousin Owen's wife is the architect."

"I want to hear more about it. Oh, there's my daughter Georgia. Come, you must meet her . . ." Delia took Chrissie by the arm.

Over the next half hour, Chrissie met so many people her head was spinning. Delia's son, Nick, his wife, India, their children. India's aunt August, who had a fondness for tossing out Latin phrases. Georgia and Matt, her husband, their kids, and Jared's sister, Rachel, whose husband had yet to arrive.

Chrissie tried to memorize one thing about each person that might help her to remember their name and relationship to either the bride or the groom. After a while, she all but gave up.

Jared had rescued her by bringing her a glass of wine.

"How're you doing?" he asked.

"I have no idea," she told him. "I thought you said this was going to be a very small affair. Just family."

"This *is* just family."

"I doubt I'll be able to keep everyone straight. Zoey, I'll remember. Georgia's the one with the long straight blond hair, and Rachel is the only one in the group with auburn hair, so she's easy."

"Plus she doesn't look like any of the Enrights," Jared said.

"That's also true, but it's the color of the hair that I'm committing to memory."

"And the guys?"

"I'm totally lost where they're concerned. The only one who stands out is Ben, and that's only because he limps."

"Old racing injury. Broke his leg in a couple of places," Jared explained. "By the end of the weekend, you'll know who everyone is. They're all very friendly, very down to earth, and you'll like them all. Trust me. I was a bit intimidated when I first met Delia's kids, but they're a great bunch and a lot of fun. You'll see."

Someone announced that Laura and Ally had just arrived and that set off another round of introductions.

"I'm not sure how she fits in," Chrissie whispered.

"Delia's daughter and her daughter Ally."

"Oh. I thought she only had the two daughters. So she's Georgia and Zoey's sister."

"Half sister," he said. "It's a long story. I'll tell you later."

"Okay."

Dinner was announced and everyone was ushered into the dining room, where a caterer's staff awaited to serve them. The meal was marked by lots of chatter and side conversations, an argument between Nick and Zoey over who got to use the kayaks first thing in the morning, and the occasional crying child, who was then tended to by a number of relatives. Chrissie had a headache by the time they'd finished eating and gone into the living room for dessert and coffee.

"You're doing great," Jared told her.

"My head is splitting open and my brains are spilling out all over this magnificent Oriental rug," she confided. "I'm not used to so many people."

"Do you have anything to take for it?" he asked.

"I do. I'll be right back." Chrissie excused herself and went back into the sunroom, where she'd left her bag. She found a container of Advil and grabbed a bottle of water from the bar, which was still set up, then tossed back the tablets.

"We've given you a headache, eh?" a voice said from the doorway.

Chrissie turned around, ready to deny it'd been the company.

"Oh, Rachel. No, it's—"

"I felt the same way when Dad first introduced

me to Delia and her kids and their spouses and their kids. It's a lot to take in at one time."

"Everyone seems so nice, but . . ." Chrissie said.

"Everyone is nice. There's not a mean bone in any one of those bodies. But that's not the point. They're just overwhelming. They all talk at the same time and their conversations are hard to follow because one person will speak and someone else will finish their sentence and then take it in an entirely new direction." Rachel laughed. "Believe me, I get it."

"I didn't want to appear rude by walking out, but yeah, overwhelming."

"How 'bout if the two of us sneak outside for a few minutes, get some fresh air to help clear our heads?" Rachel suggested.

"I like it." Chrissie followed Rachel to the French doors at the end of the room.

"The view out here is lovely at any time of the day," Rachel said as she opened the doors onto a stone patio. "But I like it best right around dusk, while the horses are still out in the pasture and the birds are just starting to hunker down in their nests."

"It's so peaceful." Chrissie stepped outside behind Rachel and closed the door, then took a deep breath. "The air smells so good here. So clean. Different from the bay. Not," she hastened to add, "that the bay doesn't smell clean. It's just different. Salty in some parts, marshy in another."

"That's right. You're from the Chesapeake Bay, that place where Jared's working," Rachel said. "How'd you meet my brother?"

"My cousin Owen works for him. They've been on dives together in the past." Chrissie took a sip from the water bottle she'd brought out with her. "Jared said you're a diver, too, and that you work for the family business. Is that what you always wanted to do?"

Rachel nodded. "I was so jealous every time Dad took Jared with him on salvage operations and left me home. They'd come back with wonderful stories of the places they'd been to and the ships they dove on, and the things they found. I wanted to be like them. I wanted to do what they did. How 'bout you, do you dive?"

"Not on your life. I don't want to go under the water and I don't want to meet up with whatever's down there."

"Hey, if you're going to be with my brother, sooner or later you're going to dive. He's going to want to share that part of his life with you."

"Jared and I are not going to 'be together.' He's not going to share his life with me, and I'm not sharing mine with him, not the way you mean. Neither of us has any interest in 'being together.' We're just friends."

"Really? Because he looks at you differently than I've seen him look at women in the past."

Chrissie shrugged. "Maybe because I don't expect anything of him."

Rachel stared at her, finally saying, "I guess we'll have to see how it plays out."

"Rachel, there's nothing to play out."

"If you say so. Oh look. The sun's starting to set." Rachel pointed to the pasture. "I should go get my husband. I left him with the boys and they're probably ready to run around a bit. Coming in?"

"In a few. You go ahead."

"Great talking to you. We'll catch up again later this weekend, I'm sure."

Rachel went inside but Chrissie remained on the patio. She hadn't been kidding when she'd told Rachel she'd felt overwhelmed. Large families and their interactions were a mystery to her. She heard a sound behind her and seconds later, Jared was there.

"Rachel said she'd left you out here. You okay? How's the headache?"

"Better. I just needed to retreat for a few minutes."

"Look at that sunset." Jared pointed out across the pasture. "If I lived in a place like this, I'd be out here every single day at this time just to see that. I bet it never gets old."

They watched as the sky turned tropical colors and the clouds took on elongated shapes. When the sun had disappeared behind them, Jared said, "I think we're getting ready to propose some toasts to the happy couple. I'm expected to give one, so . . ."

"Of course. Let's go in. I wouldn't want to miss it."

The toasts lasted for almost a full half hour because everyone wanted to express their good wishes. Some were funny, some were poignant, but everyone spoke from their hearts. There was music and lots of socializing and Chrissie found that taken one on one, the Enrights were every bit as delightful as she'd been told to expect. The only uneasy moment came when it was time to turn in for the night. Somehow someone had gotten the idea that Chrissie and Jared were sharing a room, but he handled that diplomatically so their rooms were next to each other.

Chrissie lay in bed, the windows open, listening to the owls in the tall pines outside her window. Other than the occasional breeze brushing through the branches, the night was very quiet and dark, touched by the very faintest scent of pine. It was peaceful, and it didn't take long for her to fall asleep.

Morning brought breakfast in what Delia called the morning room, which was between the dining room and the kitchen. It had windows on three sides and a fireplace, and an old farm table that had two benches on one side and chairs on the other. Chrissie sat at the end of one of the benches, someone's two-year-old on her lap. She shared her pancakes and fed eggs to Charlotte, the little girl, who turned out to belong to Georgia, and who, once fed, jumped off Chrissie's lap and took off for the yard.

"So what's on tap today?" Jared asked when he came into breakfast several minutes after Chrissie.

"Today's whatever you make it, bud." Nick poured syrup on his daughter's waffles. "There's lots to do around here, depending on your mood."

"I'm up for a row on the Brandywine," Ben said as he joined them. "Nick, you in?"

"Of course. Just like old times," Nick said.

"Nick and Ben grew up together," Delia explained to Chrissie. "They think I never caught on to any of their mischief, but they're mistaken."

"How 'bout we see some of the sights I'm always hearing about?" Jared nudged Chrissie.

"I'm up for anything," she replied.

"There's the Brandywine Battlefield, where Washington's troops were defeated by the British. That's not far from here."

"Longwood Gardens," Zoey told Chrissie. "It used to belong to one of the Du Ponts, now it's this glorious garden bonanza that's open to the public. Acres and acres of beautiousness."

"Dad, is beautiousness a word?" Georgia's six-year-old son, Zach, asked.

"I just said it, didn't I?" Zoey tried to stare down her nephew from the other side of the table.

"You could have made it up," Zach said. "You make up words all the time. Mom said so."

"Oh, did she now?" Zoey narrowed her eyes and tried to pin her sister down with a glare.

"Are you finished?" Jared asked Chrissie, who nodded. "Let's go."

They left amid the sisters volleying words back and forth. There was a burst of laughter as Jared opened the front door and he and Chrissie stepped out into a perfect early June morning. It was a morning full of sunshine and the fragrance of the flowers that seemed to bloom everywhere Chrissie looked.

"Any preference as to where we go or what we do?" Jared asked.

Chrissie shook her head. "How 'bout you?"

"I think I'd like to stop at that battlefield." He took his phone from his pocket. "And the gardens Zoey talked about—Longwood—is right down the road. And a little farther down Route 1 is the Brandywine River Museum. Heavy on the Wyeth paintings."

"That sound perfect. Let's do it."

The Brandywine Battlefield park was a series of rolling green hills right off the main highway, Route 1. For all its proximity to traffic, it was surprisingly quiet once they walked out onto the field where the bloody conflict had taken place. It was almost eerily quiet, with only the sound of the wind blowing across the hills and through the trees, and Chrissie said so.

"I know. It's almost as if you can hear the voices of the dead in the breeze coming down through those sycamores." Jared read from his phone. "'The battle was also known as the Battle of Brandywine Creek. September 11, 1777. General George Washington for the patriots, General William Howe for the British.'" He read a bit more to himself. "Oh, Washington didn't fight Howe here. That was a few miles to the west." He looked up at Chrissie. "Apparently the battle was fought across the farms and the hills. The British wanted to travel north to take Philadelphia," he said, resuming reading. "Washington wanted to stop that from happening. Lots of Quaker farmers in the area, homes were confiscated by the Americans before the battle, and by the Brits after they'd won. The Americans retreated to a place called Chester to regroup." He stopped reading and looked up again. "History is so much more interesting when you walk it, you know? I was a decent enough student, but I never felt involved in it. Walking here, I feel the connection. It's humbling."

They stopped at the visitor center and looked over the exhibits before heading out to see a few historic homes that'd been restored. Chrissie was intrigued to see the houses they visited from the very early 1700s were constructed of the same type of stone as Delia's fieldstone. They stopped for lunch at a small roadside restaurant, then drove across the road to tour the Brandywine River Museum, which had an entire floor of Jamie Wyeth's paintings. Since he was a favorite artist of Jared's, the trip had definitely been worth it, even though they returned to Delia's tired from all the walking. Chrissie'd hoped to grab a quick nap before dinner, but that had been optimistic on her part. She barely had time to shower before she was expected to be downstairs for the rehearsal for the wedding that would take place the following day in the grand living room.

Chrissie changed into one of the dresses she'd bought from Vanessa, a pretty medium-shade-of-pink sleeveless sheath with a low square neck. She remembered Cass's instructions to layer her eye shadow for the rehearsal dinner, and layer it yet again for the wedding. Chrissie applied her makeup and brushed her hair to flow around her shoulders, then left her room to join the group that'd gathered in the foyer for the rehearsal. When she came down the steps, she could feel Jared's eyes appraising her, and for the first time, she wondered what it would be like if they'd been more than friends.

She planted herself at the back of the group where she thought he couldn't see her.

Delia's minister, a woman named Sharon who was in her fifties, was running the show.

"I need the groom and his best man. Yes, you two. No ushers because there's no seating, right, Delia?"

Delia nodded. "The ceremony's only ten minutes or so long if that. There's no one here who can't stand for ten minutes."

"Exactly. So you two will stand in front of the fireplace in the living room when I tell you it's time." She glanced at the clipboard that she held in one hand. "Okay, it's time. Go."

Gordon and Jared walked into the living room and stood in front of the fireplace.

"Next up: the bridesmaids. Four of you, correct? Really? Five?" She rolled her eyes. "You walk in next. Stand on the left. Go ahead."

Zoey, Georgia, Laura, Rachel, and India went up the imaginary aisle and took their places.

"Flower girls?" Several small girls were pushed forward by their fathers, their mothers already having made their way into the living room.

"Seriously, Delia? You need them all?" Sharon asked.

"My granddaughters, and yes, I need them all," Delia told her.

"Alrighty, then. Big girls, take the hands of the little ones. That's right. Now walk nicely up there to your mommies."

The girls did as they were told.

"No maid of honor?"

"What's in a name? The bridesmaids are also my maids of honor," Delia told her.

"Then they shouldn't go ahead of the flower girls."

Delia waved a hand for Sharon to get on with it. "The little ones won't go up the aisle unless their mothers are at the other end."

"This isn't protocol."

"I don't care."

"It's your wedding. So that means that you come in next. Last, I mean. Is someone walking with you?"

"My son, Nicky." Delia turned to Nick and took his arm in an elegant motion. "Shall we?'

Nick nodded. "Indeed we shall."

Sharon followed with her clipboard, leaving Chrissie standing alone in the foyer, and in a direct line to Jared.

Jared, who was still looking at her.

At first, Chrissie'd told herself he'd been watching Delia and Nick walk toward the family gathered in the front of the room, but no. He was definitely looking at Chrissie. She could feel a blush wash through her entire body under his gaze.

The look in his eyes did not say *Hey, buddy*.

The rehearsal dinner was everything Chrissie'd expected it would be, with delicious food and wine and champagne toasts; but she escaped to her room as soon as she could, mostly because she wanted to avoid being alone with Jared at any cost. When he suggested they take a walk out to see the moon, she begged off, claiming her headache had returned. Alone in her room, she changed into a nightshirt and sat in a chair near the window where she could see the big yellow moon just fine, without complications. She knew being anything other than just friends with Jared would be a complication.

She'd been doing so well. She'd found a job she really enjoyed, working with people she liked who encouraged her and appreciated her skills. Not unlike Rob at Luna. She'd give anything to be able to call him and tell him about Blossoms, to invite him and Jim to come visit and meet Ruby and Owen, and yes, Jared. But she didn't dare make that call. She still sent Rob photos once in a while, still without captions, sometimes of the island, sometimes of dishes she'd prepared. She still didn't trust Doug to stop looking, because her gut told her otherwise. She didn't understand why, other than the fact that she'd put one over on him. His ego would not accept a blow like that. In his mind, she'd have to be punished, but he'd have to find her first, and she'd done everything possible to prevent that.

She may have put him behind her, but the effects of his abuse were long lasting. She would have expected by now she'd be able to spend time with a man and not be on edge. The funny thing was, she didn't feel that sense of dread when she was with Jared. But as soon as she realized that, she went on alert, as if she truly believed there was no such thing as a safe relationship. No such thing as a man who didn't manipulate, no such thing as a man who wouldn't try to break you.

She'd been broken once, but now she was healing. Why would she even consider being anything other than a friend to a man who could break not just her spirit but her heart as well? She wasn't sure there was a difference. Either way, something in you was broken.

Not fair, a little voice inside her whispered. *Not fair to make Jared pay for Doug's sins.* Was that what she was doing by avoiding him? Did she really think she could avoid him for the entire weekend?

Too many deep thoughts brought the headache back for real. When Jared knocked on her door later to ask how she was feeling, she sank into her pillow and lay silent, hoping he'd think she was asleep and go away. She hated feeling like such a coward; it went against everything she knew about New Chrissie. But she still couldn't face Jared alone until she sorted out how she really felt about him, and what she was prepared to do about it.

Chapter Ten

He'd scared her. He'd seen it in her eyes the moment the words left his mouth. He hadn't meant to; he couldn't help but notice how pretty she looked, and who wouldn't smile when they looked at a beautiful woman? He'd had a feeling that things would be different between them than they'd been in St. Dennis, and he'd spent several nights in hot debate with himself before he'd asked her to be his date for the weekend. He'd meant it when he'd said no pressure, that he recognized they were just friends, but that didn't mean he hadn't hoped maybe something more might develop between them.

He hadn't seen that coming, hadn't meant for that to happen, but there it was.

Chrissie Jenkins was not like any woman he'd ever met. She had a straightforward way about her, said what she thought, didn't act like a diva, didn't act like she was doing him a favor by spending time with him. If he were to be honest with himself—and he'd recently decided it was time—most of his relationships with women had been mostly superficial, beginning because he liked the way a woman looked, liked the way she moved, and ending when someone else came along whose looks caught his eye. Chrissie seemed unaware of how pretty she was, even on their walks around town, wearing no makeup and whatever clothes she felt comfortable in. He liked that about her. He liked that they'd had conversations about their families and about what was important to them, about what they wanted to do with their lives. Seeing her here—with his family, the people who mattered most to him—seeing how she interacted with them and them with her, the easy way she fit into the big picture, made him realize he wanted her to be more than his friend Chrissie. He just didn't know how to make that happen. He couldn't help the way he looked at her when she appeared the way she had tonight—and that had sent her running to her room with a "headache."

Of course, there was always the possibility that she just wasn't attracted to him. Jared didn't have a lot of experience with situations like that, but he knew he'd been a fool to think every woman he was attracted to would be equally attracted to him. If that was the case with Chrissie, he'd have to respect her feelings if they were to remain at the very least friends. He'd rather have friend Chrissie than no Chrissie at all.

Yeah, she'd really gotten to him.

For the first time in his life, Jared didn't know what to say to a woman or how to act around her. It was a totally unexpected turn of events, one that had kept him tossing and turning all night.

The morning of the wedding was a perfect June day. The dew dried early, the flowers in the gardens

were in full bloom, the sun was shining, and there
was a sweet breeze blowing to scatter the fragrance
of the peonies across the patio, where everyone had
gathered after breakfast.

Jared had been watching for Chrissie, and when
she appeared in the doorway, he'd fixed her a cup of
coffee he'd poured from the carafe on the table.

"Oh, thanks." She'd smiled, though she hadn't met
his eyes. She took a sip of coffee, then said, "It's just
the way I like it. Thanks."

"I'm very observant," he told her. "How'd you
sleep? Are you feeling better?"

"I slept well, thanks. And I do feel better."

"What would you like to do today? Anyplace
you'd like to go or see?" he asked.

"Not really. How 'bout you?"

"We don't have as much free time today since the
wedding is at four. So anything we do, we should
be back here in time to get ready for the wedding,"
he said.

"We're taking all the kids to the petting zoo this
morning, back in time for afternoon naps so no one
has a meltdown tonight. No guarantees on that, of
course." Rachel had apparently overheard their conversation. "Are you man enough to come with us,
Jared?"

"Doesn't that sound like fun, Uncle Jared?" Rachel's six-year-old son, Dylan, tugged on his arm.
"Wanna come?"

"Ummm . . . what are the other options?" Jared
consulted his phone. To Chrissie he said, "We could
do Longwood Gardens. Or the Delaware Art Museum. That's relatively close."

"We talked about Longwood yesterday. How far is that?" Chrissie asked.

"Maybe twenty minutes, give or take a few." Jared looked up from his phone. "Totally doable."

"We've been, many times," Zoey told them. "It's wonderful, a former Du Pont estate. We take the kids several times every year because they have such fun things for them. And we never miss their Christmas display. Really, you should go."

"If you go, you won't want to leave," Delia cautioned. "You'll fall under its spell and miss the wedding and Gordon will have no best man and years from now the grandchildren will be looking at the photos from our wedding and asking, 'Where was Uncle Jared?'"

"And we'll have to tell them you were tiptoeing through the tulips," Rachel said.

"Nah, there's no way I'm missing this party tonight," Jared told them. "We'll be back in plenty of time." He turned to Chrissie. "What do you say? Longwood?"

She nodded. "Sounds good."

Delia threw up her hands. "You've been warned."

AFTER WALKING THE magnificent grounds, through the park, then on to the varied beautiful gardens, Chrissie began to fade.

"There's a café," Jared said. "Let's grab a bite and then we'll see what time it is."

"Good idea. After yesterday's hike through the hills at the battlefield, I don't think I'm up to another all-day walk-a-thon."

"Half-day walk-a-thon," he corrected her. "Delia asked us to be back by around two."

"We'll make it."

Jared looked at the map again. "We're right here." He showed her. "The café is in the Terrace, over here. Between here and there is the Hillside Garden. We can go along this path, along the Allees, past the Main Fountain Gardens, and right on over to the café."

"I love a man with a plan," Chrissie said.

Jared liked the sound of that. He knew it was just an expression, but it brought a smile to his face.

"It all sounds so very French."

"As it should. The Du Ponts were originally from France, I'm pretty sure."

"I think we should have picked up a brochure in the visitor center."

"We can get one on the way out." He paused in front of the sign that pointed to the Hillside Garden. Ahead of them clouds of color swayed in the light breeze.

"Oh, lilies," Chrissie said as she walked a little faster. "I love lilies. And daisies. And oh, look at all the pretties. I can't even imagine how many people they have working here. How many expert gardeners it must take to care for all of these. And oh, look, Jared, those white flowers. Do you know what they are?"

He had no idea, but the delight that shone on her face made him want to find out so he could buy her an armful. She had the same reaction to the fountains, and for a moment she danced, a pirouette, a leap, another spin—moves perhaps remembered from a long-ago ballet class—then caught herself, remembering, no doubt, that she was in a public place.

"Sorry," she whispered, her face turning pink as

she looked around and saw other visitors smiling at her. "I got carried away."

"Don't apologize." Jared couldn't help but smile as well. "I like to see you happy. And I'm willing to bet that more than one of them"—he nodded in the direction of the others—"feel like dancing, too."

They grabbed a quick lunch in the café, then went back through the visitor center, where Chrissie nabbed several brochures.

"I want to know what else is here," she told Jared. "In case I want to come back. I feel like we've missed a lot."

"Judging from the map, I'm pretty sure we didn't see even half of the gardens. You just let me know when you're up for another trip."

Jared took her hand as they walked out of the center and into the sunshine. When they got to the car, he gave her hand a gentle squeeze before he let go so she could get in, and she squeezed back. He knew it was ridiculous for such a small gesture on her part to make him smile, but he didn't care. The entire day had been easy and had made her happy, and just then, that was all that mattered to him. She'd danced by the fountains, and the sight of her twirling around had lifted his heart. He was pretty sure it was an image that would stay with him for a long, long time.

THEY MISSED GETTING back to Delia's at two o'clock by a full half hour, but there was still plenty of time to shower and get dressed. There seemed to be a dozen florists buzzing about the house, bringing in garlands of orchids and urns filled with peonies. Huge pots of roses flanked the fireplace, and outside on the patio, tall trellises covered with climbing roses in deep pots were set in place. The entire house smelled as if it were in bloom. Delia hadn't wanted the florals brought in too early because she wanted everyone to be surprised when they came downstairs after getting dressed for the wedding.

Jared finished tying his tie, then went downstairs to await the others. In the absence of his father and Delia, Jared played host to the few invited friends: Delia's agent, several neighbors, a few booksellers who'd become close friends of Delia's, two men who'd been members of Gordon's crew for over twenty years and their wives, and, to Jared's surprise, Grace Sinclair.

"Grace. I didn't know you were coming." He greeted her with outstretched arms.

"I hadn't seen you since I'd received the invitation," she said, "or I'd have mentioned it. Assuming I'd remember. I seem to need to write notes to myself every day, then of course half the time I forget where I put them. I'm at the age where I find growing old a pain, but I recognize the alternative is much worse. Delia's home is lovely, just the way I knew it would look. Beautiful grounds, and her gardens are magnificent. I sneaked a peek on my way in."

"How did you get here? Surely you didn't drive." He moved out of the foyer with her and into the living room.

"Delia told me to bring a guest—something about uneven numbers at the tables for dinner—so I asked Barbara Noonan to come along. You know, of course, that she's the owner of Book 'Em in St. Dennis and knows Delia well from the many times she's signed her books at Barbara's store," Grace explained. "She should be along any moment, she's just parking her car."

As if on cue, Barbara entered the foyer and spied Grace and Jared.

"Jared, hi—oh look, there's Rita Cramer from Mama Loves Books in Salisbury." To Grace and Jared, Barbara said, "We belong to the same independent booksellers' organization. Excuse me for just a minute . . ."

"How nice for her to find an old friend to chat with," Grace said. "Now, is there something you should be doing instead of keeping me company, Jared?"

"I'm just door tending." He signaled one of the waiters who'd just come from the kitchen with a tray of champagne flutes. He lifted a glass and handed it to Grace, saying, "Here's something to sip while we wait for the ceremony to begin."

Georgia and Zoey were coming down the steps in long dresses in different shades of hot pink, several guests were arriving, and the string quartet had started to set up next to the fireplace in the living room. Jared excused himself to Grace and greeted the guests, made sure they had champagne, and showed them where to go. Sharon, the minister, arrived, and she, too, was given champagne and shown into the living room.

"Looking good, bro." Rachel came up behind him, a small boy on each hand.

"Wow. You look pretty good yourself." Jared kissed his sister on the cheek, for just one moment recalling how she'd looked at an Easter egg hunt one year in a dress that same color. Sometimes it was hard for him to remember that his little sister was one guy's wife and mother to two more. If he had more time to think about it, he might become nostalgic over how quickly the years had passed and how little time he'd shared with his sister. Time wasted was time you couldn't get back, their aunt Bess used to tell them, so choose wisely how you spend it. Looking at Rachel with her sons made him wish he'd spent more time with her before her life and his had taken different directions. "So is pink the color of the day?"

"Delia wanted us all to be her attendants and said the style of dress was up to each of us; she didn't care that they'd be different. But she wanted us all to wear any shade of pink, as long as it wasn't pale pink."

"I've been told the correct term is blush this year," Chrissie said.

"Ah yes, I did read that somewhere." Rachel nodded. "Oh, for heaven's sake, Jeremy . . ." Her youngest took off down the hall headed for the back door, and she took off behind him. "Dylan, you stay with Uncle Jared until you see your daddy."

Jared turned to Chrissie, and anything he might have said was lost. She'd changed into a long dress that sent shades of blues and greens shimmering when she moved. She'd done something different with her hair, pulled it all to one side so it flowed over her shoulder. She wore long sparkly earrings that swayed when she moved, and strappy high heels in shades of blue leather.

"You look beautiful," he said when he found his voice. "You look like a mermaid."

"Now I suppose you're going to tell me you've seen mermaids along with your UFOs," she teased.

"I think you're the only one."

"Well, then, thank you."

A touch of pink spread from the skin at the low V of her neckline to her forehead. He wished he could reach out and follow that pretty blush with the tips of his fingers.

"You look pretty, too." Chrissie straightened his tie.

"Jared, your dad's coming down now." Zoey poked him in the back just as Sam showed up to take Dylan off Jared's hands. "Could you make sure the strings are ready to start playing? They probably should be anyway, while we're waiting for Mom."

"Sure. Chris, they're passing out champagne somewhere. We'll get you a glass and find you a place in the living room. Oh." He snapped his fingers. "Grace is here."

"Grace? Grace Sinclair?" Her brows knit together.

Jared nodded. "I was surprised, too." He took her arm, her warm skin soft under his fingers. He hoped there'd be music later, so he could put his arms around her and slow dance her around the patio.

"Oh, there's Grace. And Barbara, too. Go do your best man things. We'll catch up after the ceremony." Chrissie tossed a smile over her shoulder to Jared, snagged a glass of champagne from the nearest waiter, and joined Grace and Barbara at one side of the room.

The musicians were given their final instructions, and at promptly four o'clock, Jared accompanied his father to stand in front of the fireplace. Next the five ladies in shades of pink made their way to the front of the room, followed by three little girls in fluffy white dresses with bright pink sashes and tiny pink flowers in their hair. Soon all the players were in place except for the bride.

The strings began to play "At Last," and Delia made her entrance on the arm of her son. She was dazzling in a long dress of blush-colored silk with elbow-length sleeves and a low back. Everyone in the room smiled as she passed by, but her eyes were on her groom.

Had there been a dry eye in the house when they repeated their vows? Jared was pretty sure he wasn't the only one to blink back a tear or two when his father said, "*I promise to swim with you every morning, and rest with you every night.*" His previous misgivings aside, Jared was happy that his father had found someone he clearly loved so deeply to spend the rest of his days with. Considering both the bride and the groom were in their midseventies, there was no way of predicting how many days there would be, but they'd face them together and with love, of that Jared was positive. As soon as Sharon pronounced them husband and wife, they embraced and kissed so long that Zoey finally called out, "Stop! Enough! There are young children here!" and everyone laughed and grabbed another glass of champagne, and the toasts began.

"That was the most beautiful ceremony." Chrissie sighed. "Imagine finding that kind of love later in life. Not that they're ancient, but they're not exactly young folk, either."

"Imagine finding that kind of love at any age." Jared watched his father and Delia, who were both positively beaming. "I'm happy for him. I know he never had that with my mother. I know she didn't love him the way Delia does."

"I wonder if they ever wished they'd found each other first," Chrissie said. "Before . . . well, before whoever came first that didn't work out."

"Dad would probably say he wouldn't change things because that would mean he wouldn't have had Rachel and me. He's always made it clear that no matter what, he'd always choose us. Delia, I don't know her well enough to know if she feels enough resentment toward her first husband to wish she hadn't married him. She did have three children with him. But then again, he left them all and just walked out of their lives."

"Oh my God. I had no idea."

"Yeah. He found out about something Delia hadn't told him . . . well, everyone in the family knows, so it's no secret. Delia had a child when she was just out of high school. Her boyfriend was killed in Vietnam, and he never even knew about the baby. Her parents were apparently the holier-than-thou type—her dad was a minister—and they couldn't face the shame of their unwed daughter having a child, so they made her give the baby away. Delia had neglected to tell her husband about that until after Georgia was born—she's the youngest—and he just up and left. That's the short version."

"Oh." Chrissie looked stunned. "What an awful man. What happened to the baby she gave away? Did she ever find her?"

Jared tilted his glass in the direction of the tall, dark-haired pretty woman standing between India and Georgia. "Laura," he said. "Sometime you can ask her how they found each other."

"I can so relate, having had my dad leave my mom and me and just disappear like that." Chrissie stared at her glass. "I can totally relate."

"Sorry, I shouldn't have . . ."

Chrissie shook her head. "It's not your fault and you shouldn't need to feel you have to sanitize things for me. It happens. Obviously it's happened to others. I'm not the only one, and my mother's not the only woman who got dumped by her husband. At least Delia's kids know why he left. Not that that's much consolation."

"I don't know that they feel better knowing what a selfish ass their father is."

"I think that's still better than not knowing at all," Chrissie whispered. "'Cause you always think somehow it was your fault that he left and doesn't want to come back. It makes you wonder what's wrong with you . . ."

Jared put an arm around her and drew her close. "If I had a daughter who grew up to be the woman you are, I'd be so proud. I hope someday I do."

"That's the nicest thing anyone has ever said to me." She looked as if she was about to cry, so he tried to lighten her mood.

"Hey, you cook, you sing, you even dance. What's not to be proud of?"

"Thanks."

She smiled the sweetest smile he'd ever seen, and he wanted to kiss her, right there in front of his entire family, old and new. But he was afraid she'd be embarrassed, so instead he promised himself that before the night was over, he'd taste that smile, and see where that would lead.

CHRISSIE HAD FELT the energy changing over the past few days, but she was pretty sure she knew when both she and Jared felt the pretext of just being friends slip away. It had been subtle, and while not totally unexpected, she just hadn't thought it would come when it did. In that moment when she'd met his gaze across the room at the rehearsal, the air had all but crackled around her, and it had frightened her. Not that she was afraid of Jared in the way she'd come to fear Doug. She'd bet her life Jared would never, ever raise a hand to a woman. Of course, she hadn't expected Doug to, either, but then, she hadn't gotten to know him in the way she'd come to know Jared. They hadn't set out to impress each other, hadn't meant for anything to happen between them except for a few walks and a few meet-ups for ice cream. What could have been more casual than that? She couldn't put a finger on exactly when she'd known that things would change; she just knew they would, though she couldn't say how she knew.

Is this how Gigi knew things? she wondered. Had Gigi's magic rubbed off on her while they lived together? Was it contagious somehow? Because she obviously didn't know things before she moved to the island. Otherwise, would she have hooked up with Doug as quickly as she had? Wouldn't she have seen what he was?

Or had she seen something in him that she'd chosen to ignore?

She stood in front of the mirror in the guest bathroom, where she'd gone to freshen her makeup and take a breath from the party that was going on outside. Sophie had been right: the Enrights knew how to party. The band had played everything from the classics to hip-hop, with everyone requesting their own personal favorites. India—Jersey girl through and through—had requested both Springsteen and Bon Jovi. Ben had wanted U2 and Zoey preferred Lady Gaga. Georgia liked romantic ballads and her husband, Matt, preferred the Stones. Jared had requested a few of his favorite country tunes, and Rachel liked Ed Sheeran. That one band had been able to make everyone happy was a miracle.

Chrissie dropped her lipstick back into the small clutch she carried and opened the door. Apparently it had been India's turn to request: the house reverberated with "You Give Love a Bad Name."

"What a party," Rachel said when Chrissie went back onto the patio.

"Best party ever." Chrissie nodded. "Everything is amazing. The flowers are gorgeous, the music is fabulous, the food was incredible . . ."

"Were you taking notes?" Jared asked. "Trying to figure out what was in the soup? How was the lobster prepared? What was that herb in the sauce for the filet? Was that a raspberry cream in between the cake layers, or as some suggested, was it flavored with pomegranate?"

Chrissie laughed as he mimicked her. "I know what was in the soup, the lobster was slow roasted, there was tarragon in the sauce the filet was served with, and it was neither raspberry nor pomegranate in the filling for the cake."

"What was it, then?"

"Elderberry."

"You're guessing," he teased. "Or you're making it up."

"Ask Delia." Chrissie grinned, knowing she was right. "Go ahead. Ask her."

Jared looked at Rachel. "I give up."

"Don't try to outguess a cook when it comes to cooking," Rachel told him. "I think I'm going to have one dance with my six-year-old, then I'm going to send him to bed so I can dance the rest of the night with his daddy. So thoughtful of Delia to hire a crew of nannies for the night."

"I can't think of anything Delia may have forgotten," Chrissie told Jared. "Everything is perfect. It's a beautiful night and a perfect party and more importantly, everyone seems so happy."

"No reason not to be happy. It's a good night for everyone." Jared sat on the stone wall and tugged on Chrissie's hand until she was seated next to him. "Rachel's boys got a new grandmother who will happily spoil them, and Delia's grandkids got a new grandfather who will teach them all sorts of fun things and take them on adventures." He chuckled. "It's like Auntie Mame married Peter Pan."

"I can see that flamboyant streak in her, and you say he took you on plenty of adventures when you were a boy. So yeah, Mame and Peter. That fits," she agreed.

Someone announced, "The groom's special request for his bride," and everyone stepped out of the designated dance area to give Delia and Gordon the floor as the band began to play.

"Hey, that's one of the songs you played in the car the other day." Jared stood and pulled her up with him.

"No, this is 'As Time Goes By.' Same era, though."

They stood on the side of the dance floor, watching the newly married couple sway to the music.

"Dad must have taken dancing lessons," Jared whispered in Chrissie's ear. "He never showed us moves like that at home."

Jared stood behind her, his arms around her lightly. "I wish I knew the lyrics to this," he said.

"And the rest of us are so glad you don't." Rachel rolled her eyes.

"What? You think I can't sing?" Jared tried to act as if he were offended, but he was clearly amused.

"Jared, you've never been able to carry a tune. It was torture growing up, you trying to sing along with the radio or one of your CDs." Rachel looked at Chrissie and added, "My room was right across the hall from his. When he started singing, Aunt Bess's cat ran from the sound."

"I wasn't that bad," Jared said defensively.

"Yeah, you were. But we loved you anyway." Rachel patted him on the back.

Jared turned to Chrissie and asked, "Did I sound that bad in the car?"

Chrissie hesitated. "Depends. Are we in the truth zone?"

He nodded.

"Well—I was pretty sure you hadn't taken lessons."

"Damn. I thought I was being so cool. Singing along with Blake, I thought I sounded just like him."

"Ahhh, no. Sorry."

"I guess I need to work on my singing." He turned her around to face him. "But I have mad dancing skills, and this is a very romantic song they're playing."

He took her in his arms and danced where they stood. "And I am feeling very romantic right now."

Chrissie knew she was at a crossroad. To back away, or to let it take its course?

She slid her hand across his shoulder and let it rest against the back of his neck.

"You know this song? 'Moonlight Becomes You'?" he asked. "Johnny Mathis? Neither country nor 1940s, but a great song all the same."

"I do. I never heard it on the radio or anything, but my boss at Luna, Rob? He used to sing it all the time to his partner. I always thought it was so sweet, but I never heard anyone sing it but him."

He sang the first line and she giggled. "Jared, think you could just hum?"

"Really? I thought I was setting a mood here." His lips close to her ear, he sang softly, "'Moonlight becomes you, it goes with your hair . . .'"

"Jared?" she whispered.

"Hmmm?"

"Maybe you should let the song speak for itself."

"That bad, eh?"

"I'm tempted to ask you what you did with the money."

He leaned back and looked into her face.

"Oh, come on. It's an old joke," she told him. "You're going to make me say it, aren't you?"

"What did I do with what money?"

She rolled her eyes. "The money your father gave you for singing lessons."

Without missing a beat, he said, "Bought my first wet suit."

He pulled her close again and resumed singing in her ear, "'And I could get so romantic tonight . . .'"

Chrissie laughed softly. "I suppose I should admire your persistence. That thick shell of yours. Or might it be a thick skull?"

"Probably all of that." The song ended but he kept his arms around her. "And it's skin, not shell."

"Whatever." She shrugged but smiled all the same.

"Let's go for a walk," he whispered.

She poked one foot out from under the hem of her dress. "In these? I don't know how far I'd get."

"Then I'll carry you. Come on." He slowly slid his hands the length of her arms from shoulder to wrist, then laced the fingers of one hand through hers.

They went in through the house, then out the front door.

"The drive is paved, so we'll stick to that and try to avoid the uneven ground. Those heels would sink a good four inches into the grass," he said. "How 'bout out toward the garden?"

"A garden in the moonlight? You *are* pushing the romantic theme tonight."

"It's a romantic night, and I'm with a beautiful woman who makes me smile every time I think of her. What could be better?"

Chrissie stopped walking.

"Do you? Smile when you think of me?"

"It's all I seem to be doing lately," he admitted. "It didn't start out that way, but something happened somewhere between that first walk to the art center and the night we had dinner at the store. I'd explain it better if I understood it myself, but that's the truth. Since that night, I haven't been able to think about much else. Okay, maybe the delay on the dive, but that's understandable."

"Totally understandable. That's your job." She nodded and tried to respond to the rest of it.

"That's all you have to say?" Jared frowned. "I think I just pretty much poured my heart out to you. Put myself on the line. How 'bout the part where I said—"

She grabbed his face and kissed him on the lips before he could finish the sentence. Words weren't coming easily to her right then, but she wanted him to know she felt the same way, and at that moment, couldn't think of any other way to get her point across. As first kisses went, it was a winner. To her sheer joy, he kissed her back, and she could taste the remnants of the shot of Glen Livet he, Sam, Ben, Nick, and Matt had shared to toast Gordon a while ago.

Finally, she pulled away from him and looked up into his eyes.

"Do we understand each other now?" she asked.

"I believe we're on the same page, yes." He was grinning like an idiot. "I've been wanting to do that but was afraid of scaring you away."

"You don't scare me, Jared Chandler. And as long as you don't sing or try to convince me that diving would change my life . . ."

"Oh, but in the right water, it would change your life."

She put her hands over her ears. "Stop. No more. I'm not doing it."

"Sorry. When you love something, you want to share it with the people you care about." He tucked a strand of hair behind her ear. "I care about you, so I want to share the good things in my life with you."

"That's very sweet." She touched the side of his face with her fingers. "But the answer's still no."

"Can't blame a guy for trying."

The squawking of geese drew their attention to somewhere behind the barn.

"What do you suppose that's all about?" Chrissie frowned.

"There's a pond down there. I'm sure the geese still have babies. Maybe a fox or an owl has come around trying to snatch one."

"Poor thing."

"Have you ever seen geese go after a predator? The fox doesn't always win, especially if there's more than one goose chasing it."

Clouds began to drift across the face of the moon, dimming its light, and a breeze had picked up, bringing with it scents from the garden. Chrissie shivered from the unexpected chill, and Jared took off his jacket and draped it over her shoulders without speaking.

"Thank you," she said. It was a small gesture on his part, one he'd barely seemed to consider, but to a woman who'd never felt like a priority to the man she was with, it spoke volumes.

The party inside was winding down, and several guests were beginning to leave. Chrissie saw Barbara Noonan walking toward the parking area not far from where she and Jared stood.

"We should probably say good night to Grace," Chrissie said. "She's over by the walk, waiting, I guess, for Barbara to get the car and pick her up."

Jared took her by the hand and they made their way back to the house. Grace stood at the end of the walk.

"She looks so tiny, standing there," Chrissie whispered to Jared. "And see how the porch lights behind her are giving her a halo?"

They drew closer and Jared called Grace's attention to the effects of the lights.

"Chrissie thinks you have a halo, Grace. I thought only angels had halos."

"Oh my. I've been called many things, but never an angel," she said with a laugh.

Barbara's car pulled up just then and Jared opened the passenger door for her, but before she got in, Grace reached out and took one of Chrissie's hands.

"You did right by coming home when you did. Ruby needs you, and the island needs you." Grace leaned closer so only Chrissie could hear. "And whether he's ready to admit it or not, Jared needs you. Let fate play its hand, dear, but do be aware. Trust yourself, and all will be well."

"Be aware of what?" Chrissie whispered.

As if she hadn't heard, Grace turned to Jared. "Lovely wedding. Simply wonderful. I couldn't be happier for Delia—and, of course, for your father. Now, I'll see you back at the inn. Enjoy the rest of the night."

She got into the car and waved as Barbara drove toward the open gates.

"Did she say something to you just then?" Jared asked.

Chrissie nodded, trying to decipher Grace's words, which sounded strangely like something cryptic Ruby might say.

"Just that she's glad I came back, that Ruby needed me. Which is debatable, but okay. Ruby claims she doesn't need anyone." No need to repeat the part about being aware, since she hadn't understood it herself. Be aware of what? Of whom? Of Jared? Of moving too quickly?

"I'm glad you came back, too, and I'm glad I was here when you did. Imagine if the dive had been shut down completely and I'd left before you got here. Or if you'd never stopped at the inn that day you brought Ruby over to have lunch with Grace." Jared draped an arm over Chrissie's shoulder, and when the taillights from the car disappeared around the bend in the road, they walked toward the house. "If you didn't know them, you might think they're an odd pair, Ruby and Grace. But there's a strange vibe that comes from both. I can't put my finger on it, but it's there."

Chrissie nodded. "It's there, and it's the same vibe. I'm starting to believe there's something in the water in St. Dennis that gives people some sort of sight."

"Oh, now who's taking a step into the unexplainable?" he teased.

"Ah, we're back to that again." Chrissie turned in the doorway.

"There you two are." Gordon opened the door. "The band is packing up and Delia and I were just about to give a final toast to our families before calling it a night. Come on out to the patio."

Gordon put a friendly hand on Chrissie's arm and escorted her through the house, Jared following. When they reached the double doors and stepped outside, Gordon replaced his hand with that of his son's, and a look passed between them. Chrissie felt that he'd somehow silently assured Jared of his approval.

Once again, champagne was passed around, and when everyone had a glass, Delia and Gordon moved to the center of the group.

"I can't imagine taking this step without each one of you here with us," Delia began. "You are my life-blood, my children, my grandchildren." She smiled at Rachel and Jared before adding, "My new children and new grandchildren, and not a 'step' in the group." She turned to Gordon. "You have enriched my life beyond words. I never thought I'd find someone I'd want to spend my days—and yes, my nights—"

"Mom!" Zoey called out, and everyone, including Delia, laughed.

"Yes, my nights. And don't think they don't matter at any age, young lady." Another round of laughter, then light applause.

Delia turned to her new husband. "Gordon Chandler, you are a remarkable man. You've shown me a wonderful world I'd never known existed." To her children, she said, "And before Zoey can attempt to silence me again, let me say I'm talking about scuba diving. And before any of you say a word, I love it. I've loved every minute I've spent with you since the day we met, Gordon, on land and at sea."

"As have I, sweetheart. But while we're on the subject, now's a good time for me to give you my wedding gift." Gordon ducked into the house and returned a moment later carrying a large box wrapped in white paper and sporting an enormous bow. "Happy wedding, darling."

"What on earth . . . ?" Delia was obviously surprised, but pleased, so she set the box on a nearby table and began to open it. When she lifted the lid, she started to laugh with apparent delight. "Oh, how perfect."

From the box she lifted something that to Chrissie looked like a black leather suit.

"Mom, is that a wet suit?" Georgia asked.

"I do believe it is." Her smile bright with surprise and pleasure, Delia turned to Gordon and kissed him. "My own wet suit. I can't wait to put it on."

"Hopefully not tonight," Zoey muttered just loud enough for everyone to hear.

"Oh, you." Still laughing, Delia tossed the bow at Zoey, who caught it with a grin.

"Mom, this is such a shock. I can hardly imagine you on a boat, but diving . . ." Nick shook his head. "I couldn't even get you into a kayak in six feet of water."

"This is totally different, love. This is exciting, an adventure we can share." She gazed at Gordon with love in her eyes.

"So many adventures to share, Delia." Gordon cleared his throat and returned his attention to their family. "A toast to each of you. We love you," Gordon said, his eyes glistening. "Our lives would not be complete without you. All of you."

His gaze met Chrissie's, and again she felt as if he'd blessed her with his approval.

"Here's to you, new dad," Nick proposed. "Welcome to the family."

Everyone drained their glasses, and in the moments that followed, they all said their good nights, and couple by couple, left for their rooms on the expansive second floor. Finally, only Chrissie and Jared were left on the patio.

"Turn off the lights before you come in, will you, son?" Gordon paused on his way out to kiss his son, then kissed Chrissie's cheek as well.

"Well, then. Alone at last," Jared quipped. He sat on the wall, holding her hand.

The caterer's crew arrived with apologetic smiles but determined to finish their tasks.

"Well, not quite," she said.

"Probably just as well." Jared stood, still holding her hand. "It's late, and it's been a long day, and we still have tomorrow. Come on, Chris. I'll walk you to your room."

Hand in hand, they walked up the stairs. At the door to her room, Chrissie turned to him, and before she could speak, he kissed her, taking his time, his lips incredibly soft, the kiss slow. It felt endless, and Chrissie felt herself drifting into a place of warmth and pleasure. When his lips moved to her forehead, she closed her eyes and savored the sensation, the sweep of emotion that washed through her.

"I'll see you in the morning," he promised.

Chrissie nodded.

"I'll have your coffee ready." He backed away down the hall toward his own room.

She nodded again.

He walked all the way down the hall backward, his eyes on her. When he reached his room, he blew her a kiss, and she laughed softly before going into her room and closing the door behind her.

Chapter Eleven

Chrissie was still awake when the earliest of the birds began to warble outside her window on Sunday morning. She'd lain awake all night, reliving every moment of the evening and everything Jared had said. She knew she was on the brink of falling for him and wanted to make sure she'd land in a safe place. She loved that he'd kissed her but hadn't pushed for more, as if instinctively understanding that she needed to sort things out for herself. For the most part, that was pretty much what she'd been doing all night. Sorting out her feelings, trying to separate reality from wishful thinking.

The acceptance and warmth extended to her by both the Chandlers and the Enrights had made her relax the first night she was there, and by the last night, she'd almost felt like one of them. The wedding had been emotional and loving, and she'd felt that by witnessing an exchange of such heartfelt vows, she'd been offered a glimpse into who these people were, and she longed to be one of them. Rachel had been especially welcoming, sharing little bits of her family life with Chrissie, like the fact that Sam, her husband, was an internationally respected marine archaeologist who'd discovered and carefully unearthed the treasures of an Egyptian trade ship the year before. The paper he'd written regarding the find had been published, won awards, and earned him the offer of a professorship at a university in Maryland renowned for its archaeology department. If he accepted, Rachel would likely be "grounded" for a while, unable to take any salvage jobs for her father because she and Sam had made a pact that if possible, at least one of them would always be with the children. Now might be the time to have that third child, Rachel had confided. What did Chrissie think?

Rachel had been a lot more open about her personal life than she herself would have been with someone she'd just met a few days ago, but she obviously thought Chrissie's relationship with Jared had gone further and to a different level than it had. Trying not to sound judgmental, Chrissie'd said honestly that she didn't know Rachel well enough and didn't know their circumstances enough to give her an intelligent answer, a response Rachel had seemed to respect.

They were interesting families, both so different from each other and from her own. While Jared's mother and Delia's husband weren't so very different from her own father when it came to family loyalty—or the lack of it—the thing Chrissie found most fascinating was that rather than turn to other people to help put them back on their feet, as her mother had done with several husbands, Delia and Gordon had worked hard to succeed on their own. Delia had become one of the most popular and best-selling authors on the planet, a position Chrissie knew must have taken a lot of late nights and determination on Delia's part as she raised three children on her own. Gordon had built his salvage company into one of the most highly regarded and often requested salvagers in the business through hard work and long hours away from home, yet still he'd remained close to his children, had overseen their upbringing and education, and gave them the tools to join him in the family business if they chose to do so. It was a tribute to him that both Jared and Rachel had wanted to follow in his footsteps.

Chrissie had no one's footsteps in which to follow, and the contrast was depressing. She didn't know what her father did for a living, but she was pretty sure he probably wasn't a cook. And Luke? She didn't even know who or where he was. At times like this, she longed for the roots she hadn't had, especially since she'd been surrounded by people who knew what it really meant to be a family.

But she did have Ruby, and she was Chrissie's anchor.

This weekend Chrissie's emotions had swung from one extreme to the other. On the one hand, she was somewhat content to be part of a wonderful family, even if only someone else's and only for a few days. On the other hand, she felt sad because it had made her realize how much she had missed growing up. When she finally fell into a brief sleep at first light, she was stuck halfway between the two.

The knocking on her bedroom door brought her around, and she sat up as if drugged.

"Chris? You awake?" Jared called through the closed door.

"Barely. What time is it?" she mumbled.

"What? I can't hear you."

"Never mind. I'll be down in a few." She rubbed her eyes, yawned, then made herself get out of the bed.

She looked out the window on a day that was overcast. Clouds had moved in overnight, and it looked as if it would rain at any minute. She stumbled into the bathroom, her lack of sleep making her feel sluggish.

A quick shower helped, and after she dried her hair in record time she put on a little makeup—a day face, Cass had called the light application when she'd been tutoring her—and hoped the concealer did its job and covered up the dark circles under her eyes. She got dressed in white pants and a fitted shirt of palest blue linen. She rolled up the long sleeves and slipped into the pair of old ballet flats she'd brought with her, then tied her still-damp hair into a ponytail with a paisley scarf.

Breakfast was just about over when she followed the chatter to the dining room

"I'm so sorry." She offered a general apology to everyone at the table. "I overslept."

"You must have needed the sleep, dear." Delia passed her a plate of toast. "It was quite a night."

"I had trouble getting to sleep." Zoey offered Chrissie a bowl of scrambled eggs. "Too much excitement these past few days, I guess. I just couldn't shut off my brain."

"It has been a busy week," India agreed. "Our kids are wiped out."

"Ours, too," Rachel said. "I think we might leave this morning instead of later today. I can't think of anything worse than being cooped up inside with a bunch of littles on a rainy day."

"Well, there's the playroom," Delia said. "And the barn. There are any number of things they could do."

"Mom, don't you and Gordon want a little privacy?" Zoey put down the mug of coffee she'd been drinking.

"Well . . ." Delia shrugged. "I certainly don't think a few more hours with the grandkiddies would be a hardship."

"It would," Zoey announced. "We'll be leaving early, too."

Chrissie could feel Jared watching her while the conversation swirled around her. She nibbled cold toast, ate cold eggs and bacon, and drank lukewarm orange juice. Fortunately, the coffee had cooled to just the right temperature.

"What do you think?" Jared asked.

"About what?" She finished the juice and the last bite of bacon.

"Staying through the day as we'd planned or leave early because of the weather."

"I think everyone else is leaving, so I think we probably should, too," she replied.

"I agree." He got a fresh cup of coffee, but it was clear to Chrissie he was marking time, waiting for her.

When she finished, she folded her arms in front of her on the table and watched his face. She liked that in addition to his being so handsome, there was character there, and humor. He was the whole package, as far as she was concerned, and she had to keep pinching herself as a reminder that he seemed to be as into her as she was into him.

"Can I get you something else?" he asked from across the table. "More coffee? There were some killer Danish if Rachel didn't eat them all."

"I heard that," Rachel said from the opposite end of the table.

"No, thanks. I'm good," Chrissie said.

"I think we'll get going." Jared stood. "We were going to go canoeing on the Brandywine after breakfast, but that's out of the question with all the rain. I think we'll just head back so Chrissie can rest up for work tomorrow."

Canoeing on the Brandywine? Chrissie didn't recall having made those plans, and tomorrow was Monday. She didn't work on Monday, but he could have forgotten that. Or Jared was merely trying to make a graceful exit.

By the time she'd packed her belongings and met Jared downstairs, others had gathered in the grand foyer to say good-bye. There were hugs and exchanges of phone numbers and email addresses, promises to visit St. Dennis and promises extracted from Chrissie to visit Georgia and Matt at their farm, Pumpkin Hill, in the Maryland countryside and India and Nick at their home in Devlin's Light. Delia and Gordon insisted Jared bring Chrissie back for another weekend, and Zoey reminded Jared that she and Ben didn't live that far from Delia, so they should plan on dinner one night. Rachel promised to call Chrissie later in the week. All in all, it had taken almost a half hour to leave. Jared had driven the car around and stopped near the walk so Chrissie wouldn't have to walk in the rain, which had begun in earnest while they were having breakfast.

"Overwhelmed much?" Jared asked as he sounded two quick beeps on the Jag's horn as they passed the house where his father and sister stood under the protection of the porch roof to wave good-bye.

"Slightly overwhelmed, yeah." Chrissie rested against the headrest.

"Everyone liked you. My dad liked you a lot and my sister thought you were the only intelligent girl I ever dated. She wants to be your friend."

"I liked everyone, too, but I doubt you only dated dummies." Chrissie stifled a yawn. "And I'd love to get to know Rachel better."

"She has very high standards and she's very astute. I couldn't argue with her." The car was chilly from the rain and dampness, so he turned the heater on low.

"Thanks for that." She was having trouble keeping her eyes open. "Were we really going to go canoeing today?"

"We were. There are several canoes in the barn, and Sam and I thought we'd take you and Rachel out on the beautiful Brandywine River. Of course, we'd have had to take one of their boys, since they couldn't take them both, but that could have been fun. I don't get enough time to spend with my nephews."

"Rachel said Sam was offered a teaching position at a school in Maryland. If he takes it, you could see them more often."

"That would be cool. I'd like that." They came to a traffic light, and Jared stopped behind a pickup truck that looked more at home in the rural terrain than the Jaguar. "What'd you think of my dad's gift to Delia?"

"Truthfully, I thought it was a little odd." She opened her eyes and glanced across the console at him.

"What was odd about it?"

"It just doesn't seem like a gift a man would give his wife on their wedding night. A wet suit isn't very romantic."

"What could be more romantic than giving her something she could use to enjoy doing something with him? What should he have given her? According to Rachel, she has more jewelry than any woman could ever wear. She doesn't need a car or obviously a house. She buys herself whatever she wants when she wants it. I think he bought it for her because it was the one thing she didn't have that she wanted. And before you ask, yes, he's taken her diving and she loved it."

"Maybe she was just saying that she loved it to make him happy." That's what Chrissie would have done, once upon a time. Would she still? She hoped not.

"You'll eat those words when you get to know her better. She doesn't do anything she doesn't want to do and she's always blunt about what she's thinking. And once you get past your first dive, you'll totally get it. I'm thinking we'll start with some warm, peaceful tropical—"

"Don't hold your breath." Chrissie closed her eyes again, ignoring his last comment and wondering if in fact she'd get to know Delia better. She hoped she might.

"Tired?" he asked, and she nodded.

"I didn't sleep well last night," she admitted.

"Why not?"

"I couldn't stop thinking about—" She really didn't want to tell him she'd mostly been thinking about him.

"Thinking about what?"

"Just . . . sensory overload, I guess. There'd been so much going on for the past few days, I think it all caught up with me. I'm used to a quiet life, you know. Life on the island is nothing like life with Delia."

"Nothing is like life with Delia. But I get it. Sometimes it's all a bit much for me, too. I spend most of my time underwater or on a dive boat."

"I thought you were the playboy in the bunch."

"Maybe in my younger days. These days . . . I'm good just taking long walks and hitting up the local ice cream shop with a special woman."

"Anyone I know?"

"If you don't, you should. She's one of those women who has it all, you know? Brains, humor, and she's a knockout. Oh, and she can cook like a demon."

"Like a demon." She opened her eyes and turned to look at him. He was smiling and looking at her from the corner of his eye. No one had ever called her a knockout before.

"Yup. What she can do with oysters . . . pure sorcery."

"Sorcerers and demons are not the same thing."

"Picky, picky. You get the general idea."

She smiled and leaned back once again. It was getting harder to keep her eyes open.

Jared turned on the radio and searched for her forties station. They listened to some early Sinatra as they drove toward the interstate.

"Jared," she said sleepily, "tell me about something else you can't explain."

He thought for a moment.

"There's a Mayan pyramid in Chichén Itzá in

Mexico. If you stand at the bottom of the pyramid's steps and clap your hands, it makes an echo that sounds like a flock of birds."

"Did you actually do that? You clapped your hands and heard a flock of birds taking off?"

"I did, and it did. And before you ask, there have been acoustic specialists who have tested it, and they can't explain it, either. Actually, some have said it sounds just like the cry of the quetzal."

"What's a quetzal?"

"It's a bird that was considered sacred by the Mayans. They believed it was a god."

"Huh." She thought it over, then asked, "Did you make that up?"

"Nope. Everything I've told you has been true. The UFOs, the disappearance of Çatalhöyük, the pyramid . . ."

"The Alaskan triangle . . ."

"That, too."

"Are there more?" she asked, her voice starting to fade.

"For another time."

The last sounds she heard were the sound of the windshield wipers and Jared singing along very softly with Frank Sinatra, but she was too tired to remember the name of the song.

"WHERE ARE WE?" Chrissie sat up slowly and rubbed her eyes before remembering she'd put on mascara that morning. She hoped she hadn't just smeared it. She'd had black eyes before, and she knew it wasn't a good look for her.

"In the parking lot in front of Ruby's store."

"We're back already?"

"If you slept through the ride, I could see it feeling like 'already.' If you were driving, it was close to two hours. That includes stopping for gas." He turned to look at her and put his arm over the back of her seat. "You slept through that, too."

"Oh, I am so sorry." She shook out the few remaining cobwebs from her brain. "I just crashed."

"All the way home."

"Again, I'm sorry."

"It's okay. You were tired, and I got to listen to some great country music after the Sinatra hour was over."

"What's the Sinatra hour?" She sat all the way up and unhooked her seat belt.

"Apparently there's a station out of Baltimore that plays all Sinatra for one hour every Sunday. We just happened to catch it on the way home."

"I'm sorry I missed that." She wanted to get out of the car and stretch, but she didn't want him to think she was eager to get away from him.

Thunder shook the car and rain pounded the hood. The stretch might have to wait.

"Why don't you go on inside? Just run. I'll get your suitcase out of the trunk and bring it in," he suggested.

"You're going to get soaked."

"I'm going to have to get your suitcase in any case, so I'm going to get wet. No reason you have to get wet, too." He reached behind her and grabbed her garment bag. "You take this, and I'll bring in the rest."

"If you're sure . . ." She reached for the door handle.

"I'm positive. Go."

She went. Getting out of the somewhat low car with her bag and her garment bag, which held several dresses, wasn't as easy as it sounded. She could feel something slip off its hanger, and her feet slid on the pebbles in the parking lot. As it turned out, running wasn't an option. She managed to get up the steps and under the porch roof where she waited for Jared, who had the larger load but managed to get across the lot without slipping.

Chrissie tried the store's front door and found it unlocked.

"Oh good," she said. "Ruby's here."

She pushed open the door and Jared followed her inside.

"Ruby?" she called.

When there was no answer, Chrissie said, "She must be in the back. Let me just go tell her we're here. Come on in, Jared."

"I'm dripping wet. I should probably stand in one spot."

"I don't think it matters." She draped the garment bag over the counter and went into the back room. "This floor has probably had a thousand people dripping water in its time."

She went into Ruby's apartment but came back shaking her head. "She isn't there. She said she'd be here." She fought to keep panic out of her voice. "Maybe she's upstairs."

Before Jared could react, she ran up the steps, opening and closing the doors.

"She's not up there, either," she said, out of breath when she ran back down.

"Whoa." In a blink, Jared was there, his arms reaching to pull her in. "What's the matter? You're shaking and the look on your face—Chris, what's wrong? You look scared to death."

"We need to call Owen." She shook him off and all but ran to the counter. She found her bag and pulled it apart searching for her phone. She found it and speed-dialed Owen's number.

When he finally answered, her hands were shaking. "Owen, she isn't here. Ruby isn't here."

"No, she's here. We brought her down to have lunch with us since she didn't expect you back until late this afternoon. What the hell's wrong?"

"Oh. Oh, okay." She could have passed out from relief. "I came in and the door was unlocked, and she wasn't here, and I thought . . . I thought . . . I was afraid . . ."

"You were afraid he'd found you and hurt Ruby? Oh, Chrissie." Owen sighed. "We should have left a note. Cass wanted to, but Ruby and I both thought we'd have her back before you got home." He paused. "Are you all right now?"

"Yes. I'm fine. Thanks." She leaned against the counter.

"Is Jared still there?"

"Yes."

"Does he know about . . ." Owen started to ask.

"No."

"I think you need to tell him," Owen said.

"I think you're probably right." Chrissie looked across the counter to where Jared stood quietly watching her.

"Like, probably now."

"You're right," she agreed. "I will."

"Otherwise he's going to think you're a little crazy, kid."

"Might be too late. Thanks, Owen."

"We'll bring Ruby back after the rain stops," he told her right before he hung up.

"So. I take it Owen knows where Ruby is?" Jared asked.

Chrissie nodded. "She went to his place to have lunch with him and Cass."

Jared folded his arms across his chest and watched her as if waiting. Which, she knew, he was.

"What did you think happened to her?" he asked softly. "What are you afraid of, Chris?"

"It's a long story."

He glanced out the window. "It doesn't look like the rain's stopping anytime soon, so we have plenty of time."

"Take your jacket and shirt off," she told him. "I'm pretty sure Owen left some things here that might fit you." She smiled weakly. "Like I said, it's a long story and it'll take a while to tell it. I don't want you sitting around in cold, wet clothes."

She went up the steps again, and a few minutes later came down with a pair of sweatpants and a sweatshirt.

"These should fit. And bonus—they're even clean. You can change in here and I'll go into the kitchen and make coffee. I think we could both use a cup or two."

She filled the Keurig she'd given Ruby for Christmas with water and set a mug beneath it while she sorted out her thoughts, then made a second mug.

She wasn't even sure where to begin. Obviously this was about Doug, but the story began way before that. Well, he already knew that part, the part about her father abandoning them and her mother being a flake. Had she explained to him just how unreliable Dorothy was? She wasn't sure. Telling him about Doug would be humiliating, but if their relationship was to move forward, he needed to know. It wouldn't be fair not to tell him, especially after the way she overreacted when Ruby wasn't in the store and wasn't in her apartment. The fear that had been dormant in her—that he would find her—had emerged full-blown. The fear that he could hurt Ruby . . . She shivered at the thought.

When she came back into the store, Jared was sitting at Ruby's table against the wall, looking out the window.

"It's turned into quite a storm," he said. "Thunder, lightning bolts flying everywhere. It always seems so much more impressive near water, don't you think?"

"I do." She set a mug in front of him.

He put his hands around the mug as if to warm them, then took a sip. "It's just the way I like it."

"You're not the only one who's observant." She tried to force a smile as she sat opposite him. She wanted to be able to watch his face, see his expressions as she spoke, so she could try to read what he really was thinking.

"Owen's things fit just fine, thanks." He pointed to the bait cooler near the door where he'd laid out his clothes to dry. "Hopefully there's no way for the worms to get out of the bait boxes."

"I'm pretty sure the lids are taped down."

"Lucky for me."

"So." She took a deep breath. "You want to know . . ." She took another. "You want to know why I got upset when I couldn't find Ruby."

"I figured it wasn't because you were thinking she'd wandered away because she's one hundred years old and forgot where she lived." He paused. "Okay, that wasn't funny. So what did you think happened to her?"

"I thought my ex-boyfriend hurt her." There. It was out. Part of it, anyway.

"Why would he do that?"

"Because I didn't tell him I was leaving before I left, and I didn't tell him where I was going."

"So you think he started looking for you, found you, and took it out on Ruby when you weren't here?"

"Yes." The thought of Doug being in the same room with Ruby made her sick to her stomach.

"Chrissie, has he ever hurt you?"

"Too many times to remember."

"I'm calling the truth zone here. I want to know everything."

She told him about meeting Doug and being swept off her feet. About thinking they were in love and moving in with him way too soon before she really knew him. About how he began to control her in little ways, then how he slowly took over her life, at first with words, then with physical threats that he soon made good on.

"This guy physically abused you? Hurt you?" Jared's tone was steady, but she could see a twitch in his jaw that he was fighting to control. "He *hit* you?"

"Yeah. I let it happen, and keep happening, and I don't have any excuse for that."

"Baby, you don't need an excuse." His voice softened to the point where she strained to hear him. "You didn't do anything wrong. This is all on him, not on you."

"I shouldn't have let it go on the way I did. I let it go on way too long."

"Because you were afraid."

"I never told anyone, I never called the police, I never did any of the things that would have been smart."

"Whoa. Listen to yourself. How 'bout he never stopped to think about what a coward he was, or how big an asshole he was? How 'bout he never stopped to think about what it meant to be a man and how he should be trying to control his temper instead of you?" His voice rose along with his growing anger. "And it must have been hard to do the 'smart' thing when you're being threatened with bodily harm."

"I know all that now, I'm just trying to tell you how it was. He did it because he could. Because I let him get away with it. Because I didn't have enough respect for myself to walk out the first time it happened. And I let him convince me that everything he said about me was true. That I was stupid and fat and not very attractive . . ."

"That's total bull. You're beautiful and you're far from fat, and no one would question your intelligence."

"I let him undermine my self-confidence and let him make me feel incompetent. For several years I stayed in jobs that were beneath me because he'd made me believe that I wasn't good enough to do anything else. I let—"

"Stop. You keep saying, 'I let.' There's no *let* when you're being coerced or manipulated and threatened." Jared got up and crouched down in front of her. "I'm trying to find the right words and they're just not coming." He swallowed hard, and she could see his eyes were beginning to fill up. "I am *so so so sorry* that happened to you. If I could change one thing about my life, I'd have met you before he did so you'd never have had to go through that."

"Me, too." She touched his face and could almost feel the pain he was feeling through her fingertips.

"Where is this guy now? What's his name?"

"It doesn't matter."

"Oh, it matters." His eyes hardened. "It matters. Where would I find him?"

"I don't want you to find him. I want to forget that part of my life ever happened."

"But you won't. As long as he's out there somewhere, you're always going to be looking over your shoulder. You're always going to react with fear first, like you did a little while ago."

"I honestly don't think he could find me." She told him all the ways she'd covered her tracks.

"Good moves, all." Jared shook his head. "But we're in the truth zone, remember? We both know you *do* think he can find you. That's why you went absolutely white with fear when you couldn't find Ruby. That's the first place your mind went."

"No one knows where I am except Rob, my former boss. And he would die before he'd tell Doug anything."

"Well, let's hope it doesn't come to that. If Doug went after him . . ." Jared stood and pulled out the chair next to hers, then sat, taking her hands in his. She could tell he was worried, much more than she'd expected him to be. The anger, she'd expected.

"Rob's married to a former NFL linebacker." Chrissie smiled. "I think Doug's smart enough not to take on Rob."

"So what do we do, babe? Do we just keep waiting for the day when he shows up?"

"I just want to put it behind me." Chrissie's frustration was beginning to build inside her. "That was the worst time of my life. I hated myself back then. I believed every horrible thing he said about me was true and I wasn't strong enough to fight back. I finally got strong enough to leave. Isn't that enough?"

"It was very brave of you to leave, Chris. And yes, it's enough until he figures out where you are."

"The police in St. Dennis know about him, they have his photo and a description of his car. If by some strange twist he was able to figure out where I am, he'll be picked up."

"That's assuming they remember to look for him, and assuming he passes by while someone's out on patrol." Jared shook his head. "I don't like this situation, Chris."

"What do you suggest I do?"

"Right now, I don't know. Maybe I'll powwow with Owen. Maybe talk to the police, see if they have any suggestions. I'm not comfortable leaving this to chance." He seemed to think it over. "Are there any weapons here?"

"A couple of kitchen knives."

"That's what I figured. The best thing would be for you to come stay with me at the inn or the boat, but I know—"

"You know I won't leave Ruby, and we both know she won't leave the store."

"And I didn't see an alarm system."

"On Cannonball Island?"

"That's what I thought."

"You're acting like there's an immediate problem. I overreacted, I didn't stop to think that Ruby had gone somewhere. It's not like her to leave the door unlocked, though, but she might have gone out the back, or thought I didn't have a key, or just forgot," she reasoned, now that she'd calmed down. "And I'm sure Rob would have called me if Doug had been in, and he hasn't. He stopped by one night after I left and asked if I'd been in, or if I was scheduled to work, but as far as I know, he hasn't asked since."

"Maybe he hasn't asked because he figured out another way."

"There is no other way he can find me, Jared, so could we please talk about something else? I'm feeling spooked now. I only brought it up because I thought you should know. I've been wanting to tell you, but I couldn't bring myself to let you know what a loser I used to be."

"Stop saying that."

"That's how I saw myself, and the fact that I know better now doesn't change the way I used to feel. *Used to* feel."

She studied his face, searching for a sign that he thought less of her because of her confession, but there was nothing there beyond understanding and concern.

The way he looked at her was assurance enough that finding out who she'd been hadn't changed the fact that he cared about who she was now.

"You have Owen on speed dial. How 'bout my number?"

She shook her head, and he gestured for her to make that change.

"The police?"

"Yes." She held up her phone to show him that she had the private cell number for the chief of police as well as the police station.

"So I don't have to tell you to call if something doesn't feel right or there's something suspicious . . ."

"No. I got that message from Owen and from Beck a couple of weeks ago."

"Okay. Bases covered. Now, come here and kiss me the way you did last night." He held out his hand and pulled her into his lap. His arms around her tightly, he kissed the line of her jaw softly before moving on to her lips.

It was easy to lose herself in him. He surrounded her and kissed her soft and sweet, then long and hard. She couldn't decide which she liked better. She'd happily indulge in either, so she took his face in her hands and kissed him back, following his lead. She was just getting into it when the sound of a car door slamming made her jump.

She looked out the window and saw Owen's old Jeep in the driveway.

"It must have stopped raining." She glanced out the window. "Yep. Sun's coming out. Bummer. I wasn't done with you yet."

"Just getting started," he murmured.

She gave Jared one more quick kiss before getting off his lap and going to the door.

"Hi, guys," she called as Owen helped Ruby out of the car. "Did you have a good lunch?"

"I SHOULD BE on my way," Jared said after the expected round of "How was the wedding?" and "Did you have a good time?," mostly from Cass and Owen.

He'd thought Ruby was relatively quiet but seemed a bit on edge. She may have overheard parts of Owen's earlier phone conversation, or more likely, Jared thought, she could have sensed Chrissie's fear. It wouldn't have surprised him if she had. He was pretty sure she knew about Chrissie's previous relationship, so it would follow that she might be hypersensitive to any possible threat to her great-granddaughter.

Then again, she did *know* things.

"Hey, nice sweats," Owen had said when he came in. When he saw Jared's clothes on the wall hanger, his eyes had narrowed suspiciously.

"I got caught in the downpour," Jared explained before Owen could even ask. "Chrissie found these upstairs, so she let me borrow them until my things dried. Which they still haven't yet. I checked."

"You can bring them to the boat tomorrow," Owen told him.

"What's tomorrow?"

"Didn't you see the email? We've been provisionally cleared to remove the artifacts from the sunken ship, as much as possible without disturbing the suspected settlement beneath it. I think they're looking for a forensic anthropologist who can dive to see if there are any Native American remains down there.

It's doubtful, though. Ruby says the Native American graveyards are up over the ridge on the other side of the river, and she always seems to know these things. But all it means for us is that we can start diving again as long as we stick to the merchant ship."

"That's great news." Jared couldn't help but grin. "I couldn't see hanging around too much longer with nothing to do. I'm not used to loafing. I'm going to have to call back the guys I sent home last week."

"Bet they'll be glad to get that call." Owen slapped Jared on the back and said, "Come outside with me for a minute."

They went out onto the porch and stood there looking at each other, each waiting for the other to speak. Finally, Jared said, "Yeah, she told me. What are we going to do about it?"

"Short of tracking this guy down first and giving him some of what he gave her—"

"I'd be up for that," Jared cut in. There was nothing he'd like more. He had no use for men like Chrissie's ex, and would happily serve up a little payback on her behalf.

"She'd have a fit. Besides, on the outside chance he's moved on, we'd just be reminding him that she had the audacity to leave."

"I think the best thing we can do is just keep an eye on her and on the store as best we can. It would probably be helpful to her if we didn't make too big a deal out of it, at least to her. I don't think we need to continue reminding her what she went through. That's only going to keep her frightened."

"If she's scared, she might be more vigilant," Owen said.

"If she's scared, she'll stop living the life she's made for herself here, and that's important to her. I don't know details, but I know she has issues about her father leaving her and her mother. She's not close to her mother, apparently—"

"No one is. Her mom, Dorothy, and my mom are first cousins, grew up together here on the island. Used to be best friends, according to my mom. She hasn't heard from Dorothy in thirty years."

"So she's been pretty much left behind by everyone in her family. Must be almost like being orphaned. It's not hard to see how she fell hard for the first guy who paid any real attention to her. Then he turns out to be a monster, she finally gets the courage to leave, and settles herself somewhere she feels safe. She won't feel safe if we keep telling her this guy's coming for her. We just need to make sure he doesn't get to her."

"You're awfully involved in this for someone who only considers her a friend," Owen said.

"I did consider her a friend. I still do."

"But . . ."

"But there's more to it than that. She's . . . she's more than that to me."

"Geez, Chandler, you can get any woman you want. You have to go after my cousin." Owen ran a hand over his face. "I don't even want to think about it."

"She's the woman I want, and I know what you're thinking, but no, it isn't like that. Chrissie isn't like anyone else. I don't know where this is headed, but I do know I will never hurt her in any way. I can promise you that."

"I can't believe it. You and my annoying little cousin Chrissie."

"She isn't annoying to me."

"Not to me anymore, either, but boy, she sure was when she was little. And now she's all grown up and one of my best buds has his eye on her. My bud who was my partner in crime for how many years and through how many bars, late nights, and beach bunnies?"

"Too many to count," Jared replied. "But I remind you, you settled down. So if you could grow up, it could happen to anyone."

"What are you guys doing out there?" Cass opened the door.

Owen shrugged. "Just talking."

"Well, come on in and have a beer with us. Chrissie made salsa and it's out of this world. Lots of heat."

"A beer and some hot salsa sounds good," Owen said.

"I'll be with you in a few minutes," Jared told him. "I want to call the guys and tell them to start on back."

"I can't guarantee there'll be anything left if you take too long, bro."

"I won't be long." Jared took out his phone, sat on the top step, and began to make his calls.

JARED LAY BACK on the bed in the cabin of the *Cordelia Elizabeth*. He'd given his crewman, Ray, the night off since he'd been on board since Thursday, and sent him to shore in the outboard motor boat he'd rented from Alec earlier and tied up off the dive platform. The first thing Jared did after Ray left was to start up the *Cordy E*'s engine and move it to a spot right beyond the cove on the other side of the island. From here he had a clear view of the general store, and while he knew it was foolish to think he was close enough to see someone skulking around with the naked eye, it made him feel he was watching over Chrissie and Ruby. He removed the binoculars from his locker and trained them on the shore, and was satisfied he could see well enough if someone was on this side of the building. That left the side closest to the bridge unguarded, but then again, he was fifty feet from the shore, so how effective his watch could be was questionable. But it made him feel he was doing something, and he needed that.

He'd been gutted by Chrissie's confession and he hadn't tried to hide it. How could anyone have raised a hand to that sweet woman? He wasn't kidding when he said he was up for tracking the weasel down and letting him feel a little of what Chrissie must have felt, even though intellectually he knew that wasn't going to make things better for her and wouldn't erase the past. What he really needed to do was help her to replace the bad memories with happy ones, to show her that she was unconditionally worth the best that a relationship could be. He wanted to be the man who did that for her.

The weekend had opened his eyes to so many things. He'd been suspecting that his interest in their historic walking tours was based on something more than a budding fascination with St. Dennis's past; the ice cream, however, had been a given. Rachel had been right about one thing: he didn't do historic walking tours. The first time he'd gone with Chrissie he'd simply been looking for something to do, something to pass the time because he was bored and the cute blonde he'd tried to pick up in the lobby had more or less blown him off. But he'd liked being with Chrissie that day, so he looked forward to doing it again. When he took her out on the deadrise, it was because he'd wanted her to see the town from his vantage point, from the water.

He'd enjoyed the weekend with her and his family, was happy that he'd had the good sense to ask her in the first place. It had pleased him to see the way she fit in with everyone, like the piece of a puzzle he hadn't realized had been missing.

While Chrissie'd been upstairs getting ready to leave, his father had taken him aside and said, "Chrissie seems like a special girl. You know I never comment on your girlfriends, but Delia and I like her very much. We're hoping you bring her back for a weekend when things aren't quite so hectic so we can get to know her a little better."

"That would be nice, Dad," he'd replied.

"Don't run from it, son." Gordon had put his arm around Jared's shoulder. "Run toward it. Love is the most—"

"Dad, no one's using the L-word." Jared had laughed nervously and held up both hands as if to ward off the word. "No one's there yet. We're really just starting to date."

"Do you know how long it took me to fall in love with Delia?"

"I have no idea."

"About five minutes. I took one look at her and felt this pull, and I knew. Sometimes it happens that way. Sometimes it's just there waiting for you to find it." His father had slapped him on the back and said,

"Talk to me again in another few months. I'm betting it won't take that long. You both have that look about you."

Jared hadn't planned on falling for her but he could see that was where this was heading—his father was right about that. He just hadn't been ready to admit it. What he felt for Chrissie wasn't something he could change or control, or even put into words just yet. It was just there as a fact of his life, that she was becoming part of that life, and while he hadn't expected it, he wasn't going to run away from it, either. Something else his dad had been right about.

He reached over and turned off the light next to the bed. His crew would begin gathering early tomorrow; they were all as eager to get back to work as he was. Owen promised he'd be there early with coffee and a couple of the scones Chrissie was mixing when he left the store. He'd gone back to the inn, picked up the clothes he'd left there, then set out to the *Cordelia Elizabeth* in the small rented outboard.

He fell asleep hoping that the feeling Owen had—that her troubles weren't over—was wrong.

Chapter Twelve

The rain had washed away the pollen from the roof and the porches around the store, leaving the air clear and fresh until the breeze picked up to start distributing the yellow dust once again. Chrissie'd gone outside to tend to the garden she'd been meaning to plant. She'd worked the soil a bit here and there, but if she was serious about growing anything this year, she had to get going today. She'd bought flower seeds, but for the vegetables she wanted, she'd gone with plants that had been started in pots. She'd bought some from Clay Madison and a few strays from the local hardware store. Today they were going into the ground.

She walked around the side of the building to Ruby's garden shed and unlocked it with the key Ruby'd given her earlier. She selected a hoe, a spade, a trowel she stuck in one of the side pockets of her cargo pants, and a short-handled shovel. As she walked back to the garden, she glanced out at the bay and stopped in her tracks. There in the cove off Dune Drive was the *Cordelia Elizabeth*. She dropped the hoe and placed one hand over her heart. Jared had moved his boat to be closer to her, to watch over her through the night. The fact that he probably couldn't have seen anyone if there was a break-in—and even if he had, he couldn't have gotten there in time to prevent something bad from happening—wasn't the point. She was pretty sure the point was to let her know he was there.

How had so much happened since that first time he'd asked to join her on a simple walk around town?

This wasn't the first time in her life Chrissie thought she was falling for someone, but it was the first time she'd had her eyes wide open. This time if she fell in love, it would be for all the right reasons.

After what she'd been through, the very thought of another relationship had made her cringe. But Jared was not Doug, and just by being himself, Jared had changed her mind about a lot of things. Kissing Jared had felt so right, had made her smile and want to kiss him again.

Her life then, her life now. The contrast couldn't have been greater.

She was determined not to let the memories direct her future or destroy what could be her chance at lasting happiness. She would take each day with Jared and see where it led them.

The garden soil was thick and damp from yesterday's rain, but she'd made up her mind that this was happening today. She turned the heavy soil over and mixed in a little bit of peat moss that Owen had left in the garden the year before when he'd planted for Ruby. She'd just finished working it in when Ruby came out onto the back porch, a glass of iced tea in each hand.

"Come here, girl, and have something cold. Your face be red as an apple. Need to set for a minute and get your right color back." Ruby set her glass onto the small table that stood between the two rocking chairs and held the other glass out to Chrissie.

"You don't have to tell me twice, Gigi." Chrissie leaned the shovel against the wall and walked through the gate to the porch. "It's really heating up out here."

"Summer be here before you know it."

Ruby lowered herself into her favorite of the two chairs, and Chrissie sat on the top step, leaning back against one of the pillars that held up the roof and stretching her legs out in front of her.

"I don't think the temperature pays any attention to the calendar," Chrissie said.

"That be true." Ruby began her slow, rhythmic rocking, which could hypnotize the unsuspecting if they stared too long. "Sun comes out when it wants, same with the rain."

Chrissie took a drink and pushed errant strands of hair from her face. It felt good to sit, and after what had seemed to be a never-ending winter, the warm air was welcomed.

"You be quiet today," Ruby said.

"I guess I'm still tired from the weekend. Four days with Jared and his family was a lot. That is one partying group."

"Expected it to be so. Delia be a lively soul."

"She sure is. She asked me to give you her regards."

"That be nice of her. Always liked that woman, liked her books before I even met her. She be on an adventure with that man, though." Ruby chuckled.

"You mean Gordon?"

"I do. He be a wandering soul, but now he has someone to wander with him. Hope that doesn't slow down her writing those books, because I be a fan."

"He gave her a wet suit for a wedding gift," Chrissie told her.

"A wet suit? Why would he give her a suit that be wet?"

"It's made out of a material that's sort of rubbery. You wear it when you dive. Like that black body-suit-type thing that Owen has?" she explained.

"I didn't know what it be called. Makes sense. You wear it in the water, it be wet."

"Jared said his dad took Delia diving for the first time and she liked it a lot and wants to dive again; that's why he bought her a suit."

Ruby nodded. "Doing new things be good for the soul and the mind. Keep you learning."

"Jared wanted to teach me to dive, too, but . . ."

"But you be afraid."

"I'm not afraid. Why would you say that?" Chrissie asked, defensive.

"Because I know when you be afraid, girl. I can feel your fear." Ruby never missed a beat in her rocking rhythm. "Like yesterday, you be afraid for me. Afraid that stupid boy had come around and done me some harm." She stopped rocking and pinned Chrissie to the deck with a stare. "That boy come around here, he won't know what hit him, that be for sure. I got no mercy when it comes to people like that. Old enough to be a man, but got a mind like a boy. Hmmph." Ruby muttered something else but Chrissie didn't catch it.

"What was that last part you said, Gigi? I didn't hear you."

"I said, be a sad day for that boy, he come around here. Don't know what he be dealing with, and that's all I have to say about him."

Chrissie guessed that Ruby'd gotten herself a little worked up over Doug, probably because of the way Chrissie'd reacted the day before. She thought Ruby was about to say something further, but she let it drop, so Chrissie did as well. She didn't want to waste another minute of her life on Doug. She wanted to sit here, drink her tea, and think about the birthday party for Ruby she and Cass had talked about the night before.

"Surprise party or no?" Cass had asked.

"We can try for a surprise, but you know Gigi. She might see it coming," Chrissie'd said.

"True, but maybe even the pretext of a surprise might be fun. As long as no one actually tells her, we won't know if she knows or not."

"Good point. Where should we have it?"

"We have choices. We could have it here at the store, or outside in the yard. Or at the point. I'll ask Lis what she thinks." Chrissie thought about what fun it would be to celebrate Ruby's 101 day. "I can make a cake . . . oh, more than one. Everyone on the island and half the town of St. Dennis knows her. And we have relatives—I don't even know who they are or where to find them, but Lis might have some ideas."

"We should get together with Lis and make a plan."

"Soon, though. Her birthday's in a few weeks. We should meet one day after I leave Blossoms."

"I can be free any afternoon. Lis probably can, too. I'll check with her and let you know."

Had Ruby ever had a big birthday party before? She didn't know.

"Gigi, your birthday's coming up soon."

"I be aware."

"Anything in particular you want for your birthday?" Chrissie asked.

Ruby appeared to be thinking, then she shook her head. "What I be wanting for?" she asked Chrissie. "Seems to me I have more than most. Less than some, but I not be worried about that. Don't need anything to make me happy. Got my store. My kin. My island." She smiled at Chrissie. "Some oyster fritters once in a while be nice, though."

"I can take care of that for you."

"I be counting on it." Ruby closed her eyes and rocked for a few more minutes while Chrissie envisioned 101 balloons tied to the porch railings all around the store. Maybe just a barbecue, she thought, something simple if we're going to have a very large group. Or maybe just dessert. The more she thought about it, the more she realized there could be well over a hundred people there, depending on where they decided to cut the guest list.

"Write down Grace's name for sure," Ruby said, her eyes still closed. "Delia, too."

Chrissie's eyes narrowed. "Write them down for what?"

"You think you and Cass be clever, but all that whispering last night, and you talking about my birthday—don't think I don't know what you're planning."

"Damn. Did you hear us or are you just, you know, feeling it?"

Ruby lifted her head and smiled.

"That's what I thought," Chrissie grumbled. "I should know better than to try to keep a secret from you."

Ruby resumed rocking, craning her neck to look out into the garden.

Chrissie followed her gaze. "What?" she asked. "What are you looking at?"

"I be looking to see if those tomatoes planted themselves yet, but no, they still be in their pots."

"I can take a hint." Chrissie finished her tea and went back to work.

By the end of the afternoon, all the trays of vegetables had been planted and all the flower seeds sown.

"I should have started the flowers sooner," she complained to Ruby later when she came inside to clean up.

"They be fine." Ruby was seated in her chair near the window where Chrissie and Jared had sat the afternoon before. "Might be late this year, but they be blooming by the end of the summer. Those others, the roses and the daisies, they be blooming soon. No need to tend to them, 'cept maybe pull out those few weeds. You be wanting some decoration for that party I don't know you're planning."

"I give up," Chrissie muttered, and went upstairs to take a shower.

She found her phone and saw Jared had texted her several times, once to see if she was okay, another to tell her he was waiting for the last of his crew to show up. Tomorrow would be their first day to dive, and he'd be moving the *Cordy E* to the site early in the morning, but he'd be coming back to the cove at night.

Thank you, she'd texted back. Knowing you're so close makes me happy.

I'm glad. It makes me happy, too.

And safe, she'd added.

That too, babe.

"SO I THINK we should just call everyone," Chrissie told Lis and Cass. "If we send out invitations, it's going to take too long. Buy them. Address them. Mail them. Wait for people to RSVP. If we call, most people will tell us flat out if they're coming or not."

They sat at the front table in Cuppachino, drinking iced coffee and watching what passed for rush hour traffic on Charles Street, which meant there might be five or six cars waiting at the town's one stoplight.

"Right. We just say, 'Would you mind checking your calendar to see if you're free that day? I don't mind waiting,'" Cass said.

"If that's what it takes, why not? And Alec thought we should have it out on the point. We can rent the tent we had for our wedding if it gets too hot," Lis suggested.

"Or how 'bout we do something like an old-fashioned box lunch? A delicious sandwich, fruit, a salad. Then we can all have birthday cake and sing to Gigi."

"That's a really good idea," Cass said. "If the number of people who accept is over fifty, I say the box lunch is the way to go." She tapped Chrissie on the arm. "Where do we get boxes?"

"I can give you the name of the place we sourced them from when I was at my last job. We did box lunches and they were very popular with our customers who wanted a lunch from Luna but didn't have time to sit in the restaurant and eat."

"Get me the information and I'll take care of it," Cass volunteered.

"And I'll get with Clay and Wade and see about beer," Lis said. "But we'll need a couple of flats of water and some iced tea or something for the people who don't drink beer."

"I can order from Tom, our supplier at the store. I can also get cups and straws and plastic utensils from him as well." Chrissie made a note to herself, then sighed heavily.

"What?" Lis asked.

"I'd wanted to tie one hundred and one balloons to the porch railing," Chrissie told them.

"You can still do that. I'll help."

"Great. That's it, then. We divvy up the guest list into thirds, we each take one of the lists, and we make all the calls before the end of the week." Chrissie made one last note, then closed her phone.

"It all sounds so easy when you say it like that," Lis said.

"It will be easy, you'll see," Chrissie promised.

"Maybe we should ask people when we call what kind of sandwich they want." Cass was thinking out loud. "Otherwise, how do you know how many of each to make?"

"We'll figure that out. The important thing is that the planning is done, we know what we're doing, and Gigi will have a great birthday."

"Too bad we couldn't have surprised her." Lis stood to leave.

"Not an option. No one else knows where the bodies are buried," Chrissie said. "I mean, how to get in touch with the relatives."

"Owen's a little nervous about who's going to show up," Cass said.

"He has reason to be," Lis told her. "This family is a mixed bag."

"Honey, every family is a mixed bag. You should see what comes out of my family tree when we shake it." Cass got up. "I wonder if we shouldn't have something for the little kids. We're going to make sure we have Owen's son that weekend."

"How is that sweet boy?" Lis asked.

"J.J.'s fine. He's adorable. He's getting used to spending time here with us and going back to his mom and stepfather without drama. Unless he's forgotten a favorite toy, then we have tears. But it's working out well." Cass smiled. "And he'll be at the party for his great-great-grandmother's birthday. How extraordinary is that?"

They disposed of their trash in the can on the way out the door, and Carlo, Cuppachino's owner, waved as they left. Chrissie'd driven, and she dropped the other two off at their homes, Lis at the house she and Alec shared at the point, and Cass at the relic she and Owen were restoring.

When Saturday night rolled around, Chrissie and Jared drove into Ballard, the next town, for dinner and a movie, and they were both half asleep by the time the movie ended. Jared'd been diving every day since the merchant ship was cleared, and he could barely keep his eyes open. Chrissie'd been doing double duty, working at the store in the morning and at Blossoms during the day, where she'd taken on more and more as Sophie's pregnancy progressed.

"Want to take a walk? It's still early," she asked after he'd driven her back to the store.

"Will you carry me?" She thought he was only half kidding.

"You're really wiped out, aren't you?"

"Yeah, but maybe a walk will revive me." He got out of the car at the same time she did.

She reached for his hand and they walked from the parking lot onto the road, which was asphalt but heavily covered with sand. There were no streetlights on the island, and it was already dark.

"So how many Jenkinses can we expect at the party?" he asked as they rounded the first curve.

"Probably none. The Jenkinses are my father's family and we didn't invite any of them. They're not from St. Dennis or the island, and there's no relationship to Gigi."

"How many are coming so far?"

"Last tally was one hundred and seven."

"That's a lot of box lunches."

She nodded. "And one hell of a big cake."

"How do you make a cake for that many people?"

"Have you never been to a wedding? It'll be tiered, like a wedding cake," she explained. "No big deal."

"Have you spoken with your mother yet?" he asked.

Chrissie nodded but didn't say anything.

"You're going to make me ask?" Jared stopped in front of one of the lots Cass was building on. "Is she coming to the party?"

"She isn't sure. She had a million reasons. She hasn't seen Gigi in years and she's uncertain whether she'd be welcome. She isn't sure Gigi likes her. She has to see if Louis—that's her new boyfriend—is free that weekend."

"Do you want her to come?"

Chrissie thought it over. "Yes and no. I know if she shows up, there will be drama of some sort, so for that, since it's Gigi's birthday, I have to say no. For myself, yes, I'd like to see her again. Anytime I've made overtures to come out to see her, there have been excuses why it wasn't a good time. She was going through another divorce. She was in the process of moving. She had the flu. She was just getting over the flu."

"I can see where it would be tough to maintain a relationship with someone like that. But—"

"But—she is my mother. So yes, I'd like to see her, but God only knows what might come of it. We'll see. I'm not going to worry about it either way. If she's here, fine. If not . . ." Chrissie shrugged. "Nothing I can do about it. But if I ever have kids, I will not treat them the way I've been treated."

Jared wrapped his arms around her and held her.

"Well, that does help," she told him, raising her face for a kiss. In the dark, he found her lips. A car came around the curve, its lights momentarily blinding her.

"Oh, my eyes." She blinked, trying to regain her focus. "How are yours?"

"Mine are fine."

"Why aren't you blinking? Why are your eyes fine when mine are seeing huge spots of yellow?"

"Because I was kissing you and my eyes were closed," he said in that matter-of-fact way of his. "I think the real question is, why were your eyes open when you were supposed to be kissing me?"

"Because I felt something, the motion of the car, maybe. Want to try it again?"

"Yes." He pulled her in close and kissed her again.

"Much better," she told him.

"No flashing lights?" he asked.

"No, but maybe a bell or two," she said.

"That sounds like wind chimes." He looked around. "I wish we had a flashlight. It sounds like it's coming from over there." He pointed toward the dune.

"I have one in my bag," she told him. "It's small but it has a powerful light. But I left my bag in the car."

"I'll run back and get it. Stay right here. I'll just be a minute."

He disappeared into the dark, but she could hear his footfalls as he took off running. It was eerie, standing there in a pitch-black night, all alone. It reminded her of when she and Lis were kids and they'd play hide-and-seek on summer nights. Owen always knew where they were hiding—well, duh. They usually kept to the same places because it'd gotten too dark to find anyplace else. When he came up behind them, she and Lis would scream at the top of their lungs and run back to the store.

A noise behind her made her jump. Fifteen feet away, something scampered out from the dune grass and dashed across the road. She could hear but not see it, just as she could not see whatever was chasing it. Then she heard the sound of pounding feet coming her way and saw the beam of light. She let out a breath she'd been holding without realizing it. She'd never been totally at ease in the dark, and even now she left the light on in the bathroom across the hall when she went to bed at night.

"Told you I'd be quick," he said as he trotted up. "Now, let's see what's back here." He took her by the hand and they went from the road to the remnants of a driveway.

"This is one of Cass's properties," she said.

"Let's take a look. Maybe the house is still there."

"Or we could come back tomorrow when it's light out and we don't need the flashlight." She followed the light with her eyes. "This is one of the old Blake properties. That's on my granddad's side. My mother's dad's side of the family." She took the flashlight from his hands and scanned the area. "There's the wind chime. Someone hung it from that pile of wood." She walked closer and aimed the light at the stack. "These must be the old floors. Cass's guys do a remarkable job saving them. Then they reuse what they can in the new houses, fill in what they need to, and then stain it all to match."

She walked around the piles of wood slowly.

"I remember my granddad Blake. He was so nice. So was Gramma Blake. He died when I was twelve and she died a few years ago. She'd asked me to handle her funeral, carry it out the way she'd spelled it out, so of course I did. Ruby was a bit scandalized because her coffin was extravagant for an island lady, but that's what she wanted and that's what she got." She paused for a moment. "Doug was incensed because I'd spent the money she'd given me for her funeral, instead of skimping on it and keeping the rest of it."

"Sounds like a real stand-up kinda guy," Jared said dryly.

She turned in the dark and hugged him. "You are the best thing that ever happened to me. If it hadn't been for him, I might never have come back here, I'd have never met you, and he's behind me now and I'm here with you. I'd say I came out on top."

The breeze had blown her hair into her face, and with his hands, Jared pushed it back.

"That's how I feel about you. Like you're the best part of my life. Well, you and that 'tea ship' at the bottom of the river."

Chrissie laughed. "That's so romantic, Jared."

"You are, though. You're the best part of my life, and I'm grateful that you got here by any means, but I wish I could have spared you."

"Water under the dam. Over the dam? Under the bridge? Whatever. It's just something that happened. And now we're together and that's what matters."

"It's definitely what matters to me." He took the flashlight from her hand and put an arm around her, leading her to the road. "Want to go sit in my car and make out?"

"Best idea you had all night."

RUBY'D BEEN SO pleased with the fact that she was having a birthday party, she'd tried to interject her ideas into the plan Chrissie, Lis, and Cass had come up with, but they didn't back down. She'd ended up issuing invitations of her own to just about everyone who came into the store. To Chrissie's dismay, Ruby told her all the early morning watermen had been invited and all of Emily Hart's nieces and grand-daughters who served illegal dinners at Emily's house on the island—illegal because she was not licensed by anyone and hadn't reported her earnings in . . . well, ever. Emily's explanation was that she served dinners in her home to a select group of guests every week, but since there were no regulatory agencies of any kind on the island, she didn't have to report to anyone. It made sense if you were an islander, Chris-sie explained to Jared, and though she didn't neces-sarily agree with Mrs. Hart's method of operation, she had to admit that a woman in her eighties who still cooked delicious meals for crowds once or twice a week, depending on demand, was a woman to be admired. She hoped she was still functioning at that high a level when she reached Emily's age.

The party was set for two o'clock, an hour when most of the point would be in shade. Jared pitched in to help Owen and Alec set up tents and rented tables and chairs, and together the three took turns using the helium tank to blow up the 101 balloons Chrissie had insisted on.

They also took turns breathing in the helium and singing rock songs in little Munchkin voices.

Lis looked out the window to watch. "Honestly, you'd think the average age of the three of them is about eight."

"Would you go out and tie the balloons on to the railing?" Chrissie asked Lis. "I don't know how securely they're tying them on, and I don't want them blowing off before Gigi sees them."

"She's still getting ready?" Cass asked.

"Taking her time. Said the rest of the world could wait for her today." Chrissie smiled. Seeing how excited the usually unflappable Ruby had been that morning made all the work worth it.

"You go on upstairs and get dressed," Cass told Chrissie. "I'll finish packing up the box lunches and then we'll go over to the point. I love the idea of the red-and-white checkered cloths, by the way."

"Everything ruby red today. Steffie made a special ice cream in Ruby's honor, and she named it—"

"I heard. Ruby red," Cass said. "Heavy on the raspberries, I understand."

"So I've been told. Thanks for taking over, Cass. I won't be long." Chrissie took off the apron she'd been wearing and folded it, leaving it on the counter.

"Jared said he'll stay here and drive you and Ruby over when she's ready." Lis stuck her head in through the doorway. "There are already a bunch of cars there, early birds, I suppose, so we should probably hurry up. I didn't recognize hardly any of the vehicles."

"It's no wonder. We get so little traffic here on the island." Chrissie headed toward the store and the steps to the second floor.

She showered and dressed in less than thirty minutes, even pausing to put on makeup, which she found herself doing more and more. She'd never bothered before, but these days, she wore light makeup to work, a little more when she and Jared went out. For the party, she'd chosen a black sundress with wide straps and flowers in shades of pink with green leaves. She'd bought it for the wedding weekend, and while she hadn't worn it then, she'd worn it twice since and Jared had admired it both times. It was her personal favorite, so she was pleased he'd liked it as well.

She went downstairs and found Ruby sitting at her table in the store.

"Ready for your close-up, Gigi?" she quipped.

"I be just about."

"I thought you'd be pacing the floor waiting for me."

"Needed a few minutes to just set," Ruby told her.

"Are you feeling all right? Do you want me to bring you some water?" Chrissie asked.

"No. Just set with me for a few."

"Of course." Chrissie walked over and sat next to Ruby instead of in the chair she usually occupied at the opposite side of the table. "Are you having deep thoughts?"

Ruby nodded slowly. "I be thinking about all them that's come before here, my folks, my Harold. All the folks on the island who came and went. None of them made one hundred and one years. My momma almost made it, came close at ninety-six. But my Harold died young. Left me with a lot on my plate." She smiled at Chrissie. "But we be strong, girl. We have the blood of those who made the crossing back in 1813. You remember that, Christiana. You be strong."

"I'm trying to be."

"There be times to try, and there be times to be." Ruby stood suddenly. "Got a party to go to. Who be driving?"

And just like that, she headed for the door, leaving Chrissie to catch up.

Jared had been waiting on the front porch in Ruby's favorite rocking chair. When the two women came out and Ruby saw where he was sitting, she stopped suddenly.

"You ask about setting in that chair?"

"Ah, no, ma'am, I . . ." Jared stood hastily.

"Good thing we be going someplace. Else there could be words over who sits in that chair." She went down the steps holding on to the railing. When she reached the bottom, she turned and said, "You two coming?"

Chrissie giggled all the way to the point, and Jared appeared to have a hard time keeping a straight face. He drove around the curve, then parked on the grass next to Lis and Alec's house.

"You ready, lady of the hour?" he asked.

"I am," Ruby said. When he came around to the passenger side to help her out, she took his hand and said, "It makes my heart glad to know you be there for her, but a woman's got to be able to save herself. You be helping her do that, and for that I be grateful."

"Thank you," he said.

As Chrissie got out of the backseat, she saw Jared kiss the side of Ruby's face. Ruby pretended to brush him away, but Chrissie could tell she'd been pleased by his gesture. The threesome, with Ruby in the middle, made their way into the party.

Ruby's appearance was met with shouts and applause, and she acted flustered, but Chrissie saw the theatrics involved and it made her smile. Owen led Ruby to the seat of honor, where she sat while her guests—Lis referred to them as Ruby's minions— could greet her and offer homage.

"She is lapping this up the way a tabby laps up cream." Lis leaned in behind Chrissie, who was stacking the box lunches on a table, and Chrissie laughed. She'd tied up the boxes with red-and-white bakers twine and slipped napkins under the ties. The napkins were white with a scattering of red tulips.

"Too cutesy?" she asked Lis.

"Adorable. Kitschy, but somehow looks just right. I think those boxes look darling. And the plastic red rubies scattered on the white tablecloths are a fun touch, along with the cornflowers in red and white vases."

"Ruby's Harold used to bring her cornflowers. I thought it would be a nice touch, to have a little bit of him here."

"Everything looks perfect. Everything has a bit of ruby red."

"I cannot tell a lie. I cheated and called Lucy at the inn and asked for some tips."

"No shame in asking the queen of event planning for a little help. I wish I'd thought of it."

Chrissie looked at the mountain of boxes. "The recycling guys are going to be busy this week."

"Alec's going to take them into St. Dennis tomorrow and put them in the recycling bins," Lis told her. "Everything else can go out in the trash."

"Good, because after all the prep, I'm just about burned out." She finished stacking the boxes and stepped back from the table, and as she looked up, she saw a face she wasn't sure she'd ever see again. The woman was looking directly at her, as if she were afraid if she blinked, Chrissie would be gone. She wore a khaki skirt and a brown polo shirt, and her strawberry-blond hair was brushed back from her face.

"Mom?" Chrissie walked out from behind the table. "You came."

Instinctively, Chrissie hugged her. At first, her mother seemed surprised, but she hugged her back. A long, warm hug that was well overdue. When Chrissie stepped back, she saw the tears in her mother's eyes, and she softened.

"Mom, I'm so glad to see you. I'm so happy you're here."

"Oh, I knew all along I had to come. I don't know why I was hemming and hawing the way I did. Ruby's my grandmother, and who knows how much longer she'll be around." Dorothy glanced at Ruby. "Though she looks damned good for having lived one hundred years on this island."

"One hundred and one," Chrissie said, correcting her.

"Oh. Right. You did tell me that. Well, that's old." Dorothy coughed the smoker's cough that Chrissie always associated with her mother. Dorothy touched Chrissie's face, then smoothed back her hair. "And you look wonderful. I've never seen you look so happy. Healthy. Beautiful. You're planning on staying here?'

"I am. I have a great job cooking in a wonderful little restaurant in St. Dennis. If you're still here on Tuesday . . ."

"Going back in the morning. Have to work on Monday."

"There you are, Dots. I've been looking all over this place for you." A man in khaki pants and a brown polo shirt that matched Dorothy's seemed to appear out of nowhere. He wore dark glasses and carried a beer in a red plastic cup.

"This is my daughter, Chrissie. *Christiana*. Meet my friend Louis." Dorothy made the introductions.

"Dotty tells me you cook in a restaurant." Louis took off his glasses and hung them from the V at the neck of his shirt.

"I do."

"Woman should know how to cook," Louis was saying as Jared walked up. "Maybe you could give your mom here some lessons." He stage-whispered, "She's not very good."

"Chrissie's a great cook," Jared said, joining the conversation. "But so am I. A man should know how to cook, too, don't you think?" Without waiting for an answer, he slipped an arm over her shoulder and said, "Chrissie, who are your friends?"

"This is my mother, Dorothy DiLenno. And her friend Louis."

"Good to meet you both." Jared looked at Chrissie's mother. "Especially you, Mrs. DiLenno."

"It's Dorothy," she told him. "I'm not Mrs. DiLenno anymore."

Dorothy took a step back and looked Jared over, obviously not blind to the possessive arm around Chrissie's shoulder. Bluntly, she asked, "So what's your relationship with my daughter?"

"I'm her guy." Jared met her gaze.

"What does that mean, exactly?"

Before he could answer, Chrissie broke in. "Mom, have you seen Gigi since you arrived? It looks like there's a bit of a lull in the well-wishers. You might want to slip over there while you have a chance."

"Good idea. Louis, come with me. Meet my grandmother." With a glance back at Jared, she tugged on Louis's hand.

"Did you ask her about your father or your brother?" Jared asked.

"I didn't have time, but I asked her on the phone when I called her to invite her, and it was just more of the same. 'I don't want to discuss it. Stop bringing up the past. I'm living in the present, you should, too.'" Chrissie shrugged. "She's just not going to talk about it. I don't know if she's being stubborn, or if whatever happened is so embarrassing to her personally that she doesn't want me to know."

"One of these days you'll find out. Today, however, we're at a party for a great lady who is having the time of her life. Owen said his mother's here from Arizona with her husband, and that Ruby was really happy to see her."

"She doesn't seem as happy to see 'Dots,' though, does she?" Chrissie observed. "She's got that look on her face, the one she gets when she's about to tell you something you don't want to hear."

"She can be tough," he agreed, "but not to me." He leaned closer. "She told me I'm the guy for you."

"You *are* the guy for me."

Chrissie looked into his eyes and saw Jared for who he really was: a caring, honest, loving man whose heart was as wide and deep as the oceans he explored. From the first day, he'd treated her as someone special, someone who deserved to be cared about. He'd listened to her, laughed with her, given her all the space she'd needed to find herself again. He'd never pushed their relationship toward anything she hadn't been ready for. Even now, when she could tell his need for her was as great as her need for him, he didn't push or try to pressure her. He'd let her take her time to find her way, made her understand with his actions more than his words that the pace of their relationship was totally up to her. Because he knew that trust didn't come easy to her, he would let her decide if or when the relationship would move to the next level. If—when—they had sex would be her decision.

He was lovable in so many ways, but she could have loved him only for giving her that power. Tonight she was going to exercise it.

"Maybe we can take a moonlit row out to the *Cordy E*," she whispered in his ear. "I hear there are private quarters for the captain. I think we should make use of them tonight."

He took a step back and gazed into her face. "Chrissie—are you sure you want to . . . ?"

"I've never been more sure of anything in my life. I've never wanted anyone the way I want you."

He took his phone from his pocket and speed-dialed a call. "Who're you calling?" she asked.

"The crew. I'm giving them the rest of the weekend off. They'll probably be at the White Dolphin lining up shots by the time I end the call."

The call was answered and the message delivered. Jared tucked the phone back into his pocket, then tugged lightly on her ponytail. "How long do you think we need to hang around?"

"Until the end. I'm sort of hosting, so . . ." She held her hands out in a *what can I do* gesture. "But Gigi turns in early most nights, and we started early in the day. I don't expect this to be an all-night affair."

"In that case, I'm going to get a beer." He kissed her on the lips.

"Look, there's my dad, Delia, and Grace. When I called, Delia wasn't sure if they could make it. I'm so glad they're here. Let's go say hello."

Ruby had fooled everyone—especially Chrissie—by keeping the party going into the evening. While a lot of the guests had left, there was still a hard-core group of St. Dennis and Cannonball Islanders partying. At ten, when someone called for pizza, Jared and Chrissie had had enough.

Chrissie took Owen aside and asked, "Do you think you could get Ruby back to the store when she's ready to leave? Take back that mountain of gifts and cards? Get her settled in?"

"Sure. Where are you going to be?"

Jared stood behind Chrissie and waved a hand at Owen, who said, "Okay. Got it. I'll stay as long as I can, but try to get back before dawn, okay?"

"I'll make sure she gets back before that. You don't have to worry about Ruby being alone," Jared promised.

"I need to say good-bye to my mother. Maybe we can have breakfast with her tomorrow before she leaves." Chrissie searched what remained of the crowd and finally spotted Dorothy.

"She's over at the second table, talking to my mom," Owen told her. "After thirty years, they're finally talking. I wonder what brought that on."

"Does it matter? They're talking. Let's take that as a sign that something good might come out of this." It had occurred to Chrissie that something must have happened in her mother's life years ago that had

caused her to withdraw from her entire family. Un-
doubtedly it had something to do with her father, but
Chrissie was no closer to finding out what that was
all about than she'd been when she was a child.

Chrissie excused herself and walked over to where
her mother was sitting. She knew that now was not
the time to get into a deep discussion about past
hurts and family drama, so she was determined to
keep things fairly light and cheerful.

"Mom, I'm calling it a night. I'm exhausted from
all the prep for this party. Could we maybe meet
tomorrow morning for breakfast before you leave?"

"I'd like that very much, Chrissie." Dorothy stood
and hugged her daughter again. "I know that you
had a lot of people to talk to tonight, so we didn't
have much time together. Breakfast would be nice,
maybe at the restaurant where you work?"

"We're closed on Sunday. Why not stop at the store
in the morning when you're ready—maybe around
nine or ten? We can decide then where we're going."

"That would be fine." Dorothy moved to hug her
again, then paused. "Chrissie, who is that woman in
the black shirt and long skirt talking to your friend?"

"That's Jared's father's new wife. They were just
married a few weeks ago."

"She looks familiar."

"That's because she is famous. That's Delia Enright, the—"

"The mystery writer. That's why she looks familiar. That's your friend's stepmother?"

"My friend has a name. It's Jared Chandler, and
Delia doesn't like to be referred to as a stepmother,"
Chrissie said.

"What does he call her?"

"He calls her Delia."

"And while we're on the subject—what happened to the other boyfriend?" Dorothy asked.

"What other boyfriend?"

"The one you were living with in New Jersey. Such a nice guy. I'm guessing you broke up with him and now you're dating this one?" She pointed to Jared.

For a moment, Chrissie froze. Then she took a deep breath and said, "Mom, that 'nice guy' wasn't so nice. He abused me physically and mentally. Leaving him was the best thing I ever did. "

Dorothy's hand flew to cover her mouth. "Oh my God, Chrissie, I had no idea."

"Of course you didn't. I didn't tell you because we almost never talked about things. But I'm telling you now. Mom, if he ever calls you, hang up. Don't tell him anything about me. He doesn't know where I am, and if he did, he'd do something to hurt me really badly."

Dorothy shook her head, her eyes spilling over with tears. "Oh, my poor girl. Why didn't you tell me? Why didn't you come stay with me?"

"It's a long story, Mom. A story for another time. One of those stories like why did Dad leave and where is my brother." Chrissie squeezed her mother's hand and said, "Someday soon we're going to sit down and we'll trade stories, okay?"

Dorothy stared at Chrissie.

"That's the price for knowing what happened to your daughter, Mom. It's long past time we were honest with each other." Chrissie kissed her mother goodbye. "I'll see you in the morning, Mom. I'm so happy you came, for Ruby's sake and for my sake. And for yours as well." She lowered her voice and whispered, "I see you're talking to Owen's mother again. Mending fences?"

"As best we can." Dorothy nodded. "It's been a long time coming."

"Yes, it has, Mom. It's past time for a lot of things. We'll talk tomorrow." Chrissie kissed her again, then went off to say her good-byes to Delia and Gordon, then Grace, then finally to Ruby, who gave no sign she was slowing down.

Chrissie'd written 101 YEARS YOUNG on the three-tiered cake she'd made. Ruby was every bit that, and more, and Chrissie said a silent prayer of thanks that she'd been given the gift of loving this very special woman.

Chapter Thirteen

❧

Chrissie'd almost had to get in line to say good night to Ruby. There were several others who were trying to leave as well, but not without saying a last word or two to the guest of honor. When Chrissie was able to get close enough, she leaned down and told Ruby she was leaving for a while.

Ruby nodded as if she knew where Chrissie was going, with whom, and what she was about to do.

"You did a fine thing here tonight," Ruby told her. "A fine party, brought all these people here just to see me. I be appreciating every bit of what you did." Then she smiled widely. "You brought my Harold to the party in those cornflowers, and that made me happiest of all, that you remembered how he used to bring them to me. You made my heart warm tonight." She pulled Chrissie closer and said, "But the night not be over for us. We be strong, and we be smart, you and me, and we be fine."

"Of course we will." Chrissie gave her a hug. "I'm glad you enjoyed your party. Don't stay up too late." Chrissie paused, debating, then did something she didn't think she'd ever done before. She leaned in and whispered, "I love you, Gigi."

"You go on now, girl." She held one of Chrissie's hands for a moment, then smiled what Chrissie called her knowing smile.

Jared stopped to say good night as well, and Ruby whispered something in his ear.

"What did she say to you?" Chrissie couldn't help but ask.

"She said she'd see me later tonight. I told Owen I wouldn't keep you out too late, but I doubt she'll still be up when we get back."

"Yeah, she said something like that to me, too. Like the night wasn't over for us. And she smiled the way she does when she knows something. Which of course made me think she knew where we're off to."

"Is there any doubt? This is Ruby Carter we're talking about."

They walked in the middle of the road, and she stopped. "Wait, the boat's out there. We're here. How are we getting out there?"

"Where there's a will, there's a way." He took her hand and started walking again.

"You don't mean swim, do you? Because I'm wearing a dress that I really love, shoes that cost more than my first apartment, and it's almost dark and the water's dark and who knows what's in there? Well, crabs for sure, and fish. Lots of fish. Sharks maybe, too. No. Uh-uh. Not swimming out to your boat." She shivered. "Sharks. No. Just . . . no."

"Well, yes, there are several kinds of sharks that you might find in the Chesapeake, but the ones that might come this far up into the bay probably aren't harmful. Most stay closer to the mouth of the bay, though there have been sharks up in this area. Not as common as, say, Florida."

"'Probably aren't harmful' is not good enough for me."

"So you're saying you'd give up our first night of bliss because you're afraid to swim fifty feet into the bay?"

"That's not a fair question."

Jared laughed. "I wouldn't make you swim."

"Then how are we getting out to the boat?"

"Patience, and all will be revealed soon enough."

They walked a little farther down the road, then Jared said, "Take your shoes off."

"I knew it," she grumbled.

Jared laughed again. "Just your shoes. For now. See where you are?"

It wasn't completely dark, but she still had to squint to see. When she took stock of the scenery, she realized that just ahead was the pier Cass's father had started building the year before. He'd wanted a place where the people who bought the houses he built could tie up their boats, but the plan was put on hold when the merchant ship was found fifty feet off the pier. The section of the pier that had been completed, however, still stood.

"We're at the pier near the river."

"And right down there is the little boat we're going to row out to the big boat."

"Well, don't you think you're clever."

"Actually, I do."

They reached the end of the pier, and the rowboat was there as he'd told her. It was tied up fore and aft, so he lowered her into the boat, then followed. He sat on the center seat and picked up the oars.

"Ready?"

"I am."

"I should be singing, like in a gondola."

"We're not having that conversation again." She laughed.

"You could sing."

"I just want to watch you row." And for a few minutes, she did. The muscles of his arms rippled as he dipped the oars in and out of the water.

"Don't wear yourself out," she said.

"No danger of that. Besides, here's the diving platform."

He rowed up to the platform, the rowboat bumping softly against it. He steadied the rowboat, then helped her out before tying it to the platform.

He took her hand and led her across the deck toward the cabin.

"Wait," she said. "Look at the moon. It's so big and bright and shiny on the water."

"It's either a romantic sight or a call to all the crazies to come out of the woodwork." He kissed her neck. "My cousin Joanie is an emergency room doctor. She hates working when there's a full moon because she swears it brings out the worst in people, especially people who have issues to begin with." He stopped and leaned back to look into her face. "You sure you're ready . . . ?"

"I am so ready, Jared."

"'Cause you know I've been wanting to make love to you since . . . I can't remember when I didn't want to make love to you. Maybe just that first time, when we walked around St. Dennis, but after that day on the boat, I knew I wanted you. But I knew you'd been hurt, and I didn't want you to think that I'd—"

"Jared. Shut up."

"Okay."

His lips moved back to her neck, then traveled to her throat, then to her chin, and by the time they reached her mouth, she was hungry for him. He picked her up and with a breathless "Watch your head," he carried her down to the cabin, ducking against the low ceiling. The small windows were open and there was just the tiniest bit of light. She reached behind her to unzip her dress, and when she dropped it on the floor, he backed her to the bed. She sat up on her knees to pull his shirt over his head, and tug at his belt, murmuring, "You don't need these."

He shed his clothes while she removed the rest of hers and fell back with her, covering her mouth with a kiss that was hot and demanding until she craved more. His hands seemed to be everywhere at once—her back, her breasts, her face, her thighs—as if he needed to touch every part of her, and it seemed he couldn't touch her fast enough, as if he was afraid she'd disappear.

His tongue flicked in her mouth and she welcomed it, meeting it with her own. When his lips started a slow, torturous slide from her neck to her shoulders, from her shoulders to her breast, she moaned softly and dug her fingers into his back. When she couldn't take any more, she whispered his name, and he pushed her knees apart. He paused and reached behind her and opened a sliding compartment. She heard the crinkling of foil and a moment later, he asked, "You sure you want to . . ."

"Oh God, yes," she murmured, her breath ragged.

Jared laughed softly and slid inside her. She felt the warmth, the rush of heat and need that became an ache, then she was spinning out of control. He seemed to know just where and how to touch her, instinctively knowing what she needed before she did. There was such tenderness in every stroke of his hands on her body, she could have cried. No one had ever taken such time, such care when loving her. Ripples of sensation coursed through her, and she rode the good wave until it crashed down on them both, leaving her wrecked and breathless, her heart racing, her mind in a jumble.

"Oh my God," she gasped. "That was . . . that was . . ." She covered her face with her hands.

"That was pretty incredible. Are you sure we haven't done this before?" Jared laughed softly. "What are you doing?"

"My brain's been rattled. Like there was an earthquake in my body and it went all the way to my brain. I'm not even sure I remember who I am."

"Let me see if I recognize you." He pulled one of her hands from her face. "Hmmm. Not sure. The eye is familiar, though. Pretty shade of green."

"You can't possibly see what color my eyes are. It's too dark."

"Then I suppose it's because I remember, which means I must know you. Now, if I could just remember your name . . ." He pulled away her other hand

and looked into her face. "I know mine must be Ohmygod, because that's what you called me. Several times, actually."

"I can't believe I did that." She covered her face again. "Don't tell me I did that."

"Oh yeah. And you must think I'm a murderer, because twice you said, 'Ohmygod, you're killing me.'"

"Enough. Stop!"

"Never would have taken you for a screamer, Chris."

"I hate you. Let me out of here."

He laughed and pulled her closer.

"If I said anything else, please don't tell me. I don't want to know."

"I'm teasing you, Chrissie."

"You made that up? You mean, I didn't say . . ."

He shook his head.

"Did I say anything?" One hand left her face.

"Just my name a time or two."

"That was so mean. I was so embarrassed. I thought maybe I'd zoned out into another dimension." She paused, then lowered the other hand. "One of those places where unexplainable things happen."

He rolled off her and onto his side, and she pulled the blanket over her.

"Now she gets modest," he said.

"I guess after you've screamed your way through sex, there's not much left to hide, but I'm chilly."

He got up and opened the chest at the foot of the bed, then pulled out a blanket and spread it over her. It was soft and just the right weight, and she snuggled under it, savoring the moment and their closeness. Jared lay next to her, propping a pillow behind his head. Chrissie closed her eyes and let herself drift in the coziness of the blanket and the warmth of his arms as they wrapped around her, the gentle rocking of the boat at anchor. Nothing had ever felt as right as loving Jared. She'd never felt so at peace with herself, and she knew she was exactly where she belonged.

"Don't go to sleep," he warned. "Owen reminded me to bring you back to the store tonight to stay with Ruby."

"I know. Just a few minutes, though. I'm so comfortable I feel like I'm floating."

"Where I come from, we call that afterglow."

"Maybe." She stretched, then curled up, her head on his arm that rested behind her. The boat rolled gently on the tide, and she had to fight to stay awake.

"Tell me something else that you can't explain," she said quietly.

He was quiet for so long she thought he hadn't heard her.

"Jared?"

"You. I can't explain you, and how I feel about you. I never expected you, or anyone like you, to come into my life and turn it around. So that's my answer. Not dragons or mermaids or UFOs. It's you. I never expected to fall in love, but I think I am." He ran his fingers lightly along the inside of her arm. "I don't understand how it happened, but it did, and for the record, I'm okay with that."

She opened her eyes and looked into his, trying to think of something to say, but there were no words, because she hadn't expected his response. When she realized she wasn't going to find what she needed to tell him what he meant to her, she pulled him down and kissed him, and decided to show him instead. Owen could wait.

"CHRISSIE? CHRIS?" JARED was prodding her to wake her up. "We need to get back. It's two in the morning, and if Owen is still at the store waiting for us, he's going to be plenty pissed off."

"Okay." She stretched her arms over her head. "This is a pretty comfy bed, for a bed on a boat."

"It's the captain's bed, so it has to be comfortable. I know I won't do as well on the other one."

"The other what?" She looked for her bra, found it under the bed.

"The other boat. My dad and I are going to Brazil in a few days and—"

"What? Brazil? When?"

"Delia has a book tour coming up and Dad didn't want to go with her. He has a crew working on a wreck down there that he thinks might be the *Santa Augusta*."

Chrissie looked at him blankly.

"It's a Spanish ship that was lost off the coast of South America in the 1500s. Dad's been researching it for years. He finally got the okay to salvage, so he wants to go down there himself, and he asked Rachel and me to go."

"Why?"

"Because it's an important ship, and an important find. I won't say it's once in a lifetime, because there have been others, and there will probably be more, but it's still exciting."

"What about the ship here?"

"Owen's going to run the job until I get back. He's more than capable. Dad wants to give him his own crew eventually so he can send him to work his own wrecks."

"Does Cass know that?"

"Yes, we even talked about it tonight. She was really happy that he's going to get that opportunity."

"Even if the ship he goes to salvage is in, say, Peru, or Madagascar, or Australia?"

"Australia has some fine salvagers of their own, but yes, she knows. She understands it's a big leap for him, both financially and professionally. Chandler and Associates is the best in the business. It's a great opportunity for him."

"If you can't brag about yourself, who will?" she muttered.

"It's not bragging if it's true, Chris. We are the best. My father worked really hard for a very long time to earn his reputation. He's proud of it, and so am I. And if you ask Owen or anyone else who works for us, they'll tell you they're proud, too."

He dressed, then sat on the edge of the bed and watched her pull her dress over her head. When he started to help her with her zipper, she said, "I have it."

"What's wrong, Chris?"

She'd lost an earring, so she looked on the floor, then pulled back the blankets, then the sheets. She found it under the pillow she'd been using and put it back into her ear.

"Chrissie, what's the matter?"

"Nothing." She tightened the earring in the other ear. Old Chrissie would have bitten her tongue. New Chrissie wasn't about to. "Okay, yeah, there's something. It's like we just had sex—several times—and I don't even have my clothes on and you tell me oh so nonchalantly that you're leaving."

"I'm leaving St. Dennis, I'm not leaving you."

"What's the difference?"

"The difference is that I'll be back to you. This wasn't a one-nighter, Chrissie. This thing between us—this is real. It's not going away. And I'm only going for a few weeks at the most. I'll be back."

"And then where will you go?"

"Wherever the job sends me. Like everyone else, Chris. I do what my job requires. Just like you do."

"My job doesn't require me to leave when things start to heat up."

"That's unfair." He watched her brush her hair with her hands. "What are we really talking about here?"

"We're really talking about me thinking we had a relationship and finding out that you're not sticking around."

"You're just going to have to trust me, Chris. You'll see. I'll go, I'll come back. I'll go again, I'll come back again. That's how it works when you're in a relationship."

"No. People leave, but they don't come back."

He sighed. "I get it. I do. But I'm not your father and I'm not your brother. I'll always come back to you. You have to see it to believe it? Fine. Not a problem. You'll see, and you'll believe, and one day, you'll understand that I will always come back. It's that simple."

"Can we go back now?"

"Did you not hear me say I'm falling in love with you? Know how many times I've said that to a woman? Zero."

"I heard. It took my breath away. And I feel the same way. It's just that . . ."

Jared sighed and got up from the bed. "Just tell me you will give me the chance to prove I mean what I say."

She nodded. "I'll give you the chance, of course I will. I'm sorry. It's just . . ."

He took her in his arms. "I know. People who should have been there for you haven't been. But this is different. This is us. Chrissie and Jared. I won't let you down. I promise."

TO CHRISSIE'S SURPRISE, he started the engine of the *Cordy E* and pulled anchor. Guiding the boat back into the bay, he kept one arm around Chrissie and the other on the wheel. A million stars spread overhead, fireflies winking across the heavens. A gentle breeze blew over the bow and kissed her bare shoulders. In the distance the lights from the opposite shore were reflected in the dark water of the Chesapeake. The full moon had dropped lower in the night sky, its light dimming as it edged toward dawn.

"I like staying in the cove at night these days," he told her as they rounded the point. "I like knowing that I'm fifty feet from shore and another fifty feet across the road and the dune to the store. I like being close to you."

"I like being close to you, too."

She rested her head on his shoulder and smiled to herself. She pushed away any thoughts of time and distance coming between them. She'd decided she was going to trust Jared and fate that nothing would come between them. He'd made it clear he was in for the long haul. She was, too. Trust didn't come easily to her, and she was only a little surprised that he'd picked up so quickly on why that was a problem for her. But he was right: he isn't her father, and he isn't her brother. She needed to see her relationship with Jared as something apart from them and not allow the past to color the future.

He drove the boat into the cove, skillfully avoiding the sandbar she knew was there somewhere, though she wasn't sure where.

"You know there's a sandbar out here?"

"It's off the right."

"How do you know that? How do you know how deep the water is?"

"Depth finder." He pointed to the instrument panel, then turned off the engine and dropped anchor.

He took her hand and said, "Come on. I'll row you ashore."

Her shoes in her hand, she stepped down into the small boat and sat on the seat facing the shore. Jared began to row, pausing to ask, "You sure you don't want me to sing? I can do country, classic rock—even learned a couple of forties tunes just for you. Well, bits and pieces of one or two. But you could fill in those parts I don't know."

Somehow she'd managed to keep a straight face. "You're such a romantic devil," she told him. "But just row."

He brought the boat as close to the shore as he could before scraping the bottom, then put the oars down and rolled his pants legs up to his knees. In bare feet, he jumped over the side of the boat, then held a hand out to her.

"There's nasty eel grass down there." Chrissie looked into the water. "It slithers against your legs and . . . ugh."

She stood and pulled her dress over her thighs so it wouldn't get wet.

"I'm not going to make you walk in it. Come closer."

With one hand, he lifted her from the boat and held her securely. His other hand held the rope that had tethered the boat to the dive platform. When he reached the beach, he set her down on the sand and walked to the jetty, where he wrapped the rope around a rock several times.

"That should hold it for a few minutes." He took her hand as they crossed the road and walked over the dune. The moon was so full and bright over-head, the path was clear, and within minutes they'd reached the store.

"Gigi must be asleep by now," Chrissie said. She climbed the front steps and tried the door.

"Ah, good, she left the door unlocked." She opened the door and whispered, "Kiss me good night here. She's a really light sleeper and I don't want to wake her."

"I thought her bedroom was in the back."

"It is, but I swear, that woman's hearing has not diminished with age. She can hear a pin drop on the second floor."

"Well, then, we'll let her sleep, and we'll say good night." He kissed her, and she let herself be molded into his body for just a moment.

"Enough," she whispered. "Or I won't be able to let you go."

"I'll be over in the morning. What time is your mother coming by?"

"I told her between nine and ten."

"I'll be here earlier. Have the coffee ready." He kissed the tip of her nose, and as an afterthought, asked, "Got scones?"

"I'll make them in the morning. Go."

She pushed him out the door, then stood in the doorway and watched until he was nothing more than a shadow in the moonlight, which disappeared on the down side of the dune.

She closed the door behind her and locked it. Swinging her shoes in one hand, she padded softly across the old pine floor. She was almost to the stairwell when she realized she was not alone.

She stopped, tilted her head, and tried to place the sound she'd just heard.

There. Again. Too late she recognized the scrape of the chair against the wooden floor. She turned toward the table and said, "Gigi?"

"Nope. Try again, Chrissie." The familiar voice that had been haunting her for months whispered through the darkness.

The scrape was louder as he pushed the chair away.

"Aren't you going to say hello? Greet me like you just sent that guy on his way?" He walked toward her, and she was frozen where she stood, too stunned to move. "Big dude."

In a flash he was there, one hand on the back of her neck, the other around her wrist, and he was kissing her.

"Stop." She tried pushing him away with her one free hand, but he was too strong. "Don't. Don't . . ."

"Was he as good as me, Chrissie?" His breath was on her face and she wanted to gag.

Old Chrissie would have said, "No, Doug. No one's as good as you."

New Chrissie said, "No. He was better." And because she couldn't resist, even knowing what it would cost her, she added, "A thousand times better."

The slap was not totally unexpected. It had merely been a question of when, not if, he would strike her.

"You think you're so clever. Did you really believe I'd let you go? Did you really think I couldn't find you?"

"How did you find me?"

He laughed. "I read *People* magazine."

"What's that supposed to mean?"

He twisted her arm and watched her face. She refused to give him the satisfaction of letting him know how much pain he was causing.

"That was a real nice lunch you made for those movie stars. Bet you thought you were hot stuff, having your picture taken with Dallas MacGregor. Nice of the person who took the shot to make sure they named that little restaurant." He gave her arm another little twist. "After we're through here, we're going to take a ride, and you're going to watch me burn that place to the ground."

Chrissie's veins turned to ice. Sophie, Jason . . . their baby . . .

"Doug, no. Please. There's no reason to do that." She fought back the panic that was threatening to overtake her.

"Of course there's a reason," he whispered, and

pulled her closer. "You need to be punished. And that's just the start."

"Where's Ruby?" She looked anxiously toward the apartment door.

"The old lady?" He grabbed her ponytail and pulled it back so she had to look him in the face. "She's sleeping peacefully."

"If you touched her . . ."

He laughed. "You'll do what? You'll hurt me?"

"Doug, tell me you didn't hurt her." God, if he hurt her . . .

"The old lady's fine. And she'll stay that way as long as you do what I want."

"What do you want, Doug? Just tell me, and I'll do it." She'd do anything—promise him anything—if he'd leave Ruby alone.

"You know what I want. I want what he had." He slid one strap of her dress over her shoulder.

"Don't do this, Doug." Her mind raced. She had to find out if Ruby was all right. She could deal with anything else he might do to her, as long as Ruby hadn't been harmed.

"If you're thinking you're going to scream and the old lady will come running—that ain't gonna happen." His mouth was at her ear again. "I locked her in. Even if she hears you, she can't get to you."

He pulled down the other strap of her dress and began kissing her neck. She closed her eyes and tried not to scream. He pushed her up against the wall and started to pull up the hem of her dress. "You be nice, and I promise I won't touch the old lady. If you struggle . . ."

"I'll be nice." She knew what being nice meant to Doug, but if that was what it took to keep Ruby safe, then so be it. She gritted her teeth and willed herself not to cry. And there was still Blossoms. There was no way she could let him do what he'd planned.

There was a clicking sound from across the room and he froze, his lips still against her skin, his hand still on her thigh.

"Son, I think you best be walking away right about now." Ruby's voice was clear and strong. "While you still can."

Without letting go of Chrissie, Doug turned and looked over his shoulder. The light from the moon spilled in through the big window next to the table, and Chrissie knew he saw what she did.

Ruby stood in her bathrobe, her feet bare, holding what looked like a rifle up to her shoulder.

"Been a while since I shot a man, but I still remember how," she said.

"Who are you kidding, old woman?" Doug turned around slowly and laughed. "You're not going to shoot me. I doubt that thing's even loaded. You even know what to do with one of those things? Put it down now."

She braced herself against the wall and pulled the trigger. The shot hit two feet in front of him.

"I guess it be loaded, and I guess I know what to do with it."

Doug started walking toward Ruby.

"You calling my bluff, boy?" she said softly.

Before he could answer, Chrissie picked up the nearest chair and struck him over the head as hard as she could. He went down in a heap on the floor.

"I called Beck," Ruby said calmly. "He be along anytime now."

She walked closer, the rifle still pointed at Doug. Chrissie burst into tears.

"Where did you get that?" She pointed to the rifle. "How did you know . . . ?"

"Now, you come here, girl." Ruby reached one hand to her. "Nothing to cry about. No one hurt but him, and that's all right." She looked down at the man on the floor, who was just beginning to come around.

Flashing lights lit up the night outside the store, and a car door slammed, followed by footfalls on the porch.

He started to get up, and Ruby said, "Police just pulled in, boy. You stay put or I be putting a slug in you."

The door opened and Chrissie heard heavy boots crossing the floor.

"Where the hell's the light switch?" Beck asked as he came in, his gun drawn.

"Chrissie, you go put on those lights so he doesn't shoot you or me." She pointed the tip of the gun at Doug's head. "Him I don't be caring about."

Chrissie ran across the floor and turned on the overhead lights. For a moment she was blinded, but she could see Beck moving toward Ruby, his gun drawn.

"Miz Carter, you can put that down now." Beck holstered his gun and flipped Doug onto his stomach, none too gently, Chrissie noted. He snapped handcuffs around Doug's wrists but let him lie facedown on the floor. "Actually, I'd appreciate it—a lot—if you did."

Another car with flashing lights pulled in out front.

"That would be Duncan Alcott." Beck stood. When the newcomer came into the room, Beck said, "Officer Alcott, please remove this piece of"—he glanced at Ruby—"the prisoner. Read him his rights and get him out of here. I'll be out in a minute."

"Sir, you've got this all wrong. I know what this looks like, but . . ." Doug began to babble.

"It looks like exactly what it is. Home invasion, assault, attempted rape. I'm sure there's more." Beck brushed him off. To Chrissie, he said, "Are you okay?"

She nodded, but then started to quietly cry. "I can't believe he found me. He could have hurt Ruby." She felt the tears roll down her face. "He said he was going to burn down Blossoms."

"But he didn't now, did he?" Ruby handed the rifle to Beck and wrapped Chrissie in her embrace. "Didn't I tell you we be strong and we be smart, that we be fine?"

"You did. You knew." Chrissie stared at the remarkable woman who'd just turned 101 years old.

"I be feeling it coming for a time. I be ready." She pointed to the rifle in Beck's hand. "That belonged to my Harold. He loved that thing. Remington, it be. He taught me how to load it, shoot it." She smiled with no small amount of pride. "Had to lean me against the wall, though, lest the kick put me on my kiester. Might have shot clear through the roof."

"Could you have shot him, Gigi?"

"Didn't bring that thing out here for show. My Harold always said you don't load it if you're not about shooting it." She looked Beck in the eye and told him, "I'd'a blown a hole right through him if he'd harmed my girl."

"Can't say I blame you, Miz Carter." Beck patted her on the back.

"You thinking about arresting me, Gabriel Beck?"

"For what? Shooting a hole in your own floor?" He shook his head. "I would put this in a safe place, though." He left the rifle on the table.

"Keep it where I always kept it," she told him. "Under my bed."

"You sleep with a loaded rifle under your bed?" he asked.

"Doesn't everyone?"

He laughed and headed out just as Jared came in, soaking wet.

"What the hell's going on? Chrissie . . . ?" He rushed across the room.

"The short version? Doug was waiting for me here, in the store, in the dark, when you brought me back. Ruby shot at him with Harold's rifle, and I hit him over the head with a chair." She looked at Ruby. "Oh, Gigi, I broke your chair."

"No matter. There be another one just like it in the storage room. You can go on in and get it for me. I think I'm going to need a cup of tea and a place to set while I drink it." She shuffled off toward her kitchen.

"Gigi, how did you get out of the apartment?" Chrissie called after her. "Doug said he locked you in."

"Don't know how he could'a done that. Only key be in a drawer in my kitchen." She paused and turned around. "Must'a used that old key I keep hanging on the wall here."

Ruby ran her hand along the wall. "Yep, that's what he must'a done." She chuckled. "That old key only worked one door, and it not be this one. My

Harold hanged it there when we moved down here from the point." She paused and looked back at Chrissie and Jared. "That be the key for his grand-daddy's house. Burned down about seventy years ago. 'Course, it hardly matters which key he had. That lock be broke inside for maybe ten, fifteen years. He could turn that key all he wanted, lock still be broken and the door still be opening."

She continued on into her living quarters to make her tea. "Don't you be forgetting that chair, Christiana."

Chrissie buried her head in Jared's shoulder and he wrapped her in his arms. "Are you crying or laughing?" he asked.

"Both. My ex shows up—he's probably going to rape me before he kills me, and probably kill Ruby as well. Oh, and he's going to burn down Blossoms before the night is over. My great-grandmother shows up in the dark with a shotgun . . ."

"Rifle," Jared corrected her.

"Whatever. He's taunting her and she shoots the damned thing." She pointed to the hole in the floor. "She shot right there. Just to show him she could, and she would have shot him. I feel terrible that she was put in harm's way." Chrissie took a deep breath. "Looks like Ruby can take care of herself."

She let him hold her, even though he was soaking wet. "Why are you wet?"

"When I heard the gunshot, I dove in and swam. I figured it would be faster than untying the boat and rowing. I'm sorry I didn't get here sooner. I'm sorry I left you here. I should have stayed."

"There's no way you could have known he was

here. With all the traffic on the island today because of the party, no one would have noticed an out-of-state car. He must have parked down near the point and left the car there, walked up."

"I'm so grateful to Ruby, but damn. I wanted to be your hero."

"You are my hero." She nuzzled the side of his face. "Just not tonight."

"I don't see a chair there in my place." Ruby shuffled into the room.

"I'm on my way, Gigi."

WHEN CHRISSIE AND Jared made their way downstairs in the morning, they found Ruby, Dorothy, and Louis drinking coffee at Ruby's table in the store. Dorothy looked up when she heard them.

"Ruby told me everything." Dorothy's hand flew over her heart and her jaw dropped. "Oh my God, he could have killed you! Both of you!"

"I think that was his endgame. He probably would have succeeded if Ruby hadn't come in when she did," Chrissie told her.

Dorothy's mouth still hung open. Finally, she said, "Thank God for you, Ruby. Thank God you kept that old rifle of Harold's." She paused. "I remember that rifle. He had that thing forever. It must be, oh, close to eighty years old."

Ruby nodded. "His daddy gave it to him when he was twelve. He was always proud of that rifle."

"Where is it now?" Dorothy asked.

"Back where it belongs," Ruby told her. "Under my bed."

Chrissie had to turn her back on Louis, whose eyes

were big and round as dinner plates. He hadn't said a word. She guessed if you didn't know Ruby, it might be a little tough to take.

"Why don't you let me make breakfast for everyone?" Jared poured himself a cup of coffee from the old pot on the counter near the cash register, which Ruby preferred to the new Keurig. To Chrissie he said, "You should spend some time with your mother."

"Do you know how to make scrambled eggs?" Chrissie asked. "Cook bacon? Make toast?"

"I'm going to forget you even asked. Go." He pointed to the door. "Do I know how to scramble eggs," he pretended to grumble.

"There are some scones in the refrigerator that need to be warmed up. Would you put them in the oven, set the timer for ten minutes, then take them out? You know Ruby is dying for one." She smiled. "So am I."

"Sure." He rubbed her back for a second, then told her, "You finally have some time together. Use it."

"Good point. Thank you." She turned to the table. "Well, Mom. Looks like we'll have some time to catch up after all."

"Okay. Sure." Dorothy nodded.

"Girl time," Jared told Louis. "You can come on into the kitchen and watch me scramble some eggs."

"I think I be coming along too. Someone's got to be keeping an eye on those scones." Ruby rose and followed Louis and Jared into the kitchen.

Chrissie sat in her usual seat, sipping her coffee and wondering where to begin.

"Dear God, Chrissie, I can't believe what went on here this morning. Who'd have thought that Ruby—

where she got the strength . . ." Dorothy blew out a long breath. "I just can't get over that man wanting to hurt you."

"I'm having a hard time believing it myself, but it's over and done with and Doug's sitting in the jail in St. Dennis, waiting for someone to come bail him out, I suppose. I'd be surprised if anyone showed up." She smiled. "As for Ruby, she's the strongest woman I ever met. I want to be just like her. She was like an avenging angel, Mom. She was just not going to let that man hurt me again."

"I'm still having trouble understanding how this happened, Chrissie. Why you didn't leave him sooner."

"It's hard to explain, Mom. And it's more involved than I want to go into right now. Someday. For now, I'll just say it was a situation I got myself into, and eventually I was lucky. I got myself out. It wasn't easy. It never is with a man like him."

Chrissie took her mother's hands. "Now you know my secret, but there's still the elephant in the room. Why did Dad leave? Why did he take Luke? Why didn't they ever come back?"

"I know I should have told you a long time ago, but it's not a nice story, honey. I'm embarrassed to even think about it, but you should know." Dorothy tapped her fingers on the side of her mug. "Your father left when he found out . . ." She swallowed hard. "When he found out that he isn't your father."

For a very long moment, Chrissie couldn't react. It was as if the words were spoken in a foreign language she'd never learned.

"Dad . . ."

"Wasn't your father. I'm sorry, Chrissie, but that's

the fact. When he found out, he took Luke—who was his—and he left. Didn't tell me where he was going, but I knew he'd never come back. That's why he never came to see you, never sent a dime in child support." Dorothy couldn't seem to look up to meet Chrissie's eyes. She stared into her coffee, her voice a monotone. "I wish I'd been able to tell you, so you'd have understood. But that's not something you tell a child."

"If he wasn't my father, then who . . . ?" Chrissie was trying to comprehend the unexpected news. "Who's my father?"

"A waterman who sometimes fished with your . . . with Stephen." Dorothy finally raised her face. "We'd been having some troubles, Stephen and I were. Stupid little things, but I was being a little pissy about it. He started drinking, then I started drinking, and he came home one night with some other woman's lipstick on his shirt." She laughed harshly. "Is that the biggest cliché in the world?" She laughed again, then coughed. "You know how things get to be clichés, right? They happen so often they become a common theme in a lot of stories."

"So you and this fisherman . . ." Chrissie's head was spinning.

Dorothy nodded. "Stephen finally did the math and figured out you couldn't be his, because we hadn't been together while I was with this other man and your father was with this other woman, and that was that. Once he'd figured it out, there wasn't even a good-bye. Just packed up his things and packed up Luke. I can still see him standing in the doorway, looking at me like he wanted to kill me, told me not to come looking for him. And he closed the door and that was that."

Chrissie's head began to pound. "What was his name? The fisherman?"

"Does it matter?"

"Are you kidding? Of course it matters. He was my father."

"Andy O'Connor. He died not long after your father left. They said he fell off his skipjack in a storm and he drowned."

"Is that true, or are you telling me that so I don't look for him?" After all the lies over all the years, how could Chrissie trust her mother to tell the truth now?

"Go look it up at the library here. There's a local paper. The *St. Dennis Gazette*. Ruby's friend Grace Sinclair owns it. I know they covered the story. I read it."

"How did you feel? When you read about it?" Chrissie asked. She couldn't help but wonder. After all, Dorothy's husband had left because of this man.

"Just numb. We'd planned to be together, then *bam!* Gone. But I'd been numb ever since the day Stephen left and took my little boy." Dorothy began to cry. "Luke was gone, then Andy . . ."

"You never heard from Stephen again? You never heard from Luke? How could he not find you? How could he not be in touch with you?"

"Luke started calling me a few years ago," she admitted.

"What? Are you kidding me?" Chrissie nearly exploded. "Where is he? Why didn't you tell me?" Chrissie slammed a hand down on the table. "How could you keep all this from me?"

"Because I'd have had to tell you the truth. Stephen had already told Luke, and I didn't want you to know. I didn't want you to think I was . . . all the things your father called me. The things he told Luke that I was." Dorothy's shoulders began to shake with each sob. "I was between a rock and a hard place. I couldn't tell you, and the longer I hid the truth, the more impossible it was for me to tell you even when I knew I should. I'm sorry, Chrissie. More than I can say. I cheated on my husband and you were the result of that affair. I was ashamed of myself and I was a coward. It was easier for me to lie to you than it was for me to tell you, and that's the sad truth." Dorothy ran a hand through her hair. "How do you tell a child that her father isn't her father? That he left you behind when he found out that a friend of his—someone he'd worked alongside of—had fathered you? How does a child understand that?"

"After a while, I wasn't a child anymore, Mom. There's been plenty of time to tell me the truth. At least I'd have understood why he left, why I couldn't see Luke."

"Like I said, I was a coward. I was afraid you'd hate me for . . . well, for everything. I couldn't risk losing you, too."

"Did you care about him? Andy O'Connor?"

Dorothy nodded. "That's one of the saddest parts of this whole mess. I would have left your father and married him if he hadn't died. We talked about it, Andy and I. Even talked about sharing custody of Luke with Stephen. But then there was a storm that Andy shouldn't have been out in—" She left the rest unspoken until she added, "He was the love of my life."

"Where's Luke now? Where's my brother?"

"Luke's in Montana. That's where he and Stephen

settled when they left. Stephen wanted to get as far away from me as he could."

"I need to call him. I want to talk to him."

"He wants to talk to you, too." She looked up at Chrissie with swollen eyes. "He got married about eight years ago. Had two children. His wife passed last year. Breast cancer. I guess it got him thinking. I told him about the party this weekend for Ruby, told him he should come, but he wasn't ready for that. He's ready to see you, though. Ready to talk to you if you want to. He said I could give you his number if you want . . ."

"Of course I want it." Chrissie stared at her mother, then finally asked, "If I hadn't pushed, would you have told me the truth? Would you have told me about Luke?"

"I like to think that before I left today, I would have." Still, Dorothy couldn't meet Chrissie's eyes.

Jared came to the doorway and called to them. "Breakfast is ready, and Owen and Cass just got here. If you want bacon, better get in here before Owen eats it all." He walked into the room and looked from Chrissie's face to her mother's and back again.

"Chris? You all right?"

"I'm fine," she told him. "I know why my father left and didn't take me with him. And I know where my brother is."

Chapter Fourteen

Chrissie stretched out on the beach towel, her body warm in the hot Florida sun. When Jared's shadow crossed over her, she pulled on her sunglasses and looked up.

"It's time for your lesson," he told her.

"Later. Right now I'm relaxing." She closed her eyes behind her dark shades.

"No, right now you're going to get onto that boat and you're going to dive with me." He bent down and pulled her up to a sitting position.

"I did it yesterday. And the day before." She knew she shouldn't tease him, but she just couldn't help herself.

This was their third day in the Florida Keys, her third day snorkeling with him on the reefs, and she still hadn't admitted how much she was loving it. Oh, it hadn't been easy, that first time she'd strapped on gear and lowered herself over the side of the boat. The water had been warm and crystal clear, so she could see all the way to the bottom, but that meant she could see things swimming there. Even the smallest fish looked like man-eaters to her. But it had meant so much to Jared, she had to buck up and go for it. And she, like Delia, had found a whole new world beneath the surface of the water. Once she realized the fish had no interest in her—other than at best a mild curiosity—she'd been fascinated by their colors and shapes, by the beauty of the silence and the way the sunlight had shimmered below the surface, just as Jared had promised. She was looking forward to a lifetime of sharing that beauty with him.

"All right. If you insist. Where are we off to today?"

"Today it's Islamorada. Middle Keys. Great snorkeling."

"If you say so."

"You'll thank me later."

She picked up her towel and her bag and followed him across the sand. They were staying in a house Gordon had bought years ago and occasionally rented to people he knew. Jared had gotten the keys from his father before they left Maryland.

She'd called Luke the day after Ruby's party, almost immediately after Dorothy'd given her his number, and after a long, tear-filled conversation, asked if he could meet them in Florida, a place that had no memories for either of them. The earliest Luke could take off from work was a week in late August before school started—not ideal vacation time in sunny Florida, but Chrissie would have agreed to the hottest, most humid day of the year just to meet him. She'd had to wait another six weeks, but he sounded as if he needed the time, so she'd gladly agreed. He and his two children could stay in the house with Chrissie and Jared, get to know each other as adults, and find out if they liked each other.

As it turned out, they did.

"Besides, we want to be back before Luke and the kids get back from Grassy Key. He was taking them to the Dolphin Research Center this morning. I promised them I'd take them to the Shipwreck Museum in Key West later this afternoon. We can have dinner there in this great restaurant I used to go to with my dad and Rachel when we were kids."

"Okay. Lead on."

Gordon's boat was tied at the end of the newly rebuilt dock. Damaged in the last hurricane, it had taken Gordon's favorite flat-bottom boat with it. He'd replaced it over the winter with a new one that he hadn't taken out yet, so he was happy to have Jared test it. Chrissie followed Jared to the end of the pier and she tossed her things into the boat, then got in. Her mask, fins, goggles, and snorkel were waiting for her.

"Gear up, girl. We're going sightseeing."

He drove the boat to the reef they'd found the day before yesterday and anchored. Once they were both fully geared, they dropped over the side of the boat into water that was barely six feet deep.

Then came the part Chrissie was learning to love. The reef was home to dozens of colorful fish that darted around her, for the most part ignoring her as she swam weightless through the crystal-clear water. She'd never dreamed it would be like this. She'd heard Jared and Owen talk about diving in the cold, deep waters where sunken ships lay lost at the bottom of the sea, but this was a colorful paradise. She pointed to Jared when a blue fish swam close to her face, and he shook his head, rightly thinking she was going to laugh.

"Don't take the regulator out of your mouth when you're underwater," he'd told her the first day out.

But she'd gotten so excited at her first glimpse of the underwater world she forgot where she was and started to call out to him, earning her a mouthful of water and a quick trip back to the surface.

"I'm sorry." Water had sputtered from her mouth and her nose. "I just got so excited . . ."

"Try to contain yourself when you're down there. Save your excitement for the surface."

Today their swim was short because he knew she wanted time with Luke, so after an hour in the water, he'd waved to her and they made their way back to the boat.

"So I can see you still hate me for forcing you to go down into that hell pit," he said as he climbed onboard.

"I do. It's torture. Never make me do this again." She hoisted herself over the side and took off her mask. "I never knew how beautiful it was. It's magical. It's everything you promised it would be and more."

"I am so tempted to say 'told you so.'"

"Go on, say it. You're entitled. When you're right, you're right." She leaned over and kissed him. "Thank you for sharing this with me. I love it—and I love you."

"I love you, too." His lips lingered on hers for a moment. "Maybe before we leave next weekend, we can have you outfitted with a wet suit." He grinned. "In some circles, it's the preferred wedding gift from a man to his bride."

She narrowed her eyes. "You better not be playing

with me. You do not tease a girl with bride-talk and wedding gifts. Especially when the gift has such deep sentimental meaning."

"I wouldn't think of it." Jared touched his forehead to hers. "Give me one good reason why we shouldn't get married."

She sat silently, her mind racing. Was he really proposing to her? Was this really happening?

"Ha! See? Can't think of one." He kissed the side of her face. "So will you?"

"Will I think of one?" She smiled, knowing what he was really asking.

In typical Jared fashion, he laughed.

"Of course I will." She held his face in her hands and looked deeply into his eyes. "I cannot think of one thing that would make me happier than to spend the rest of my life with you."

"Then that's what we'll do." He held her for a moment. "We'll look for a ring and we'll pick a date and we'll do it."

"Just like that." She could have laughed, knowing there had to be more to getting married than merely buying a ring and picking a date. She had a feeling she'd be calling on Lucy—the acknowledged best wedding planner on the Eastern Shore—sometime very soon.

"Yes," he said. "Just like that." He started the engine and headed toward shore.

Moments later, he looked over his shoulder and said, "To be continued. We have company."

Luke's children, four-year-old Maddie and six-year-old Finn, were waiting on the end of the dock, jumping up and down as the boat drew closer.

"Can we go for a ride, too?" Finn asked. "Just a little one?"

"Just a little ride?" Maddie repeated.

"If it's all right with your father, it's okay with me," Jared told them.

"Life jackets, kids."

Chrissie went into the screened porch and picked up the orange vests they'd worn the day before. Gordon had bought them for Rachel's boys when they were roughly the same age as Luke's children. Chrissie took them out and strapped them on, first Maddie, then Finn. Jared lifted them into the boat and sat them down.

"You remember you have to stay in your seat, right?" Jared asked.

They both nodded, Maddie's sweet little face wide with excitement, Finn with his brown hair and dark green eyes so serious and concerned.

"Okay. We won't be long. We want to go see the shipwreck museum, right, guys?"

Both kids nodded vigorously.

Chrissie looped her arm through her brother's and looked up into his handsome face. She hadn't remembered what he looked like because she was so young when he left, yet he was familiar to her somehow. He was tall and had the same blond hair and green eyes she did, but where she was petite, he was tall and broad shouldered. They watched the boat slowly glide away from the dock, and while she turned back toward the house, his eyes were fixed on the boat that carried his children.

"They'll be fine. He won't go far or keep them long, and he'll take good care of them," she said.

Luke nodded, his eyes shielded by dark glasses. "I know." He exhaled. "They're all I have."

"I understand. But he'd die before he'd let anything happen to either of them."

He nodded again.

"Come on inside. I'll make us lunch, and you can tell me all about what it was like growing up in Montana on a cattle ranch." She took his arm and they walked toward the house. "I always wanted to go there."

"Maybe you and Jared could come out and visit sometime," Luke said. "Though I'm not sure how much longer we'll be there. I'm not sure it's where we belong."

"You should talk to Ruby about that," Chrissie told him. "She knows about such things. As a matter of fact, you should just talk to Ruby, period. You should know her. You and Maddie and Finn."

She glanced over her shoulder at the sea, where the man she loved and trusted with her whole heart was driving the boat around in huge, slow circles in the water, Maddie's and Finn's laughter floating to the shore. Someday it would be their children, hers and Jared's, in that boat along with her brother's children and Rachel's.

Chrissie followed her brother into the house. There was still so much to talk about, so much to discover about each other and their lives growing up, their lives now. She was grateful for this time with him, grateful that Jared had understood and had been content to share her time with Luke.

She smiled as she closed the door behind her, her past and her present—and her future—coming together at last.

Diary~

Oh my, what a time we've had here in our little corner of the world lately! I'm so overwhelmed I hardly know where to begin. But good newswoman that I am—I did, after all, run a newspaper for more years than I care to think about—I did get the story.

First, lest I forget in all the excitement to follow, I have it on good authority that Cass Parker's little reclaimed historic homes are going like hotcakes. Ruby tells me people are coming from all over since that article appeared in the *Times* about Cass's nondevelopment development (that's how she referred to it, and who am I to argue?). I understand there are only two lots left. How amazing to see Cannonball Island reinvigorated and reinvented in such a way. There are some who fear the island's culture will be lost with all the new people coming in, but I look to St. Dennis as an example of how to grow while maintaining one's identity. If we here in town can do it, surely the island can as well. Especially with Ruby here to keep an eye on things; and yes, she'll be watching over the island and her family for a very long time to come, from one side of the veil or another. It's not mine to say when, but I can say she'll be with us for a while yet. There are babies waiting in the wings to meet her, and knowing Ruby, she won't go anywhere until she's satisfied that all is well with those who are dearest to her.

Speaking of Ruby's dearest—Owen and Cass are almost ready to move into their new home. Who'd ever have thought that old, run-down place that once belonged to Ruby's Harold's father could be restored, but Cass is the idea girl and she got her contractors on board. Suffice it to say, I can't wait until the open house. Ruby says it's lovely.

The work on the sunken merchant ship is moving right along. I understand the divers have brought up some interesting items: crocks that were sealed over two hundred years ago were found with tea still inside, barrels still holding fine china, and crates of silver items—candelabras and things of that sort. Once they've finished cataloging everything, they'll remove what they can of the ship. I heard Owen say he wished they could salvage enough to rebuild it on land, but he didn't think that was going to be possible.

All the work on the ship has kept our friend Jared Chandler around for longer than he'd intended. Oh, of course it isn't just the ship that's keeping him around. Ruby tells me there are wedding bells in the near future for her Chrissie and Jared—as if that were a big surprise. Ruby and I knew even before that boy set foot off that ship that he was destined to stay, that the love of his life would be waiting for him here. And of course, she was. That girl came home with a hurt so big, she thought she'd never recover. But Ruby knew she was meant for better than what she'd left behind, and that once she'd learned to believe in herself, the world would open to her and wonderful things would pour in. Which is, of course, exactly what happened.

Ruby also tells me that one of Cass's little houses was purchased by Jared as a surprise for his bride-to-be. I believe he'd requested the Singer house, but it had been sold. But he found the old Blake homestead to be even more suitable. It's a stone's throw over the dune from the general store, for one thing. For another, Chrissie's kin are buried there, so for her, it'll be just another way of coming home.

Which, of course, will leave Ruby alone again. Not that she minds, but we both know it's only a matter of time before another lost soul shows up on her doorstep, looking for home and healing.

She'll be waiting.

~Grace

*Blossoms is the up-and-coming
hot spot for great food in St. Dennis—
even the Hollywood elite have discovered
its goodness! Turn the page for some of the
recipes Chrissie and Sophie prepared for
Dallas MacGregor and her crew.
Enjoy!*

Sophie's Oyster Stew

Yield: 4 servings

1 pint shucked oysters in their liquid
6 tablespoons unsalted butter
2 green onions, white and green parts, finely chopped
1 small garlic clove, minced
1 teaspoon salt, depending on the saltiness
    of the oysters
⅛ teaspoon freshly ground black pepper
4 cups milk
2 cups heavy cream
Dash of Worcestershire or Tabasco sauce
Oyster crackers

Lift the oysters out of their liquid and clean them to remove any traces of shell.

Strain the liquid to remove any sand. Chill the oysters and liquid separately.

Melt the butter in a 4-quart saucepan over medium heat. Stir in the green onions and sauté until the onions are softened.

Stir in the garlic, salt, and pepper.

Stir in the milk, heavy cream, oyster liquid, and Worcestershire sauce and cook for 2 minutes until it starts to gently bubble but not boil.

Turn the heat to low, add the oysters, and cook them just until their edges begin to curl, about 1 to 2 minutes.

Serve with oyster crackers and a smidge of butter swirled into the top of each bowl.

Chrissy's Oyster Fritters

Yield: 16–18 pieces

1 pint shucked Maryland standard oysters
2 cups all-purpose flour
½ tablespoon mixed herbs (tarragon, thyme,
    rosemary)
1 teaspoon salt
¼ teaspoon pepper
½ cup milk
¾ cup olive oil

Drain the oysters, reserving the liquid.

Combine the flour, herbs, salt, and pepper in a bowl and mix well.

Stir in the milk, then add the oysters.

Heat the oil in a large skillet over medium-high heat. Drop the batter by tablespoonful into the oil (2 oysters per fritter).

Fry for 1 to 2 minutes, or until browned on one side. Then turn and fry the other side until browned. Drain on paper towels. Serve immediately.

Watercress, Avocado, and Citrus Salad

Yield: 4 servings

Dressing
3 tablespoons extra-virgin olive oil
2 teaspoons orange juice
1 teaspoon balsamic vinegar
2 teaspoons honey

Salad
2 tablespoons freshly squeezed lemon juice
1 medium red onion, finely chopped
3 tablespoons extra-virgin olive oil
2 firm ripe avocados, chopped
2 oranges, or 1 ruby red grapefruit, peeled and sliced
½ cup toasted almonds, chopped
2 (12-ounce) bunches watercress, thick stems
    removed and discarded
Salt
Freshly ground pepper

Whisk together the oil, orange juice, vinegar, and honey and set aside.

In a large bowl, combine the lemon juice and chopped onion and let stand for 10 minutes.

Gradually whisk in the oil and the dressing.

Add the avocado, orange, almonds, and watercress to the dressing and toss well.

Season the salad with salt and pepper. Serve immediately.

Asparagus, Spring Onions, and Goat Cheese Quiche

Yield: 6–8 servings

1 store-bought piecrust
2 tablespoons unsalted butter
2 cups thinly sliced spring (green) onions
1 bunch fresh asparagus, trimmed and cut into
    1-inch pieces
2 teaspoons sea salt
¾ teaspoon pepper
1 cup heavy cream
8 large eggs
2 tablespoons thinly sliced chives
¾ cup crumbled goat cheese

Preheat the oven to 350°F.

Prepare the piecrust according to the package directions. Let cool completely.

Melt the butter in a large skillet over medium-high heat. Add the onions and cook, stirring, until tender and lightly browned. Stir in the asparagus; sprinkle with ½ teaspoon of the salt and ¼ teaspoon of the pepper. Remove from the heat and let cool for 5 minutes.

Whisk together the heavy cream, eggs, and chives and the remaining 1½ teaspoons salt and ½ teaspoon pepper.

Spread half of the onion mixture (about 1 cup) in the piecrust. Sprinkle with ¼ cup of the goat cheese. Spoon half of the cream mixture over the cheese. Repeat the layers once and sprinkle the top with the remaining goat cheese.

Bake until set, about 1 hour. Cool on a wire rack for 20 minutes before serving.

Bacon-Wrapped Potatoes
with Dipping Sauce

Yield: 16 wedges

2 medium baking potatoes, cut into 8 wedges each
½ teaspoon salt
16 bacon slices
½ teaspoon pepper
1 tablespoon olive oil
½ cup diced onion
2 tablespoons minced garlic
8 ounces sour cream
2 tablespoons hot sauce

Place a lightly greased wire rack in an aluminum foil–lined 15 x 10-inch jelly roll pan.

Preheat the oven to 425°F. Sprinkle the potato wedges with the salt. Wrap each wedge with 1 bacon slice. Arrange the potato wedges in a single layer in the prepared pan. Sprinkle with the pepper.

Bake for 40 to 45 minutes, or until the bacon is crisp and browned.

Meanwhile, heat the oil in a small nonstick skillet over medium-high heat and sauté the onion for 5 minutes, or until tender. Add the garlic and sauté for 1 minute more. Let cool slightly before making the dipping sauce.

Mix the sour cream, hot sauce, and the onion and garlic mixture. Serve as a dip for the potatoes.

Roasted Tomato Tart

Yield: 6 servings

4 Roma tomatoes
½ teaspoon sea salt
½ (17.3-ounce) package frozen puff pastry sheets,
   thawed
¼ cup shredded mozzarella cheese
1 teaspoon lemon zest
½ teaspoon freshly ground pepper
1 tablespoon chopped fresh basil

Preheat the oven to 400°F.

Cut the tomatoes into ¼-inch slices. Sprinkle the tomatoes with the salt. Let stand on paper towels for a few minutes.

Unfold 1 puff pastry sheet onto a lightly floured baking sheet.

Arrange the tomato slices in a single layer on the pastry.

Stir together the cheese, lemon zest, pepper, and basil in a small bowl. Sprinkle the cheese mixture over the tomatoes.

Roast until the pastry is puffed and golden brown, about 20 minutes, or until pastry is golden brown and cheese is melted. (Note: Check at 15 minutes, depending on your oven.) Cut into squares.

Mini Crab Cakes

Yield: 16 mini crab cakes

⅓ cup mayonnaise
3 green onions, thinly sliced
1 teaspoon Old Bay seasoning
2 teaspoons Worcestershire sauce
1 tablespoon Grey Poupon mustard
2 large eggs, lightly beaten
Light sprinkle of Tabasco sauce
1 cup bread crumbs
½ pound fresh lump crabmeat, carefully picked over to
   remove shells
Oil, for frying
Lemon wedges

Stir together the mayonnaise, green onions, Old Bay seasoning, Worcestershire sauce, mustard, eggs, and Tabasco in a large bowl.

Gently stir in the bread crumbs and crabmeat.

Shape the mixture into 16 cakes (about 2 table-spoons each).

Heat the oil in a large griddle or nonstick skillet over medium-low heat and cook in batches for 4 minutes on each side, or until golden brown.

Serve with the lemon wedges.

Chrissie's Rhubarb Upside-Down Cake

Yield: 8–10 servings

Topping

5 tablespoons unsalted butter, melted
½ cup all-purpose flour
¼ cup sugar
¼ teaspoon sea salt
¼ teaspoon ground cinnamon

Cake

1 pound rhubarb, trimmed and cut on a diagonal about ½ inch thick
1⅓ cups sugar plus ½ cup for the rhubarb
1½ sticks unsalted butter, plus more for the pan, at room temperature
1½ cups all-purpose flour
1½ teaspoons baking powder
1½ teaspoons sea salt
½ tablespoon finely grated orange zest
2 tablespoons fresh orange juice
2 large eggs
1 cup plain yogurt

Preheat the oven to 350°F.

Make the topping: Stir together the 5 tablespoons butter, ½ cup flour, ¼ cup sugar, ¼ teaspoon salt, and cinnamon until crumbly. Set aside.

Toss the rhubarb with the ½ cup sugar; let stand while other ingredients are mixed.

Make the cake: Butter a 9 x 2-inch round cake pan. Dot with 2 or 3 tablespoons of butter.

In a medium bowl, whisk together the 1½ cups flour, the baking powder, and 1½ teaspoons salt.

In a large bowl, beat the 1½ sticks butter and 1⅓ cups sugar with a mixer on medium speed until pale and fluffy.

Beat in the orange zest and juice. Beat in the eggs, one at a time, scraping down the sides of the bowl.

Beat in the flour mixture in three additions, alternating with the yogurt, until smooth.

Stir the rhubarb-sugar mixture and spread in the pan.

Spread the cake batter evenly over the rhubarb. Crumble the topping over the batter.

Bake until a toothpick inserted into the center comes out clean, about 1 hour.

Let the cake cool for 10 minutes before removing it from the pan. Rhubarb will be hot, but if it stays in the pan too long, the fruit will stick to the bottom.

Note: Can substitute lemon zest and juice for orange.